–YOUR NET MATERIAL IS ALL PASSWORD
PROTECTED. TO ACCESS ANY SPECIFIC IN-
FORMATION, YOU WILL HAVE TO PROVIDE
SPECIFIC CODES. WHAT AREA DO YOU WISH
TO GO TO?

Theo thought for a moment, then typed, ACCESS
BY SUBJECT.

–VERY WELL
–HOUSEHOLD SECURITY, she requested.
–THREE SPECIFIC CODES ARE NECESSARY
TO ACCESS THIS INFORMATION.

YOU HAVE TWO MINUTES TO ENTER THE
FIRST. IF THIS CODE IS INCORRECTLY EN-
TERED, OR THE TWO MINUTE MARK IS
REACHED, THE HOUSEHOLD ALARMS WILL
GO OFF. TIME BEGINS NOW.

Great gods of scholars! Theo leaped out of the
chair. Then she stopped, leaned over, and typed
END.

–THIS DEFENSE PROGRAM CANNOT BE IN-
TERRUPTED. . . .

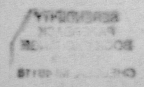

THE GATE OF IVORY

DORIS EGAN

DAW BOOKS, INC.
DONALD A. WOLLHEIM, PUBLISHER

1633 Broadway, New York, NY 10019

First Printing, February 1989

12-90

1 2 3 4 5 6 7 8 9

Printed in the U.S.A.

For Yu Wen, who has always known that which of us
is the tymon depends on where we are

for Sam, the unseen critic

and for Mary Lou Egan, wherever she is—
don't say I forgot.

Chapter 1

I was laying down cards in the marketplace when I got the latest job offer. "Here comes money," Irsa, the vendor next to me had said and moved out of the way so as not to scare him off. So I'd given him his fortune, all the usual sort of nonsense, and out he came with this. I hadn't expected it of him; he looked too respectable. True, he hadn't mentioned the exact nature of this job. But I'd been in the Square long enough—I thought—to know what that meant.

"I might want to hire you," he repeated, as though he expected a dim-witted foreigner like me might need it said twice.

"Move on," I said, picking up my Tarot cards. "Your fortune's been told."

"I'm serious," he protested.

"Please, noble sir. I'm well aware that people hired by Street of Gold Coin procurers are never seen again. Unless you want me for one of the Great Houses?" I smiled with polite rudeness. It was obviously out of the question. By Ivory standards, I'm not even pretty. Eight centimeters shorter than everyone around me, hair auburn instead of black—they wouldn't let me into a Great House as a domestic servant. Not that I felt I was really cut out for prostitution.

"I'm not talking about Gold Coin *kanza*." The word he used was Ivoran, and meant rotten flesh, animal dung, scum to the tenth power. I looked at him in surprise, as he'd intended. "I like your card-reading."

"Thank you, noble sir." I was as phony as any other market fortuneteller.

"I'm not a noble sir. 'Gracious' will do."

So he wasn't part of the nobility, although he dressed like it. More and more interesting. And it hadn't been easy to read his cards. Usually the marks responded, gave you answers, hints, facial expressions. "Someone I know has had an accident? Why, you must mean my great-uncle Hobar." Not this man. Total silence as I interpreted the pictures. It was unnerving.

He said, "You're not Ivoran. How did you end up here?"

I shrugged. "If you really want to know, pay me." To my surprise he brought out another coin and laid it on the ground before me. I shifted position on my rug. "Know, oh gracious sir, that this humble person who is I was born on Pyrene, far from—"

"You can skip the formalities. I'm not paying you as a storyteller."

I sighed. "I left Pyrene and went to Athena as a student. A classmate of mine had a father who was first mate on the *Queen Julia*, one of those big luxury liners out of Tellys. One of his wealthy passengers had reserved a suite for the full run, from Tellys to Athena to Ivory, and left at Athena. My friend talked his father into letting him use the suite—it was booked round trip—and take some friends along. It seemed like a great opportunity. You know—I mean, the gracious sir must be aware of what starship passage costs. If I hadn't gotten a scholarship to Athena, I'd never have gotten even that far. So I came along. That was two years ago."

When I stopped he said, "But you're still here."

"The gracious sir asked me how I came here. Not why I remain."

He dropped another coin. I scooped it up and added it to the others in my pouch. "I spent a happy month on your lovely planet, which is how long the *Julia* was in orbit. We went to the Lantern Gardens, the Great Obelisk, and the Lavender Palace. I'd heard about the sorcerers and magicians of Ivory, and while I knew they

were fakes, I still wanted to see them. How many chances
would I get to play tourist? My friends weren't interested
in phonies, though. The night before we were due to
leave they wanted to visit the Lantern Gardens again—
they were fascinated by the naked floorshow, we don't
have things like that on Athena. So I left them and went
off to the Street of Gold Coins by myself—''

"Why the Street of Gold Coins?''

"Well, I didn't know where else to find a sorcerer.
And I'd heard you could buy anything there.''

He nodded. "Go on.''

"I wish I could; unfortunately, I don't remember a lot
of what happened next. I don't even know which building
I went in. I have a vague memory of a small woman in
a green robe, with black hair down to her knees, opening
a door.'' I began shuffling my cards. This next part was
embarrassing. "I woke up the next afternoon in an alley.
My money was gone.''

He laughed. "You were rolled.''

"I was rolled.'' Because it's an old story doesn't make
it funny. "The *Julia* was gone, my friends were gone—I
did have some money, because they'd left it for me at the
hotel. I've spent the last two years trying to make enough
money to buy passage back.'' And barely making enough
to live on. But if I let myself see how impossible it was,
I'd go crazy.

"Have you made friends here?''

"I don't see that that's any of your business, gracious
sir.''

He brought out another coin. This was a good day for
me.

"No real friends, no relatives, no guildmates. No one
to care if I live or die, which was a problem when my
tourist badge expired.'' Among the higher classes of
Ivory, murder is considered a practical craft, rather like
needlepoint. A noble who wants to keep his hand in
might pick off a passing stranger on the way home from
a hard day in government. Tourists are exempt, by Imperial decree; they wear large red badges, prominently

displayed. When mine expired, flickering to a burnt-out black, my spirits went out with it.

"I want to hire you," he said, a slight variation on his first statement: I *might* want to hire you.

"For what?"

"To read cards. Not these," he said, seeing my eyes go to the Tarot deck in front of me, and dismissing it with a contemptuous gesture. "I have my own cards. Come with me and I'll test you on them."

This could get too deep for me to swim out. "Gracious sir, I'd better tell you right now that I'm as phony as any other magician on Ivory. I can't read cards. I just make them up."

"You think our sorcerers are fakes." He smiled. "You've been here two years, but you still haven't learned much about Ivory. Rest easy, your lack of talent doesn't matter. The virtue is in my cards, not in the person using them."

He put out his hand and helped me up.

And so I met Ran Cormallon. His office was a house in a street I had never seen before, in a quiet part of town. The furnishings told me he was wealthy, but I had known that much from the way he was dressed. There were six beautifully appointed rooms—tapestries, paintings, computer screens in cabinets of inlaid marblewood—all empty of people. We walked over wine-colored rugs embroidered with intricate calligraphy.

The innermost room of the top floor contained one large marble-topped desk with one chair behind it. I thought that Cormallon would sit, but he motioned me to it. "Open the drawer." I did so, slowly. A corner of gold caught my eye—a case for a pack of cards? Seeing my hesitance, Cormallon reached in and brought it out. He opened the case and spilled the cards on the desk. "Shuffle them," he said, "stack them, do whatever it is you do." When I had them shuffled and stacked neatly on the marble desktop, I looked at him. "Now read them," he said.

I turned over the top card. It showed a man sitting in

shadow, bound and gagged. It was very realistic, with gradations of shade I'd never seen before in a deck of cards. "I don't even know what they're supposed to symbolize," I protested.

"When you're more used to them, you can tell *me* what they symbolize. This one is The Prisoner. Go on; you're doing better than you know."

I turned over the next one. It was an ancient water ship, with a smoke stack; as I put it down a picture flashed through my mind of a different ship, a modern pleasure vessel. I touched the card again, and this time I was looking through a porthole into one of the cabins. Ran Cormallon was stretched out on a bed, reading a notebook; a young woman sat cross-legged on the carpet, her dark hair held back by a red jeweled pin. I couldn't see what she was doing. I took my hand away from the card and looked at Cormallon. "I don't suppose you've been on a boat recently."

He smiled. "Go on. This time see if you can tell me something new."

"With a woman," I said slowly, "who pins her hair up with a red pin."

"Go on," he repeated. "The next card."

I turned over the next card and dropped it hastily. It felt hot. I looked at the picture and saw an Ivoran house on fire, flames shooting up around the white stone.

Cormallon was watching me closely.

"It's hot. I can't touch it."

"Try the next one."

I put my hand on the deck, then drew back in pain. "They're all hot, gracious sir. I can't get near them."

He nodded, replaced the three cards in the deck with no apparent difficulty and returned it to the drawer. "You can drop the 'gracious' . . . since I'm to be your employer."

"You're taking it for granted, aren't you, that I'll take the job?" Though there was no doubt in my mind that I would. The money alone would have decided me, and I was overwhelmed by what had just happened.

"If you hadn't already decided to take it, you wouldn't have been able to do what you just did."

"I didn't get very far, though." When he didn't reply, I said, "Why did the cards become hot? And what about that building on fire—"

"A temporary problem, I'm sure—it may have something to do with your predecessor in this position. She was involved in an accident, which is why I had to find a replacement."

I was ready to ask more questions when he brought out my advance. It was more money than I'd seen in the last six months.

"Thank you, gracious—ah, Ran."

He blinked. "A plain 'sir' will do. I know Athena makes less use of formality than we do, but there's no need to go overboard."

"Yes, sir." I took the money.

On the way back to the market I realized what the woman on the ship had been doing. She had been dealing out cards.

Trade Square Marketplace is the loudest, busiest, and most dangerous corner of the Imperial Capital, which is the loudest, busiest, and most dangerous corner of Ivory; which is not a planet known for its peaceful style of living. But it was the only place lawless enough to let a stranger earn a living, and the only place well-organized enough to protect me while I earned it. The Square only *looks* like chaos cubed; those of us who sold there knew it was as carefully run as a Pyrene military maneuver. I paid a weekly fee to the Merchant's Association—a non-official, profit-making organization—and was not disturbed by thieves, cutthroats, pickpockets, or policemen. Irsa sponsored my membership in the Association; she was the closest thing to a friend I had here. I went straight from Ran Cormallon's office to her fruit stall in the market.

"Cormallon," she said thoughtfully. "They're big fish. Not one of the six Houses, but one of them that claims to be seventh. Specialize in sorcery, I hear, and other things less respectable. Lots of money there. Didn't I tell you when I saw him?''

"But how much of that money am I likely to see, do you think? Can I trust him to let me stay around when the job is over? Burial fees are so much cheaper. And I didn't like—'' I paused. I hadn't liked the way his offer of employment came hard on the heels of my admission about my lack of family. I may be a dim-witted outlander, but I was well aware that I was probably the only person in the market that day who wasn't protected by some sort of kinship web.

"If you ask, I'd say the Cormallons are rich enough to be able to afford a little honesty. They've got their good name to consider, too—they've always honored their contracts. I'd work for them myself if they made the offer. For certain, if it was that young sparklehawk who was here today doing the offering.'' She grinned. Irsa was fifty-eight; she had nine children, and about as many teeth. "I don't ask questions,'' she went on, ''no, I was well brought up. But if he's paid you already, that's a good sign.''

I'd trust Irsa's judgment about the ways of Ivory before my own, or in fact before anyone's I'd met so far. I said, "What about my membership in the Association? If I let it lapse, will I be able to get in again?''

She shrugged. "It's a risk. If you—'' A man in a red embroidered robe leapt suddenly on an older man in brown who had been fingering the bronze cups in an adjoining stall. The two fell, pushing Irsa's cart back and upsetting one of her piles of fruit. She pulled the cart back farther as they scrabbled on the ground. She was standing perfectly still, her eyes following two rolling pellfruit across the dirt. The man in red had a hotpencil, which he pressed against the other's temple. The victim's face contorted. "It's not fair,'' he said, in a shaking voice. "You weren't—supposed to—''

"I was within touching distance,'' said the man in red.

The other was dead. Irsa went to pick up her pellfruit, stooping with a look of disgust on her face. "Aristocrats, both of 'em,'' she said as she returned to me, one large round fruit in each hand. She raised an arm to wipe sweat off her face with the back of her robe. "You'd think they had better places for that sort of thing. Why, dear," she said to me, "you look a bit scretchy. It's all this sun, makes everything seem more important than it is. I know you weren't brought up to it, dear, but so what if two fools choose to end their quarrel in front of us? It's happened before, it will happen again. Ishin na' telleth!" She looked around for something to give me to cheer me up, and ended by giving me what she gave anyone in distress: a piece of fruit. It was all she had to offer.

I asked the innkeeper where I stayed for the name of a reliable bathhouse. I usually carried jars of water from the well in the innyard up to my room, but I felt I deserved a treat.

"Asuka baths are good," he said to me. I'd just paid my last week's bill, and I could see him wondering.

"A good day in the Square," I said, smiling. He'd been patient about my not knowing the customs when I first came here. I could have paid him the next three months in advance, but I didn't want him to wonder *too* much. At that time I still had to carry all my money in the belt around my waist. No Ivoran bank would accept me, since I wasn't on the Net.

"Well, it'll make up for the fluteplayer. He's off."

"The fluteplayer's gone?" I'd heard him play every evening since I came.

"Dirty kanz skipped without paying for the last two weeks. Said he had a job in the north, and the next thing I know his room's empty." He shrugged and spat into an engraved copper vessel behind the counter. "Ishin na' telleth. It's too hot to get excited about." He went back to his record book. "Try Asuka," he called to me as I headed for the door. "Good family."

Asuka was expensive, but well worth it. It was one of the tallest private buildings in the capital, over twenty stories high, with grayglass walls and an aviary garden in its inner courtyard. I was met at the doors by two female guards, both dressed in gray, who gave me a rather perfunctory weapons search and handed me over to the people inside with a friendly slap. "Facial, massage, manicure, body painting?" they asked me.

"Just a bath." The man behind the desk handed me some towels and a woman took me up the grav to the tenth floor. We walked down a long hallway, the woman first with a gun in hand. She coded an alphabox in the wall and a steel door slid aside. "All steel walls and floors," she said, stepping inside. "Weapon-proof glass—good view of the park. Soap and extra towels here; this controls the temperature. The rooms on either side of you are empty. Please note that Asuka personnel all wear gray. If anyone in gray is harmed for any reason, we hold the client liable. If you have any questions, this will call the desk." She bent over, twisted the taps on and off, then straightened up and looked at me. "Is everything to your satisfaction?"

"Fine."

"How long will you want the room?"

"Two hours, I think."

"Should we notify you when that time is up, or wait for you to call?"

"Ah, no, you can call me."

She nodded and stepped into the corridor. "Enjoy your time with us." The walls closed seamlessly behind her. I threw the towels down on the floor and stepped into the bath. It was almost two meters long, and wonderfully deep. If I filled it all the way, it would go past my head. I faced the window and let the water run over my feet. Oh, this was more like it. I hadn't had such a bath since Athena—no, I'd *never* had such a bath.

In the park below it was spring, all green and white and budding. A hot day for spring, though, a reminder of how bad a summer in the capital could be. I wondered how many more summers I would have to spend here before I made my passage money. I'd begun to think it was impossible, and now here was this Ran Cormallon, dripping gold coins, providing me with hope and this lovely soak in the tub. "As long as it's not too dangerous,'' I said aloud, swishing about in the water. My voice echoed off the walls.

I was just a scholar, trying to get my degree. I hadn't planned on a two- or three- or five-year hiatus, but I was handling it, I thought, in the true spirit of Athenan rationalism. Mmm—they should have tubs like this on Athena. They wouldn't dream of having them on Pyrene, my birthplace; nonutilitarian, a waste of time and space. I had no kind memories of Pyrene, not of my crèche-guardian, my teachers, my classmates. It was years before I could acknowledge that anyone could be happy on Pyrene; that, in fact, most citizens were. The best thing they'd done for me was to give me my scholarship to Athena at the age of twelve. They had expected me to come back with my degree, of course, and revise municipal sewer systems, or some such. I changed my citizenship as soon as I touched ground on Athena and never looked back.

Brian Lonii, a guide for new students, met me at the port. I told him what I wanted to do, steeling myself for his contempt; and wonder of wonders, he did not speak of my debt to the state, but only laughed and took me to the top of the Scholar's Beacon, where I could see the parks and buildings and labs of North Branch spread out to the horizon. He took a picture of me there, with the railing and the sky behind me. I wish I had thought to bring it with me when I boarded the *Julia*.

Within a week I'd moved in with Brian's cluster. In two weeks I changed my field of study from technical administration (Pyrene's designation for me on my application) to cultural anthropology; and a year later I changed it to cross-cultural legends and folk literature. I spent half my waking hours getting language implants— I was the only undergraduate I knew who spoke Ancient English, Chinese, and Hebrew. I completely overlooked Ivoran. But then, it was a living language, and what folk tales can be gotten from contemporary life?

One day Brian came to me with the news there was a suite free on the *Queen Julia*. I took a hasty implant of the spoken (but not the written) language of Ivory, and here I was, two years down the path—Ivoran years, which made them even longer—an illiterate fortuneteller for the world at large and Ran Cormallon in particular. Well, ishin na' telleth, as they said here, being the strongest way of saying "I'm not about to care" that it can be said. I had heard of monasteries in the hills nearby where the men and women spent their days thinking and tending gardens. "Saying 'ishin na' telleth' to the world," it's called. I doubted I could ever match their fine and careless composure.

It was too bad about not being able to read, it had made life difficult for me—though it was not all that unusual on Ivory, not the badge of shame it would be on Pyrene or Athena. But I *had* picked up some compensatory skills along the way.

Those cards, now, those were unusual. . . .

Chapter 2

"Welcome, noble sirs. Can I get you some refreshment?"

The bald man harrumphed, returning Ran's bow. He ignored me, which was understandable, since he didn't know I was there. I was in my alcove, well within earshot, behind a satin curtain. The alcove was just big enough for me to sit comfortably, spread my cards, and get a good view of the office from the automatic projection on the curved wall. The more I knew of his affairs, Ran kept telling me, the more specific I could be in my card-readings. I found I had no more trouble with the deck; in fact, it was a joy to me to have this sudden, sure skill, to see the rich pictures and feel the new emotions tumble into my mind, and, to be truthful, to be able to look through a window into the lives of strangers and know there was nothing they could do about it.

The three officials sat themselves on raised platform cushions that tended to put their eye levels just below Ran's. The woman and the younger man took silver cups from Ran and sat holding them mechanically. The bald man ignored his cup. He folded his hands over his chest, just where his robes parted to accommodate his bulging stomach.

"I don't think this need take too much of your time, gracious sir. Our request seems pretty straightforward, as I understand these things."

"So it is. I just want to make sure you know what you're asking."

"I'm asking for a simple removal. And if I may speak plainly, your fee seems a bit high for a service we could easily perform ourselves."

"You're free to perform it, noble sir." When the bald man didn't answer, Ran went on, "What you are paying for in this case is untraceability. Two of you belong to a particular house, no need to mention names, and you want that house to remain uninvolved in this. All of you are colleagues in the Department of Water and Power, and all of you will be advanced through this action. You don't want to anger your victim's family or alienate your own. Very well. His death will not only appear to be a natural death, it will *be* a natural death. Stroke, heart attack, whatever you like. Sorcery partakes of nature, after all. And if you considered my fee too outrageous, you wouldn't be here."

The woman's bracelet tapped the cup in her hand. She seemed startled by the sound. The bald man looked at his two colleagues, then back to Ran.

"How long would this take?" he asked.

When they had filed out, Ran pulled back my curtain. "Well?"

"I don't like them."

"I'm not pleased by their company myself, but that wasn't the question I had in mind."

I sighed. "The cards don't like them either, Ran."

"Sir."

"Sir. There's something funny about them and their designated victim. Something to do with a blood relationship. Necessary information we haven't been given—"

He was already going to his shelf of hand-held books, pulling down the current year's volume of the *Imperial Rolls*. "Hideo, Hideo . . . here it is. What a victim our victim is—no major family support, no powerful relatives. A gift from heaven, apparently. You're sure of the cards? Could it be that a blood relationship with one of our three visitors is what you're seeing?"

I ran the cards again. He was always patient at this

Doris Egan

point, almost deferential. "I can't explain it, but I get the same answer both ways. Our target or our clients: a powerful person involved, a blood tie. And possibly illegitimate—it's on the left side of the configuration."

"Huh. Well, I'll put them off for a day or so while I make inquiries."

"I'm sorry."

"Why apologize? That's what you're here for, to warn me off dangerous ground." He went over to the small round window behind his desk, unscrewed the locks, and pulled it open. The smell of late-flowering cinnatree came in with the summer breeze. It's strange how deeply smells go in the memory; the antiseptic smell of my crèche when I was small, the smell of old books in the artifacts library of Athena's North Branch. The Square was always filled with the aroma of food cooking. Cinnatree is a wonderful smell to enter a tiny room, it seemed to pull down the walls to the world outside. I stretched and let my legs dangle from the alcove niche. "This is the first negative report you've given me," Ran went on, "and I'm glad. You're coming more into tune with the cards. Are you doing as I said, keeping them with you and sleeping with them at night?"

"They're always in my pouch," I said, patting the leather bag I had slung beneath my outer robe.

"The more you do, the more you'll be able to see." He unlocked a drawer in the desk and pulled out a green candle and a small plastic packet of dried leaves. "There's no need for you to wait around, I won't be seeing any more clients this afternoon."

"Well, I was wondering if I might use one of the terminals in the other rooms."

"Go ahead; you don't need my permission. Polite of you to ask, of course."

"The problem is, I need an access code."

"Why can't you use your own code?" His voice changed. "Are you involved in anything you didn't tell me about?"

"No, no. I don't *have* a code . . . I'm not on the Net."

"That's impossible."

"No, a lot of people in the market aren't on the Net. They don't like to be kept track of, and when I started to work the Square they told me not to register. It's not compulsory, you know."

"Great bumbling gods in heaven!" It was the first time I'd seen him surprised. "How do they *tax* you, woman?"

"Oh, they don't. The Emperor sends census takers into the market every now and then, but they never get very far. I saw one get pretty badly beaten, and he was one of the lucky ones."

After a moment of wonderment he said, "I knew the Emperor always has notices up for census takers willing to travel out to the Northwest Sector to try and register the outlaws, but it never even crossed my mind they might also be trying to register people in the very shadow of the capital. I've been leading a sheltered life." He took out a scrap of paper and wrote down a number. "Here. Since it's a family number, I've got to know what you'll do with it."

Feeling my face get a little hot, I said, "I want to learn to read and write."

He shook his head. "Theodora, I have ceased to be surprised. Memorize it, burn it, and use it as much as you like."

So I took it to one of the other rooms. It was the first time since my classmates left Ivory that anyone had called me by my name.

It was a silly thing to be so pleased about, I thought, especially as I had rarely heard my full name anyway, not since childhood. It was a nice enough name but nothing special; we only used one name on Pyrene, so we dug deep for variety. My crèche-guardian named me from a random-historical program, after an ancient empress. On Athena I was usually Teddy, or even Teddy Bear, which latter I left behind as one of the few advantages of my exile. (It's hard enough looking small and cute—and in a totally asexual way, I might add—without having your nose rubbed in it.) But this casual human contact had warmed me more than anything else on Ivory.

Sentiment, however, did not stop me from making my usual daily cash-count, as I walked back to the inn:

Third class passage to Athena:	520,500 dollars
520,500 dollars =	140,166 tabals Ivoran
Weekly salary =	760 tabals
which makes today's earnings =	108 tabals
My total savings to date =	9,120 tabals
140,166 - 9,120 =	131,046 tabals still to go.

I could save the necessary in about three years, provided I remained the single-minded miser I had become.

It was odd: When I was pulling in two or three tabals a day in the market, I was never so obsessed with money. Now that I was making a higher salary than I could ever make on Athena (where even the most honored scholars saved for decades to make their one trip on a starship), now that my goal was a serious possibility, I regarded every spent coin as an enemy.

I stopped to buy a bag of apples in the market, mentally subtracting the price from my savings:

```
  9,120 tabals
-    63 kamb. (rounded to one tabal)
  9,119 tabals.
```

Which increased, you will see, my tabals-still-to-go amount by one. This may not seem like much, but when you figure in this same amount every day it comes to quite an unfortunate total per month. I decided against getting any meat or rice with the apples.

I found myself doing calculations like this one all the time, and I didn't like it. I also found myself lying awake at night, worrying about my money belt, wondering the best way to approach one of the nonNet bankers who operated so informally in the market. They charged a ridiculous interest rate for the "favor" of looking after your money; but I'd heard they were reliable. Of course I could have used Ran's access code to get a legitimate account; but then the account would belong to Ran, and I wasn't quite that naive.

One of my ancient literature texts had been a piece called *Moll Flanders*—an English story about a woman making her way in a hostile, male-dominated society. I remember that this woman couldn't pick up a pewter tankard without reappraising her general net worth. She was beginning to look more and more sensible.

Anyway, I took my apples home and had them for supper. It seemed to me that they'd tasted better in the days before I reduced them to numbers. But then, maybe they were just off-season.

The next day Ran met me at the door. "Good news," he said, "in a manner of speaking. Your report on our threesome of yesterday checks out. They failed to tell us that their chosen victim is the illegitimate son of our Noble District Magistrate. It seems to be an open secret, that's why he's rising so fast in the department, and why our friends are so nervous." He took a bite out of the piece of fruit in his hand. "Have you had breakfast? Have a plum." He tossed me one. "I've already warned the magistrate about them, and he's sent us a reward. Not what we would have gotten from our almost-clients; but not ungenerous, I think. They'll be in the Imperial Prisons by lunchtime."

"Is that a good idea? Won't you be making enemies?"

He shrugged. "Nothing we have to worry about. Hardly anybody ever comes out of the Imperial Prisons. It's not like the army." (The army being where most Ivoran criminals end up.) "There's not even a trial." He grinned happily, a row of perfect white teeth in a brown face. The level of physical beauty I encountered on Ivory was depressingly high; if I hadn't kept in mind that my stay was temporary, I might have gotten an inferiority complex.

"That's not why I'm so pleased, though," he was going on. Or possibly I was just showing the effects of two-plus years by myself.

"Sorry," I said, into a pause in the stream, "I missed that. Who are 'they'? What do they want?"

"It's a lovely idea. One of the Great Houses, of course. Who else would own prostitutes? Do you think I'd take a commission from some Gold Coin rattrap? An advisor at the Yangs' has come up with something new. Something new!" He practically sang it. "You don't know how boring this job can be, Theodora. Nothing but routine, day in and day out. Everybody has the same three or four problems. 'Cast me a curse, gracious sir, I need a luck-spell, gracious sir,'—I'm tired of hearing it. We sorcerers can be creative enough for ourselves, but nobody knows how to make use of us. I only get about three halfway interesting assignments in a year."

"But what *is* it?"

He looked sheepish. "Sorry. I don't usually let myself get enthusiastic. Well, ishin na' telleth. Here's what they want—"

One of the Great Houses had come up with the idea of using sorcery in their business. Every boy and girl in the House was to be given what we decided to call an *over-texture,* a sort of double tactile image. A client who stroked a girl's breast would feel that, in addition to warm flesh, he was touching something else—silk, perhaps; or leather, or steel, or the petals of a rose. Ran was intrigued, but before he accepted he wanted me to run the cards. There was to be some small trouble, I reported, but with people rather than the assignment itself. That was good enough for him.

The next few weeks were busy ones; it was a complex project. Each of the House entertainers had to decide what image he or she wanted to project and, proud ego-ists all, none of them wanted to repeat another's sensory texture. It was a new concept, and Ran had to work out the spells from scratch. Our house suddenly became filled with people using vidiphones, using computers, running back and forth between our office and the Yangs'.

That was how it happened. The overtextures were to

be attached to the entertainers themselves, rather than planted as an illusion in the minds of the customers, and so lengthy spells had to be placed on every one of them. It was time-consuming, and since Ran charged a high fee for his time, the House hired another, cheaper sorcerer to assist him in the actual placing of the spells.

I was on a terminal in an empty room, practicing my reading, when I happened to look up at the spy projection of Ran's inner office on my wall. His new assistant was there, measuring one of the boys from the Great House. I was so engrossed with the boy—as I said, the level of physical beauty on Ivory is high—that it took me a moment to notice the woman. Ran's assistant looked very familiar. I wasn't sure why, but I had a very uncomfortable memory associated with her . . . then I got it, and the surge of anger that went through me was a new experience.

I linked with the room, voice but not visual; this is not considered strange on Ivory, where no one gives away any information if they can help it. "Is Ran Cormallon around?"

"He's in another room. Shall I call him?" That was the voice, all right.

"Yes, please. Tell him it's a private call." In a minute Ran was there. "It's Theodora. I don't believe it myself, but I've met your new assistant before. She's the one who rolled me when I first came here and made me miss the *Julia.*"

"Are you sure?" I could see him in the spy projection, turning to look thoughtfully at the door. The door itself was out of my line of sight, but I knew it was closed, since I had said the word "private." "I don't suppose," he said wistfully, "that you would be interested in revenge."

There's nothing a well-brought-up aristocrat likes better than the chance at a good bit of vengeance-taking. As an Athenan, I should have been beyond that sort of thing.

"The hell I'm not," I said. "Two years of my life—I could be a Master of Arts at North Branch by now."

"Leave it to me," he said with delight. "You'll allow

me to participate, won't you? I mean to say, as my employee, it's as much an offense to me as to you."

That seemed rather convoluted to me; if not for her, I wouldn't *be* his employee. I wasn't about to object, though. I said, graciously. "I'd be happy to hear any ideas you have."

"Thank you." He cut the link. On the projection I saw him smile.

The Great House commission took a few more days. Ran worked closely with his new assistant—Pina was her name, I learned—then told the House he had to take care of family business for an afternoon. He left her to finish placing the spells by herself.

When Ran got back to the office there was a message for him on the Net. The House was not pleased. Somehow it had happened that one of the girls our new assistant cast her spell on—a nice girl who thought it would be fun to feel like polished mahogany—ended up with skin of dragon hide. And a boy with the look of a statue of some ancient god, who had asked for the texture of marble, found that he had sprouted thorns. His first customer actually bled.

"Let's go," he said. "I hear the Yangs can be very rough on people when they want to be."

A Yang representative met us in their public room. "Something will have to be done. Curran—" (the boy with the thorns) "—is scheduled to sing at Lord Degrammont's birthday party tonight."

"Oh, it shouldn't affect his singing," said Ran calmly.

The man glared at him. "And who is this person? You can't bring strangers into our House."

"A member of my own House," he answered politely, "although not my family. Theodora, this is the gracious sir Tyon Yang. Theodora is my assistant. I usually like to choose my own, when I get the chance."

The man's mouth tightened. "Please come with me, gracious sir and lady."

I was moving up in the world. I hoped I would be around long enough to enjoy it.

* * *

The Yangs had a disciplinary chamber in the private section of their House. It was shaped like a pit; old-fashioned, trite, psychologically formidable. Pina stood in the pit's center. There were only four other people present, aside from Ran and myself. Three men and one woman, in formal robes with the circled Yang "Y" on their chests, sat in the front row. Empty seats rose behind them. I wondered what they filled them for.

"Madame Pina," said one of the men, when we had been seated, "this hearing is to determine whether your actions today stemmed from simple incompetence or were a deliberate attempt to sabotage the reputation of this House." A ring of fire sprang up around Pina, knee-high. "All questions are to be answered truthfully, on peril of your life." Like all entertainment Houses, the Yangs went for a good show. They knew how to go about it, though, and I speculated on what Ran's and my roles were to be in this.

To give her credit, Pina's voice didn't even waver. "I will, of course, answer truthfully, my lords. I have nothing to conceal. Ask your questions." The circle of fire blazed up a bit, but that was all. A good sign for her.

"We will first hear testimony from Ran Cormallon, a witness and possible co-defendant. Please enter the ring."

Oh-oh. Ran went down to the pit, and the fires parted to let him through. He ignored Pina. "At your service, gracious sirs."

"Sir Cormallon, please give us your estimate of Madame Pina's capabilities as a sorcerer."

"I can only answer for what little I've seen. She did the jobs I gave her well enough. Passable, I would say, but little creativity or style."

"Could she make such an error as this, in your opinion?"

He shrugged. "It's possible, gracious sirs. I really couldn't say."

The Yang woman spoke. "Did you have any inkling when you left that she might be planning this?"

"No," said Ran carefully, "when I left, I had absolutely no idea that she had anything like this in mind."

"Thank you. Please return to your seat. We may have other questions."

He sat down again beside me.

They questioned Pina for about half an hour. She denied having intended any harm, protested that she didn't know what had gone wrong with her spells, and speculated that some lesser, and jealous, sorcerer was trying to make her look bad. She asked for mercy. The four Yangs debated for several minutes.

"Madame Pina," said the first questioner finally, "we are willing to grant that your harm was probably accidental. However, regardless of intent, you have damaged the reputation of our House. We rely on the trust of the public. You will have to restore our integrity in their eyes." He looked around at his colleagues, who nodded, and turned back to Pina. "To redeem ourselves and show we had no connection with this unfortunate incident, we must condemn you professionally. We will make it clear that you are a risk, and that anyone who hires you does so at our displeasure. Most of your clients are not the sort who could afford to annoy us, and we regret ending your career in the capital."

Pina looked white.

The man went on, "But we have no wish to be vindictive, and though we may claim otherwise publicly I assure you we will not pursue this matter beyond the city boundaries. I would recommend a change of name. Thank you for your presence—"

"No, wait! My lords, please! I've spent years getting a name in this city—I won't go back to the provinces! Please, give me another chance. I can remove the spells, I know I can. Please." To my discomfort, she started to cry. The Yangs were filing out. I felt a tug and realized Ran was standing beside me.

"It's over," he said. I stood up.

"Wait, please!" called Pina. "Listen to me! How could I know this would happen? Please! Oh, please!"

The Yang judges were gone. Ran and I were at the

chamber door. I looked back, and my last image was of her standing in the empty pit, an old man in green standing beside her, waiting patiently for her to finish so he could show her out.

We walked back to Ran's office, scuffing through the cinnaflowers that were all about on the sidewalks. The breeze ruffled through my robes with an unexpectedly cool tang, and I realized I had been sweating.

"It wasn't the way I thought it would be."

Ran was disappointed with my response. "It wasn't as severe as some would have made it," he said defensively, "but I thought you foreigners didn't like that sort of thing."

"Maybe we went too far."

"*Too* far?" He sighed. "If there is one thing I'll never understand, it's outplanet thinking. You people start fights as much as anyone, kick and claw as much as anyone, and then you pick your enemy up out of the dust, brush him off, and send him away with gold coins and 'Better luck tomorrow.' If Pina hadn't cried, you wouldn't be acting this way."

"She did cry, though, and I feel rotten."

"What have we done that was so terrible? All right, Pina won't be living her life where she planned on living it. How is that different from what she did to you?"

"She didn't know that what she did to me would be so serious—"

"When you interfere in someone's life you have to take the consequences."

"—and at least, with me, it's not for life. I'll be going home eventually."

He was silent for a while. My robes swished over the white cinnablossoms. I stepped on one, deliberately, and as I lifted my foot the petals sprang back into place. Hardy flowers, the cinnas. They last until the autumn rains carry them down the gutters.

When Ran spoke there was a trace of anger in his voice. "You foreigners have no concept of honor—not to mention self-defense. You think you can forgive your enemies. That's crazy. One day your new friend is going to bring you down with your own knife, and serve you right." He muttered something under his breath. It sounded like "ishin na' telleth." "Look," he said, "I'm going out to celebrate. You can come if you like. Otherwise I'll see you tomorrow."

"Go on ahead, then. I'm tired. I'm going home."

So he went on to the office and I turned to go through the market to the inn.

I lay on the bed, soaking in nothingness. This room was very valuable to me, the closest thing to peace in the city. I looked at the ceiling of plaster and wood, the discoloration under the beam that showed when the light from the high slit window ran over it. It was quiet. I missed the fluteplayer.

A restless night followed. I got up for the third time to use the privy down the hall. By the hall window I stopped to feel the breeze; this window faced the courtyard, rather than the street, and so was cut bigger than mine. Moonlight shone on the well and I saw lights in the windows across the way. I made my way back to my room. Outside the door I stopped.

I was usually far from intuitive, but the sudden and compelling feeling pricked at me that something was wrong. I reached out hesitantly to touch the door. It was red-hot.

I backed away, stood for a moment in confusion, and ran down the stairs to wake the innkeeper.

I left them pouring water over what was left of my possessions. My money was gone; I'd locked the door and left the money belt under the mattress (the first place anyone would look but my choices were few) and the last I saw of it was as a charred heap of metal among wet ashes. Whatever was salvageable from it my neighbors got to before I could. After an hour or more of people rushing through with buckets—there are better ways of fighting fires on Ivory, but the protective association my inn belonged to couldn't afford them—I decided to slip out before the innkeeper thought to stop me. It had just occurred to me that I might be held liable for the damages.

I found myself stripped down to my skivvies on a dark street, without money, my card pouch still dangling by my waist. I was never without the cards, at any rate; being cautious to the point of fanaticism, I literally wore them everywhere. (''Detail-oriented,'' my advisor used to say on Athena. I just looked at it as avoiding trouble in advance.)

But I hadn't been quite as fanatic about my money, which was strange, but this wasn't the time to analyze the matter. I needed clothes and shelter, meaning more money. I naturally thought of Ran. He would be out celebrating somewhere by now; looking at the moons I saw to my surprise that it was only about the fifth hour. I found a quiet corner and began laying out the cards on the pavement.

The Lantern Gardens are not the sort of place where one goes in one's underwear. On Athena—although somehow I couldn't see the situation rising on Athena— I would have blushed and hidden behind a bush. But since then I had spent two years in Trade Square, where anyone can do anything, and shame has yet to be invented. The manager told me that sir Cormallon was not there (I knew he was from the cards) and said I simply *could not* walk through the restaurant like this. I told him he'd better supply the tablecloth to wrap me in, because I planned on going through. Really, I thought, how can this man be so upset? And the Lantern Gardens famous for their naked floorshow. Unless he felt the sight of my particular body would ruin his patrons' appetites, and I couldn't argue with him there. On Ivory, at least, I'm not to everyone's taste.

Ran was at a table with a woman, which did not surprise me; he'd had me run the cards several times on matters dealing with his private life. She was exotic by local standards; blonde hair piled up with a jade pin, slant black eyes. She caught sight of me first, making my way to their table, and the black eyes opened wide. I suppose I did look rather alarming, in a red-and-black studded tease-gown belonging to one of the performers, and far too big for me.

Ran turned to see what his companion was staring at. To my disappointment, there was no surprise at all in his face. "Something come up?" he inquired laconically.

I told him about it. "So I need an advance, for clothes and food and that sort of thing—"

He was getting up. "Sorry to cut things short, my dear," he said to the woman. "I'm afraid I'll have to be leaving." He started to count out some coins onto the table. "Please feel free to continue the evening as my guest. I hope I can ask for you again?" He turned to me. "Let's go."

"What? Look, you don't have to leave. I just need some money. I left the inn before there could be any trouble, you don't have to worry about my being arrested, or having to pay anybody off. . . ." He was drumming his fingers on the table. He gave me a few seconds to realize that there might be more going on than I knew about, and he might not want to explain in front of someone else. "All right," I said, shifting gears. "Let's go."

In an attack of upper class formality, Ran took my arm. Necessity had carried me beautifully through the evening up till now, but all at once I became acutely conscious of what I was wearing. Ran didn't seem to notice.

"Let's go out that way," I said, pointing to a shadowy area of the restaurant.

"Nonsense." We started down the main aisle. By the time we were halfway to the door I had to stop myself from laughing. The manager was staring from the side with a horrified look on his face. Some patrons stared openly, while others studiously looked around their winecups and over their forks and just past me. My partner was serenely oblivious. I was taken by a great feeling of fondness for him at that moment.

Near the door I spotted a face that looked familiar, a face that didn't seem to belong in the Gardens. I recognized the Athenan embassy officer sitting at a table. He ought to know me, as well; I'd practically camped out in his office for weeks after the *Julia* left, begging for a loan, either official or personal; at least a subradio check with Athena so he could know whether to extend me credit. Surely his budget covered that, I kept saying. The bastard—the *kanz*—claimed he couldn't do anything without my I.D.—stolen, of course, along with everything else.

I waved at him as we went out.

"What's going on?" I asked outside.

"I'm not making the same mistake twice," he said, and shook his head because the carriage he'd been hailing pulled up. The horse was six-footed, but rather old, and I could sense Ran straining to hurry the driver on. We got out at the office, where we climbed briskly up the four flights of stairs to the roof. I'd never been up there before. Under an overhang in the corner of the empty cistern was a small aircar.

"*Where* are we going?" I asked, climbing in.

He fiddled with the controls. "Home," he said, leaning back in the seat with a sigh. For the first time since I'd known him I saw him relax.

Chapter 3

We flew until the sun came up. All around us I saw the shadows of what by day were sun-browned fields, irrigation channels, small groves and lakes, followed by vineyards, followed by hills covered with trees at the height of summer growth. We had come far to the northwest—far, at least, to me, who had never been more than three kilometers from Trade Square.

"It begins here," said Ran, and I opened my mouth to ask *what* began there, when the air shimmered, wavering before my sight like the capital on a hot day. Then it straightened again, and I knew we had just passed a sorcerous barrier.

More hills then, and trees, and in the midst of them, fast approaching, an expanse of greenery that flaunted human attention: streams, gardens, arched bridges, and small houses tucked away here and there. In the center of all rose a huge house of white stone, with steps leading to the front doors. I caught a glimpse of the inner courtyard and then we were down.

Ran sat for a minute tapping on the controls. No one came out to greet us; the early-morning quiet felt very strange after everything I had been through. "This is going to be awkward," he said. "Getting you inside, I mean."

I knew what he meant. It's not that members of one family never visited another; if your families have been allies for the past five hundred years, and nobody has offended anybody in all that time, you might be asked over. My own position was less clearly defined.

"Well, waiting won't help," he said. So we got out and climbed the steps to the high green doors. He rested the palm of his hand against them and said, "I've come home."

The doors opened, gently, with an inward swing. As we passed through, I saw they were at least ten centimeters thick. A long, wide corridor led to the heart of the house; at its end a man appeared, jogging down the length toward us. He was gray-haired but vigorous, in a short green robe, bare-armed, with a gold band around his wrist. He stopped and stared at me.

"Don't panic, now," said Ran, not to me but to the man. "In fact, Jad, don't pay any attention at all. She's not really here yet."

"I, ah, see," said Jad, recovering. "I was sent to tell you breakfast is being served. Your grandmother is aware that you're back, and expects you at the table."

"She would."

"She also wants to talk to you about the—foreign object—you brought through the barrier." He carefully did not look at me.

"Mmm. Yes. Tell her I'll be right there, that I have to wash first."

"I will." He turned to go, but looked back again for a moment. "Best of luck, youngster," he said to Ran, and then he vanished quickly down a passage.

"Better hurry," said Ran, pulling my arm, and like Jad before us we were jogging down the corridor. It ended in a staircase; we trotted up without even a pause. A woman passed us coming down, a gold band on her wrist. She halted in shock. "Never mind, Herel. She's not really here," said Ran, hustling me past. I looked back and saw her staring up at us, her mouth an O.

We entered a small room on the second floor. I sat on the bed while he paced. "All right," he said, "there's no need to worry. I'll go down first and explain to Grandmother why you're here. She'll understand; she's very radical, in her way. I should have gotten you clothes.

Never mind. I wonder where Tagra is.'' He stopped pacing, which was good, as I might have gotten violent. ''All right. Wait here, don't go out, and I'll be back in a few minutes.'' The doorway had a red curtain over it; he flung it back and left.

I waited. And to think that just a few hours ago I had been sleeping in my own room at the inn, refuge and symbol of whatever peace Ivory had to offer me. I decided there was no reason not to lie down while I could.

Someone was trying to wake me up. ''Here,'' said Ran's voice. He let a white silk robe slip from his arm to the bed. ''I found some clothes for you.''

''I look stupid in white.''

''Wake up, come on. It's all I could find, anyhow, so it will have to do. Grandmother's waiting.''

I got up and slipped it over my head. Ran was pacing again. I unhooked the absurd Lantern Gardens gown underneath and it fell around my feet. They were still dirty in their sandals from the fire.

He said, ''Be polite, I don't have to tell you that. You don't have to mention why we're here—''

''Good, because I don't *know* why we're here.'' We started down the staircase.

''And Grandmother is nobly born, so remember to address her that way. I'll show you where to sit. And don't hesitate about taking any of the food, it would be a mortal insult.''

''Why would I—oh.''

''And don't speak to anybody until I've introduced you. And don't—never mind, here we are. No time for anything else.'' He squeezed my shoulder. ''Don't worry, you'll do fine.''

We were in a high hall flooded with sunlight. Screens were open at intervals in the arched ceiling above. Four people sat at the long table, leaving most of it empty. They watched me enter with noncommittal expressions that reminded me of Pina's inquisitors. Ran steered me to the old woman at the head of the table. She wore an old-fashioned gown of midnight blue, and above the neckline I could see her pale, smocked skin. Her white hair was done up in a braid that encircled the top of her head. She wore it like a crown, holding her neck stiffly as she turned to me. Ran bowed and said softly. "Grandmother, this is the one I was telling you about. Theodora Cormallon."

I was too startled for a moment to move, to take the outstretched hand she offered me. Then I realized that of course he was using Cormallon as my house name; as an employee I was entitled to it, and he wanted to play down my outsider status for his grandmother.

"My dear Theodora," she said, quite easily. "Welcome to our table. I hope you like hermit's eggs?"

"Thank you, noble lady. I don't know, I've never had them."

"Then it will be a treat. Ran, will you show our guest to her seat?" She unwrapped her napkin.

Ran looked toward the three others at the table. "Grandmother, I'd like—"

"I have every intention of introducing Theodora. Sit *down*."

He did so, motioned me to my cushion first. I learned later than Grandmother was committing a slight breach of etiquette; as Ran was technically the first in the family, it was for him to introduce me to those he felt I should know. However, as he had said, she was radical in her own way.

"Theodora, please recognize Kylla, my granddaughter; and Ane and Stepan, my great niece and nephew, Ran's cousins."

Ane and Stepan nodded. Kylla smiled and said, "I'm pleased to see you again." It was nice of her to join in the pleasant fiction that I was not a stranger invading their home; she didn't have to be that polite just for me. And Grandmother's use of the word "recognize" was more appropriate to a second meeting than a first, implying that I already knew everyone. For the first time in my entire life, as I sat among these courteous people, I felt that I was out-bred. It made me more nervous than Ran's earlier hints of physical danger.

Kylla's seat was across from mine, and I decided to

copy her table manners with whatever came up. It was
prickly-strange watching her. On Pyrene siblings are
brought up separately, and I wasn't used to seeing people
the same age look so similar. She was very like Ran. Yet
somehow what on Ran was quietly masculine, on Kylla
was flamboyantly feminine. Her eyebrows were thin and
upswept. Two dove-pins held back a mass of black hair,
showing delicate ears with gold shell earrings. Gold shine
covered her eyelids and swirled on her cheeks. She smiled
at me and picked up her fork with her left hand.

I picked up my own fork with my left hand and had to
stop, because there was nothing on my plate. But Grandmother must have already given orders. A gray-haired
man appeared beside me with a platter of eggs and some
sort of meat; he began spooning out the eggs, the gold
band on his wrist showing beneath the sleeve of his robe.
Two slices of meat followed onto my plate. Everyone
seemed to be waiting politely for me to begin eating. The
servingman crossed over to my left to pour tah into my
cup. As he bent over, I saw the blue tattoo of a "C" on
his leathery right cheek.

"C"—Convicted criminal.

Only a small minority of Ivory's criminals actually go
to prison, as did the three officials we sent up not long
before. Most are taken care of quite simply with an in-
duction into the Imperial Army. In realistic terms this is
as much a life sentence as prison would ever be; the blue
tattoo never comes off. All deserters and even dischar-
gees from the army were criminals through necessity,
severed from reentering society by a mark on the face. It
was common knowledge that in the Northwest Sector
many of these deserters had banded together, robbing
and plundering travelers and small villages. The Emperor
could have cleaned out these pockets of bandits, had he
troubled to do so, but no one lived in that sector anyway
but a few farmers and small ranchers, hardly worth bothering about.

So I did not miss the significance of the fact that Ran's
family chose their servants from army deserters. They
were people whose loyalty was assured. They had no ties

with the outside world, and nowhere else to go. I realized
how lucky I was to be admitted to the house and still be
sitting here alive. The Cormallons were breaking at least
ten different laws.

I also realized what I had in common with the deserters, why Ran had chosen me. I had no friends, no relatives, and no ties with any other family.

Grandmother tapped on her glass. I looked up and saw
her watching me. "You must try your tah, my dear. Our
neighbors to the south, the Ducorts, grow the tah plants
themselves, and the leaves are quite unequaled." Ran
was watching me, too, his eyes tense. *Don't hesitate
about taking any of the food.* But I hadn't known my
position was this dangerous when he told me that.

I picked up the cup of cool red porcelain. The tah
steamed gently pink inside. It wasn't fair; I had avoided
ever drinking tah, no mean feat on Ivory, because it was
physically addictive. I now felt it would be nice to live
long enough to become addicted. I took a few sips.

It was delicious.

Thus began one of the most awkward meals of my life.
Ran's grandmother would occasionally initiate a line of
conversation, which one of the other four would try to
pick up, only to have each topic trail off into silence after
a few minutes. At one point Stepan tried to bring up
something about a sorcery assignment he was working
on at his home in the north. Grandmother looked at him
benignly and said, "Family business, Stepan." No one
said anything after that.

At the close of the meal Grandmother said, "Ran, I'd
like to speak with you in my room." She was struggling
to rise off the cushions, and he came forward at once and
took an arm. She said, "It's this business of a personnel
exchange with the Ducorts." They were leaving the hall.
I started to get up, uncertain about interrupting. Kylla
caught my eye and shook her head. I let them go.

Ane and Stepan were leaving as well. Kylla came
around the table to me. "Grandmother's been waiting to
pounce on him about this particular business for days

now. She'd have been annoyed if they were interrupted. If there's something you want or need, let me help you.''

"Right now all I need is a bed, and about twelve hours alone.''

She smiled. "I'm glad it's something easy. There's a room connected with mine, you can sleep there. It was just cleaned this morning, so no one will bother you.''

"If Ran asks for me—''

"If Ran asks for you, I'll tell him you've got important business of your own. Don't worry about Ran. In any case, knowing him, he'll probably be snoring himself within five minutes after Grandmother is through with him.''

She took me to the room, another small but pleasant place with green hangings on the walls and a window facing east. A bar of light crossed the bed. "If you want anything I'll be in my study. Just ask one of the gold-bands, they'll take you to me. Pleasant dreams.''

She was gone. I pulled off the robe and dug in under the coverlet. There was an early morning chill in the room and the bed was more comfortable than I remembered a bed could be.

The bar of light was gone. There was a sound some-where, like bare feet on stone. I swung my legs down and went to look out the window. It was still light; the sun must be somewhere on the other side of the house. The hanging in the archway across the room swung back and a head appeared. "Sorry. Did I wake you?'' It was Kylla.

"How long was I asleep?''

"It's almost dusk. You haven't missed supper, though.'' She came in. "Do Athenans all sleep during the day?'' she asked curiously.

"Only the eccentrics.'' I looked around for my san-dals, found them under the bed. I felt the grime against my fingers when I picked them up. "Sorry, Kylla, I don't wake up very well. Thank you for the bed.'' I really looked at her for the first time, and was astonished.

The makeup and bangles of that morning were gone,

and it was the first time I'd seen a respectable aristocrat without her public robes. She wore a short tunic and wide blue trousers, and her hair was tied in a thick braid. There was a dagger in a decorated sheath in her belt. One foot was in a short furry boot, the other still bare. She sat down on the bed. "I'm going night hunting," she explained, "anything to get away from doing the records, and the kitchen needs game. If you and Ran aren't going to be busy, maybe you'd like to come along. You can't get much hunting in the capital."

Great Plato, that incredible fringe of eyelash must actually belong to her. "Er—no, I don't really get to hunt in the city. I don't know what Ran has in mind, though. He might want me for something."

"Too bad." She got up and went into her room again. I could hear her rummaging around. "I haven't seen Ran since breakfast," she called to me. "I don't know where he is."

"Oh."

"If you get bored, try the gallery, or the library. Or there's a bath in the courtyard that's big enough for swimming."

"Thanks."

"I'll see you tomorrow." Her footsteps faded away. I went to the narrow window and rested my chin there on folded arms for a while. I saw Kylla's figure appear below with a bow slung on her back. She walked steadily out past the trees, over the hills, until she was too small to follow. Less light was coming in the window now.

No sense putting it off.

I made my way downstairs, not sure where I was going. The dining hall was empty. A man with a gold band passed me in the main corridor and as he went by I tried to look without staring for the "C" on his cheek. "Excuse me," I called after him.

"Yes?" He turned. It was there, all right.

"Do you know where I can find Ran?"

"No, I'm sorry, I don't know where he is."

"Thanks." He went on.

Well, there was the gallery—whatever that was—and the library. There was also the bath, but I didn't feel like stripping in front of people I didn't know. Especially since sitting with Kylla just now had reminded me of what a comparative ugly duckling I was around here. That's what I would leave Ivory with: an inferiority complex, and chronic back pain. Why were there so few chairs on this damned planet? For the moment my worries about money, dealing with corrupt officials, and murderous aristocrats paled before these two considerations.

My bad mood ended, to my relief, when I saw Ran through the open doorway of one of the rooms I passed. I went in.

"About time you became conscious," he said. "Take a look at this."

I looked. It was a rather basic Net linkage terminal, small screen.

"This is one of the first pieces of the Net to come to Ivory. They brought it straight here off the ship from Tellys, and my grandfather put it together. The cabinet's Ivoran, of course."

That went without saying. It was a complex, over-ornamented border of marblewood, with stars, moons, leaves, faces, and fish all leaping and tumbling together. Though perhaps I was being unfair. The last time I had walked on Foreigner's Row, the Athenan embassy, which I used to find in perfect taste, had seemed rather bare and pathetic beside the carved and decorated exterior of Merchant's Bank.

"Nice," I said politely. "Ran, I'm starving. Is it too early for supper?"

He pressed a button on the set. "Could somebody there bring me some food? I'm at the terminal in Grandfather's study . . . seed-bread, I guess, and cheese and fruit." He looked at me for each one, and I nodded. "Thank you." He released the button and grinned at me. "The first thing Grandfather did was set up a link in the kitchen."

There was something . . . *easier* about Ran, here on

his own territory. I sat down on a tasseled pillow to wait for the food. "Would you like to tell me why we're here now?"

"Oh." He looked uncomfortable. "I suppose you mean here on Cormallon, not here in this room. . . ."

"Yes, that's what I mean. What's so special about a fire that we had to run off like this?"

"All right." He swung out of the terminal seat and dropped down on a cushion beside me. He had eyelashes just like his sister, I noticed. "I told you that you weren't the first person to hold your job."

"I remember." And I knew more than he thought, too. I'd had a lot of time to experiment with the cards. Ran's previous card-reader had been connected with Ran's fortunes, and was therefore accessible to me through the deck. She was twenty years old, beautiful, clever, with a bluestone pendant she never took off. She came from somewhere in the mountains. She was somehow related to Ran. And she was dead.

"My cousin used to run the cards for me," he said slowly. "She died in a fire. It started quickly, but there was no reason to think it wasn't an accident. I was suspicious, of course. You're *supposed* to be suspicious. But time went by, I found my replacement . . . I was very careful with you, you know. You stayed in the alcove and nobody saw you. But nothing more happened, and I decided I was being over-cautious. This matter with Pina came up; it seemed a shame to deprive you of witnessing your revenge. I let us be seen together. But when your room caught fire that very night, it was hard to think of it as a coincidence."

"You think it was deliberate."

"It's possible. A sorcerer can easily cause fire from a distance. Spontaneous combustion: it's one of the first tricks one learns."

My stomach was beginning to feel a little queasy. "Why should anybody care about me? I haven't offended anybody . . . not anybody important, at least."

"Nobody does care about you," he said, not conscious of any brutality, only describing the rules of Ivory. "But

Cormallon has plenty of enemies, like any Great Family. I've even got a few of my own. By now you must know that without the guidance I get from the cards I wouldn't be able to function. There are too many twists, too many enemies—just too many variables in each case to try to work without the edge the cards give me. I'd have been dead my first month as a sorcerer without them. And of course I've never told anyone that I have to depend on someone else to read them for me. If the wrong person became suspicious, wondered why I always take an assistant with me when I travel—well, they might want to test their theory, and leave me without a reader. I'd be working blind, open to any attack—''

''That's what I've never understood. Why don't you read them yourself? Other sorcerers do.''

''I wish it were possible. I did a stupid thing once, and now I'm paying for it.''

''I don't understand.''

He looked pained, and even a trifle embarrassed. ''When I was ten, they took me to see my grandmother. She'd been ill for several years—most of my life at that point—and I barely knew her. It was a formal interview, held right after my tenth year initiation. There was to be a party afterward and I was impatient to get to it. I stood there in my best clothes while she asked a lot of questions and tested my learning in sorcery. Then she made the remark that, since I was the last male to be initiated in the immediate family, she supposed she wouldn't have another boy to test until I got married.'' He coughed. ''I was something of a brat in those days. I told her I didn't like girls, and I was never going to get married. She passed it off as a joke, but I insisted. Even a ten year old in our family is supposed to know his duty.''

He paused, and smiled. ''I had a curse put on me. Grandmother said that I didn't have the proper familial respect for women, but I was damn well going to learn. She got out the pack of cards that belonged to my grandfather—the pack you have in your pouch there. She said that when I was given these cards at the age of sixteen I wouldn't be able to read them. I would never be able to read any deck. If I wanted to have the cards read for me, I would have to find a woman to do it. And I would have to keep her happy doing it, because no one else would be able to read for me while she lived."

Unpleasant thoughts were going through my head. This was to be a lifetime job? But what about Athena?

Ran was still talking. "I tested it, of course, when I turned sixteen. The cards were dead to me, their pictures turned up randomly and showed me nothing when I touched them. The first woman I tried was in the terminal ward of the city hospital. She could read them, but no one else could. When she died, I hired Marla. Marla was a distant cousin of mine who wanted to visit the capital and make some money."

"Ran—"

"She stayed with me for five years. She hadn't planned on it being that long, although I warned her when I gave her the cards. We ended up hating each other. I had to have her information, and I had to trust what she told me. What could I do? She was family." He took a deep breath. "It was a relief when she died. Then there was the problem of a replacement. I saw you in the marketplace, reading that ridiculous Tarot—no Ivoran, that was clear. I thought my luck had turned."

"But Ran, what—"

"Sir. Not Ran."

I let it pass. Considering the circumstances, it might be best not to annoy him too much. After all, the only people Ivorans were honor-bound not to kill were members of their own families, and that only because there had to be *someone* they could trust. "Tell me the truth. Just what were you planning to do when I saved enough to book passage home?"

"Well . . . I had a few ideas." He grinned. "Raise your salary, for one thing. Force you into debt—that was my second idea—or arrange to have your money stolen. Or prevent you from reaching the ship on time. They're not in port that often, you know, and passage money isn't refunded, so that would really slow you up for a while."

What fine, nonviolent scenarios. Although if all else

fails, the way would have to be cleared for the next reader. . . . "Do we have any work to do right now?"

"No. Why do you ask?"

"I'd like to be alone for a while. I've got a lot to think about."

"Certainly." He helped me rise like the well-brought-up gentleman he was. He was so damned charming about everything, so sure I knew all the rules of the game, it's all in fun, so sorry if you almost got killed.

A young woman appeared in the doorway with a bowl of cut fruit and cheese. Her hair was brown and tied back, and her face was lovely in a very clear and young way. I stood up. My stomach was still whirling and standing up made it feel twice as hollow as before. "Thanks," I mumbled as I pushed past her, taking a piece of melon from the bowl. Perhaps I could get it down in a few minutes. I looked into her face when I thanked her.

Some people are allergic to the ink they use in the tattoos. From the midsection of her cheek back to her ear, the right side of her face was a hideously swollen, red-purple mass. She saw my eyes widen, and for a moment I thought she would run away. Then she turned away from me and walked inside, her head high. She set the bowl down with a thud. "Do you need anything else?" she asked Ran.

"No, thank you, Tagra," I heard him say. "This is more than enough." I fled down the corridor.

Chapter 4

I wandered blindly around the house for a couple of hours. Suppertime must have come and gone. I passed few people in the halls, though once I saw the serving-man from breakfast puffing up a flight of stairs with a loaf of bread. Twice I found myself in the inner court-yard, and the second time I sat down on a bench in the colonnade. The water in the pool rippled softly.

No cinnatree scent here, although the air seemed fresher and cleaner than in the capital. There's something about moving water . . . I began to wonder just why I'd been upset. My life had been up for grabs since the morning I woke up in an alley. Naturally Ran would take advantage of it; that was what he was. And the game remained to be played out. By the time an Athenan-bound ship touched ground I planned on being ready for it.

Torches flared up under the pillars. No warning, no one to light them: Cormallon household magic. I went over to inspect one, cupping my hands around the flame. It was almost completely dark now and the courtyard looked suitably barbaric, with the torches mirrored in the black water.

Across the yard an electric light snapped on and the sound of two women arguing came clearly out the window. There goes the mood, I thought wryly. True, electric light is also quaint . . . but when you think of torchlight you think of ancient armies, processions, banquets. Electricity, on the other hand, is more likely to bring to mind turbine generators.

A slight attack of culture shock, I told myself, that was all it was. It was bound to recur every now and then. . . . Well, if I was still in the game, it would help to learn the rules. I wondered where the library was.

It was in a cavernous room on the second floor, densely carpeted, softly lit. I had passed it by before, and the goldband I pestered into leading me there had to insist before I would go in. "There are no books, no tapes, no terminals. How can it be a library?" I asked him. He shrugged. Like all the goldbands, he didn't say very much; at least, not to me.

The room was lined with shallow wooden shelves from ceiling to floor, with sliding ladders against each wall. The shelves contained everything except books. There were pieces of pottery, necklaces, pendants, and rings, odd bits of stone, and miscellaneous specimens of daily life, some of which I could identify and some I could not. On a shelf nearby I saw a brass shoehorn.

By far the greater number of pieces were stone, and most of them were the milky red or bluestone found in Ivory riverbeds. Stone has always tempted me; I picked one up.

"Would you like some makel?" asked my host. "No, thank you," I answered, cleaning the sauce in my bowl with a piece of bread. We were gliding on Lake Pell on a late summer evening, the lanterns on the prow swaying gently over the water. "More wine, then," said Bakfar. "More wine, by all means." I was well content. My business with Bakfar was almost concluded, and the profits for Cormallon should be substantial. My girl from the Great House handed me a cup, and I kissed her as I took it. Her hair was warm and fragrant. Bakfar provided for his guests like a gentleman, a good omen for our future association. All at once I was stabbed by a searing pain in my side. I looked down, expecting to see a knife, but there was nothing there. The stabbing came again. I gasped for breath. The

*cup rolled out of my fingers and struck the boards
of the boat. The girl stared at me. The night sky
framed her white face. I looked with effort to Bakfar. Poison or sorcery, I didn't care. I would kill
him.*

I dropped the piece of stone. It hit the carpet sound-
lessly and I turned to look for a chair. I needed to sit
now. You fool, I thought, seeing none, there are only
about ten chairs on all of Ivory. Sit on the floor if you
must.

It's not easy to stop being a fifty-year-old man, let alone
one who has just been murdered, in the space of a minute. I needed to sort things out. I sprawled pretzel-
fashion in the position I dropped, not bothering to get
comfortable. I remember paying a great deal of attention
to the feel of the carpet on my fingers.

After a while I looked at the shelves. If every one of
them held something like *that* . . .

That man had really existed, nobody made him up.
Sitting in that boat on Lake Pell I'd been conscious of
the unbroken memory of Seth Cormallon, stretching back
through childhood. That was fading now, but I still had
the central incident, the one I'd lived through—his murder.

I ought to put the stone back, I knew, but I didn't want
to touch it again. I started to get up when my eye was
caught by a bronze plaque in the base of the wall. It said,
in simple lettering: "Immortality is a privilege to be won
and not a right. Rest in peace knowing you will live in
honor and love as long as Cormallon endures." The
stones, the jewelry, the random flotsam of several hundred lives—this library was Ran's family.

There was a sound to my right, a whirring, mechanical
sound. I leaped to my feet.

"Didn't mean to startle you," said the voice. "But you
really should pick it up. We can't leave relatives on the
carpet. People would step on them, and how would we
explain it to Grandmother?"

He rode out into the dim light—rode, on a floater horse,

the kind I'd seen used in Athenan hospitals for nonam-
bulatory patients. His legs were strapped to the sides.
"Eln Cormallon, at your service."

I supposed I would have to get used to seeing echoes
of Ran's face in the people here. But the resemblance
was strong in him—if not for the lines around the eyes
and mouth, if his hair were black instead of brown, he
would be Ran's reflection.

"And you must be my brother's mysterious guest. Is
your name really Theodora?"

I nodded. I had never thought of myself as mysterious
before.

"But what's your family name? Ran's keeping it a deep,
dark secret."

"Cormallon, I guess, at the moment. I don't really
have one."

"Amazing." He maneuvered the floater to just above
the carpet, reached over, and picked up the stone I'd
dropped. He could just reach it with the tips of his fingers. "But Theodora is far too long. I'll call you Theo
. . . in case there's a fire or something, and I have to
shout for you in a hurry." He leered with melodramatic
wickedness.

I couldn't help laughing. At the same time I wondered
what Ran had told him about fires.

He reached behind the floater and pulled out a bottle.
"Will you join me? Vintage Ducort. For your christen-
ing."

"Some other time, thank you. I couldn't handle it on
an empty stomach."

"Empty stomach? What happened to breakfast, lunch,
and dinner?"

"There was a breakfast back there somewhere . . . and
I've got a piece of melon in my pocket."

"But this is horrifying. What will happen to our reputation for hospitality? Still, no need to panic, we'll fix
it right away." The floater carried him off toward the
door. I followed.

"Look, you don't have to—"

"Just how weak are you? Are you going to faint? I'll dismount, noble lady. You can ride and I'll walk."

I wasn't sure if he was kidding or not. Rather than put it to the test I accompanied him to the kitchen.

It was a big room with a central plank table where a substantial, broad-shouldered woman was rolling dough. It was clear from the air that she was already responsible for something wonderful baking in the oven. "Hello, Herel," Eln said to her. "Just thought I'd ride through. Where are you hiding the good tah? And didn't I see some hermit's eggs here this morning?"

"Now, Eln—you know supper was hours ago. Grandmother wants you at table with everyone else. You can't keep showing up here at all hours—"

"Herel, Herel, you misunderstand me. We have need of your noble talents. Our guest here is about to collapse from lack of nourishment. Have pity. —Theo, look pale, or Herel might not feed us."

Herel shook her head, a broad, involuntary grin on her face. She began pulling out bowls and cutlery and laying them on the long wooden table. Eln brought his floater over to the table and I took a seat on the bench. My feet didn't quite reach the floor. The table was huge, the room was huge, Herel—pretty huge herself—was dealing with pots and pans of a suitable size for mass cooking; all in all, I felt as though Eln and I were children who had wandered into a giant's kitchen.

Eln took up a paring knife and started peeling an apple. "Have you been on Ivory long?"

"Over two years now." He finished the apple and handed it to me.

"And from what fantastic planet did you come?"

I told him my story, in a general sort of way. He listened closely and asked questions about Pyrene and Athena, my friends and what I did there. "And you've been working in the capital for two years. Doing what?"

Well, it would be easy for him to find out, if he wanted to. "Telling fortunes. In Trade Square."

"But I've never known foreigners to have the talent

. . . ah. A light begins to dawn. You're Ran's new card-reader, true?''

I said nothing. He laughed and said, "You don't have to worry. It's an open secret, at least in the family. Poor Ran . . . and Grandmother's so easy to deal with, if you don't get her angry. Well, I hope you're charging all the freight will bear. You're irreplaceable, you know.''

I remained silent, shifting uncomfortably. I watched Herel's broad, workmanlike hands deftly kneading bread dough. Eln said suddenly, "Have you heard the Emperor's latest speech? It's priority one on all the terminals. Every time I punch for the racing scores from the capital it keeps popping up . . . 'In view of the, er, dipping balance of the trade situation . . .' ''

I had to laugh. It was the Emperor's favorite phrase, and Eln had captured the pompous tones with cruel precision.

Herel fed us royally. Eln made her sit down and have some wine with us while he told the story of the flyer he had backed in the last Imperial races. "Came in last in a field of forty-three. Do you know what the odds are for that? If only I'd known, I could have bet the other way.'' He imitated the flyer's owner making his excuses; he had a gift for imitation.

Other stories and talk followed. I lost track of time. It must have been near sunrise when the door opened and Kylla came in. She looked tired and disheveled, and was unslinging her quiver as she spoke. "Herel, I'm glad you're up. Can you give me a hand? I've got three ground-hermits outside, they'll need to be plucked . . .'' She saw Eln and me at the table, looked from him to me and back again. "Oh, dear,'' she said.

"It's not a good idea to spend much time with Eln,'' Ran said to me later that afternoon. We were in the study, where he was searching through the files on his heirloom terminal.

"Why not?'' I asked.

"Eln is . . . a very moody sort of person. He gets

upset about things sometimes. No, not exactly upset . . . he's unreliable.''

"You don't trust him?'' For I wasn't very clear on that.

"Of course I trust him. He's my brother,'' he said, with an air of self-evident logic. ''But he's not reliable, and you shouldn't spend your time with him.''

I shrugged, a response I often found useful in the face of Ivoran thinking, and changed the subject. ''Why are you always on the Net now? You never used to spend much time on it back in the city.''

He watched the screens flick past on the terminal. ''I'm making sure there aren't any enemies lying around that I've forgotten.'' He halted the flow of data and made a note on a pad beside the terminal. ''It's incredible that the people we've got investigating this haven't come up with any strong possibilities. They keep *eliminating* suspects. It's very irritating of them.''

"What if you don't come up with anybody? Do I stay here for the rest of my life?''

"I've thought about it,'' he said seriously. ''I suppose we could handle the business by vidiphone for a while, with me in the capital and you here, but I don't think it would work in the long run. You really need personal contact to make your judgments. You'd have to come back with me.''

Praise Wisdom for that.

"Meanwhile, I almost forgot—see that book on the table? The one with the red binding. Yes, there—take a look through it.''

I picked it up; the cover showed a single symbol in white against a blood-red background: ⅄. I remembered Ran had a crystal block in his office etched with the same symbol.

"It's a book of sorcery,'' he said. ''The Red Book, for beginners. Start studying it.''

"Ran, you know I've got no talent for sorcery.''

"True, but the more familiar you become with technique, the better your understanding of our work will be. Besides, there are some things anybody can pick up, and they might do you some good. How to avoid certain spells, for instance.''

"How?"

"Read it and see." He went back to writing in his pad.

I read in the shade of the courtyard until dinnertime. Grandmother wasn't there for the meal, nor had she been present at lunch or breakfast. Ran said that she was often ill and ate in her room. For the Cormallons dinner was a meal of many tiny courses; the whole thing together didn't make up their usual breakfast, but was somehow very satisfying to the mind and palate. Kylla passed me a tiny seed-cake, the dessert, and poured me a little bell-glass of white wine. "Are you coming with us tomorrow?" she asked.

"With you?" I looked around at Ran. "Where?"

"We're going on our jaunt," he said. "It's a family custom, at least with Kylla and me. We ride out into the hills and camp for a couple of days. We do it every year."

"If you're sure I won't—" I cut it off. Inappropriate response. These were Ivorans; if I were in the way, they would not have asked me. "Thank you . . . we'd still be within the barrier, wouldn't we?"

Ran smiled. "We'll be within the barrier. It's a jaunt, we're not looking for trouble. Think of it as a long picnic."

"Will Eln be coming along?" I asked. As usual, he was not at the table with us. Ran's cousins were gone as well, I didn't know where; so the three of us were alone.

Kylla looked at her brother, who was silent. "Will he?" she asked.

He got up and walked around the table. A servant began gathering up the plates. Ran brushed by him and left the room.

Kylla watched him go with a worried look on her face.

"I'm sorry if I said the wrong thing," I told her.

"It's not your fault." She started to pile the plates at one end of the table, where the servant was scraping them into a large wheeled bucket. "Eln used to come with us . . . until a few years ago." A slight tremor appeared in her voice, so faint that I could not be sure if I imagined it.

There was only the scrape, scrape, scrape of knife against plate, and the sound of food hitting the bucket.

Ran reappeared in the doorway. "If you want him to come, then ask him," he said.

Chapter 5

Kylla handed me a pack. I slung it over my back and then staggered under the weight. "I hope you don't expect me to walk very far with this," I said.

"Don't be silly," she smiled. "You don't have to walk at all with it. It's a jaunt, not a hike."

I followed her out the door and down the front steps. "Then how are we going to—Great Plato, what's that?"

Ran came up to the edge of the lawn leading two huge animals. "Olin will have yours in a minute, Ky," he said. He slapped one of the creatures on its flank, a move which alarmed me but which the beast seemed to tolerate. "This one's for you," he told me.

The hell it was. "What *is* it?"

"It's a horse," he said, "the old-fashioned, unmodified kind: straight Terran stock. Her name is Patch."

Well, in an intellectual way I was delighted; so these were the guardian animals so often mentioned in Terran legends, partners of battle and adventure. I had imagined them to be about four feet tall, and covered with armor plate.

I approached the creature very slowly. It stamped its hard front foot onto the ground and made an ominous noise through its snout.

I stepped back. It was so *big*. "It doesn't like me."

"Nonsense. You just have to get to know her."

"I'm not getting up on one of those things."

"Then how are you going to keep up with us? A dead run all the way?"

"Can't we take the aircar?"

Eln's voice came then, startling me. Apparently he had joined us while my attention was, well, focused on the monster. I've noticed before that fear makes me overly attentive. "Ran, I could get her my other floater. It's modified for speed."

"If she won't mount a horse, why would she mount a floater?"

"No, it's a good idea," I said quickly. "I'm willing to try it." It was at least mechanical, not a huge unpredictable beast with teeth the size of my fist. Machines are different.

So it ended with two of us on mechanical horses and two on flesh and blood. Cormallon, I found, covered a lot of territory. There were brooks, streams, woods, even the beginnings of mountains. Ran and Kylla kept a slow, sight-seeing pace, and Eln showed me how to match my speed to theirs. But when Kylla broke into a gallop over a meadow flecked with white hearthwhistle and golden violets, and Ran laughed and went after her, Eln put out his hand to the front of my floater. "Don't try it," he said. "They're going too fast. You're new to this, and your legs aren't strapped in like mine." It looked as if it would take us a while to catch up. As we rode after them, he said, "Are you having a good time? Nature can be horribly boring, if you're not in the mood for it."

"I'm having a wonderful time. I never realized there were so many different plants here," I said, for while I'd been aware intellectually there was a whole planet around me, until then I had only seen the more cultivated flowers for sale in the market, cut to uniform length and with thorns removed. "That's hearthwhistle," I told him, pointing. Kylla had been telling me names all morning, far too many to remember, and I was proud of the handful I had managed to retain.

"So it is."

"It's beautiful."

"It's a weed, and it's everywhere." He looked the meadow over with a jaded, supercilious air, a connoisseur searching for the truly fine, and not finding it.

"Aren't you having a good time?"

"I tend to prefer my entertainment on a more verbal level." Seeing my disappointment, he said, "But I agree with you, it's beautiful. Beauty's cheap on Ivory . . . the weather, the sky, the hearthwhistle . . . that doesn't stop it from being a weed, though."

I was tempted to ask him why he had stopped coming on these expeditions with his brother and sister, but knew it was forbidden territory. Besides, he might answer, and I was already more involved with these people than seemed good for me.

We camped by a lake that afternoon. Ran and Kylla busied themselves tending to the horses and setting things out for the night. I thought that for people who were used to a troop of servants in their house, they seemed perfectly content to take care of themselves.

The idea of servants had bothered me, scratching at the corner of my mind, since I arrived at Cormallon. Pyrene is a fiercely egalitarian place, and Athena likes to think of itself as a meritocracy; neither system had prepared me for where I was. And it puzzled me that the Cormallons would want so many people not-of-the-family in their home. Only after much thought did I realize that they *needed* servants. It was a big place, on a technologically backward world. They could hardly set dust-catchers loose in the rooms—I hadn't seen one on the entire planet. Naturally they could have imported them from Tellys, but if it was the first time the import fees would be astronomical. (They explained this to us on Athena: Tellys knows it can't hold onto its technological lead forever. But when it runs out, they'd like to have a good bank account to fall back on. So the very first model of any item imported by any planet from Tellys is stamped with a fleur-de-lis, meaning "new and copyable technology." For that fleur-de-lis you pay two thousand times the actual price of the item. It's a nice system, for Tellys.)

Ivory wasn't a poor planet, but they didn't seem to import much. I remarked on it to Eln as I unwrapped the bedrolls. Ran and Kylla had gone off to collect wood for the campfire.

"Well, what do you expect, Theo," he said. "You know aristocrats. A century ago the emperor managed to bully us into pooling our resources and bringing in the Net. And the aircar. And a few other things. But how long can you expect nobility to cooperate? Not to mention semi-nobility." He grinned.

Eln had a more detached way of looking at things than most Ivorans, a more historical perspective. History to anyone else I'd spoken to seemed to mean their immediate family tree. I told Eln so.

"It's the way I was brought up," he said, rather cryptically I thought, and taking his bedroll off the back of the floater he dropped it at my feet. "Don't forget this one."

"Thanks a bunch." I put it with the others. "Don't you import anything from Tellys these days?"

"One or two things, privately bought."

"What sort of things?"

"Theo, darling, why this fascination with our balance of trade? The Emperor talks about it all the time, but you don't have to."

"I'm interested," I said, a little hurt. "I get interested in things."

"Well, try to get interested in something else. It's not a subject I long to pursue." He was silent for a moment, then said, "Let's find a topic more in common. Your situation, for instance. One can't help but notice that you and Ran arrived here rather precipitously. I hope you're not in any trouble?"

I couldn't tell if he was genuinely concerned or not, or how much he knew already. "It's not a topic *I* care to pursue," I said.

"Ouch." He reached into his sidebag and pulled out another in his never-ending supply of wine bottles. It was amazing that he never seemed to be drunk. "Will you join me? We may still find a lawful subject for conversation, after a few swallows."

"Why not?" I took the bottle. "May dawn follow night." It was a toast I'd heard in Trade Square.

"And night follow dawn," he said, taking it back. I'd never heard that one before, but it had the ring of "ishin na' telleth" about it. "Did I hear Ran questioning you about sorcery this morning? It seemed a little odd. I was under the impression he knew more about the field than you."

"He's teaching me." I took another swallow. "It's not going well."

"Oh? What seems to be the problem? I can imagine my brother isn't the most patient teacher."

"It's the book. It just isn't very clear about some things. I've memorized all I could—"

"Aah, now that's always fatal. Rote memorization. You have to pick up the patterns, the reasons for things. Then you won't have to memorize."

"There *aren't* any damn reasons," I said, more sharply than I'd intended. But trying to fight my way through that vaguely written mishmosh of a textbook was very frustrating. They seemed to have a whole other way of looking at scholarship here.

"There are always reasons. Look, what part are you reading?"

"Part One." There are only two parts to the Red Book. Part One's title would translate as: Things Tend to Become More Diverse. Part Two reads: Things Tend to Become the Same. Neither of them made a lot of sense.

"How would you find someone who wanted to remain hidden?"

"Location spell," I said, glad to have something easy.

"What's the hierarchy of search in a location spell?" When I didn't answer he said, "Outside to inside? Or vice versa?"

"The book doesn't say. I couldn't find it, anyway."

"All right, break it down. What are 'outside' traits?"

"Outside traits are those most liable to change," I parroted. "They would usually include color of hair and eyes, name, and clothing. And inside traits," I went on as he opened his mouth, "are more fixed and less easy to change. These are often intangibles, and would include hobbies; entertainment preferences; handwriting; and height, which is hard to change without surgery." I took a deep breath.

Eln applauded. "So now," he said, "which does the spell search for first? Inside or outside traits?"

"I don't know! The book doesn't say."

"Oh, Theo, this isn't like you at all. Is this how they train Athenan scholars? You're letting yourself be thrown by the strangeness of it all. Think of it as a problem in logic."

"What's the answer?"

"I'm not going to tell you. Think about it tonight before you go to sleep."

"And you criticized Ran's teaching methods!"

"Getting testy? It doesn't become you. Have some more wine."

"Thanks." I always get a nice glow from alcohol. I thought about location hierarchies, and Eln sang a song about "a girl of the open sea," who had apparently had an interesting life. It was about then that Kylla came out of the trees with an armful of dry sticks.

"Oh, no, he's singing," she announced. "Theodora, you shouldn't encourage him. His mouth will be open the rest of the night."

He raised one eyebrow and took out a harmonica for the refrain.

We were camped that night near "the very skin of the barrier," as Eln put it. Perhaps the Cormallons liked to go as far as they could, when they had the chance, without actually crossing into strangers' territory.

Kylla passed around cups from the pot of tah she had resting over the fire. "Temple's not far from here, is it? We could visit. Theodora's never been there."

"It's about a mile over the hill," said Ran, with a slight tilt of his head toward the northeast. "But aren't you tired?"

"Well, I was thinking of tomorrow."

"Let's go now," said Eln, poking at the fire. I'm not tired."

Kylla said, "Oh, yes, Ran. Can't we go now? Theo, you want to come, don't you?"

"I'm willing," I said, not to disappoint her.

Ran looked tired himself, but he let the majority rule. We went to see the temple.

It was more like the ruin of a temple. Moonlight cast a bluish tinge on the light stone at the top of the hill. We came in through the gaps in the circular wall and stood on a marble floor that still showed a clear picture of a burning torch at its center. The torchfire was inlaid red and yellow strips of stone, its smoke black and gray. Part of the flooring around the picture had been pulled up, and grass grew high there.

"Ishin na' telleth," said Ran softly.

I was surprised. I thought there was still enough beauty here to be worth caring about. Then I realized he was paying respects to the purpose of the temple.

There must have been a dome once. Now we stood under naked starlight. "It was damaged," said Ran, seeing my glance run over the broken masonry where the roof should have joined the walls, "during one of the wars of succession. Which dynasty was that, Ky?"

"The Prian," said Eln. "Eight centuries ago."

A historical mind. "Who won the war?" I asked him.

"We did. At least, our candidate won the throne. Otherwise we wouldn't be here."

There had been no war on Ivory for the past two hundred years. They still kept up the barrier, of course.

"Let's sleep here," said Kylla.

Ran said, "All our things are back at the camp."

"We can get them tomorrow. Who's going to take them?"

He shrugged. But the marble was too cold for sleeping, so we laid our cloaks down on the grass. Kylla offered her cheek for her brothers to kiss. There was a pause, then Eln, followed by Ran, kissed me good night as well. I lay down near Kylla. She reached out her hand and took

mine. "Good night, Theodora," she said. It was a long
time before I went to sleep.

"Where is everybody?" I asked Kylla when I woke.
The sun was well up, and Ran and Eln were nowhere to
be seen. Our camping gear had been deposited in a pile
nearby and her horse was contentedly chewing the grass
beside the temple wall. "Won't that stuff hurt him?" I
asked her, pointing it out worriedly.

She laughed. "I'm glad you're here, Theo. Everything
seems new and different when you're around." She
handed me a jar that proved to be berry-flavored tah; the
smell when I unstoppered it was heavenly. "Grandmother said I could have an outbuilding of my own, for
when I want to be alone. Eln and Ran have gone to argue
over where it should be."

"Shouldn't you be there, then?"

She shook her head. "It's men's work."

I knew that the great families were old-fashioned, but
it was the first time I'd heard *that* phrase. I was shocked.

"Kylla, it's going to be *your* place."

"I know," she said, unruffled. "I'll veto anything I
don't like. Meanwhile, it's a nice morning, and I'd rather
sit on this hill with you."

There was nothing I could say to that. She broke off a
piece of bread and handed it to me. "Just a minute,"
she said, going through her pack, "there's jam in here
somewhere."

I munched and thought. I found myself remembering
the story of Ran's curse, and exactly what his grandmother had said: He was the last male in the immediate
family to be initiated. And Eln had said that he was Ran's
older brother. So why was Ran ranked first in the family?
Shouldn't it be Eln? How had he lost the rights of inheritance? Unfortunately it was not the type of question one
could ask.

I said instead, "Is there some reason I shouldn't talk
to Eln?"

"It's an awkward subject," said Kylla, "but I suppose
it's made no less awkward by confusing you about it. Eln

can be . . . difficult, sometimes. It's hard to explain unless you've seen it happen. He gets hurt, and he doesn't
hold back. Well, I suppose it's not easy for him, being
the most intelligent of us and seeing all the rewards go
to other people. He can't even be sure he'll have a place
in the library when he dies. . . . He *is* the brightest of
us,'' she said, seeing my look. "If you'd grown up with
him you'd know. He has Cowper's Disease. He got it
when he was ten . . . a side-benefit of Tellys' contact
with us. It doesn't affect them the way it does us. You've
wondered about the floater, naturally. Artificial limbs
wouldn't do any good. The nerve damage goes too far.''
She put her breadknife jam-side down in the grass, not
noticing. "Our father couldn't stand it. We have high
standards in the family . . . and I found out later he'd
had Eln's cards read at his birth. I don't know what they
said, but this seemed to confirm everything. He tried to
trade Eln to another family, but Grandmother wouldn't
hear of it. After that . . . he just paid no attention to Eln
at all. It was horrible. Father died a couple of years later,
but meanwhile. . . .'' She was silent, then said very quietly, as though sharing a great shame, "Eln declared ishin
na' telleth on the family. He moved away to the capital.
After Father's death, Grandmother had him brought back.
He was very ill. Cowper's Disease makes you vulnerable,
you know, it does something to the part of your body that
fights sickness.''

"The immune system.''

"I suppose. When he was himself again, he just stayed
on. Grandmother never lets anyone remind him he declared ishin na' telleth.''

That was the shame, not that he declared it but that he
went back on it. When done sincerely—not just as an
expression of discontent, the way I'd heard it a thousand
times in the capital—you were not supposed to be able
to care again. The object of your declaration was no
longer part of your world. The man who went back on
ishin na' telleth had never done it properly in the first
place. He was beneath contempt, a buffoon, worthy of
whatever happened to him now. Because such things

could never work out. As sure as the moons rose and fell, he would be hurt again.

"Ran reminded him once," she said softly. "He was first in the family by then, and Eln said something to him. Things were very bad." she repeated, "Things were very bad."

We ate bread and jam. The sun rose higher.

When the brothers came back, we packed up and began riding again. Ran decided school was back in session and started to quiz me on what I'd learned of sorcery.

"How do you find someone who doesn't want to be found?" was his third question.

"Do a location spell," I said, and added, when he did not seem disposed to question further, "the hierarchy of which is, of course, from inside to outside."

"Why 'of course'?"

"The spell works by elimination. Inside traits are less liable to change, so the subject pool is more likely to contain the person you want. For example, say you're looking for a man with blond hair who likes classical music and lives in the Northwest Sector. There would be more variables, but I'll just use those three."

Ran was looking at me. I went on smugly. "The blond hair would be easiest to change. If you began with an *outside* trait like that, the spell would isolate, say, a few hundred people in the Northwest Sector with blond hair, and then begin eliminating those who don't like classical music. But the man you're looking for probably isn't even there among the ones you've isolated—he's probably changed his hair color and moved out of sector. If you start from the *inside*, the odds are much higher that somewhere along the line you'll find the one you want." I paused. "It's also easier to recast—"

"All right, you've made your point." He turned to Eln. "What's so funny?"

"Nothing," said Eln.

Since I seemed to be getting the hang of things, Ran let his questions go for the rest of the afternoon, and time passed pleasantly. That evening he and Eln went off to look over another possible site for Kylla's outbuilding. When they came back, they weren't speaking.

"I'm sorry the jaunt turned out so badly for you," Kylla said to me.

We were in the dining hall of the main house, setting up for supper. Kylla was gathering hearthwhistle into vases for the table. "I'm sorry it was spoiled for *you,*" I replied.

The last night out had been awful, the tension between Ran and Eln unable to be ignored. We all tiptoed around it, Kylla speaking to Ran, Ran to me, Eln to Kylla . . . pretending things hadn't changed. It was no use, we cut things short the next morning and came back. I did feel partly responsible; I was the one who brought up Eln's coming along in the first place. Ran and Kylla, at least, might have had a good time alone. "I'm not looking forward to supper with them, either," I added.

"Perhaps Eln won't come," she said. "He often doesn't."

But he did come. He came and seemed totally unchanged, his attention bent on keeping Grandmother and Kylla and me amused. The fact that he never addressed Ran might well have gone unnoticed had we not known the way things were.

Grandmother looked brighter than she had when we left. She let herself be charmed by her older grandson, who seemed to be her favorite. She allowed him to help her up when the main meal was complete, so that she could take dessert in her room.

She grasped her cane with one hand and Eln's shoulder with the other, and peered at Ran. "Have you given thought to your problem?" she asked him.

"Yes, Grandmother. I've decided that we'll be returning to the city tomorrow."

It was the first I'd heard of it.

"You'd best take care of Theodora, now," she said sternly, in the tone of one who says, "these things don't come cheap."

"Yes, Grandmother."

"Kiss me good night, then; and come see me tomorrow morning."

He did so. She and Eln left the room.

I looked at Ran.

"I was going to tell you after supper," he said.

"You said that you hadn't been able to find out who did it."

"Maybe no one did it. The fire could have been a coincidence, you know."

"You don't believe that any more—" I began, and Kylla said, "If she's really in *danger,* Ran—" when Eln walked back into the hall.

"I certainly know how to quiet a room, don't I?" he said. "Pass me the wine, will you, Ky?"

She handed him the bottle. He didn't bother to pour it, but wiped off the lip with the palm of his hand and took a swallow. "Sorry to hear you're leaving, I should say. I should say it, brother, but I won't. Don't feel you have to hurry back for my sake."

Ran touched the rim of his fragile crystal wine bowl, gently twirling it a half-circle. There was a thimbleful of red wine inside that raced after the tilt of the bowl.

"Don't feel you're under any obligation to answer me, either," Eln went on.

"Why should I answer you?" Ran said idly. "Ishin na' telleth."

Eln's face grew very red. " 'Ishin na' telleth' is a good refuge for the incompetent," he said. "For the sort who can't afford to care if he succeeds or not, because he fails so often. The sort of person, I'd say, who annoys someone enough to have a curse put on him. Who loses his card-reader, the life of a family member, through his own negligence. Who's probably about to lose another reader the same way. Don't tell me about ishin na' telleth." I *knew,* from what he said and how they took it, that Ran's problem had never been spoken of before, and that Eln was trampling on a Cormallon taboo in order to inflict the greatest hurt with the least amount of effort.

Kylla said, "Stop it, Eln, please. You're going too far. You know what happened last time—"

"I don't need advice from someone who's admitted strangers into her bed within the very bounds of our property."

A servant who had come out to scrape and clear away the dishes dropped a knife. It clattered into the bucket. We all looked over at the sound. The man bowed stiffly and walked away, leaving the dishes out and a wine bowl balanced on top of the bucket.

I wanted to make him stop. I felt hurt for Kylla's sake, and acute embarrassment at being there at all. But if he could hurt *Kylla* . . . if I spoke, what would he find to say to me? I didn't want to know. And it was none of my business anyway.

She said hoarsely, "I'm not fighting with you. Listen to what I'm saying. I love you. Haven't I always loved you?"

"And you've always supported our brother. Don't change now."

"I'm *not* going to fight you, Eln," said Ran. "Give it up. I'm older now."

"Then tell me you don't care—" "Na' telleth" was the word he used, "—*really* tell me. Declare me out of your life. Why put us through all this?"

Ran said nothing. After a moment he stood up. His hands tightened on the wine bowl; he seemed about to speak. Then he lifted it up over his head and brought it crashing down on the table. Crystal shards and wine spilled over. He left the room.

Eln looked as though he were trying not to cry.

In the cool of early morning I packed to leave. I'd brought nothing with me, but now I had three robes, undergarments, belts, a bracelet, and a spare pair of sandals—all presents from Kylla. When I'd tried to give them back she had said, "Don't be silly, Theo," in her best aristocratic manner. She had her brothers' high-handedness, sometimes. I put it all in a canvas pack—that was from Eln, another present; he gave it to me for the jaunt.

There was a knock on the door-post, and someone

pulled the curtain back. It was Tagra, the lovely girl with the spoiled face.

"Grandmother wants to see you." She spoke tonelessly.

"Ahh . . . I think Ran's expecting me outside."

"He knows he has to wait." She lounged against the wall and looked contemptuously over my possessions. "Are you coming?"

I left the pack on the bed and followed her through the halls. I was uncomfortably conscious of her dislike, and found myself wanting to explain . . . but explain what? How can you apologize for a look? No words had actually passed between us. There was nothing I could take hold of.

She stopped at a door with a violet curtain. "Here." She pulled it back for me.

The room was blue, diffused with morning sunlight from the latticed window at one end, where Grandmother sat on a wooden bench in her nightrobe. The window was the largest I'd ever seen on this planet, almost as tall as I was.

"Come in, dear. No need to be shy." She put her hairbrush down on the stool by her feet and held out her hand.

I took it. "Good morning, noble lady."

It seemed strange to see her without her braid pinned atop her head; it hung down like a sculptured chain of ivory over her right breast. "How long have you been reading the cards for my grandson?"

"Almost half a year now, noble lady."

She nodded and took down an inlaid marble box from the bureau beside her. Her fingers played with the lid. "You didn't know Ran when he was a child." I shook my head. "That was no loss to you; he was insufferable. He has improved since then, but he still has a long way to go." She wore the ghost of a smile. "I have plans for the boy, and I want him to be able to meet them. Tell me," she said suddenly, "I've heard that you come from Athena. What is it like there?"

So I told her about the university, and the people I'd

known, all the while wondering why I was there. No
Ivoran does anything without a reason. What did this
woman want from me? Presently she said, "Thank you,
my dear, I never had much opportunity to hear firsthand
of other worlds. And now I'd like to show you something." She grasped a corner of the bureau and pulled
herself up, groping for her cane. I handed it to her. She
led me slowly from the sitting room into her bedroom. I
had never before seen anyone walk with the care and
concentration she put into the act.

I stared about in surprise. The bedroom was covered
with maps. Star-maps, land masses, continents, city
plans—they filled the walls. One half of the wall nearest
the door was covered with pictures of places I'd never
seen—though one of them, I recognized, was the Scholar's Beacon on Athena. A carved wooden bed pushed into
one corner was the only concession to conventionality. A
long marble table cut the room in two; it was piled with
maps and charts, and an ornate astrolabe stood in the
middle.

She smiled at the look on my face. "It's just a hobby,
child. Cormallons are curious about things, and I haven't
been off the estate in more than forty years . . . yes, it's
true. Don't look so surprised at everything, Theodora.
Not everyone is brought up the way you were. See, this
is where I was born." She pointed to a dot on a large
map displaying five great land masses; on a peninsula in
the southern hemisphere were the tiny words "Ducort
estate 3." Looking further along the map I saw written
"Imperial Capital" and "Cormallon main estate." I felt
my own ignorance wash over me. I had not had much
time for research before I came to this world, and after I
arrived my time had been taken up by more immediate
concerns. I had not even known that I was living in the
southern hemisphere! But then, shouldn't it be warmer
here at Cormallon than it was in the capital? I studied the
map's notations and realized that Cormallon was much
higher above sea level, as was most of the Northwest
Sector not too much farther on. I had not known, either,
that Cormallon was so close to the sector—was that why

it was so easy for the family to find deserters to put in their employ?

Grandmother went on, "Times were different then. I grew up on a Ducort tah plantation and only left it when I married into Cormallon. I only left *this* estate when I went to family gatherings with my husband. From what I hear, young women in the cities—those not of the Great Families, anyway—are very free indeed in what they do and the jobs they hold."

"People without money can't afford this sort of chivalry," I said boldly, for the sake of Irsa, whose cart was next to mine for two years. It did not seem to displease Grandmother.

"It is not quite . . . chivalry," she said. "It is custom, which is much more important. You may be surprised, by the way, that I know the word 'chivalry.' The home tongue of my first people—I mean the Ducorts—is French. We lost much during the settlement of this world, but the families cling to their ways."

This time I tried not to let the surprise show on my face. I had heard of French and knew that it had not been spoken as a native tongue anywhere for more than five standard centuries. Custom *was* important to the families.

"Let me tell you a story," she said.

"I am the only one old enough in Cormallon to remember the days before we made contact with Tellys and the other planets of this sector. In those days there were no aircars, there was no Net . . . and women of respectable families were never seen by outsiders. Women criminals could not even be held guilty for violation of the law; their families were assumed to be responsible for everything they did. For me, you understand, this does not seem so long ago.

"The tah plantation where I lived bordered the sea; there were five other families to the north and south of us, all allies of long standing. And far to the other side of us was a road, parallel to the sea, which led inland in time to the capital. We sent our tah to market along this road.

"But the road was difficult to get to. Our workers carried sacks of tah by foot over the kilometers of undergrowth that separated us from it. All the families agreed it would be a good thing to build a road of our own, to connect us with the Imperial road, and we would send our wagons of tah along it. It would be a major undertaking, but we could all share the expense.

"So they made the agreement among themselves and then said, through whose property shall we build this road? No man wanted it to be through his own property, for then strangers would see his women. The arguments over this took many weeks, and at last our family was forced to agree to have it built on our land.

"They sent for builders from the capital and these builders brought a great machine with blades and a huge wall on its front, to clear a way for this road. We saw it drive up and sit near our house, ready to work the next morning.

"We women knew what was happening, and much as our men did not want the road, we wanted it even less. You know, my dear, that we are often rather free in our way of dress when here on the estate."

If Kylla was a sample to judge by, this was certainly true. I nodded.

"We knew that if the men of other families would be passing through our property, we would be made to wear veils and robes from head to toe. No one wanted that. So the next morning the women of the household all filed out to the construction site, led by my great-grandmother. She sat down in the dirt just in front of the great machine, and we all sat down around her. I was perhaps five or six years old. The construction manager was horrified. He had to pretend not to see us . . . but he could hardly start up his machine and crush us all. He begged and pleaded with thin air, and cursed his luck. 'If there were women of the house here, I would ask them to be kind to me!' he cried. 'I have my job to do! I would ask them to take pity on a man with children to feed!' My great-grandmother did not move. He went to my great-grandfather, who did not want the road built there either, you will recall. My great-grandfather said mildly, 'Women will have their way in these things.' And he went inside to smoke his pipe, and did not come out again. This went on for five days, until the construction manager took his machine and went back to the city.

"So you see, Theodora," she smiled, "Custom is a weapon as well as a disadvantage, and women of Cormallon and Ducort have ways of accomplishing what they want."

I never doubted that for an instant, Grandmother. "Yes, noble lady."

She looked about and took the inlaid box she had been holding all this while and put it on the table. "The mortality rate of males in the Great Families is regrettably very high. That is why women still are not often risked outside estate boundaries. We keep the records, run the family councils, bear children to replace the ones lost in inter-family disagreements; so we are far too valuable to risk. Did you know that while the men of the Great Families keep the businesses going, much of the art and literature of the past four centuries has been created by women?"

I shook my head. If it were not absurd, I would think that she was trying to convince me of something. But what could my opinions possibly matter to her?

"But all this does not necessarily apply to you, my dear. You are precious to us in terms of the safety of our family, but your role requires a certain amount of risk. You could never be bound by the confines of an estate."

Now, why did she want to reassure me of that? And just what did the noble lady want from me?

"Well, enough," she sighed. "You must be going, and we come to my purpose in asking for this visit. I am grateful for your telling me of other places; and I'd like to give you a gift in return." She reached again for the inlaid box and played with the lid a moment, thinking. Then she opened it. She removed something shiny and black, about the size of a ripe plum, and held it in her fist.

"You see, dear . . . I know that you may be facing

some danger now, with no family to look out for you, and it may be hard to know whom to trust.'' She showed me what she held in her hand. It was a plump black cat, carved of onyx. ''In old-fashioned times, girls would take these to dances and hold them to cool their hands. This one is special. Give this to someone to hold, and when you take it back you will know his thoughts concerning you. Wear gloves when you touch it, or else pick it up with the sleeves of your robe; otherwise it will betray your own thoughts.'' She placed it in my hand gravely, flesh against flesh.

I looked at her, startled. Grandmother liked me. She wanted something from me, yes, something complex that I couldn't grasp, but she liked me. She wished me well.

''Good-bye, child.''

I hesitated. ''Noble lady? What happened to the road?''

She had to recollect for a moment. ''Oh. They never built it, after all. We went on sending the sacks of tah by foot. Of course, now they have aircars, so perhaps we saved them some expense. Run along now, child, my grandson must be waiting and I'm feeling tired.'' She took my hand. ''Good-bye, cherie.''

''Good-bye, noble—good-bye, Grandmother.''

I went downstairs in a daze. Eln was waiting for me at the doorway.

''How's Grandmother?''

''All right. A little tired.'' I wasn't sure how to act with him; I hadn't seen him since last night's dinner.

''I wanted to say good-bye.'' He leaned over from his floater and kissed me on the cheek. ''Theo, if you *are* in any trouble . . . I'm willing to help.''

''I'm all right, Eln.''

He nodded, and said, ''We're bound to meet again. Safe journey.''

I was wondering if I were being a fool, refusing help when it was offered; when Eln maneuvered his mount around in the corridor and the sunlight that streamed through the open front doors hit the niche just under his seat. I saw the shining outline of a fleur-de-lis stamped on the black metal.

A fleur-de-lis: new and copyable technology.

How much had that cost the Cormallons? I would have given a lot to know when Grandmother bought it for Eln—before he left the family, or afterward, as a bribe to come back. We have high standards in the family, Kylla had said. Ran hadn't been exactly gentle with my life, but he did me the honor of assuming I could play the game without any help. But someone had loved Eln too much, had made exceptions for him. And that was what he couldn't forgive.

I went down the front steps into the sun, where Ran sat playing with a white puppy. He stood up. "Ready?" he asked me.

Chapter 6

It was dark before we passed over the crumbling line of the old city wall. Ran stopped several times to call ahead and make arrangements for us. It seemed like pointless dawdling to me; he could have called from the car just as easily. I had plenty of time to think about Eln. Whatever his problems—and it was clear I had no real understanding of what they might be—I couldn't get over the feeling that, somewhere along the line, Eln and I had hatched out of the same misfit egg. The country of his birth made no place for him that he could accept, a feeling I knew something about. What would I have been if I'd been fool enough to stay on Pyrene? As pathetically vicious as Eln, perhaps, but without the saving grace of Eln's wit.

I longed to turn the car around, go back and tell him there were other places he could go to, other things he could attempt and win, planets where he would be respected. All he had to do was let go of the game he was playing here and learn new rules. Fine, Theodora! Tell that to an Ivoran, who believes in his heart that all foreigners are barbarians, and that the Imperial capital and his native estate are the twin centers of the universe. Tell that to Eln in particular, who couldn't even loosen his grip by the rules of his own people long enough to make his ishin na' telleth declaration respectable.

There was something else, too.

"Eln reminds me of somebody," I said to Ran somewhere over the foothills.

He grunted, which meant that he was either acknowledging my remark or thinking of something else.

"I can't seem to pinpoint it, though," I went on.

"Maybe someone from Athena," he said. So he was listening.

"If I'd met anyone like him on Athena, I'm sure I would remember."

"An actor, then. Or a politician. Or a picture you saw once on a terminal." He spoke with Olympian disinterest, swerving to avoid a startled hawk.

So I followed the thread of memory in silence, not getting very far. Soon enough we saw the yellow square of Ran's house and were parked on the roof, under the lip of the cistern.

Once inside, Ran stalked about making sure all the shutters were closed. As soon as I entered the office, I saw that a cot had been set up alongside the desk; I went over and bounced on it tentatively.

"I'll be sleeping in the room outside," said Ran, appearing in the doorway.

"I thought you said we were being too cautious and the fire was a coincidence."

"I said it *could* have been a coincidence."

"What's to stop this hypothetical pyromaniac from starting a fire in here?"

"Watch." He took out a match and twisted the bottom. Nothing happened. He twisted it again. "Try it yourself. This room is so well protected, even an ordinary fire can't get started. Ane and Stepan are in the house across the street, they'll be keeping an eye on the place. They spent the day setting up a monitor in here—the slightest whiff of any sorcery but my own and they'll be over immediately. Other than that, the business goes on. I'll screen the clients and you stay locked up at night."

"I stay where?"

This was my first argument with Ran. Hitherto I had silenced all thoughts of disagreement with the private incantation: Well, he's paying you. If the disagreement was strong I added: And he's paying you a *lot*.

I had many occasions to repeat these chants over the next few weeks. In Ran's eyes I was simply too valuable a commodity to risk out on the street, at least until we had a better idea of where things stood. I passed the time observing clients, using the Net, and going through Ran's sparse collection of hand-held books. In the evenings he brought home dinner for us from market cookshops and we ate on the rug in the office. There are about twenty cookshops in and around the Square, and he varied his choice randomly every day. I mean that literally. Since the human brain is incapable of generating true random patterns, he assigned each shop a number and pulled the numbers from the Net. I began to understand that Ran was nothing if not thorough.

Sometimes Ane or Stepan joined us for dinner; never both. One always remained across the street, in touch with the monitor. We played cards and drank great amounts of cherry wine; sometimes Ane sang or played the kitha. Ran was trying his best to keep me entertained. Unfortunately the effect was too premeditated. Ane seemed a nice young woman, but she and Stepan were both naturally quiet and the effort involved in their good fellowship was painful to watch.

I might at least have had the satisfaction of knowing that Ran's social life was as curtailed as mine; but since he was doing it of his own free will, to be polite, it just made me uncomfortable. I told him so, and after that Ane or Stepan would occasionally come over with dinner for one and a message from Ran saying he would not be home that night.

And sometimes in the middle of the night, alone in the office, I would lie down on the inconceivably expensive carpet and beat it with my fists and pull up tiny tufts of shadowy crimson. I had been freer in the marketplace.

It was Anniversary Day, the anniversary of the founding of the current dynasty, and cooks and bakers throughout the capital were making the stuffed rolls and green tah, sticky cakes and sugared fruit that were customary on the occasion. The Square will be a madhouse today,

I thought; and I unscrewed the window a bit so as to look down disapprovingly on Ran's quiet, residential street.

I could hear horns and cymbals, very faintly, in the distance. Ran was out somewhere, probably enjoying himself; no clients today. They were all off celebrating instead of scheming. Schemers without peer. When you think about it, I said to myself, why does a man come to a sorcerer but to gain an unfair advantage over someone else? What a lousy business we were in. I made a face out the window—take it any way you like, Ane or Stepan; I'll bet you wish you were outside, too.

It was perhaps symptomatic of my state of mind that I saw everything in the worst possible light. I knew well enough that plenty of our clients came to escape trouble, not to cause it. Sometimes we attacked, but sometimes we defended, like any warriors; and Ivory found us honorable enough. I pulled down a book, flipped through it, put it back, and heard Ran come in downstairs.

He was carrying a box of stuffed rolls and swinging a jar of green tah. He set them on the floor. "Happy Anniversary Day, Theodora," he said.

"Ran, I'm bored."

"Sir," he corrected.

I glared at him. He cleared his throat. "Well, uh, let's see. How much farther have you gotten with the Red Book?"

"This isn't going to cheer me up, I'll tell you in advance."

"How does one cast a love spell? People always seem to find that topic interesting."

"There's no such thing, as you know perfectly well. We can't make people fall in love, it's too complicated. We can only make them fall in lust."

"And just how is that accomplished? Not the casting, just the effect on the victim."

"A lust spell creates certain physiological effects in the victim when he is in the presence of the person in question. Increased heart rate, sweating, pupil dilation, and a long list I didn't bother to memorize. Since these are symptoms of sexual attraction, the victim interprets them as meaning he's attracted to this person and behaves accordingly.''

"And that's why—"

"That's why the victim can't know he's under a spell, or it won't work. He'll feel the same symptoms, but he'll just interpret them as a bunch of artificially caused metabolic changes. And we can do similar things to convince someone that they're afraid of something, or that they're hungry, or angry, or whatever. And come on, Ran, can't I just go out for a day?''

"You know, it's rather charming," he said, "But although the book won't tell you this, the effects of these spells can be quite long-lasting. A few years ago a rather plain young woman came to me—daughter of Benzet, the architect—and asked me for a love spell for a certain young man. I explained why I couldn't help her, but she said she was willing to take anything I could give. Well, by the time they'd made love a few times and talked together and spent their afternoons together . . . she told me I could lift the spell, that she had enough memories to comfort her, and she didn't want to tie him down when he might be happy with someone else. So I lifted it. They were married a week later, have a nice farm out on the Ostin road. Didn't seem to make a bit of difference in their relationship, as far as she or I could tell.''

I sighed. "All right, so you don't want me to go out."

"The effects of a fear spell can also build to such a pitch that, even when removed—"

"We can celebrate here, I guess."

"Now, that's a good idea. The smell was beginning to drive me crazy." He popped a stuffed roll into his mouth. "It won't be much longer, you know. Take heart."

"You've found our pyro? Or have you decided there isn't one?''

"I've decided that if nothing happens in the next three days, there isn't one."

"Fine. Send me out to get killed."

"There's no pleasing you either way, is there? Please, have a roll.''

"Thanks." I *was* hungry. "Are you going to open the tah or leave it there as a conversation piece?"

"Sorry." He pulled out the stopper. "Sticky cakes are in the bottom of the box."

I gave myself over to gluttony for a while. By the time I'd gone through half the provisions I was feeling a little sheepish. "Sorry I've been so short-tempered," I said.

"Quite understandable," he said politely. "More tah?"

"No thanks. I'll be pissing all night." I was glad I could match his politeness. It is considered good form, in the better circles of Ivory, to give a physical reason for refusing a host's food. Otherwise it might be interpreted as a lack of trust in your host. That didn't apply to Ran, but still—good manners.

"That's what holidays are for." He finished the jar. "Kylla should be by later."

"Tonight? She's in the city!"

"Tomorrow—she's attending a dance here tonight, she'll be staying as a houseguest of the Ducorts. I may drop in on them later myself, so don't be surprised if you wake up tonight and I'm not here."

"Stop worrying, I'm not going to panic. I can take care of myself." And so I can, except where the people I'm dealing with are bigger, stronger, more numerous, or carrying weapons. That covered just about everyone on this planet, but I was damned if I was going to let it affect my peace of mind, such as it was.

I turned in early that night. Lying on the cot it suddenly came to me whom Eln had been reminding me of. Not a professor or a politician, either—although, in a sense, it was on Athena that I met him. It would be pleasant to tell Ran how wrong his guesses were, but he wouldn't get the reference anyway. Eln reminded me of Loki. Red-bearded, resentful, entertaining Loki, an aspect of the Terran trickster god. That's an Athenan scholar for you—track down our associations and you'll find they all come out of books.

I suppose it was something about his sense of humor, and the way he was-part/was-not-part of the family. I thought of Ran sleeping in the next room. If Eln was Loki, who did that make him? Thor, I supposed, but he was really too sophisticated for Thor.

It was a pity, I thought, as I settled sleepily into the mattress, that these metaphors never quite worked out.

Too much tah can keep you awake, just as everyone says. I woke up twice, the second time apparently irrevocably. I was annoyed with myself. Ran had clients coming in the morning and I would be falling asleep over the cards—the alcove niche was warm and stuffy and lent itself to that kind of thing. A quiet check of the outer room showed me that Ran was gone, doubtless to Kylla's dance. Lack of sleep never seemed to bother *him* in the morning.

I resolved to lie motionless on the cot until sheer boredom sent me under. This had never worked before, but there was always a first time. I lay down accordingly.

Within minutes I began to hear creaks, rustlings, and the other night sounds that are reserved for empty houses. That one was *almost* like a door opening . . . that one *almost* like a footstep . . . It went on for the better part of an hour. I refuse to give in to this, I thought; I refuse to put on the light.

Then a hand reached down and grabbed me.

I don't know when I woke up, but from what I learned later I must have been unconscious for at least half a day. I was in a small, steel-walled room whose metallic anonymity reminded me of the Asuka baths, except that here one could not even begin to guess where the door was. Plato, Athena, and all gods of scholars stick by me now, I thought; I had no idea what was going on but I knew I was in for it.

It is a tribute to the habit of months that the first thing I did was check to see if I still had my cards. I did. Then I looked around at the drab walls. There might easily be observation equipment, but if so, it was hidden. I took stock of myself—no headache, nausea, or needlemarks. Athena was with me so far. But how had they put me out? Sorcery? No form that I had been taught—it had happened too quickly. I felt the walls, searching for the door; nothing.

There was a low table on casters nearby. The only other object in the room was the bedroll I'd awakened on; I went over and sat on it.

After about an hour a seam appeared in the wall opposite. The metal parted and a man came in. Tall, broad, middle-aged, with carefully curled beard and ruby earrings. His robes were plain and white, and his belt was brown leather. He walked like a wrestler.

"Don't worry," he smiled. "We haven't taken your cards."

I didn't say anything.

He motioned to the table. "Won't you sit with me?" There was a cushion beside it; he sat, and I took the floor. His perfume was strong in the tiny room. I recognized the scent—it was one Ran used at times, and it cost more per centiliter than I made in a month. "I gather that you *are* Cormallon's advisor," he went on. "Either that or his lover, and I tend to think it's the former."

When I still didn't answer, he said, "You may as well admit it. Why else would you be holding the pack of cards?"

I said, "I'm Cormallon's pupil. He's instructing me in sorcery and he gave me a deck for my own guidance. What does that have to do with you?"

"It's a rich deck to give a beginner."

"I paid a lot of money for it."

"I see. Well, I'm going to test my theory." He took out a pipe, a rather gaudy one, no different from the cheap synthawoods on sale in the market but for the silver plate on the stem. Possibly it was a signal, for a boy came in then in short gray robe and scraped knees. He carried tah, one cup, which he set in front of the man. It was insultingly rude. I was his guest, albeit an involuntary one, and there should have been two cups. I ought to have been grateful for one less thing to worry about, but I felt anger, and it surprised me—before this I had only been scared. "It would stand to reason," he said, "that if Cormallon has to depend on one specific person to give his readings, then the power can't be transferred until your death." He was watching for my reactions. I hoped I wasn't giving any.

"So," he went on, "you're not going to be touched. For the moment. We'll give Cormallon a little time to get nervous, notice he's lost something. Then we'll make our offer: a slight payment to me, the nature of which doesn't concern you, and we'll send back his cards. And we'll kill you, so he can be free to get a replacement. I mean no offense by the last statement; but after all, we can hardly return you. You've seen what I look like."

"Then why," I said, "did you let me see you?"

He smiled.

I thought, Ran, if you ever decide to take revenge on this man, I swear I'll never give you a hard time about it.

He said, "There isn't anything you'd like to tell me?"

"About what?" I asked sincerely. He seemed to have the whole story, and he'd be proved right soon enough.

"Well, then," he said courteously, and stood up, a host taking his leave. I put my palms on the table, shifting my weight to rise also.

He lifted his sandaled foot and brought it down on the back of my right hand. I rocked back, gasping. I could feel a tear starting down one cheek, and I turned my face aside.

"Perhaps I'll come back later," he said cheerfully, "and you can run through the cards for me. That would be very enlightening, I'm sure." He paused at the door. "You don't really believe, I hope, that Cormallon won't agree to these terms?"

I clasped my right hand. Any revenge you want to try, Ran. I set no limits, use your fine imagination. But I wasn't fooling myself. Of course he would agree to the terms. He was an Ivoran. There was no reason not to.

It felt as though at least a day, and perhaps more, had gone by. My hand was bruised but not broken; it throbbed only when I paid attention to it. I expected my captor hourly, but he had not returned. One meal had been served by the boy with scraped knees, a bowl with an impersonally tasteless grouping of meat and rice. The meat was unidentifiable. I tried smiling at the boy. He smiled back, rather shyly. "You have a name?" I asked. "I'm Theo." He shook his head nervously, his eyes looking toward the door. He never came back for the empty bowl.

I ran the cards four or five times; there was nothing else to do. They told me that Ran was in danger, which irritated me. *I* was the one in danger. Ran had a few problems, certainly, stemming from my kidnapping; but nothing he couldn't handle. The Prisoner card kept turning up. "How helpful," I murmured, finding myself talking to the deck. Why not? I'd become obsessed with these painted pieces of cardboard. I ran them daily, ate with them, slept with them, and half the time dreamed about them. I'd been so relieved to find they hadn't been taken. Identifying their safety with mine . . . it wasn't healthy. And this was what I was, in Ran's eyes, in the eyes of the man with the vulgar pipe. They paid me in gold or they stamped the back of my hand for it, but here my profession was what I was.

I picked up the cards and threw them against the wall. Let them lay there. Eventually someone, maybe the boy, would come and put them carefully together and send them off to Ran with a note saying I was dead. And Ran would find someone new to test them and know it was true. It was a pity I couldn't burn them, but I had nothing to start a fire.

Time passed, and finally I gathered them up and put them back in my pouch.

The lights had gone out. I got up quickly, not knowing what to expect. There was only dark, and silence. Then a seam of gray light appeared where the door ought to be; I moved to a diagonal position across from it. My heart was pounding as though it were about to leap out of my chest. It was lighter outside the door—I could see a man's silhouette on the threshold. Before his sight could

adjust to the darkness I ran the space between us and
rammed him, head first, in the stomach. He gave a
breathless groan. As I did I was thinking, "the eyes—
you've got to find the eyes." I was no match for an adult
Ivoran and my only chance was to fight dirty, a choice I
felt Ran would have approved.

"Oof," said Ran's voice in the darkness. "Enthus . . .
iastic, aren't you."

"Ran! What—" I dropped my hands from his face.

"Never mind. We've got five minutes before the lights
come on."

He grabbed my hand and we started running down the
corridor. It was lit with a ghostly gray luminescence,
some kind of secondary power source, I guessed. We
rounded a corner and ran into a man coming from the
other direction, in a gray tunic and cap that seemed
vaguely like a uniform. He blinked, startled. His hand
went to his side. I kept running, straight into another
tackle, and Ran got an arm around his neck as he went
over. (I learned this art of the tackle as a child on Pyrene,
where we played a game called football. At the time I
hated it, but now saw that it did indeed prepare one for
life.) "Very nice," said Ran to me, polite as always. He
had the man's weapon and was holding it against his
cheek. I turned away, not wanting to see how my employer handled the matter.

I closed my eyes and tried to concentrate on something
else. This man was wearing a uniform, but I was not
well-educated enough to recognize the colors of a family
livery. It must be a powerful House, though. Where were
we? The Shikibus'? The Degrammonts'?

I opened my eyes. To my surprise it was hard to do.
Hadn't he finished yet?

He was whispering—no, chanting—in the man's ear.
He held him by the shoulders, his head in the crook of
an arm. The corridor seemed to waver; I put out a hand
to the wall to steady myself. "Theo!" Ran hissed. I shook
my head fiercely. He lowered the man gently to the floor
and stood up. "Come on!"

"There's a grav bank," he got out as we pounded on,

"at the end . . . but we need the power . . . to come back . . . on time." I could see it in the distance. Suddenly the corridor lit up to full brilliance. "Too soon," he said. "Hurry."

We reached the end and the grav opened. Ran punched the speed float and we shot up to the roof.

It was dark and windy. I could see row upon row of aircars—the building must be enormous, I thought. Some of them were huge shapes, like freight trucks. One of the cars had an open door, and Ran motioned me into it after him. "Wait a minute," I said. "This is a—"

"I know," he said, pulling me in.

We took off. "Ran," I said, "You're stealing a *police vehicle.*"

"What other kind of vehicle could I steal? Theodora, don't you even know where you are?" He stopped fiddling the controls and turned to me in disbelief. "We just broke out of the city detention units, under police headquarters."

We flew out of the city, through the night. I never seem to travel in the daylight anymore, I thought. I looked over at Ran, sitting at the controls; he wore the rough-weaved uniform of the Imperial jails, gray shorts and overtunic. But a sweet smell was in the car, a scent much like the one I'd recognized on my interrogator. That was a Cormallon for you. He would wear the uniform, but he refused to wash off his perfume.

"Are we going home? Your home, I mean."

"No." He punched in the automatic. "That direction wouldn't be safe for us right now. We're going to another city. You've cost me a fortune in bribes, you know."

"I didn't expect you to come."

"I don't know why not," he said, sounding hurt. "When it was my fault you were picked up. I was so damn careful to watch out for sorcery, I forgot about brute force."

"Why was I picked up? Why should the police care about me? Or you either, for that matter."

"Well, sorcery *is* illegal. There are conventions. Painful though following the law may be, sometimes it is enforced—"

"Don't joke," I said, sounding as irritated as I felt.

"Where have you been for two and a half years? It's the truth."

"But everyone uses it. Some of your clients were policemen."

He was smiling, I suppose at my naïveté. It's a strange universe—magic illegal on the one planet where it's known to exist.

"Still," I said, "If they never arrested you before—"

"And they haven't arrested me now, not as Ran Cormallon. No, there's just one person behind this. The only one who could have the power to lock you in a holding cell and keep it a secret would be the man who runs the place—the Chief of Police. He keeps too tight a rein on his people for it to be anyone else." I described the man who had spoken to me in my cell. He nodded. "I can see his point of view. It would be a three-way success for him: putting a Cormallon out of business and impressing his superiors; getting blackmail payments from me; and using me to ruin other sorcerers. Still, he's taking a lot upon himself . . . if he is. Maybe it's arrogance, but I don't believe anyone would take on the Cormallons all alone. Damn. I wish I could question him, but as my late father used to say, the one thing you never do is dance around with the cops. Father had a quaint way of expressing himself."

"So what do we do?"

"We'll kill him. Safest thing under the circumstances."

I remembered my promise and said, "Good."

He smiled, surprised but pleased by this rare evidence of my good sense.

I said, "But Ran, how did you find me?"

" 'Sir,' not—oh, never mind. Call me Ran. Stepan picked up that there was something wrong in the room and followed the men who took you. He called me at the Ducorts. Then I had to make a lot of bribes." He began listing them on his fingers. "To get myself arrested under a false name. To make sure my cell was unlocked. To find out where you were—it was sheer luck I got to you so fast, I knew what level you were on but not what cell. To have the power and the first back-up power cut off. There was an extra fee to see that your level was unpatrolled at the right time, but they did tell me that might not work out perfectly. No amount of bribery would let me bring in a weapon, though. That's a death offense, for the guard and the prisoner both."

"I'm sorry about all the money."

"That's all right. I can take it out of your salary." He said it quite seriously.

We stayed that night in a branch house of the Cormallons in the town of Braece, the only town on an island about two hundred kilometers off the coast, and a good five hours' travel from the capital in a direction just opposite Cormallon itself. The family here lived in a tall gray tower near the ocean, with dull reddish-brown waves breaking on dull brown rocks at the cliff beneath the tower's base. Mournful birds, as seem to fly over every ocean on every world, soared past the windows. The family was a small one, father and mother and aunt, little boy and girl. They were far removed here from the intrigues of the capital, seemingly quite content to be so. They also seemed the slightest bit in awe of Ran, but not in any uncomfortable way. They took us to a suite at the top of the tower, gave us clothes and towels, and left us alone.

Ran went to the Net as soon as they had left. I ran water for a bath and laid out my clothes from what they had given us. The water was too loud for me to hear Ran as he spoke to whomever was at the other end. I knew what he was doing anyway. He was arranging the police chief's demise. The details were just business; I had no interest in them. "All done," he said, when he came over to the tub. I sat on the edge, my legs dangling in the water, half in and half out of my robes. It was a family-size bath, deep enough to stand in, with enough room for six or seven people. A waste of resource in this case. "I'll turn off the water," I said. "Unless you want it deeper." I got up to do so, dropped back down into a cushion and took a deep breath, hearing my heart beat like the tide outside the windows. I felt hot and weak, as though I hadn't eaten in days.

Ran swung down beside me. "You look *awful*," he said. He put his hand on my forehead. "Shall I get you water? Should I have our hosts bring you some food? When did you last eat?" He sounded genuinely concerned, and it was more than I could bear.

"I'm not hungry. I'm all right." To my embarrassment I heard my voice shake. Theodora of Pyrene, jailbreak-artist, ruthless criminal mastermind. And my hand still hurt. I turned my face away and got up, a little unsteadily, to go to the taps.

"Wait a minute," he said, taking hold of the sleeve of my robe.

"I'm sorry. I guess I've been more worried than I thought—"

He unhooked the top of my robe and started to kiss me. It was so startling I forgot I was upset.

I had thought about this happening since the first day I read the cards and long ago decided that I could not afford to get any more entangled in Ran's life. I was still going to leave as soon as I could, save myself and ruin his career. This sort of thing was what we referred to on Athena as a conflict of interest. Not to mention it was a violation of the employer/employee relationship. . . .

Luckily Ran continued to take the initiative, because it might have taken me years to work out the ethics of the situation. He pulled me back down on the cushion and I slipped off what remained of my clothes, holding onto him as though I were drowning.

"What's digging into my back?" asked Ran some time later.

I investigated and found that I still had Grandmother's onyx cat lost at the bottom of my pile of robes; I was glad no one had taken it from me. "It's a present from your grandmother," I said sleepily.

"Present? Show me."

I pulled aside the robes and held it out.

I heard his breath draw in. "Where did you get *this*?" He took it gently from my hands.

"I told you, it's a present from Grandmother."

He was looking at me strangely, and I suddenly realized what I had done. I tried to take it back, but he held it out of my reach and, wrapping it carefully in his cloak, said, "I think I'd better give it some time to wear off first." It was late, and I decided I was too tired to try to understand.

A shrieking bird outside the window awakened me. Ran's cloak was tangled around my legs, and I had a panicked moment when I couldn't find my card pouch. Then I saw it on the floor across the room. I *must* have been in a confused state of mind, I thought. I heard Ran's voice from the other room; he was on the Net again. I dressed and went out just as he was logging off. "It's been taken care of," he said, "we can go home." As easy as that.

Well, it wasn't that easy for me. He made no move to touch me, or kiss me, or wish me good morning, as my Athenan lovers (none of whom had meant over-much to me, or vice versa) had been polite enough to do. Last night had clearly been erased. Granted, we had both been running on adrenaline since leaving police headquarters; there had been more of physical reflex than anything else in the timing of what happened; but there had been something else, too. I wanted it acknowledged.

I walked over to him. "Good morning," I said, more like a challenge than anything else, and I kissed him. He returned it, impersonally. Then he picked up my onyx cat from the Net counter, grasping it in a towel, and held it out to me.

"Better hold onto this," he said. "Grandmother doesn't give out gifts casually."

I took it from him and jammed it into my pouch, beside the cards. I went into the other room, found my outer robe and belt and made sure there was nothing I'd forgotten.

He was closing up the Net when I came back in. "Shouldn't we be running along?" I asked.

"Give me a hand with the cover? It's a guestroom Net; it will only get dusty if we leave it out."

So we closed it up, like courteous guests. He led the way down the circular staircase and I followed, with savage politeness.

We said good-bye to the family group downstairs. The aircar was perched on the hill above the rocks and the winds blew up around us. The little family was lined up outside the tower, red-faced in the wind. The father bowed nervously and the others followed suit. When we reached the car, there was a flash of blue smoke. Ran pulled me by the arm and we both fell onto the hard-packed dirt, rolling out of the way.

Nothing happened. I'd landed on my bad hand and sat up, blinking with pain. Ran jumped to his feet. "Just who is responsible for this?" he said angrily.

They looked at one another. The little girl's face puffed up a dark reddish tan, and she began to bawl.

Ran stopped glaring immediately and went over to her. "Here, here, darling, it's all right. I'm sorry. I was just surprised, that's all." He knelt down and hugged her. "You wanted to show us what you could do, didn't you? You wanted to make an illusion?" She nodded, her face buried in his shoulder. Clearly words were still beyond her. "Well, and it was certainly a good show you put on, wasn't it? It took our attention."

She heaved, between sobs, "There—were—supposed to be—d-d-doves."

"Oh, darling." He kissed her. "There'll be doves one day, I promise." He reached to his shoulder and ripped off the silver clasp on his cloak. "Here, look." He showed her the diamond-shaped clasp with its long pin. She sniffled. He put it into her hand. "Keep it, now, be very careful with it; it's a magic talisman. You keep it with you when you work your spells. And if you study hard and practice long enough, I swear to you, one day you'll make beautiful doves.'' Magic talisman, indeed! The clasp and the cloak both had been supplied to Ran by her own parents to replace his jail uniform.

She stared at the clasp. "But don't you need it?"

"Not any more, honey. It's a gift, from one sorcerer to another."

A smile broke out on her face. She threw her arms around him and clung to him. I turned away and looked out to the ocean.

The sun was high over the water as we flew west. We ate as we flew, a boxed meal the Braece family had put up for us. A sea blossom wrapped in a piece of red-striped silk was in the box beside the food. I opened the card case from time to time and flicked through the deck.

"You're pretty quiet," he said.

I shrugged. "Sorry."

It took us several hours to near Cormallon territory. Ran bypassed the capital and took a straight line for home.

We had often been silent with one another, but where before it had been companionable, now it grated. He shifted in his seat and would tap the controls, make an effort to stop, and then tap again. The green and brown hills, the vineyards, passed away beneath us.

"Look," he said, and stopped. When he spoke it was to state the obvious, and I felt that it was not what he had meant to say. "Look, at least we won't have to worry about any more attempts on your life. The police chief seems to have been the active figure, and he's out of our way."

We reached the Cormallon barrier. The air shimmered obediently around us, and the car caught fire.

Chapter 7

Time passed. It was dark and I was asleep. One dream kept recurring, the time when I was three years old in the crèche kitchen on Pyrene, and I spilled boiling water on my hands. I yelled and screamed and dropped the container I was holding, and the kitchen worker went to get my crèche-guardian, who sat and held until they came with salve and painkillers, and took me to the infirmary.

I hadn't thought of her in years. The dream-memory of her face was sharp and clear, and didn't go with the voices I heard, familiar voices, but somehow removed from the place where I was dreaming.

Kylla's voice. I tried to open my eyes and couldn't. "Kylla!" It came out a croak.

"Theo, sweetheart, don't move. We've got you all strapped in."

"I can't open my eyes."

"You're wearing a bandage. Don't worry about it, it doesn't mean you're blind, we just can't take it off yet."

"Ran—"

"Ran's fine. He generated a personal shield right away. He extended it to you as soon as he could, but it was a few seconds too late. He's just downstairs, wait a minute." Her footsteps went away and I heard her talking outside the door. She returned to my bed. "He'll be right up. How do you feel? Any pain?"

"No." There was a delayed surprise to that realization; shouldn't I be, in fact, in a great deal of pain? Or

how long had I lain here? Long enough for burns to heal?
"Ky, how long—"

"Not too long. Don't worry about—"

Running footsteps. "Ky, is she awake? Theodora?"

"Hello, Ran."

I heard a released breath. "Theodora. How do you
feel?"

"All right. I guess. I wish I could see you."

He sat down on the bed. "Tilt your head forward."

Kylla's voice was sharp. "Brother, what do you think
you're doing?"

His fingers were loosening the bandage around my
eyes. "Come on, Ky, it's almost time for it to come off
anyway. Another day or two won't make any difference."

"Theo, if the light hurts your eyes, you speak up right
away. Understand?"

The bandage came off, all of a piece, and I blinked.
Ran sat blurrily before me, looking anxious. Kylla came
over next to him and swung back the bar that held in my
legs. She said, "Can you see me?"

"Yeah. Your hair looks nice up."

She smiled. "So much for Tellys medical advice," she
said airily to Ran, and went over to the little table by the
door. The top was covered with jars and white cloths.

Ran kept looking at me.

"Is there something wrong with me?" I felt my face;
it seemed all right.

"What? No. You look fine. How do you feel? Can you
sit up?"

I tried it. "It seems I can."

"Good. You don't know how worried I've been." He
reached into the pocket of his robe. "Do you feel well
enough to run the cards?"

"Damn you, Ran!" Kylla looked as though she were
very close to hitting him.

He looked faintly surprised. "I'm sorry," he said to
me, and inclined a head to Kylla. "Of course we're glad
to see you recovered, and of course I hope I convey our
relief and happiness. But there's no need to be imprac-
tical. In fact, Kylla, if we want to avoid such incidents

as these in the future, we'd better get to work on them now." He fiddled with the pocket of his robe and brought out the familiar deck.

Ran and his priorities, some things never change. Suddenly it struck me as funny, and I began to chuckle.

He was taken aback. "Have you been tranking her up?" he asked his sister.

"No, no," I said. "Sorry. The cards, by all means." Lay 'em down, read 'em out, I almost added, but then I would have lost all credibility as a rational human being.

I ran the cards. It was odd; it was as if they were any pack of cards. No visions, no intuitions . . . at any rate, no intuitions that felt as though they carried any weight of truth. I didn't panic over it; already the power seemed so natural to me that I assumed it was bound to come back. I missed it, though. "I'm sorry," I said. "Maybe I'm not well enough yet."

"Don't worry about it," he said, as he gathered them up. He laid the pack on a tray beside my bed. "We'll try again later."

"Do you feel like eating?" asked Kylla. "The healer said you could have soup. Nothing stronger, for a few days."

"Yes, thanks."

She went away. Ran looked at me speculatively. "Kylla had a hill-healer in, as well as a doctor trained on Tellys. She sent to Perbry Monastery for the healer. One of the ishin na' telleth monks."

"Oh?" I bent an arm experimentally. Whatever they'd done, I seemed to have survived it. "What did he say about my injuries?"

"He didn't say anything about them. He said you don't get enough exercise. He also said you don't live in your body enough."

"What's that supposed to mean? Where the hell do I live, if I don't live in my body?"

"I wouldn't know. Anyway, one shouldn't take these ishin na' telleth people seriously. They don't even take themselves seriously."

"What did the doctor say?"

"He said you had a concussion and second-degree burns."

"Good for him."

"Yes. But when he left, you still had second-degree burns, and when the healer left, you were all right."

I thought about it. "He must have been some kind of sorcerer, then."

"Apparently. I thought I knew what could be done with sorcery and what couldn't. I always assumed these hill-healers lived on superstition . . . I don't like feeling like a novice."

He got up and walked around the bedroom. "There are too many mysteries in my life right now. I'm tired of this siege business, I don't want to lock us both in again and wait for something else to happen.

"So."

"So I'm leaving you here at Cormallon for a while. If you're safe anywhere, it's here. I have research to do."

"I just woke up, so I'm sorry if I'm slow . . . research?"

He smiled. "Know Thy Enemy."

That wasn't the way they taught us Socrates on Athena. But I guess each society finds the path that suits it.

I was in and out of consciousness several times after that, but the basic thing was, I felt fine and healthy for someone who by rights ought to be dead. It was a pretty shaky thought. *I* hadn't done anything to save myself (nothing I could have done), and the idea that I'd been plucked out of harm's way and nursed back to strength by people and forces outside of me was not really a pleasant one. Suppose I hadn't been saved? It took your innocent notions about having some control over your own life and trashed them rather ruthlessly.

Kylla said later that in a way my rescue was my own doing; in that, if I weren't a good enough person no one would have gone to the trouble of helping me. She meant that as reassurance. However, it struck me more as black humor, since it suddenly brought back a childish illusion of mine from about the age of six or seven: that if I was

nice enough, I would never have to die. Teams of doctors
would work round the clock to save me, donations would
pour in from around the planet. . . . What a charming
thought—had I really ever believed that? Obviously my
world-view had undergone a material change since then.
I was much closer to the Ivoran ideal of keeping myself
to myself, and assuming that any time you let other people "help" you it was more likely to damage you than
anything else. I wasn't going to try to explain all this to
an Ivoran, though, and let Kylla think that my muffled
laughter was some kind of physical reaction. She brought
me more soup.

I spent a week in bed. Eln played chess with me, at
least for two games, until we saw I was so bad in com-
parison with him that there was no point. We talked about
a lot of things, things I had no chance to go over with
Ran or anybody else—most Ivorans having no inclination
for scientific or philosophical speculation. They are too
intensely concerned with daily profit and loss, or in the
case of the ishin na' telleths, too intensely *unconcerned*.
(Well, they would always make time for songs and plays,
they liked the dramatic arts. But why make time for what
won't bring you any juice personally?) So these hours
were a vacation, a return to late-night sessions with Athenan friends, a chance to play with concepts which would
never affect my life directly.

I said, "Magic bothers me."

Eln sat on the edge of my bed that afternoon, his floater
hovering beside him, laying cards on the blanket. Not
my cards, regular playing cards; it was some form of
solitaire. Like an old Earth painting: the heavy sunlight
through the window, the slender, tanned fingers tapping
the ace of spades, dark eyes following the deal-out, and
on his face the look of mild interest which was the closest
he came to revealing full concentration. I wondered how
I ever could have thought he and Ran looked alike.

He finally acknowledged my remark with a grunt.

I said, "Yes, Ran gives me these helpful explanations
also."

He smiled. "Magic bothers you. Does this mean you're

under a spell? Or does the concept itself bother you? Or
are you implying your sorcerous education leaves something to be desired? Specific questions, Theo, are what
lead to specific answers.''

''You do this to annoy me, don't you.''

''Yes. All right, you were trying to open a conversation. 'Tell me, Theo, what bothers you about it?' ''

''Take me seriously, Eln. I can't talk to you when
you're this na' telleth.''

He said, not entirely happily, ''This is as serious as I
ever am. If you can manage to separate the content from
the style, I don't think you'll have any complaints.''

I thought about that for a while, then said, ''I beg your
pardon.''

He smiled, not a teasing smile this time. He lifted my
right hand and kissed my fingers with gentle courtesy. To
cover my surprise I started to talk quickly. ''Magic works;
that's obvious. I'm not going to waste my time debating
the reality of what I've already perceived. I outgrew those
sorts of arguments when I was twelve.''

''All right,'' he said, promptingly.

''But so far as I can tell, it only works *here*. Surely if
it worked anyplace else, I would have heard about it. And
yet I can't believe the laws governing the universe were
changed for this one particular planet. That's just . . .
ridiculous.''

''I agree. Although 'ridiculous' and 'impossible' aren't
the same thing. Still, I don't like the idea either.''

''So how do you explain it?'' I folded my arms and
stared at him.

He began picking up his cards. ''How do *you* explain
it?''

''I don't. I just use it.''

''A good Ivoran answer. As I understand it, the human
race did the same with electricity for a long time.''

I wriggled with frustration under the blanket. ''That
isn't good enough!''

''No. Well, there are theories.''

Now I froze. ''There *are?* Ran never told me.''

He shrugged. "I doubt if he's studied them; he's very practical."

"But you have studied them?"

"Well, I am the theorist of the family—it makes up for having no talent of my own, I suppose."

Was I hearing right? "Are you telling me you're not a sorcerer?"

"My dear, not in any shape or form. What gave you the idea I was? I'm someone who studies sorcery and designs new ways to use it. I can't use it myself, though."

In a family like the Cormallons it must be like being crippled twice over. "I always assumed . . . when you helped me study, you knew so much about it. . . ."

He smiled. "I know more about it than anyone you're likely to meet on this planet. Which makes it lucky for you, Theo, that you come to me with your question. Not that I can actually answer it, mind you, but I can recite more unproven theories than you or any sane human would really want to hear. Shall I start? If you don't stop me I will. Number One:—"

"Wait a minute. You're not making any of this up, are you? It wouldn't be a funny joke." I saw his face and said, "I'm sorry. I would like to know these theories. Please go ahead and tell me."

He said, "The most popular one for the last couple of centuries is the genetic engineering explanation."

"Genetic engineering? Come on, Eln, Ivory hasn't been capable of anything that technically sophisticated, not ever. And I don't see—"

"Theo. Darling. Lately when you talk your brain seems to disconnect from your vocal cords. Possibly a side effect of your injuries."

I shut up.

"What do you know about the Pakrinor?" he asked.

"I saw a picture of one once," I said cautiously. "But they didn't photograph well. It was pretty blurry." The Pakrinor: the one and only alien species ever encountered by humanity. Date of encounter, somewhere around 100 or 200 post-Spaceflight. A fleet of fourteen ships, first sighted past Jupiter; as they put it, "just passing through." "They only stayed on Earth for a few weeks, as I remember. Not long enough for any good information on them, anyway. And as I understand it, the communication level between them and us wasn't all that reliable."

"So the books say. But they gave us the first practical star drive. Not as good as the present one, but enough to change history. Communication was reliable enough for that." He started dealing cards onto the blanket again.

"What does this have to do with magic? Are you trying to tell me—"

"I'm trying to tell you that Ivory is a hitchhiker planet."

I said, finally, "I've heard the phrase . . ."

"The star drive," he said, "was not free of charge."

"No, I understand that quite a few museums were gutted. They traded it for works of art."

"Works of art, yes." He gave a short laugh. "Not only canvas and stone."

"I don't know what you mean."

"Surely you've read that the aliens took riders along with them. Colonists, who agreed to be set down at the first habitable planet. Nobody wanted to wait for the twenty or thirty years it would take to build the first human starship. Pakrinor ships are *big*. Freighters, with huge holds. Several thousand people went, not to mention the records and tools and livestock."

"Yes, I think I did read about it. Wait, you're saying Ivory is one of those lost colonies? You mean people have been here since 200 PS? Great Plato, no wonder there's been genetic drift—we might not even be the same species anymore," I said, and stopped dead.

Eln didn't notice; his thoughts were less personal than mine. "I'm not talking about *drift,*" he said. "Our stories of that time are very explicit. The Pakrinor regarded one-tenth of their passengers as part of the payment—they kept them, never let them disembark. We don't forget things like that here, no matter how long ago they happened. As for the other nine-tenths . . . there was a great deal of medical experimentation."

"Experimentation—"

"It's too late to prove anything now. Maybe the government really did agree before we left." He paused. "I wonder sometimes what they did to the people targeted for the other hitchhiker worlds."

We were both silent. Magic as a force to be accessed only by beings of certain genetic background . . . that took some thinking about. Probably several days at least. I said finally, "I can wait to hear the other theories."

He laughed. He picked up my hand again and dug his knuckle in playfully. "So be it." Then he said, "Still. If the Pakrinor ever come back . . . I don't think they'll be made welcome. Quite the opposite."

"I get that impression. I'm glad we're on the same side, Eln."

He grinned. "I feel the same way. It's the quiet ones you have to watch out for." He cut one of his card piles in two and balanced the second one on my left shin. "Hear anything from Ran? He's been gone a week now."

"He calls Kylla every night. I've spoken to him a few times."

"Any news?"

I said, "Why don't you ask him the next time he calls?"

"Why don't I?" he said. He patted the bump in the blanket that represented my knee and slipped off the bed onto his floater. "Get lots of sleep tonight, Theo-my-darling. We start your exercise program tomorrow."

"We do, do we?"

"Forgive me if I presume. But your healer did suggest it. And you need to live more in your body."

The way I heard it, Eln had not been present when that judgment was made. I said, "You always have to know everything that goes on, don't you?"

"Lots of sleep, Theo."

"Right. Lots of sleep."

He waved and left. Several piles of cards remained perched just out of easy reach. The hell with them, I thought, and decided to start on that sleep right now.

* * *

In fact there wasn't any useful news from Ran. Or if there was, he wasn't about to reveal it over the Net link. I tabled the matter for the time being and concentrated on the present.

Which included the matter of exercise. Eln appeared at my door next morning with towels and two wooden staves. It was a shock to me—I hadn't thought he got up before noon.

"We're going to do sa'ret," he announced, and he handed me a staff.

Sa'ret: The River. "I think I've heard of this."

"Good," he said. "I'm glad Kylla got you a pair of trousers. Put them on, bring your staff, and meet me outside in five minutes."

"I haven't even had breakfast!"

"Ah. I'd almost forgotten." He reached into his pouch and pulled out a small loaf of bread. "There's more later if you work hard. Chew as you dress, I hate to be kept waiting." He gave me a mock salute and went out. I glared at him as he went. Was this any way for a hedonist to behave?

The River. That was my first day, my introduction to the way of movement that was sa'ret. We did the Old River first, the flowing stretches and bends of a river that wound over well-known lands. And we did the Middle River, the balancer; you use the staff most in Middle River. We finished with the Young River, the current with wild leaps over rock and down canyons. I was sweating hard by that time. It was clear that Eln was not only a better chessplayer, he had a lot more endurance. Particularly since he had to modify the movements so they could be done solely with his arms, using apparatus he had set up in the garden. His verbal instructions to me about what to do with my feet were quick and clear, even as he was twisting on a set of movable bars several meters over my head. His staff rested, an unused talisman, on a perch nearby, while he grasped the bars in its place. His legs were strapped together at the thighs and ankles, giving him a merman look from below.

He was graceful on those bars, as if he were flying. It

made me feel clumsy. Nor did I really understand what The River meant. It was several weeks before I came to realize that it didn't mean anything, and that that fact didn't matter. I came out every morning after that with Eln, and struggled and sweated while he flew gloriously overhead. But I did learn; at least I had the basic postures and positions down, after what seemed like an eternity but was only a week. A few days later Eln told me to close my eyes while I did it, and stop watching him. Another week went by. Then he put up mirrors all around the practice area; so what was the idea, I asked, am I supposed to watch or not? No answer from Eln, he just smiled and pulled up on the bars. So I did watch. How appalling—I *was* clumsy. What of it, I was a scholar, wasn't I? I didn't have to do this, did I? I could go in the house right now . . . I sighed as I shifted to Middle River; what was the use of trying? I closed my eyes and twirled the staff, opened them and watched the mirrors from the corner of my eye.

I was as graceful as anybody! I stopped utterly short.

"What's the matter?" His voice came down through the dappled morning sunlight.

I looked up through the shadow of the bars. I shrugged.

"Well?" he said.

I hesitated. "I don't think I was bad that time."

"You haven't been bad," he said, "since the sixth day."

We regarded each other. "Well," I said. I returned my feet to Middle River Seven position. As I did so, a leaf let loose from one of the garden trees and floated to the ground. "It's almost autumn."

"So it is," he said.

It was over a month since Ran had left to do his "research." It bothered me that he wasn't letting me know just what he was trying to find out. And when I was honest with myself I knew that that wasn't all that bothered me. Grandmother never came to meals anymore, and between her absence and Ran's, and Eln ignoring proper dinnertimes, the dining hall was a sad place. Kylla seemed busy and abstracted. Grandmother was ill, although just what the sickness was was never made clear to me, and from something Eln said I gathered that she didn't even know I was at Cormallon. This was somehow more shocking than anything; I'd been under the illusion that Grandmother knew everything that went on, at least where her family was concerned.

One afternoon I passed by Grandmother's sun-washed doorway, watching Tagra hand Kylla an empty lunch tray. "I'm glad she's eating, at least," I said to Kylla.

"Yes, but not much." Kylla swung back her hair out of her eyes, balancing the tray as she moved. Usually she put her hair up when there was work to be done, but she seemed to have little time for amenities these days. She looked tired and worried.

"What do you care?" said Tagra. She frowned at me and went down the passage.

"Sorry," said Kylla.

"I haven't even said anything to her this time."

"She's probably upset at the time you're spending with Eln. Don't know why—she's got him most nights."

"What?" I said.

She leaned against the stone wall. "Could you hold this for a second?"

"Sure—of course." I took the tray. "You look done in."

"I'll rest. But first I need to go down to the kitchen and talk with Herel. Come with me?"

I carried the tray. ". . . Tagra and Eln?" I said, cautiously, as we went down the stairs.

"For years," she said, resignedly. "And you'd think she'd relax by now. She's the only person at Cormallon who fits Eln's requirements."

Which brought up a lot of questions which were none of my business, but which I was quite interested in. While I was thinking how to phrase them we reached the kitchen, and the thought of continuing the subject in front of Herel was just beyond the limits of my indiscretion. Later during my visit I could find no way of slipping into the topic gracefully.

So there we were: Tagra hated me, Kylla was too busy to talk to, and Eln made me work. I also felt a bit of a fraud. After all, I wasn't *doing* anything. Just The River for two hours in the morning, and rooting through the library in the afternoons. And for this I was pulling down an enormous salary? Not that anyone else even hinted at such an attitude; on the contrary, they treated me more like a soldier honorably wounded, which just made me feel more uncomfortable.

So it came as a relief when Ran finally showed up, over a month after he disappeared. Even if I had to leave the safe cocoon of the estate, it was better than marking time in this strained atmosphere . . . although just why the atmosphere was strained, I could not have said.

I looked up from a new set I was trying of Young River Six-Three-Two and there he was, standing under a tree in the garden. I wiped the sweat out of my eyes and threw down my staff. The garden seemed to tilt for a minute; I knew I really shouldn't stop so suddenly.

"I didn't mean to interrupt," he said.

"Too late," I said cheerfully, "you have." And I walked out from under the bars, feeling as though a pressure had been lifted.

I was not the only one who had stopped suddenly. I'd forgotten Eln. "Theo," his voice came down. I looked up and saw that he'd swung himself over to the platform with his rest-seat. "Cut off my timer," he said, nodding to the floater down below. He usually had it set to rise to the platform after a certain span of time had passed.

I looked over at Ran, and back up to the platform. "You don't have to stop," I said, "we can leave."

"Cut off the timer," he repeated.

I went over and switched it off. When the floater reached platform level, Eln swung into the seat. He pulled off his sweatband and let it fall to earth. Then he took the floater down to safety level and rode it back into the house, without saying another word.

Ran chose a good-sized boulder off to the side of the practice area and sat down. "We need to talk," he said.

Was he going to give me a hard time about my being

with Eln? I was annoyed with them both. I was beginning to feel that the Pyrene crèche setup made more sense than all this family intensity, and I was tempted to say so. Luckily I did not; for, as I found, it was not what was on his mind at all.

"I've been checking into this sabotage," he began. It was just another example of a moment I was glad I'd kept my mouth shut. "And I can sum up my findings by saying I have no idea who is behind it or why. It's not that I don't have enemies . . . but what would they have to gain by it? At least twice the attacks were not against me at all, but focused on my card-reader. Why?"

I said, "Why? You've said yourself that eliminating me would be a neat way of making you vulnerable."

"That motive only works if the person doing this *knows* about you. I've been very careful, Theodora. And I've spent the last month checking everywhere and everyone I could think of. The secret is still a secret."

"The Chief of Police knew . . . suspected, anyway."

"And someone had to tell him. I know. And yet, I swear, it's not general knowledge."

"Eln and Kylla know, I think."

"Eln and Kylla," he said, dismissing them. "I'm talking about a threat."

"So this month was wasted effort, then," I said.

He spoke reprovingly. "Elimination of wrong data is never wasted effort. And there is another possibility I've been considering."

"Oh?" I had the impression that I wouldn't like this possibility.

"Someone tried to kill you because someone doesn't like you."

"I'm a likable person, Ran."

"Yes, of course you are. But let's look at—"

"Besides, that assumes the death of your cousin was accidental."

"Accidents happen. Let's look at—"

"And the Police Chief's actions were unrelated."

"Theodora. Try to think about this possibility rationally for a moment. Don't talk. Just think about it. Yes, the Police Chief's actions could be unrelated. He could have been making a move on his own—these things happen, you know, they happened before you came here and they'll go on happening.''

I was silent.

''Well?'' he said.

''I'm thinking, all right?''

He cleared his throat. ''I would like to hear what you're thinking.''

''It's a nice theory, except for one thing—I don't have any enemies. I keep a low profile. I'm polite. Even in the market I always addressed customers by the highest title possible. I don't like to be noticed.''

He said, ''You've got at least one enemy, and so do I. Her name's Pina.''

Oops. That was another story. I said, slowly, ''She didn't know we were behind her being blacklisted. She knew it was a trick. But she didn't know about us.''

''Possibly she found out. There's no reason to think she's an idiot.''

I was quiet for a moment, then said, ''I'm thinking some more.''

''Good. I've been doing that for the last week. After I finished, I asked some questions. Pina's not in the city anymore. Her friends—of which she hasn't many, I might add—think she returned to her birth village.''

''And you've got the name and location of the village.''

''Yes.''

I paused. ''Have you been there?''

''Not yet,'' he said. ''I thought we'd go together.''

Chapter 8

I was glad to be leaving Cormallon. It was beautiful, it
was peaceful, everyone was very nice to me; and there
was something wrong with it. Something in the undertow
that I couldn't identify and therefore irritated me. I hadn't
felt this way on my previous visit, and didn't know why.
Perhaps I'd simply been too unfamiliar with the family
to be sensitive to these nuances. Anyway, I was more
than willing to accompany Ran on this "business trip."
That was the phrase we used to the captain of the *Summer
Ice* to describe our reason for wanting to travel down to
Issin at this time of year—and I suppose it really was
business, although not, as we claimed, the export business.

We spent a couple of days in the capital waiting on the
ship's schedule; and I used the time to ask a favor of my
old market-mate, Irsa. She approached a couple of the
illegal market bankers on my behalf, and we discovered
that the ones who'd claimed they had to charge interest
on handling my savings were taking advantage of a foreigner. They made profits on that money, illegal or not,
and they were supposed to *pay* interest. I gave Irsa a split
on my last week's pay, most joyfully, and made the necessary arrangements. By the time I boarded ship for Issin
I'd made three payments into the account.

Issin is a good way down the continent, three days for
a little freighter like the *Summer Ice*. Autumn was coming on, the captain pointed out, and we'd have slow going
down Issin-way, watching out for the first ice. We had a

good cabin, he said, and it was true. Of course it was the only passenger cabin on the ship.

I slung my pack under the narrow bunk and said to Ran, "Which of us gets the floor?"

"You do," he said.

"I was thinking we would match for it."

"I was thinking I'm senior to you."

"I was thinking how I hate rolling over onto the cards in the middle of the night. With a mattress it's not so bad. . . ."

"All right, all right." He threw some of the blankets on the floor. I bent over the bunk to hide my grin and offered thanks to Grandmother Cormallon. Ran *hated* to be reminded of my nonexpendability.

I did the cards that night; again they were unhelpful and I was left wondering if I were reading things into them. There was no clear sense of what was coming from them and what was born of my frustrated imagination. I joined Ran on deck afterward.

It was a cool night. Moonlight spilled in twin trenches over the water. I looked blankly up at constellations I didn't recognize; usually I saw that I was safe indoors after sundown.

"Where's your coat?" asked Ran.

"I left it on the bunk."

"You should be wearing it."

"You hate that coat," I pointed out.

"It's a secondhand disgrace," he said, "and unfitting for a member of our house. You ought to have gotten a new one when we were in the capital."

I shrugged. It was only cold for a few weeks anyway in the capital. "New coats cost too much. This one's cheap."

"And I assume it's warm. You should go down and put it on."

I decided to get him off the subject. "Ran, when you were at Cormallon, did you get the feeling everything was not quite right there?"

"Grandmother's ill. The house routine was thrown off. Is that what you mean?"

"I don't think so. Or maybe it is, I don't know."

"I was only there for a couple of days."

"And I was there for a month, and I still don't know what I'm talking about." I shivered.

"You should—" he began.

"I know," I said. "I only planned on staying here for a minute. I'm going to bed, don't wake me up when you come in." And I went down to the cabin. A long time later it occurred to me that I was nervous about Cormallon because it had come to represent, for me as well as Ran, a safe haven in a paranoid universe. The thought was upsetting when it came; I didn't want to rely on anything Ivoran.

We came into Issin harbor on early morning of the third day. Not a sign of ice anywhere, and I was beginning to think that the captain had ice on the brain. It was autumn, after all, even if we were pretty far south. It was go-through-your-bones chilly, though, and I wore my old blue coat on deck, wrapping the straps of my pack over the thick shoulders. Underneath it I wore a long wool robe, and underneath that a thin silk one.

Ran was already at the rail, looking over the harbor. "Not a land of excitement," I said as I joined him. A half-circle of rippling gray water, old wooden boats bobbing at their moorings, and maybe twenty or thirty stone houses on the hills around the bay.

"Every house there belongs to Cormallon," he replied. "And they do their share. You wouldn't think they could, just from fishing, but every year they send money into the treasury instead of taking it out. I only wish some of the flashier branches could do as well."

Hooray for them, I thought, and was immediately ashamed. This wasn't the most hospitable spot I'd ever seen. If they could wrench a good living from it, they were doing better than I'd been doing before I hooked up with Ran. I said, "Why do they call this ship the *Summer Ice,* anyway? It's a cold autumn, and I still haven't seen any ice."

"The captain and crew are Andulsine. It's summer up

there when it's winter down here. That's where their regular route starts—comes by way of the capital, by Sebral,
and down to Issin. I guess it's sort of a message to their
Andulsine customers about their route. Anyway, even if
they weren't from above the equator . . . icebergs have
crumpled up a few ships in these waters even at high
summer. *Our* high summer.''

I was glad I hadn't known.

Ran looked toward the shore. "Our welcome," he
said.

A rowboat was heading out to us. A man and a woman
sat in it. The man had his back to me but I could see the
woman's scarf blowing on the wind, rippling above the
ripples on the bay. They both wore scarves wrapped
around their heads, covering their ears, with green caps
pulled over the scarves. At last the boat bumped against
side of the *Summer Ice*. "Sir?" the man called up.

"Ran Cormallon," said Ran, as though answering a
challenge. He added, one hand on my shoulder, "Theodora Cormallon."

"Welcome," called the woman. She looked up with a
red and wrinkled face.

"Welcome, and come down," echoed the man. Ran
glanced over at the captain, who motioned to have the
ladder lowered. It was a rope affair, not at all like
the elegant way we walked on board from the pier in the
capital. I hitched the ends of my robes into my belt and
felt them balloon out as the wind bit my legs, and tried
not to picture what the Cormallon representatives below
thought of the figure I must cut. Still, I had no intention
of taking a tumble in that cold gray water for the sake of
decorum.

They said nothing about it, though, as they helped me
in. I noticed as I sat down that they both wore trousers.

"Beth and Karn, happy by your presence. It's a fine
time for you to honor us," said the man. He was solidly
built, on the late side of middle age, and his face was as
ruddy as the woman's. He smiled at me as he said, "Luck
for us all, the timing. We've a wedding at the house."

"My son," said the woman, Beth.

"Fine food and drink in plenty," said Karn.

"We only hope you remember all the words of the service," said Beth, and they both laughed.

Ran looked taken aback. ". . . Service?" he said, in a voice that was the pattern of noncommittance.

Beth and Karn exchanged glances. Some of the light left their faces. "We assumed," said Beth, "that as first in the family you would do the ritual yourself."

They looked at him warily, like children waiting to be told there would be no birthday gifts this year.

"Well, of course," said Ran.

"That goes without saying," I agreed, and though Ran's eyes flicked past me he gave no other sign.

"Is it today?" he asked.

"This afternoon," said Beth. "When we heard you were coming, we postponed it."

"I'm honored," he said, as gracefully as possible.

The wedding proper took place in a long, low stone hall attached to Karn's house. The bride and groom seemed about twenty years old; they both wore long red silk tunics with woven belts, and looked shy and silly. Everyone present was dressed up. I hoped I wasn't disgracing Ran with my own clothes, but probably not; the outer robe was from Kylla, and I had great faith in her judgment.

In some ways it was more like a night club than a wedding. I sat at a round table with half a dozen strangers, and the half of the table not facing the couple had to crane their necks for the service. The hall was filled with similar tables. Not that anyone had to crane for long; whatever Ran was mumbling over the bride and groom only lasted about a minute, the two exchanged their bluestone pendants, and everyone sat down for the main event, which seemed to mean: food. And there was food. One course after another of the most amazing, wondrous, deliciously prepared food it has ever been my privilege to partake. I didn't know what any of it was, and I gave up trying to ask and remember all the names of the dishes. Where had they been hiding this stuff while

I was in the capital? I sat in a glow of calories and thought how mad I must be to consider leaving this fine planet.

Ran had to sit at the bride and groom's table, but I was in an expansive mood after the first two courses, and more than willing to try small talk with the people on either side of me. The girl on my left was Cara, the bride's cousin, and she told me that the exchange of pendants was temporary and took place so that "there would always be a little of them mixed together," come what may. That seemed a bit messy, I thought, considering that (for all I knew) they might not even be acquainted yet.

The boy on my right was more interesting. He was eighteen, and a medical student. Medical studies on Ivory cover a wide range, depending on where you do the learning; and since about half of it was secondhand knowledge from Tellys and the other half from a tradition of folklore, magic, and consmanship, it made for a fascinating topic. He held forth for quite a while, until I interrupted him by dropping the latest small dish of delicacies I'd been handed.

I'd been staring down at the dish, wondering if I were imagining the *eyes* I thought I saw there . . . not to mention the . . . *beaks?*

"Those are *heads*," I said to him.

"Yes," he said.

"Those are birds' heads," I said.

"Yes," he said again, and taking the one I held frozen in a pair of tongs away from me, he proceeded to pull the skin off the top of the skull. Then he pointed to the quartered brains inside and began explaining some neurological experiments he had been performing recently. Afterward he popped the brain into his mouth and smiled happily.

"They've done some excellent food, haven't they?" he said. "I came all the way from South Port when I heard they were planning to use the traditional dishes."

"Yes, I can see why you would." I hoped I hadn't eaten anything too strange underneath all the sauces. Perhaps I shouldn't get a list of the ingredients after all.

After a good deal more wine and more courses than I thought possible, the party started to break up. I parted amicably from my dinner partners and went to join the line of people waiting for their coats. Ran found me there. "We're to stay the night at Beth's house," he said.

"Yes, I know."

When the line reached me, Ran took my tattered and disgraceful blue coat and held it for me to get into. It was a gesture no one else on the line had yet made. He held it, I thought, no differently than if it had been the most expensive tanil-lined fur available in the Imperial stores. As I turned to put my arms in it, I saw the face of the woman behind me. Her eyes widened and she seemed impressed. Her glance flickered toward her own escort, a short, balding man who was looking at his watch. As I turned back to Ran, from the corner of my eye I saw her elbow jab out viciously, though not lethally, into her escort's side. "Hey!" he said suddenly. Ran and I headed toward the door. "What was that all about?" the short man went on. The door closed before I heard her answer.

The next day was clear and bright. Ran borrowed a landcar for us, the ferocious, hill-climbing, snow-ignoring, rock-crumbling kind they use around Issin. A closed car with internal environment—they like having that kind of option at Issin, too. We headed west toward the hills. Not many villages out there, the Issin people said, and what there were were definitely *provincial*. Ran let that pass, since in the capital Issin would be provincial.

It was dull. Two days' ride into the real hills, nibbling packed food and water and exchanging conversation about the environment, mostly on the order of "should we stop and ask questions at this village" and arguments over which direction we should be taking. The hills were pretty much dirt and grass, the sky was uniformly gray, and the occasional sheep herds only served to remind me how far off the beaten track I was. I entirely reversed my pleasure-induced estimate of Ivory made at the wedding banquet. This place *was* provincial. I passed the time recalculating the interest I should be earning on the last payment I made to my nonNet banker.

Some of these villages didn't even have names; they were just six or seven houses clustered together. We had reached the foothills of the Skytop Mountains when a local informant told us he had indeed heard of the village we were seeking, and we were on the right track. Just keep going *up*, he pointed; and the looming range of mountains shivered in the heat from the car's system.

Well, there was a pass, more or less, where he was pointing, and we could take the car most of the way. "*Most* of the way?" I asked Ran. He got that grim look I was beginning to know, and we climbed back into the car without further discussion. Anyway, it wasn't as if I had other plans.

So we walked into Pina's village. It really was Pina's village, too, and one could see why she'd been in no hurry to return to it. In fact, I began to seriously think that she probably hadn't. Sod huts and a lot of clothes-lines seemed to make up the main portion of the place. We walked past rows of damp, flapping laundry, while a gaunt woman with a sheet in her hand turned her fixed, unhappy gaze from the clothes to us. "I'd look unhappy too," I said to Ran, my hands in my coat pockets. Her hands were red and worn-looking. "Can we leave her a pair of gloves?"

His mind wasn't on secondary considerations. "If this isn't the right place," he muttered, as though it were a complete sentence. Thematically, it was.

There was a group of men in open fur jackets sitting by a fire. They were playing a game with tablets. "We're looking for Pina," said Ran, into the silence our appearance brought.

"I'm Pina," said a man's voice. He came out of a nearby hut, stooping to get through the door. About fifty to sixty years old, stocky, with a huge knife stuck through his belt. There was fresh blood on his hands. "Beg your pardon, gracious lady," he said, seeing my glance. "I was skinning a jack." He looked to the men at the game and back to us. "Can I offer you mountain tea? We haven't got any tah, it's hard to come by here, strangers prefer it, I know."

"Excuse me," said Ran, "You're Pina?"

"Tregorian Pina, headman of this village."

Ran and I looked at each other. Was this whole thing a mistake? I said, "We're trying to find a woman named Pina. About twenty-five, dark hair—" of course she has dark hair, you idiot, I thought, and went on desperately, "she worked as a sorcerer in the capital for a while—"

"My daughter, you mean."

I hoped very much we meant it. I found myself smiling at the man and he returned the smile.

"You're too late, gracious lady. I welcome you if you're friends of my daughter's, but you've made your trip for nothing, and I must tell you unhappy news. My daughter Katherine died last summer."

The silence seemed to lengthen, and I found that I was uncomfortable and even a little embarrassed. I was ready to leave immediately, but I'd forgotten that Ran never took anybody's word for anything.

"Last summer?" said Ran. "She was not home long, then. It's a pity, since we came all the way from Issin to offer her a contract. We'd heard that there was a sorcerer from the capital here, and thought it would be better to deal with her than with the local talent. Local Issin talent, I mean."

"Yes, I understand she had a fine reputation. I know very little of the trade, myself. I'm sorry you came all this way for nothing, are you sure you wouldn't like some tea?"

"What did she die of?" Ran went on.

There was a long silence. One of the players by the fire grunted. Tregorian Pina said, "It was very quick. Merciful for us all that way. If you don't want to stay—"

"Tell him," said one of the players.

"That's right," said another. "Tell him what your fine daughter who was too good for her village did."

"Tell him," said a third.

The headman's face screwed up. "She was very un-

happy. She never thought she was too good for the village, I swear she didn't. She was just unhappy.''

"When she came back she talked different," said the
first player.

"Had clothes that wouldn't last a season."

"Did you see her shoes? Made of paper, I swear to
you."

"Didn't want to do real work."

"Enough!" roared Tregorian Pina. The comments cut
short. He glared at them until they sullenly returned, or
pretended to return, to the game. "She hanged herself,"
he said to us. He looked down at his bloody hands. "I've
got to get back to work," he whispered. He turned and
went back to the hut.

Ran and I stood there for a minute. Then we started
the long walk to the car.

It was much longer going back. "When you interfere
in someone's life, you have to expect the consequences,"
Ran had told me a long time ago in connection with this
same Katherine Pina. Maybe he was thinking it over in
those terms. Or maybe not; maybe he thought that she'd
started this chain of events and it was up to her to take
care of herself. I can only speculate because we did not
talk about it at all on the way back to Issin. Nor did we
ever talk about it.

When I wasn't thinking about Pina, I was thinking what
a relief it would be to get out of that whole part of the
world and offering thanks that we would be back in the
capital in a few days' time.

As it turned out I was wrong about that, too.

A siren started to wail as we came in sight of the Issin
buildings. Our car rolled onto the dirt road that led to the
pond just west of town. As we took the road east, men
and women spilled out and lined up just outside the circle
of houses. They stood in a knot on the road, about a
dozen of them. A good portion, I noted, were tall and
male.

I said, "Something's wrong, isn't it?"

Ran did not dignify this observation with an answer.

I said, "I mean, this isn't some quaint custom I haven't heard of . . . is it?"

"I haven't heard of it either," he said quietly.

We rolled to a stop at the knot of people. Ran opened his door and leaned out. "What's wrong?" he yelled, over a strong sea wind. "What happened?"

"Get out of the car," said one of the men.

Ran hesitated. Then he jumped down, slamming his door.

"Both of you," said the man.

I found myself pausing as well. I looked at Ran, he nodded, and I didn't have any better ideas. So I got out.

"We repossess this car in the name of Cormallon," said the man, and he motioned to the others. Two of them climbed in and started throwing out our belongings.

"Hey!" I said. None of this made any sense. Wasn't Ran Cormallon entitled to use Cormallon property? Certainly more entitled than minor-branch provincials! Who did they think they were?

Ran just looked blank. He scanned the faces there and called, "Karn! What's going on?"

Karn hung back, looking embarrassed. Someone said, "Karn doesn't have to talk to you, he's disgraced himself enough by accepting you before."

"Have the decency to leave him alone!" called a woman.

Ran looked at Karn for a moment, then turned and climbed up on the front of the landcar. "I *demand* an explanation," he said.

"Demand? Who are you to demand anything from respectable people?" cried the woman who had spoken before.

"Cheat!"

"Thief!"

"No-name!"

He looked angry at that. "I'm the first in this house and family, and you'd better have a very, very good explanation, because right now I'm wondering how much Cormallon will lose by cutting out a few fishermen."

"First in nothing!" said the woman.

"I'll tell him," said Karn suddenly.

"You don't have to—"

"No," said Karn, "I'll tell him." He came to the front. "We know about you. We know about your cheating the treasury—"

"What?"

"—about your private bank account—"

"There is no private bank account!"

"—against all the customs and laws of the family."

The woman said, "Taking money away from all of us who earn it!"

That met with muttered agreement from everybody.

Ran said, "Listen to me. I don't know where you got this idea, but it's a lie. Why should I have a private bank account? I can take money out of the treasury any time I want."

"We got the idea," said Karn, "from our message-taker, who got it straight from the message-taker at Cormallon main estate."

Ran went pale at that.

"I have to get back there," he said to me. "Now."

"Not in our car," said a man.

Ran said, "I don't want your kanz car. Freighters call in every morning—"

"None that will take you as a passenger—not unless you've got enough gold in your bags. Cormallon won't pay for it."

"If he has gold in his bags, we should take it out. It's ours by right."

Karn said, "Enough—"

Ran was picking up our bags, throwing mine to me. "I don't know what's going on, but I have a right to be heard at Cormallon. I can't believe anything could happen without my being there—"

"Unless the evidence were overwhelming," said Karn. "And they say it was. Do you think Cormallon *owes* you something? Do you think we have to go through needless forms, like the Imperial Courts? When something is clear enough to see in the dark, we don't need to file a report on it to take action. Action's been taken. The disowning ritual's been read—by your own brother and sister—and only a fool would say that could happen without cause.''

Ran had been growing paler and paler as Karn spoke. When he said, ''disowning ritual,'' Ran looked as though he'd been punched in the stomach.

''You come here,'' said the woman who'd done the talking earlier, ''in your fine clothes. You disgrace us by reciting the wedding service. You take our property off to who knows where—''

''Enough,'' said Karn again. His voice was weary.

''In the company of a notorious foreign assassin,'' went on the woman.

''What?'' I said. I glanced at Ran, who still looked sick.

''Poisoner,'' she said, and spat at my feet. I had the feeling she would have liked to spit higher up.

''I don't—''

''Brin almost *died,*'' she said. ''He might still.''

Brin? It came to me suddenly. The young medical student who sat next to me at the wedding feast. But that was impossible. Poisoning isn't that uncommon on Ivory, but practically everything at the feast had been passed around in communal bowls. It was probably *because* of poisoning that shared dishes were such a tradition. Why blame me . . . then I remembered the little delicacy dish of bird's heads. Little individual plates. I remembered his taking one and popping it into his mouth. . . .

He'd taken a couple of others from my plate, too, when he saw I wasn't going to touch them.

I looked around at the faces of the Issin folk. Someone was probably trying to kill me again, and there was nothing I could say to these people. They were all closed up against me.

''Leave,'' said Karn very quietly.

It seemed like a good idea. I strapped on my pack and grabbed Ran by the hand and pulled him away. We went toward the north. It was warmer that way.

* * *

It was all rather depressing. First Pina, now this Brin. I'd liked him at the feast; he was nice about being seated next to the eccentric foreigner. And then there was Ran. Ran hadn't said a word since we walked out of Issin. I'd never seen him like this, with all the fight taken out of him. It was frightening. Particularly since we were a long way from anyplace I knew how to get to, and minus his endless store of gold coins.

If we just went north, we should end up on the same parallel as the capital, eventually. Maybe in months or years.

We'd tramped a couple of hours when I heard a faint whine behind us. It was the damned landcar. Two Issin men, vaguely familiar, got out and approached. I wondered if killing us without witnesses would save Issin paperwork. "Ran, maybe we should run?" I said. Ran paid no attention. Of course, I'd always been the lousiest runner in my Healthful Sports class on Pyrene, and sometimes when you run it gives people ideas they didn't originally have. . . .

"Theodora of Pyrene?" said the taller man.

"Yes," I said, only because there was no point in denying it.

"We're here," he said, as though he didn't like the words, "to give you a safe ride back to Issin and provide you with passage money for the next northbound ship. When you're in the capital, a Cormallon representative will meet you. I'm to tell you specifically that your services have not been terminated. Cormallon still wants to employ you. Legally it does still employ you. All measures will be taken for your safety and comfort."

Well! I looked at Ran, who continued unhelpful. So I considered every aspect I could possibly think of for about ten seconds. But what did this really change?

"I'm sorry," I said. "My employment wasn't from Cormallon proper, but from Ran Cormallon in particular. So I'm ethically bound to stay with him. Thanks anyway. . . ."

He shook his head. "We were told you're a house member, a family employee—"

"Thank you for all your trouble," I said as firmly as I could. "But I'm afraid I have the best understanding of the circumstances of my employment. Safe trip back to Issin."

It must have come out as strongly as I meant it. He shrugged to the other man and they both climbed into the landcar, turned it awkwardly about, and drove away.

I watched them go unhappily. Maybe it was a mistake, but between an unknown reception in the capital and sticking with Ran, I chose Ran. Besides, he was acting pretty strangely—I wasn't sure he could make it without help.

"Well," I said. And started walking again.

He matched his strides to mine. He said the first words he'd come up with since Karn said "disownment." And they didn't sound like a compliment to my intelligence.

"Crazy foreigner," he said.

Chapter 9

Crazy foreigner I may have been, but I know a long walk when I see one. The next few months were an entirely new way of life, and if I made them seem as long in the telling as they were to live through I would have to go on for volumes. The routine was monotonous enough, yet soon the routine was all I thought about, all I anticipated, all I dreamed about. The walk through the southern woods all morning, the rest at noon; then walking till late afternoon, then the stop at the closest village. We kept near the coast, where most of the towns and villages are. Nor did we actually sleep in the villages, that would be asking for trouble—we just showed up at the town hall steps at sunrise, pretending we'd spent the night. Then the hall servants would give out the "indigent's breakfast," and we got our one meal of the day.

It's a custom of the southern towns to discourage vagrants. Anyone who chooses can appear on the town hall steps and get a free meal . . . provided they leave town immediately after. If the village is small enough, the breakfast is whatever was left over from the communal supper the night before. I preferred that; there was usually rice and fish and eggs in the bowl then. When it was a larger town, the hall cook would make up the breakfasts himself, generally tired vegetables and undercooked rice. Seagrass was a big favorite of the town hall cooks. I hate seagrass.

I say "we"—but I was mentally alone in this journey. Ran may as well have been a ghost. It scared me. I'd always had the impression of massive energy in Ran, of a mind with clear purpose, sharp and ready for anything. He'd always been so sure of himself—annoying, but you could forgive it since he was generally right. Now it was as if he weren't there at all. I had to make all the decisions—where to stop, what village to head for, when to rest. I didn't even know where I was going. He was supposed to be the expert, I was the barbarian outlander.

I just didn't understand how a thing like this could throw him so hard. He'd been disowned. I'd walked out on a crèche-family on Pyrene and lost an academic family on Athena, and it didn't mean anything to me. I hadn't even liked the former. Did the simple fact of shared genes make such a difference? It was eerie. It was as if the engine for all that energy and purpose had been Cormallon, and now he had no motive power.

That was Worry Number One. Worry Number Two was the cold. Winter was coming; already the wind was blowing in off the sea and we had to stay well inland, among the trees. The lining of my coat was nothing but tattered strips. I didn't know how we would sleep when it snowed, nor did I feel that one meal would keep us warm and moving through the day. I told Ran everything I was thinking about. (I usually did, during the noon rest stop, and as usual he said absolutely nothing.)

Teshin Village was on a peninsula that extended into a good-sized bay. There were some hills just to the north, and the ocean was about eight kilometers to the east. The village wasn't too big, which was good; I'd picked up some bad feelings about towns because of the lousy breakfasts they served. So one bright morning when the water birds were making an enormous racket, Ran and I walked across the muddy flats by the bay and into Teshin.

And here at last was our one piece of luck: it was the day before a holiday. Tomorrow was Imperial Guardian Venrat's Birthday—which no doubt meant as little to the people of Teshin as it did to myself, but it did mean a day of no work, feasting, and drinking. Which made the day before the feast a day of a great deal of work, planning, and preparation. The village hall was in chaos.

I was rebuffed and insulted by several busy people (a barbarian outlander learns to expect these things) before someone pointed me to Hall Manager Peradon. He was an elderly, stocky man seated at a chipped wooden table in the back of the hall. There was a line of people waiting to talk to him, so I just joined the line. From what I overheard the sole function of these people was to explain to the Hall Manager why what he had ordered had not been done. By the time I reached him I felt quite sympathetic to the old man.

Still, I hadn't expected to be seized on like a long-lost friend.

"My child," he said to me, "I have just the place for you. Five bakras for the day, and all you can eat."

"I was really looking for something long-term," I said.

"Long-term! This *is* long-term. As long as you like. And if you decide you don't like it, we'll try to move you into something else." As he spoke a little boy with a blue cap was tugging on his arm. "I know, Piece-of-My-Heart," he said to the boy. "Don't joggle me. Tell your mother we have just the person." He looked up at me. "Sign your name here in my book, right next to '5 bakras'—we like to keep everything honest and on record here."

"My feelings exactly," I said, and signed "Coral Passuran."

He turned his book around and peered down at it. "That's a good, sensible name for a barbarian," he said.

"Thank you," I said.

"Just go with little Seth here to the kitchens—tell the Kitchen Chief you're taking Dana's place."

"Thank you," I said again.

Seth led me off to the back of the hall. "Hold on a minute," I said to him. I stepped up onto a bench and peered over the heads in the hall. There was Ran—still waiting by the door. Well, he wasn't going anywhere.

"Mother's in a hurry," said Seth, looking up at me distrustfully.

"Fine," I said. I climbed down.

The kitchens seemed to have even more people in them

than the hall itself. Seth led me to a woman in a white apron, a sensible middle-aged woman who reminded me a little of Herel. "Here she is," said Seth.

"Here who is?" said the woman, frowning at me.

"I'm taking Dana's place," I explained.

"Ah!" she said at once, and the frown was replaced by relief. "About time Peradon found someone. The food has to go in the hot-pots *now*. Come over here . . . now, I'm Berta, the Kitchen Chief for the hall. We have three meals a day in the hall, but not like tomorrow, believe me. We're making Cream Hermit Soup, Wine-Steep Runner Stew, good dishes that they don't see too often here, but that'll keep in the pots. I'm sure you're familiar with them."

"Well, not *very* familiar."

"No matter. And the cakes and pies we'll get to later. This is the ledge where we keep the pots . . . the servers will bring them over here to you."

"And I put the food in the pots."

"No, no—Penda and I will do that ourselves, it has to be done right or it won't keep properly." She paused. "You don't know how to do it, do you?"

"No, I'm afraid not."

"Well, then. Stick to your job, stranger, that's all we ask." She raised her voice and yelled at a young man over by a table. "No, no, the *soup* first! The stew can wait! Bring the soup!" She sighed. "You have no idea what it's like," she said to me. "Oh, if you get tired, we can bring over a chair for you."

Just then the first shipment of soup arrived. "Penda!" she yelled, making me wince. A girl in her teens rushed over and they opened the first hot-pot. Berta ladled out a bit of the soup and handed it to me. "Here," she said.

I tasted it. It was a little gamy, but I suppose you have to expect that from groundhermit. "Very nice," I said.

"Thank you," said Berta. "Into the pot, now. Careful, sweetheart." They tilted the huge bowl just far enough, and when the pot was full they pulled down the hinged top and adjusted the metal braces that kept it airtight. "Mark it 'one,' " she said. She raised her voice and turned her face toward a woman seated across the kitchen, on a high platform against the wall. "We're marking it 'one,'" she yelled. The woman waved back.

"Who's that?" I asked.

"The observer, of course." They filled another pot. "We should really put stew in this one," she said to her helper. "It's too big to waste on soup." She filled her lungs and yelled "Stew!" to the world at large, and soon enough someone brought over a bowl of stew. She ladled around in it, sniffing. "Let's get some nice vegetables on it for you," she said. Then she handed me the ladle and I tried the stew.

It was delicious, and I said so. Berta said, "My own recipe. Bet you can't tell there's seagrass in there."

"I couldn't. I usually don't like seagrass."

"Sensible child. Hold the pot, will you? Gently now."

A few bowls later Berta set down her pot and put her hands on her hips. "Are you making fun of me?" she said.

I was taken by surprise. "Who, me?"

"You—tymon—is this your sense of humor, stranger? Why do you keep telling me about the dishes? Are you passing judgment on my cooking?"

"I, uh, no, of course not. But you gave it to me to taste—"

"Of course I gave it to you to taste! You're taking Dana's place!"

A voice called, "Is there a problem?" It was the woman on the platform against the wall. She was standing up now, looking over at Berta and me.

Berta said, "Now we'll have the observer staring at us the rest of the day!"

"Look, I'm sorry," I began. Then I stopped. All right, I can be stupid sometimes—but remember, I'd been on the edge of exhaustion for days. Here I was, in a communal kitchen among the population of the most suspicious, paranoid planet I'd ever heard of—why would they want somebody to taste the food, now? And pay hard Ivoran money to someone to observe the kitchen workers and see that the pots stayed locked and nobody did anything they shouldn't? I said, slowly, "Do you get much food poisoning here?"

"You *are* trying to insult me!"

"No, please, believe me. It's just that I'm a stranger. Peradon didn't say what my job was, that's all. It's not a problem, really. I don't think. *Do* you get much food poisoning here?"

The girl helping Berta said, "She's just nervous, is all. Well, really, how can we criticize? None of us volunteered to take Dana's place."

Berta said, mollified, "I suppose that's so. I'll overlook it, stranger," she said to me.

"Thank you," I said. After a pause I asked, "What happened to Dana?"

"She's not feeling well," said the helper.

"Oh?" I said.

"But don't worry. She'll be up and around in a few weeks."

"I see."

"Next pot," said Berta, "and try to look casual. I can't stand having the observer watch over my shoulder."

I sought out Ran several hours later. He hadn't moved from the hall door. "Five bakras," I said, jingling the contents of my pocket. He did not appear impressed. In fact, he didn't appear totally conscious.

"Now what we need is a place for the night," I said. "There's no inn, but the Kitchen Chief told me about a family who might have some extra rooms."

He stood up, which suggested he must be paying attention to what I said on *some* level. It didn't seem to interest him, though. Damn. We followed Berta's directions easily enough and they took us to a large house overlooking the village square. I knocked.

The door was opened by a girl of about twelve. She looked at me, then looked at Ran. "Yes?" she said. It was not a proper greeting, even if we did look a shade disreputable. Anyway, we'd washed in the bay that morning.

"Your mistress, please," I said.

"What?"

"Gracious lady Coral Passuran to see your mistress. Please tell her I'm here."

She closed the door gently and went away. A moment later it was opened again, this time by a more matronly figure in a good woolen robe. "I'm the mistress," she said, "Karina Mullet. May I ask your business?" The tone implied that she did not seriously expect us to have any.

"The Hall Kitchen Chief recommended you to us, gracious lady." (It was an adjective I felt it never did any harm to throw in, although she really wasn't quite up to it.) "We're looking for a place to stay."

She seemed faintly disbelieving.

I said, "We can pay three bakras in advance. If it suits, we'll probably want to make a longer arrangement with you."

She said, "Please give me a moment, uh, gracious visitor. I must consult my husband."

Again the door closed. There was no one in the street to watch, so I put one ear up against it. A brief but intense argument was going on inside. I couldn't quite catch most of it, or tell who was on what side, but the word "tymon" was used. Also the word "bakras"—that one mostly by the wife. Probably she was the one on our side, then. "Tymon" was spoken by a male voice. "We'll kill him later," I said to Ran, knowing he wouldn't pay attention. "Tymon": not only a barbarian outlander, but a Barbarian Outlander With No Manners. Most unfair.

I pulled my ear away from the door just in time. Karina Mullet swung it open and stepped back, waving us in. We were greeted in the inner entranceway by respectable husband Mullet, in his houserobe and socks, tobacco falling out of the pouch he was gripping in one hand. He was round-faced, middle-aged, and either a little bit drunk or very ruddy for someone of his dark complexion. Well, if you can't do it at home, where can you do it? I bowed, and jabbed at Ran to do the same—I wasn't sure he would, but his training in courtesy ran deep. I said,

"Your hospitality honors us, gracious sir." Take that, name-caller!

He blinked. "Uh," he began.

"You must forgive our appearance, sir, we've had a long journey. We're greatly fatigued. I wonder if we might impose on you to let us see our rooms at once?"

"Certainly we can," said his wife. "This way, up the stairs."

I bowed again to her husband, just to rub it in. "I regret the postponement of our acquaintance until to-morrow."

"Oh. Yes. Me, too." He finally made his return bow. About time, too.

Madame Mullet said, as we went up the stairs, "Will you be wanting one room or two?"

"I suppose two rooms cost more than one," I said thoughtfully.

"Oh, yes, of course." She seemed amused.

"We'll only need one. This is my br—my husband," I said, remembering in time that we looked nothing alike.

I saw her thinking: your br—, your husband—fine. Maybe I should collect the money now.

Sure enough she said, "I wonder if you could give me those three bakras before you retire? Then we won't have to worry about it in the morning."

I went down an hour later to ask if I could buy a meat pie from her, the market being closed. I still had two bakras left, and Ran hadn't eaten all day.

"Certainly," she said, and heated it up for me as well. "Your friend—I mean, your husband doesn't talk much," she remarked as she set the pie in the oven.

"He's been very ill," I said. "Affected his vocal cords. Nothing catching," I added at once.

"Ah," she said noncommittally. A moment later she said, "Would you like some tah to go with it? No charge, of course."

"Thank you, no," I said. I'd been as addicted to tah as any Ivoran. It had been hard enough getting my body to accept the decline to the one cup a day that went with the indigent's breakfast. If I got used to it again, how would it be later? And Ran's withdrawal pains had been worse than mine.

It's not the addiction; it's the expense. Still, I felt badly, since I knew Ran would have liked a cup.

My hostess took the meat pie out of the oven and wrapped it in waxed paper. Then she put two glasses on a tray alongside the pie. "Water, at least," she said. "The pie's too spicy."

"You're very considerate," I said, and found myself yawning.

She chuckled. "I can't get over your accent." She steered me to the stairs.

"What accent?"

"What accent, indeed. You talk like one of those high-toned nobles that come over the Net from the capital. That's why my man's eyeballs were popping when you said hello."

"I haven't *got* an accent."

She laughed. "Good night, gracious visitor. Don't bother about the tray; you can bring it down tomorrow."

I went up to our room and found Ran sitting on the bed. I handed him the pie and put one of the glasses on the night table.

"If I have an accent," I said, "it's *your* fault."

He raised his eyes to my face briefly, then started eating the pie. He did that sometimes; it could drive you crazy wondering if it meant anything.

I said, "When we've got a few more coins in our pockets, we'll see if there's a healer in this village. I mean, I guess you've noticed that you've got a problem." He went on eating and I pulled off my outer robe and sat down on my side of the bed. "If you've got something to say about seeing a healer, you'd better say it now."

After a minute I said, "I didn't think so."

Sleeping with a ghost is a very chaste experience. In case you wondered. The next morning as I washed at the basin, I heard sounds from out in the square, a voice raised in command and the tap of wood on stone. I looked out the narrow window that faced the street (like all well-planned houses, the good, wide windows of the house faced in toward the inner courtyard, not out on the dangerous world) and saw a dozen villagers, young and old, standing in the square holding wooden staffs. They were doing The River.

I hurried down to see if I could join them. I didn't have a staff, of course, but for Young River and Old that's not so important. I had a pair of trousers I'd not slept in more than twenty or thirty times; they would have to do.

I crept in on the far left of the group, hoping no one would object. The practice leader stopped everyone at once.

"What's going on here?" he said. He was about thirty, light-skinned for an Ivoran, with unexpectedly blue eyes that looked out from under a head kerchief that reminded me of Eln. Like Eln, there was something "off" about him; perhaps it was the coloring. Unlike Eln, he stared at me coldly.

"I'm sorry," I said, since I was the invader, after all. "I was hoping to join you. If this is a private group, I didn't mean to presume."

Someone muttered something that sounded like "tymon."

"Well," said the leader, with pure sarcasm in his voice, "Maybe our gracious visitor would like to lead the group this morning. We'd be honored, wouldn't we, friends?"

I said, "Thank you, but I'd rather not."

"Oh, come now, you can't be so rude. We'd love to see how it's done in the outworlds, am I right?"

There was general agreement. They were enjoying themselves.

So I walked to the front and stepped up to the practice leader's place. "I'll need a staff," I said, and he grinned and gave me his. Then he joined the other villagers.

There was a Middle River set I'd done perhaps five hundred times in the garden at Cormallon, trying for at least one set to achieve grace rather than simple memorization of movement. I could do it in my sleep . . . or I could if I weren't nervous.

I cleared my throat and said, "Middle Six-Eight-Eleven, Six-Eight-Two, Six-Two-Two, and repeat for a dozen. Staff horizontal to begin."

They looked at each other and shuffled around and held out their staffs.

"Now," I said, and went to position Middle Six. I felt stiff and mechanical as I moved through the set. Of course, they were probably surprised to see me do it at all, they may as well see an ape dressed up leading their sa'ret. The hell with them. I closed my eyes and pretended I was back in the garden, with Eln moving over my head. I closed them all out. Third set, fourth set, fifth set. I stretched the movements farther, just to see if it would work that way, and it felt right. I counted eleventh set and twelfth, mildly surprised that we were so far along. Maybe I'd left something out, but never mind, this wasn't as bad as I'd thought.

"And twelve." I opened my eyes. They were standing in a semicircle, sweaty and bright-eyed—probably the way I looked, too.

"Woh!" said one of the men. He laughed.

"I agree," said the woman next to him. She stamped her foot and started to clap. The others took it up and now I felt my face really get hot.

"Hey-oh," said the woman when it died down, "we should have outlanders lead us more often. Tanit always does Young River because he likes it."

Tanit, the practice leader, looked sour.

She called, "So what's next?"

"Yes, what's next?" a few others called.

"I'm just a novice," I said. "I'd really rather learn than lead. If Tanit doesn't mind, I mean."

Tanit shrugged, but I thought he looked rather relieved. He came back to the lead position. I held out his staff, but he said, "Keep it. I can lead without it, and I'll bring you an extra one tomorrow."

He stepped up into place. "Back in line, tymon," he

said, but he said it ironically, like someone who's just had the joke on him.

From then on I heard the word "tymon" a great deal in Teshin Village, but it was no longer an insult, it was just a nickname. I didn't mind. By then I'd lived in a lot of places, and been called a lot of things.

Chapter 10

The practice session made me late for the hall breakfast tasting. Luckily not that many people showed up for breakfast on the morning of a holiday; they sleep late and save their appetites for later, or have something cold at their own homes. (The house where I was staying was one of the few in the village with an oven, and the Mullets were pretty snobbish about it.)

I went to Hall Manager Peradon, who was surrounded by even more people than yesterday, and tried to get his attention.

"Manager Peradon," I said finally, "you didn't tell me yesterday what my position was."

He smiled pleasantly. "I'm sure I must have, my dear, you probably weren't paying attention. But I hear you've been doing a splendid job, so just keep it up."

I launched into my speech. "You said that if I didn't like it, I could change to something else. That sounds like a good idea. So I've been thinking: I know I'm not a cook, I know the best jobs go to people who are related to other people. I'm not fussy. I can do scut work, I can sweep the floors—"

"Sweeping floors is only two bakras a day," he said regretfully.

"I'll take it."

The hall master looked down around his feet. "It seems to me the floors are clean enough already—I don't think we need any more sweepers. In fact, I believe the only opening at the moment is the one for Dana's position. And you've been doing such a fine job of it.''

I looked at him, unimpressed. He went on quickly, ''Although, if you want to expand your duties, help out in the cleaning and such—we could probably find a way to raise you to six bakras a day.''

''Seven,'' I said, to my surprise. I really hadn't planned on keeping this job. But still, seven a day . . . and a clean bed. And I really should get Ran to a healer, the sooner the better.

''For you, flower petal, we'll make it seven.''

I couldn't help returning his smile, the old crook. But I remembered to add, ''Paid each night in coin.''

''You can't wait till the end of the week like everybody else? Trust your Uncle Peradon. You can't have any safe place to keep it, staying at a place like Mullet's, and I'm the village banker.''

Did everybody in the village know where the tymon was staying? Probably. ''Once a night,'' I said. ''Be reasonable—I might not be around at the end of the week to enjoy it.''

He grinned—probably just what he'd been thinking. ''So be it, child, but you're tearing the meat from my heart.''

''Thank you, Uncle. Meanwhile, I was wondering if there's a healer in Teshin?''

''Not in Teshin,'' he said, ''but in the hills just outside. It's not a half hour's walk to his house, and he's as fine as anybody in the capital. Have little Seth show you the way this evening after work, if you like.''

''I will. Thanks.''

''My pleasure. Seth won't want more than a bakra, either.''

Peradon went back to his account books, probably a very different set from the one he kept on the Net—if he kept any on the Net at all, which was a doubtful matter.

Seth took us out to the hills that evening. It was a clear, starry night, with one moon showing as we circled the edge of the bay and made our way north. Wind blew through the grass.

"He cured my mother of arthritis," announced Seth.

I looked over at Ran, his face lit by moonlight, and wondered if the healer could do anything with a case like this. Maybe I was expecting too much. A Tellys psychiatric ward was the more likely place to go for help, but under the circumstances that was a little far away.

"What's the healer's name?" I asked Seth.

"Here we are," he said, and pointed to a hut in a clump of trees, halfway up the hill, facing the bay.

We climbed up to the door. Seth knocked. "His name is Vale," he said suddenly, pulling off his cap.

The door opened. A man of about fifty standard years stood there, thin, balding, looking like a breeze would carry him away. Delicate and birdlike, as though his bones were hollow.

His glance took in Seth, the tall stranger in the expensive but tattered clothing, the short female barbarian. An eyebrow was raised very gently and a smile passed over his face so quickly I was never sure if I'd seen it or not. "Can I help you, travelers?" he said.

"I don't know," I answered. "My friend . . ." I made a vague motion toward Ran.

"You'd better come in," he said.

Inside there was a clean wooden floor and a brick hearth. A striped cat was sleeping by the fire, and I paused when I saw it. "What's the matter?" asked Vale. Sharp eyes, I noted, and I wasn't sure I liked that.

"It's nothing. I'm allergic to cats," I said.

"Not this one," he said.

I'd had to use the Ivoran phrase "I have an aversion to," since they had no word for allergy, and I wasn't sure that we'd managed to communicate here. Possibly he only meant that his own cat was a likable creature. However, in all the time I spent in that hut—and as it turned out, I spent a lot of time there—I never sniffled or sneezed. And the last time I'd had to stay in a room with cats I'd felt my nose turn into an ever-expanding faucet, my eyes

tear, and I'd left the home of my Athenan friends wishing
I could bury my head in the dirt and just die.

Vale led Ran to a mat beside the fire and offered him
a cup of tah. Then he watched Ran while he drank it.
Seth and I sat in a corner and waited.

The firelight flickered over them. Vale helped Ran to
lie on the mat, then knelt beside him. His hands moved
quickly, lightly, over Ran's chest, shoulders, legs, feet.
He cupped a hand on Ran's forehead. He pulled his ears
and peered inside. Then he tapped him affectionately on
one shoulder and helped him up again. That final touch
was not diagnostic, but meant as reassurance, and was
my first inkling of the many differences between healing
outworlder style and healing Ivoran style.

Then he pulled off Ran's boots and examined the soles,
leading me to wonder if I'd brought Ran to a sane man.

"Yes," he said. He turned to me. "Now, please tell
me why you've come."

"He doesn't talk," I said.

"Maybe he has nothing to say."

"Look," I said, and started to get up. Vale raised a
hand.

"Please humor me." He smiled. For the first time I
realized that this was a being of great personal charm,
when he cared to exercise it. No wonder the Teshin villagers thought he was great stuff. Take care, Theodora,
I thought.

He said, "This happened all at once? The not-
talking?"

"Yes. He'd had a shock. He heard something bad, and
the next thing I knew he was like this."

"No words at all?"

I flushed. "Well, he called me a name. But he hasn't
said anything since."

Vale nodded. "He is a sorcerer, is he not?"

Taken by surprise, I said nothing.

Vale said, "Seth, you will wait outside."

The boy left. Vale came over and knelt in front of me.
"He is clearly a sorcerer."

"Probably. You're the expert."

He said, with a touch of irony, "I am if you will let me be." The cat came over from the hearth, and Vale leaned back on his heels to make a lap for him. He stroked the cat's fur and said, "This is more than shock, I think. Does your friend have enemies?"

"Doesn't everybody?"

"Some of us more than others. I think that someone may have tried to hurt your friend. It may be worse than you know . . . it's hard to say. It's good that he called you a name, at least. A hopeful sign, that."

"Can you do anything for him?" At last the question. I wasn't sure I wanted the answer.

"Maybe. I'll need to make an examination."

"I thought you just did that."

"I just introduced myself. He knows I'm here and I'm a friend. He learned a little about me and I learned a little about him. The examination will take longer, about an hour."

"All right."

"In private."

I said, "No."

He knelt there, petting the cat. Then he said, "Would you like a cup of tah?"

And one cup of tah and some polite conversation later, I found myself waiting outside on the hill with Seth.

Seth said, "Do you know any stories?"

"No, do you?"

We sat in the grass under the trees. The wind shook the branches, and I wrapped the coat around me tighter. Luckily it was warm for the time of year, and the wind wasn't the enemy it would become in a month.

"I know lots of stories," he said. "I thought you'd have a new one. Being an outlander."

"Well, I can't think of any right now. You tell me one."

I said it because I wanted to think, but he went ahead and told a wonderful, harrowing, magical story about Kata the Mother of Soldiers and the evil Emperor of the tenth dynasty. I wished I had a notebook with me. From time to time I looked back at the hut where a suspicious-looking green glow seeped through the door frame.

"He'll be all right," said Seth once, interrupting the fight between the Clay Soldiers and the Emperor's griffin.

"I hope so."

"Vale's the best, everybody says. He's been here as far back as I can remember."

Seth was maybe all of ten. "Don't stop the story," I said.

He finished the story, and I applauded and stamped one foot against the side of the hill. Seth ducked his head. "You're a prince of storytellers," I told him.

"Don't make fun," he said.

The door to the hut opened. "Come in," said Vale.

We went inside. Ran was sitting by the hearth, the striped cat leaning against him.

"I don't know," said Vale. "I'm sorry to give you an answer like this. I do know that it will take time."

"What's *wrong* with him?" For the first time I felt ready to cry.

"Shock, as you said. But that was just the stimulus. His life-force has been blocked."

" 'Life-force'—oh, really, what garbage! I didn't come out here and sit on your damned hill to hear about kanz like a life-force. I thought you could help." I grabbed Ran's hand and pulled him up. "Come on, Seth."

Vale stepped in front of the door. "*Listen* to me. He's a sorcerer. He draws on magic for his energy. Now he can no longer touch that source of power."

I said, "Get out of the way."

"Think a minute. I haven't even mentioned a fee yet, have I? Do I have something to gain by lying to you?" He said, in despair, "What is it about you foreigners that you can't see magic when it's in front of you?"

That made me pause. I remembered the jokes my Athenan friends and I had made about magic on the liner voyage out. My judgment of the situation had changed a great deal since then. I'd had to accept the reality of a lot of things I hadn't quite approved of . . . was I going to maybe wreck Ran's last chance because I didn't like the way Vale talked?

Then it hit me. *Blocked.* Ran's source of magic was blocked—and it was really Ran's ability to read cards that I used for his benefit, thanks to the curse. Except that I hadn't been able to read the cards for months.

Vale was watching me. He stepped away from the door. "I can help him," he said, "maybe."

"What do you want to do?" I asked.

"Bring him here every day. I'll work to wear away the blockage—it has to be done little by little, and he has to help me."

"He can't even help himself. He's been like this for months, he doesn't care what happens to him. I could have left him in the woods and he wouldn't have lifted a finger to stop me." What's more, he seemed supremely uninterested in this conversation now.

"Oh, he's not quite as na' telleth as all that." Vale smiled. "He cared enough to call you a name. And you cared enough to remain hurt by it for months."

I could really learn to dislike Vale.

"Need another cup of tah?" he asked pointedly.

"All right, you win. I'll bring him back tomorrow evening."

"Morning," said Vale. "Drop him off on your way to work." And as I left the hut with Seth and Ran, he added, "And if you experience any abdominal pains connected with your new job, see me immediately."

I hadn't mentioned my work. Apparently even the recluse outside of town knew what the tymon was doing.

Winter on Ivory is officially equal to five standard months. Which is really just saying that five standard months is equal to one-quarter of the Ivoran year. In real life, winter defines itself, and along the southern coast it blows in fiercely and stays for half a standard year, at the very least. I was glad to have settled in Teshin before it came in earnest.

I dropped off Ran every morning and went by after work to pick him up again, jingling my seven bakras all the way. (Seven bakras minus two bakras a day for rent and one for food—since I got all the food I wanted on the job, I only needed to pay for Ran—left four bakras to accumulate under the loose floorboard in our room. Which came to a total of three tabals profit per week, not bad compared to the nothing we had before entering Teshin.) As I waited for Ran in the evenings, I saw that a number of villagers made their way to and from Vale's hut.

Most of them seemed pretty healthy. I passed Hall Master Peradon once on the way down the hill, and asked him about it. "Well, of course," he said, "you don't want to climb up this hill when you're sick, do you? The whole point is not to get sick."

I thought Peradon was the last visitor of the day, so I went right up to the door and knocked. Usually I respected Vale's wish not to be disturbed when he was with someone.

"A moment," called Vale. He opened the door. "Oh, it's you, tymon. You'll have to wait a bit, I'm with someone right now."

Behind him, on the mat by the fire, I saw one of the young fishermen lying with his shirt off. His head was resting on his arms. As I stood there he turned his face to the door and called lazily, "Oh, she can wait in here if she's cold. I don't mind."

Vale bowed and motioned me inside. I sat down in a corner where Ran was waiting for me. The cat was in his lap.

Vale knelt down by the fisherman and placed his hand gently in the center of the man's back. Then he closed his eyes and breathed quietly. A moment later he knelt up higher, bent over the body on the mat, and began moving his hands down the sides of the back, a few inches from the spinal column. It was some form of massage. I watched the procedure for about forty minutes. He did the back, the legs, the rump, the feet; then rolled the man over and worked up from the feet to neck and face. He did not spare the area around the pelvis, which caused me to look away into the darkness of the hut for a few minutes and try to stop the redness I was sure was covering my cheeks. He worked cheerfully but quietly, and I didn't know what to think; it was by no means impersonal, but it wasn't sexual either. I wasn't used to seeing physical contact that didn't fit into one of those two baskets.

When he was finished, the man just lay there on the mat for a few minutes while Vale brewed tea. "Not tah," said Vale to me, when he offered me a cup, and the fisherman sat down beside us with his. "You shouldn't have tah just after a session. It overstimulates the system. And as for you, little tymon, you've drunk more tah in your time than is good for you—I can tell from the color of the whites of your eyes."

I peered into the shininess of my cup, trying to make out the whites of my eyes. As far as I could tell, they were fine. "That was interesting to watch," I said to Vale.

The fisherman—his name was Pyre, and I came to know him very well over the next few months—grinned at me and said, "Interesting to do, also."

I asked, "You really liked it?"

"Why would I come three, four times a week if it were boring?"

"Pyre is one of my more enthusiastic clients," said Vale. "But given the things he asks of his poor body, it's no wonder."

"I'm a chakon dancer," explained Pyre.

"I thought you were a fisherman."

"I'm a fisherman the way you're a poison-taster, tymon. It pays me through the winter." He finished his tea and poured another cup, topping mine off as he did so. Pyre was of middle height, brown-haired, and wiry-looking. It was only when his shirt was off, as it had been a few minutes ago, that you saw the well-defined muscles of his arms.

When he'd left, I said, thoughtfully to Vale: "I wish I could do something like that. It's a simple thing, but he left happier than he came in, I'll bet. And when it comes to really helping another person, it's usually a pretty hopeless task.''

''You could do it if you wanted to.''

''Ha.''

Vale said, ''Yes, it is a simple thing, and like many simple things it takes years to learn. But it's like The River that way; you can learn the basics quickly, and then you let your clients teach you. That part only takes a lifetime.'

''I've got several months.''

He laughed. ''It will have to do, then,'' he said.

''Come on, Vale, don't sell me kanz instead of a calf. I'm clumsy, that's just the way I am. I accept it. I can do other things.''

''You can do this thing, if you want to.''

''I'd better be taking Ran home now,'' I said.

''Wait,'' said Vale, and he called out, ''Ran, would you mind picking up the dishes and helping me carry them to the bucket?''

Ran got up, came over to the low table, and began lifting the cups. I stared. ''. . . Ran?'' I said, tentatively.

''Not yet,'' said Vale. ''He's not all the way back yet. But he's watching. I think it does him good to be here when the different clients come. The fluctuations in the energy fields draw him out.''

Vale would *say* things like that just when you thought he was beginning to make sense.

''Think about it,'' he said as we left. ''I haven't had a student in two decades, and it would do some of my clients well to have a different touch.''

''Different, yeah,'' I muttered, as I led Ran down the hill. He almost tripped over a groundhermit hole, and I said, ''Fluctuations in the energy fields, my maiden aunt.''

But in fact he did seem better, and could respond to simple requests although he still wouldn't initiate anything. I thought about that, and I thought about not living enough in my body, whatever that may mean, and decided that a course with Vale might be good for me. It's hard to explain; it's not that I was looking forward to it, it's not as though I thought I would enjoy it; it was more like going for a blood test because it's a necessary thing to do.

So I knocked on Vale's door a few days later and said, "Maybe I'm interested in learning from you after all. Let's talk about money, Vale."

He said, "Sir or Teacher, not Vale."

I said, "You like to keep your relationships clear on this planet, don't you?"

He smiled and gestured me inside.

Chapter 11

Money was, of course, the first concern. I found that Vale
expected me to appear on his doorstep first thing in the
morning, and work through the evening. "It's the only
way," he said. "You told me that you have just a few
months."

"It's the only way to starve," I said. "What am I supposed to do without the coin I get from the kitchens?
And how am I supposed to pay you?"

"You can't afford me, so don't worry about it. When
I see a penniless barbarian working her way up the coast
in clothes like yours, I really don't expect her to meet
my tuition."

I said, suspiciously, "So you're not charging me? This
is free?"

"It is not. It's only deferred. When I see a penniless
barbarian in the company of a high-level sorcerer—in
clothes that must have cost him a great deal once—I sus-
pect she may one day come into better fortune." He
added, "Especially when the sorcerer is Ran Cormallon.
I saw him in the capital once."

I stared.

"A most impressive young man. We'll speak no more
about it, though. Here is your mat—you see I've gotten
you your own, and I expect you to keep it clean."

"You never said anything."

"I had nothing to say. On the floor now, and I'll show
you the proper beginning positions. Kneel down, back
straight, weight even—"

I did so. By the time the day was over, my knees and arms and calves and buttocks all knew they had been through a great deal more than they had ever expected. I had also settled with Vale that he would pay four bakras a day to me to make up for my loss of income, at an interest rate of twenty percent, compounded weekly. He said it would be unethical for me to charge money to any of the clients I would be working on, since I was only an ignorant apprentice. I asked if twenty percent interest struck him as unethical, and he said no.

I ate, breathed, and slept work for the next few months. When I wasn't practicing at Vale's, I was studying body charts in the room at Mullet's. I had to give up The River in the morning, I was too exhausted; studying with Vale was more physically demanding than I'd dreamed, and a second workout on top of it was more than I could handle. But I learned what I set out to learn. I'd come to this place a well-trained scholar, with, as Vale later said, a soul that needed a good turning-out; and had spent my time studying the crueler arts of Ivory instead of the kind ones. I had barely noticed there were kind ones. And if I had, I wouldn't have expected them to be this complicated.

Tinaje was what I was studying; Vale gave me a choice from three forms of touch healing: Bratelle, Perthes, and Tinaje, in descending order of roughness. Tinaje was the gentlest. That other stuff *hurt*. "They're very popular," said Vale. "Not with me," I said.

So Vale let his clients know that he had a tinaje apprentice, should they want free sessions, and many of them did. The most accommodating was Pyre, who showed up every day, and sometimes twice a day.

As he lay there on his stomach, Vale would walk around me while I worked, pulling my legs back and tapping my back unexpectedly with just enough force to make me bend the way he wanted.

"That's better," he said.

"But this way all my body weight will be on him!"

"Exactly," he said.

I said to Pyre, "Doesn't it hurt?"

"Nooo," said Pyre smugly.

"You're a feeble little barbarian," said Vale. "He's a big healthy boy. Don't be so timid."

After Pyre had left, Vale got out his charts and lectured me on the incomprehensible nature of Ivoran energy-flow theories. As far as I could tell he considered the body as practically imaginary, a convenient peg for dealing with the actual human condition, which he called "energies in flux." ("We'll save the muscle groups and rib counts for later," he told me. "Were you Ivoran, I'd begin with those. But we start with the most alien system first.") I really didn't know how to accept this sort of thing, which seemed firmly grounded in folk-belief. But I decided that Vale was the Teacher, I was there to learn, and I'd make up my mind later when I'd gathered enough experience. Meanwhile, if it worked, it worked . . . an acccptance system which had weathered me safely through Ivoran thought to this point.

I sat there thinking despairing thoughts about the length of time it would take to learn these theories. Each chart was full of complex diagrams, and there were dozens of charts. I'd thought I was doing well to get the strokes and pressures down.

"All right, tymon, lie down," said Vale.

"What?"

"On the mat," he said patiently. "I'm going to demonstrate the fire lines and the major points. We'll do legs and back tonight."

"On me?" I lay down and pulled up my shirt. Mostly tinaje is done clothed, but the lower back is often bare-skin.

"Who else is here to demonstrate on? Besides, you look as though you haven't been touched very much."

"What's that supposed to mean?"

"My, look at those back muscles tense up. Now: Fire line one, the Point of Gathered Thunder."

He did it, he said, a little deeper than was necessary, almost perthes rather than tinaje, and when I got up I could see why. I could still feel the pathway tingling down my back and legs. It would be hard to forget, at least for the rest of the night, and I could review the points on my way home. Or so he suggested.

But in fact on the way home I ran into Seth, who'd come up the hill earlier on an errand for Hall Manager Peradon, and I let him tell me another story about Annurian the Outlaw and his band in the Northwest Sector. There seemed to be a lot of stories about Annurian, he was a popular legendary figure in the provinces. There were at least three Annurian tales in my new notebook (purchased for half a bakra after much soul-searching) and Seth said he knew dozens more. When I got back to Mullet's rooms, I should have studied the tinaje points, but instead I scribbled down Seth's tale and then lay awake dreaming about an adventurous life in the Northwest Sector. But doubtless such are the dreams of all provincial apprentices.

It was a few weeks into my training when the unusual thing happened. Vale sent me to see a client of his who was too old to come to the hut himself. But he was a connoisseur and hard to please, said Vale, so I was to do my very best.

"Won't he mind taking tinaje from an apprentice?" I said.

"Not at all," said Vale, which surely had to be a lie.

So I found myself on the ferry that made the once-a-week crossing to Kado Island, in the middle of the bay, on my way to see Curran Lormer . . . which was his name, I found after much digging, although the only thing the villagers ever called him was the Old Man of Kado Island.

The ferry was an actual little steamer, down-at-the-heels and elderly, but still a cut above the boats Teshin usually used. There were about fifteen people on it besides myself. I hadn't expected so many would have business on the island, but there were twenty or thirty families living there, and I suppose many of them had weekly errands. The boat would make two trips back, one at noon and one at sunset, taking care of everyone, inbound to out and outbound to in. But if I missed the sunset run, I would be stuck for a week.

We docked in the little inlet at the foot of the hill. A long series of wooden steps led up the hill to the blue sky above, and that was all one could see of Kado Island. As I stood on the dock, I saw two men in fisherman's trousers and jackets making their way down the steps, the wind whipping the trousers against their legs, scarves tied around their caps to keep them on. As they came closer, I saw they were gray-haired, with wrinkled, leathery faces. They smiled and nodded to me in passing, and headed for the boat. "Excuse me!" I called. They turned and bowed, their hands stuffed in their jackets. "Can you tell me where to find Curran Lormer?"

They looked at each other. "I am sorry?" said one. They seemed polite but faintly off-balance, as though to say to each other, well, one can't expect a foreigner to make sense.

"Curran Lor—the Old Man. The Old Man of the Island."

The smiles broke wide. "Yes, of course," said the first man, relieved I spoke the language after all. They directed me over the hill and down to the island settlement. I thanked them and they bowed and hurried off to the boat, talking excitedly to each other about this encounter with the cosmopolitan.

I couldn't have missed it anyway. There were over a dozen cabins in this settlement, with wells, livestock, dogs, and children. Everybody knew the Old Man; they were thrilled to show off their knowledge to an outlander. An old porch with peeling paint and soft floorboards led up to the door of the cabin. Wooden wind chimes hung from a string above the doorpost.

I knocked. "Gracious sir?" I called. He might be hard of hearing.

He opened the door slowly. He was indeed very old, and pale-skinned. He was stocky, with alert black eyes, totally bald, and wearing a thick green robe with an orange undertunic. And he was short! He wasn't much taller than I was. "Curran Lormer?" I asked.

"Yes. And you are the little tinaje artist?"

Little, indeed—that was nice, coming from him. "Coral Passuran," I agreed.

So our relationship began with a lie. However, at the time, I thought I was the one who was lying.

He was a restful person to do tinaje for. He knew exactly what he wanted and needed, having dealt with Vale for at least ten years, and was willing to direct me when I asked for it. He was very tolerant. Looking back on how little I knew at that time, I realize that he must have been. He told me that he was in the last stages of hemgee poisoning, given him by an old enemy many years ago. He kept it at bay through herbal treatments and touch healing, but it was gradually winning.

"So my fire lines need especial attention, little one," he told me from the mat on the floor.

Poor man, I could see why he chose tinaje rather than the other arts. For all he looked so stocky and vigorous, I could barely lean against him without feeling the delicacy of his bones and seeing him wince. His skin had the texture I came to associate with the very old, at least on this planet; it was gray-looking in the cabin, under the two candles that were our only light source.

"Where are you from, little one?" he asked.

I pulled his pendant out of the way. "Here and there," I said. I didn't like the idea of putting this much force on his body. Vale had taught me to lean over and let my weight to do the work, and not be afraid . . . but he also said that every case was different. Well, this was my decision then: I put one foot on the floor in a genuflection position, and rested some of my body weight on my own knee.

He didn't seem in as much pain after that. "Do they do tinaje differently in the land of Here and There?" he asked.

"Oh, much the same." I worked down the dorsal fire lines. "How could it dare be different, when Ivory is the center of the universe, and Teshin the center of Ivory?"

There was a rumble in his body, like a subdued chuckle. "You're not content in the provinces, are you?"

I grunted. An honest answer to that would be insulting. I said, to change the subject, "Do you know any stories?"

And he told me a story, and because it will tell you a little about how Ivorans regard the hill-healers, I will repeat it here.

The Tale of Two Families

There once was a healer named Old Kenthik, and he was a member of the family Solovay. They were enemies with a family named Davis, a very old and respected family indeed, who lived just next door. The Solovay men came to the Davis house and said that they wanted to make peace, because they all lived in a town on the coast (but bigger than Teshin) and wanted to combine their shipping line with the Davis one. So they agreed to pay the Davises a face-price of two hundred bolts of silk and eighty oil-jars. After the Davises collected the payment, they called peace and invited the Solovays to a feast. All the important Solovay men came to the feast, including Old Kenthik, who was invited down from the hills. After the first course was served, Old Kenthik became ill and vomited on the floor, which was embarrassing because they had an Andulsine carpet of intricate design in the banquet hall. So he apologized and went out to be sick in the garden. But one of the Solovay women was walking in the garden next door, and she looked over the wall because she was curious about what was going on at this party she hadn't been invited to. And she saw Old Kenthik being sick under the rose bushes. And she said to herself, Old Kenthik's done The River every day of his life for the last fifty years, and his body is a friend of his. So she sent a note over to her young husband that said, "Husband, you've been poisoned." And her husband went carefully around to his relatives and

told them so. One by one they excused themselves
for some air, and went into the garden and made
themselves vomit out the poison, and the young wife
passed their knives and short swords to them over
the wall. And when each one came back to the party
he was armed. Then the young husband gave the
signal, and they fell on their hosts and killed them,
and set fire to their house. When the neighbors heard
the noise, they came to investigate, but seeing the
bloody weapons in the hands of the men, they were
too timid to say anything. And the men said, "Go
back to your homes, good neighbors. This is not
because of anything you've done, and it's not because we're angry with you. It's just one of those
things that happen because we are in this world."

"Well," I said to the Old Man, "that's a good story.
I'll write it down when I get back to Teshin."

"It's not the real ending," he said. "The real ending's
that the Imperial Police used to collect bribes from the
Davises every week, and they resented the Solovay family for what they'd done. So every male in the family
cleared out of town overnight and ran off to the Northwest Sector."

"Northwest Sector . . . say, do you know any Annurian stories?"

"Dull stuff," he said, and then he said "ahh," because I was going to work on his feet.

"I like them," I said, disappointed.

"I like true stories . . . I'll bet *you* have a story," he
said. He grinned and wiggled his toes.

I gave the soles of his feet a gentle slap. "Dull stuff,"
I said.

"Dull," he repeated lightly. "You know, that's why I
like the provinces. Someday when you're old and white-
haired, you'll be glad for a place where nothing happens."

When the session was over, I thanked him as was customary for being so good as to trust me and took the
sunset ferry back to Teshin.

"Name," Vale would say to me these days, as he demonstrated a certain point on the tolerant corpse of Pyre. "Soft Rain," I would say. "Line," Vale then said. "Earth," I replied. "Organ," said Vale. "Liver," said I. "Poisons which affect," said Vale. "Hethra, genroot, tiril . . . that's all I can think of." "Treatments," snapped Vale, who didn't like to see hesitation. "Liquids. Red tah and crushed tannis seeds. No purgatives." Then he would either make me do it all again, while I wondered what I'd missed, or he'd move to the next point and say: "Name."

We did anatomy at the same time, which at least I understood. Vale would have me count down the ribs and show what point was at what intercostal space, where the pericardium was, what to look for where the rib cage ended. By now I firmly grasped the fact that I'd gotten into a lot more than I'd bargained for when I decided to study with Vale. Before this I had never considered the knowledge of five hundred kinds of poisons and the proper treatment of stab wounds to be part of general health maintenance, whereas in Vale's mind it seemed to be what every young girl should know.

It was a relief to have the stories to look forward to. The clients always offered to leave me money, which I had to refuse, and I often said, "But if you have a story to tell, I'd like to hear it." Vale didn't mind, because he got to listen. There's nothing an Ivoran likes more than a story, and the blank pages in my notebook were growing few. I was beginning to think: This could get you a doctorate back on Athena . . . there's no point in thinking of your years here as wasted.

As for Ran: I saw no difference, but Vale told me to keep close to him at all times. He was heading for some kind of crisis, and it was important—so Vale said—that he come out of it in as gentle a fashion as possible. So I even took Ran with me on the ferry to Kado Island once a week, and let him sit on the porch while I did tinaje for the Old Man.

It was very late in the winter on one of my weekly visits, when I stood on the dock and saw the two gray-

haired polite men who'd directed me to the cabin on my
first trip. They were making their usual way down the
steps, trousers flapping back from their legs, smiles for
me and Ran as they passed. They had to wait for one of
the ferrymen to do something with the plank, and as they
hung back one of them approached me. "You know," he
said confidentially, "he's Annurian."

"I beg your pardon?"

"Our Old Man," he said, with the same insane smile.
"He's Annurian."

"*Vathcar* Annurian?" I said, for lack of anything else.

He nodded. "He thinks we don't know. But everybody
knows."

"Annurian is a historical figure," I said, although actually I wasn't sure. Maybe he was a legendary figure.
But in any case, he certainly lived a long time ago.

"He is, of course, historical. He retired thirty years
ago. It was thirty years, was it not?" He appealed to his
companion, who nodded.

Seth had never actually told me when his stories were
supposed to have taken place. I'd only assumed it was a
thousand years ago.

"It is, of course, an honor," said the other man, and
they both hurried onto the boat. I wasn't sure what was
an honor, talking to me or harboring a famous fugitive
on their little island.

If he was, technically, a fugitive. Annurian: The leader
of a raider band in the Northwest Sector that drove the
Emperor crazy for years. That was the time that most of
the stories were set in, the outlaw years. Later he was
captured and sentenced to the Imperial Army. He worked
his way through the ranks and, very likely, arrested many
former colleagues; ending as Chief General and later
Prime Minister. It was a Cinderella story, bloody but
Ivoran.

"Gracious lady!" called a voice.

I turned. A few feet away, over the water, the man I'd
just spoken to called, "Don't mention it, gracious lady!
I don't think the new Emperor likes him."

* * *

It was probably just a story. I told myself that as I walked up the hill with Ran. Suddenly I froze. I remembered moving the Old Man's pendant out of the way when I worked; I didn't have time to think about it at the time, my mind being mostly concentrated on the tinaje and partly on the Old Man's stories; but I remembered the feel of it now as though I were holding it at that very moment. It was warm, warmer than body heat should make it; and it was carved from that favorite material of the Cormallon library, the material that best held psychic memories—what was an old man living in poverty doing with a bluestone pendant?

What did that prove? It proved Curran Lormer was a very suspicious fellow, that was all. It proved he had more of a past than the rest of the people on Kado Island. As for anything else, it was impossible to say . . . no, it wasn't. He couldn't be Annurian. Where was his tattoo?

At once I was relieved, reality was restored. Although, when I started to think about it, I realized I'd never seen him full-faced in the sunlight. Only by the light of two cheap candles in a dark cabin . . . and we could assume that his tattoo would have faded over the years.

"Come in, little artist," said the Old Man when I knocked.

"Who's little?" I asked, because he liked that kind of thing. But I was sad to see when I entered that he was even more tired and shrunken looking than usual. That was the way it was over the last few weeks; the poison eating away at him.

I had to do the tinaje more softly and carefully than ever. His skin was unnaturally warm. As I finished the neck and head I tilted his face gently to the right . . . and there it was, in the flickering candlelight, a faint gray over the lighter gray-white of his cheek: the letter C.

His eyes moved up to meet mine. "Well, little artist," he said calmly. Upside down like that, the friendliest face can look threatening. "Did you see what you wanted to see?"

"Pardon?"

"Didn't anyone tell you, tymon of mine, that a fine

intuition develops between people who work on tinaje together? I felt what you were thinking then, like a cold gust of wind."

"What I think is dull stuff," I said carefully.

He said, "You're a novice. It takes years to learn the craft, but you show promise or I would have sent you back to Vale. Let's not cut your career short, you and I, with a misunderstanding."

By all means, let us not.

He went on. "I'm an old man, the oldest man on Kado Island. But I sleep with a knife under my mat, and a short sword over the door post, and if you think you could get to either of them faster than I could, I can only say—you're wrong."

"I see."

The neck muscles under my hands were very tight. I wondered what would happen if I closed my fist around his throat. The outcome looked uncertain; he was old, but I was a feeble barbarian. "So the question is, my friend, are you going to go back to the capital and tell anyone where I am?"

"Would you kill me if I said that I would?"

"Most certainly."

"In that case," I said, "I won't mention it."

The neck muscles relaxed, and he laughed. "Oh, my dear barbarian. If we can't trust someone who's done tinaje with us through the whole cold winter, whom can we trust?"

I made the ferry crossing in a daze. When we docked, I took Ran with me to the market to pick up some supper, and that's when I got my third shock of the day.

We were walking down the narrow street that ran behind the village hall when I heard voices just around the corner. There was something both out-of-place and familiar about them. I frowned, feeling there was something about these particular voices it was important I should know; then I got it, just as they came round the bend and we were face-to-face with a dozen tourists. Of course they had to be tourists; they were speaking Standard with Athenan accents! They ranged in age from about eighteen to sixty, wearing Athenan clothing with the occasional robe thrown over their thermal suits, and they were talking the sort of nonstop, interested, meaningless jabber that made me homesick. What could they possibly be doing in a backwater town like Teshin?

By the looks of things they wondered the same about me. A couple of them caught sight of me and halted their arguing colleagues, mostly by pulling forcibly on their clothing, and we stared at each other. "Hello," I said, in Standard.

"Hello," said the youngest, a girl—probably a first year student. Very likely these were her topic relations, and a wealthy group they must be, to afford the Grand Tour. But then, the retirement-age adults outnumbered the younger ones. I'd planned on saving up myself, and taking the sector round to Ivory and Tellys when I was retired; I was willing to save the money and skip Pyrene, the usual third point on the tours.

So here we were. About half the group didn't want to give up their argument, something about provincial art forms, but the other half clustered around me. "Are you Athenan?" asked the girl. She sounded uncertain.

"Legends and Folk Literature," I said, extending a hand.

"You must talk to Clement. He's Cross-Cultural Myths," she said. "I'm Annamarie, and I haven't decided yet."

"We're on a tour of the provinces," put in a boy who looked not too much older than Annamarie. "Clement wants to study the mental structure of the provincials."

"Oh, does he?" I said.

"Their world-view, you know. It's what he's famous for."

Annamarie said, "We're very lucky to have the opportunity of traveling with him."

"Who's your friend?" asked the boy, nodding to Ran.

Meanwhile the man Annamarie had gestured toward when she said "Clement" was raising his voice to his companion.

"Let's face facts, Tom," he was saying. "Our hosts in the capital are one thing, particularly the aristocrats. Abysmally ignorant, of course, but that's hardly their fault. They know how to behave, at least. But we're among primitive people here—you can't expect sophisticated visual expression from them. Of *course* the murals in the hall are representational. Do you think they've heard of Kohler dual-effect abstractionism here? Maybe we should ask one of them. How about that young savage over here?"

He was clearly referring to Ran.

I said to the boy with Annamarie, "He's my guide." Meanwhile I wondered how "Clement" would look staked out on the shore during high tide, when the clickers come out of the water looking for food.

"Oh," said the boy.

Annamarie said, "But listen, this is wonderful! Who would think we'd meet someone from home out here in the middle of nowhere? You *must* come and have dinner with us—we'll be here for three days, you could come any night."

"Where are you staying?" I asked, knowing very well there was no inn in the village.

"We've a boat docked on the bay side of the harbor. It's a wonderful thing, we rented it in the capital. It's got cabins and a kitchen and a big dining room, and it's all *luxurious,*" she said in happy awe. With reason, things tend to be a bit more functional back in the schoolroom.

"Clement, really," said his debating partner, "You tell me these things as though you're teaching me something new. I don't expect children to fly. But many of the people here have quite modern minds. Look at the trade suggestion put forth by that fellow in the city—I forget his name, the head of Cormallon."

I felt Ran stiffen beside me.

The man went on, "Quite a sophisticated plan. If we got together privately, I think we *could* pry a few new designs out of Tellys before they got wise to us and cried monopoly. He's right, these things shouldn't be in the hands of governments; governments can't keep secrets, it's not in their nature. And my department could surely use that new scanner system."

"If you say so," said Clement tolerantly. "I stay away from technology, it's not my field. I'll give you this, though, Eln Cormallon puts on one colossus of a welcome party. My insides are still quivering. I'm just not sure," he said, lowering his voice, "that we should have brought the youngsters."

Ran was walking quickly up the street. I started after him.

"Wait a minute, friend!" called Annamarie. "Will you come to dinner?"

"Tomorrow," I said.

"We don't know your name!"

"Coral Passuran," I called, without stopping to think.

Ran was sitting on the bed at Mullet's, muttering. "Eln," he said. "I knew it was Eln. It had to be. I knew it all along."

I was alarmed. Vale had told me specifically that when Ran came out of it, it should be in "an atmosphere of gentle reassurance." This did not seem to fit that description . . . if he was normalizing at all, which was still uncertain.

"Ran? Do you know where you are?"

He looked up irritably. "Mullet's house, in Teshin, a long way away from where we ought to be. You know Eln is behind all this, don't you? I don't know about Kylla."

"Uh, are you aware of how things have been for the last few months? You remember?"

"Naturally." He emptied my pack on the bed. "We'd better start getting ready to move. There's a lot to be done . . . the important thing is not to trust anybody."

He was scary this way. When an Ivoran closes down that circle of trust to exclude his family, it gets awfully confining.

He said. "Take out the cards."

"I haven't been able to get anything from them. I haven't run them in ages."

"They'll work now," he said.

I started to take them out, then stopped. "Look, can we wait a little while on this? It's just . . . they make me nervous right now."

He was alert. "Nervous how?"

"You make me nervous, too."

He relaxed. "Just the jitters. No wonder you're scretchy. Never mind, we've waited this long. Where are your weapons, anyway? They're not in the pack."

I said, "Well, I've got a knife. And there's a hotpencil I stuck under the mat, but it de-energized on the way here."

"Contact weapons," he said with scorn. "I'm talking about the real thing—the Issin people confiscated my pistols."

"I never had a pistol. They're expensive."

"Really, Theodora, I paid you a high enough salary—"

"I was saving up!"

He raised his hands. "All right, all right." He laid back on the bed, thinking.

After a while I said, "Are you going to lie there thinking all night?"

"Probably," he said.

"Yeah, well, it's good to talk to you again, too." I crawled under the blankets. After a minute I added, "If you can think in the dark, you'd better put out the candle. We pay the Mullets extra for those."

And he put it out, without another word.

When I woke up, he was already gone. There was a note on the bedtable that said: "Running errands. You'll find your wallet two bakras lighter." No signature, because discretion as well as courtesy form the two rivers that run deepest in a Cormallon. In truth I could not actually read the whole message, but I recognized the symbols for "errands" and "bakras" and the rest was self-explanatory.

I washed and went out to the square, where The River was breaking up. I waved to the participants. As I turned the corner out of the square, I looked down the street and saw Ran standing in the shadow of the village hall, talking to a man I'd seen from time to time in The River sessions. He was one of the more disreputable citizens of the village, and I'd picked up the idea (although no one had specifically warned me) that I should avoid his company.

I put it out of my mind and went out to the hills to do my class with Vale. I was at a difficult time in my training; I was somehow supposed to synthesize all the modes of thought and all the physical techniques and anything else I'd picked up on the way into some glorious whole.

"You shouldn't even have to stop to think about it," said Vale, grinning like a shark.

"I can't stand much more of this," I said. "It gets more and more impossible. Each time I think I've made progress you spring something on me that I see at once will mean months of study. I can't win. There's too much to absorb, it takes *years*, Teacher, and you knew that when you let me start."

"Well, well," he said.

"I'm not even a novice! I'm not even qualified to be a novice! I'm still at the beginning of the beginning!"

"Well, never mind that," he said. "I've been doing this for half a century, and I'm just at the beginning of the middle."

"Is that supposed to cheer me up? If *you're* not an expert, what does that make me?"

"That's not for me to answer," he said. He knelt down beside me. "You have to begin somewhere, tymon, or you'll never begin at all. I don't know what this obsession is with *expertness* you foreigners have. You're not a machine. None of your clients have complained to me, let that be enough for you right now." There was a knock on the door and he sat back on his heels. "That's someone I asked by to test you on. I can ask him to come back later, if . . . is there something else bothering you? You didn't bring Ran today, and you say he's normalized. . . ."

"He is." I sniffled. For a moment there I'd felt the

threat of tears, but it was gone now. "Let him in, Teacher. Do your worst."

So he let in the client, age forty to forty-five, dressed like a fisherman but not anyone I recognized. "Where would you begin to work?" asked Vale, so I knew there was a trick somewhere. I looked the client up and down and watched the way he walked—there was something off about it—and asked him to lie down, and observed how his limbs fell when he relaxed. Then I picked up his boots and saw from the soles that he avoided putting weight on the inside of his left foot. So I said to Vale, "Tinther arthritis?" And Vale said, "Don't ask me, ask him." I thought about that and said to the client, "Excuse me, gracious sir, is there anything you would like to tell me before we begin?" And he smiled and gave me a beautifully classic description of tinther arthritis. I traced the twist in his muscle up the leg, and did a little extrapolation to figure where he would have to shift his weight to compensate. I moved up to the shoulders, and put my hand on the knot of muscles by the right side of the neck. "Here," I said.

Vale applauded and stamped his foot on the floor of the hut.

The client grinned at me, upside down. "Not bad for a tymon, I guess," he said.

Vale put me through a lot that day. I was glad when my old friend Pyre came in, last of all. Pyre was tolerant, he would take anything, and I wasn't sure I was up to much. But as I knelt over him something occurred to me. Vale was always telling me to "de-energize my telleth" before I began a session, and I'd always listened with a straight face and thought: De-energize, indeed. I'll begin when I begin.

But I felt wrung out, and didn't want to shortchange Pyre. So I knelt there and calmed myself down and cleared all the trash out of my mind, and told myself to just concentrate on the session. And as I put my hands on Pyre's shoulders he said, "Oh, *tymon.*" I felt distant surprise but went on with it and when it was over he said, "You're really getting good at this, aren't you?" With just enough surprise in his voice that I wondered what his previous opinion had really been.

Pyre asked me to work on his hands afterward, because he'd been practicing the hand-walk scene from *Clerina,* the classic chakon theater dance. Vale was sweeping the floor, as he did once a day, trying not to hit the cat. I'd pulled my outer robe off a long while back, and Pyre had his shirt still off. We were sitting there on Vale's hearth, laughing comfortably over a story Pyre was telling about his dancing partner, as I held his hand in my lap, putting pressure on the palm muscles. Ran walked in.

We'd been laughing too hard to notice the knock, and anyway my mind was focused on the session. Ran looked us over, and I let go of Pyre's hand. It was the first time since the beginning of training that I felt embarrassed to touch somebody. Ran said, "I came to talk to Vale." I resented his attitude—if anyone ought to understand tinaje, it was an Ivoran—at the same time I wanted to let him know that if Pyre had sexual interest in anybody it was not in women.

Pyre said, "I have to go anyway." He put on his shirt and fisherman's jacket. "I'll see you tomorrow, tymon."

"Tymon?" said Ran, raising an eyebrow. He turned to me. "You'd best go as well. I want to speak with Vale privately."

If his edict about not trusting anybody was going to extend to me, he was going to hear about it. "Look, if you've got something to say—"

"You'll hear about it soon enough," he said.

Vale spoke up. "I think it's for me to decide if I want to speak privately to your friend. Why don't you wait outside, tymon?"

"Wait at Mullet's. This will take a while." Ran didn't look at me.

Well, so be it. Later he would have to listen to me.

When Ran hadn't shown up within an hour, I went to the Athenans' dinner without him. It would have saved the price of a meal if he'd come along, and that, I told myself, was the only reason I was annoyed.

Their boat was as opulent as advertised. Annamarie met me at the top of the plank. "I'm so glad you came, we're all dying to talk to you."

She took me into the dining hall, which had a long table (high enough for foreigners) and dining couches with satin covers. "Must be hell for the servants to clean," I said, and she responded with a look of puzzlement.

"We've put you next to Clement," she said.

"Thank you," I said, keeping sarcasm out of my voice.

It was a good enough dinner, not half the meal I'd enjoyed at the wedding at Issin, but a few notches above village hall kitchen fare. Wine was passed around freely, but I kept at one glass. Clement did not.

I thought I would have to bring up the work I was doing on Athena, and it had worried me a bit, as many of the details had faded in my mind. However, this was not required of me. Clement told me about his planned article on provincial myths and mind-sets. He told me about his last three articles and last two promotions.

He told me that his wives didn't understand him.

Eventually his chin rested on the pillow of his couch. One of the pleasanter aspects of horizontal dining was that it lulled people like Clement to sleep long before they started sliding one hand up your thigh. After that I could join in the general conversation.

And it wasn't bad. They were pleasant people, on the whole, and I even remembered a couple of relevant points from my experiences on Athena that added to the conversation, and we exchanged anecdotes about traveling on the *Queen* liners. I liked them.

Someone brought up the topic of the University Extended Research Institute, which was trying to open up a branch on Ivory to add to the ones on Tellys and Pyrene. But they couldn't seem to find a building of the proper size for sale, nor could they get a permit to build one of their own.

"Can you imagine," said the man who was telling the

story, "the last time they applied, the official at the permits bureau wanted a *bribe*? He wanted five hundred tabals—god only knows what that comes to in dollars."

There was shocked murmuring around the table.

"Not only that," said the man. "The official before that one wanted six hundred tabals."

"They should have taken the second one, then." I finished off the sip of wine left in my glass.

A silence descended on the table.

I looked up. "Well, they're not going to do any better if they wait," I pointed out.

The man said to me, as though repeating for a child, "It's a *bribe*, you see. He wanted a bribe."

"Yes. I understand the word."

"Are you saying," said a woman slowly, "that we should encourage corruption? Be a party to extortion of this sort? I must say, that's a strange view for an Athenan."

"On Athena it would be a bribe. On Ivory it's business as usual. I don't see the point of sticking to one's personal customs if it means you can't do business with anyone else—I mean, do they want to open a branch here, or not? Because without a bribe—without a lot of bribes, actually—they're just not going to."

Someone said, "But it's *wrong.*"

"I don't know," I said. "On Athena you have to tip waiters for good service, and on Pyrene they consider that blackmail. It's just geography. Face it, nobody goes to the bathroom on Ivory without paying somebody else off."

I looked around the table. Annamarie was staring at her plate, embarrassed. Nor was she the only one who seemed uncomfortable. I saw their faces and I just knew that there was no way, no way in the world I was going to get through to them.

I got to my feet. "Excuse me," I said. "I'm afraid I have to leave early. Thank you for the excellent dinner."

There were a number of "you're quite welcomes" and "not at all, not at alls"—but nobody tried to stop me.

I walked down the plank and stood on the dock under

the starlight and the crackling torchlight from the boat-
deck. Water slapped the side of the dock. I took a long,
deep breath of the crisp night air. Then I started back to
Mullet's.

Chapter 12

Ran still wasn't back by the time I got to our room, so I went to bed. Nor was he back the next morning. I rose, feeling a vague grudge against Ran, Vale, and all Athenan tourists, and tried to deal with a mind and a stomach equally unsettled. By rights I should have gone straight up to Vale's, but some contrary stubbornness kept me in the village. I worked on my notebook, did The River by myself when I thought I could handle it, and talked to Seth about his Annurian stories. I wondered about going back to see the Old Man when the next time came; I'd like to show him how my abilities had improved, but at the same time it didn't seem particularly safe. On the other hand, it would look strange if I didn't show up when I was expected . . . and there was no law that said the Old Man had to stay on the island if he didn't want to. He was probably good with a short sword anywhere.

I remember that day with special clarity. When evening came I went to the early supper at the village hall, saying hello to the kitchen staff before I sat down. Dana the food-taster was back on the job, and better her than me, I thought. The table I chose was already occupied by five women in fisherman's trousers and jackets, but they made room for me courteously.

They were strangers to Teshin and we stared at each other with mutual curiosity. They drank an enormous amount of wine, and spoke and moved with the wide, free gestures of the lowest-class trading families. One was only fourteen, but the others were in their thirties and forties.

I asked them who they were, and they told me they were boatwomen from the Kiris River (in the west) but they'd brought their barges down the Silver to the bay and thence to Teshin. "And what about you, outworlder?" asked the oldest. "Farther from home than we are, I think."

"What makes you think I'm an outworlder?"

There were chuckles at that, and I told them a little of my story—the high points, at least, and I changed Ran's name. There were clucks of sympathy in the right places, and a couple of the women made the gesture disassociating themselves from bad luck.

"Now," I said, "What brings five boatwomen from across the mountains to run the Silver River?"

And they told me, amid much mutual promptings; but since it is not part of my story I will not repeat it here. Anyway, bits of their explanation were highly personal, albeit highly interesting, and I suppose you can take the scholar out of Athena but you can't stop her blushing after you've done so.

It was a more successful dinner, socially speaking, than my previous night of Athenan hospitality. The upshot of it was that the boatwomen gave me their trading address in Bentham City and told me to look them up if things got too hot for me in the capital. Apparently life was a bit looser over the mountains; or, as the oldest said, "It's not the Northwest Sector, but it's as close as you can get and still be legal."

I left the hall feeling less of a clod and idiot than I had since the unfortunate events of yesterday. But as I walked down the street outside I saw Annamarie and the Athenan boy (whose name I never did get straight) walking toward me. It was too late to duck around a corner, so I went on hoping they wouldn't notice me.

"Oh, hello," said Annamarie.

"Hello," I said, still walking. But she stopped, so I had to stop or be openly rude.

"I'm sorry about last night," she said. "I hope we

didn't seem too impolite. There was a lot of wine, you know."

"Yes, there was. I'm sorry if I offended anyone."

"No, no, it's we who should apologize, you were the guest. Free speech is the cornerstone of Athena progress," she said primly, "and Clement was very annoyed with us when he came arou—when he woke up. What I was wondering, was . . . people asked me, you see, and I'd forgotten . . . what I mean to say is, what *is* your name again?"

I caught the reflex in time and said, "Actually, it's Theodora."

Her eyes widened. "Theodora of Pyrene?"

"Why, yes—"

At that moment Seth came running down the street. He barreled into me and grabbed me by the hand. "You must come at once," he said. "Ran sent me. You must come at once." He was panting.

"What, what's the matter?"

"You must come," he said. "Vale's been arrested."

"Two Imperial cops," said Ran. We were in our room at Mullet's, stuffing things into our packs. "They were on Vale's doorstep over an hour ago. They've got him in the basement under the village hall—for interrogation, I assume."

"Imperials? In Teshin? That makes no sense."

"No point in staying to figure it out. See if you can get food from the Mullets before we—no. Cancel that. We say nothing to the Mullets and we leave through the window."

"We're on the second story."

"There's a ledge over the downstairs window. We can reach there and drop from it. Anyway, the street outside is just dirt."

I thought about it. "Ran, it might not be us they're asking about."

"What do you mean?"

"Vale is the known friend of a fugitive who lives over on Kado Island. They might have heard . . . no. It still doesn't explain the timing.'' Annurian had lived on the island for years. Ran had broken out of his trance just yesterday, and one day later the nearest healer was brought in for questioning.

Still, what about Vale? Maybe if I got word to Annurian, he would able to do something for the healer; over the past winter I'd developed a lot of respect for the Old Man of Kado Island. If I could hitch a ride over on one of the fishing boats, I could warn him . . . try a little logic, Theodora. With two Imperials in the village you would leave a trail leading to Annurian's door? The Old Man really would kill you for that one, and you would deserve it for stupidity of such magnitude.

"Well?" asked Ran, waiting for me to continue.

"Never mind. We go out the window."

"Right." He handed me my pack.

"How did you find out about the arrest?" I climbed up on the sill. This narrow slit was going to be hell to get through, and even if a dwarfish barbarian could do it I didn't see how Ran was going to. I threw the pack down first.

"Manager Peradon sent word with Seth, right before I sent Seth to find you. I don't know if Peradon knows anything, or if he just decided on principle that Imperials and foreigners shouldn't come together. Just think, if the Imperials had offered him a split of their juice we'd probably be in the basement instead of Vale. Save the cops a lot of trouble. Are you ready to go?"

I looked down. "Maybe."

"But they were typical Imperials. Rudeness never pays, Theodora, remember that."

First thing Grandmother ever taught you, I was about to say. But Ran said, "Try to roll when you hit," and gave me a friendly push.

I hit the dirt. It was like being smacked by a giant fist. All the breath left my body and I was paralyzed for minutes.

"Theodora? Are you all right?" Ran was kneeling over me, fear in his voice. I *was* all right, although in pain, but I couldn't get my breath back to tell him so. "Theodora?"

After a bit I said, "M'okay."

"What?"

"I'm all right," I whispered. "Just give me a minute."

He sat back on his heels. "I told you to roll when you hit," he said.

"You said . . . there was a ledge, too."

"Oh, that—I realized as soon as you got up that that window was too narrow to get through without being pushed from this side. You would never have been able to get into position. But it's not that far up! I told you to roll!"

"Yes, well . . . when I can move again, I will."

A few minutes later I got up and started moving stiffly after Ran, heading out of town. "How did you get through that window?" I asked.

He smiled. "There's no point in being a sorcerer if you can't cheat," he said.

There was a clearing in the woods a few minutes' walk north of Verger's Ford. We dropped our packs and sat on them. Ran said, "We have to wait for somebody."

So we waited. I was still stiff and careful about jarring my back. I thought about a lot of things: Vale, first of all, and Seth and the Old Man and the people I used to do The River with and the kitchen workers. I hadn't said good-bye to anybody. Now it was too late.

Hours went by. "Who are we waiting for?" I asked.

"Friends," he said.

More time passed. Then there was the sound of rustling, and Ran stood up. He looked as though he wished I'd bought a pistol, and I was beginning to have similar thoughts. Then somebody broke through the trees.

It was Seth! He ran over and hugged me. "Tymon," he said. He lifted his face to Ran. "I brought them," he added.

Two men followed, one of them the disreputable character I'd seen speaking with Ran earlier. He was about forty, bearded, with the bead-rim cap of a follower of the Quiet Way (a na' telleth organization, a contradiction in itself which made one wonder about the logical faculties of the man wearing such a cap). He lived alone in a small house in Teshin and had a reputation for being able to get you cheap beer when the hall was closed. The other man was much younger, in his late teens, but tall and well-muscled; I didn't know him. "My uncle and cousin," said Seth to me, bowing.

"Peradons?" I asked.

"Somerings," he said.

"But perhaps not for long," said the older man, as he bowed also. "I'm Karlas, and this is my nephew Tyl. Seth and Tyl are both my nephews, from different lines." He smiled as he struck Tyl's lower back, and Tyl bowed uncertainly.

I should have known; everybody in these little villages was related in some way.

"Not for long?" I repeated.

Ran said, "I've promised them membership in Cormallon if this works out."

"I see."

"For my brother Halet as well," said Karlas, "but he'll have to join us later."

"I see," I said again.

Ran took my arm and pulled me aside. "Vale says they're all right. That's why I went to see him, to consult him about which villagers might be suitable."

"Ah," I said, not wanting to say "I see" anymore.

"Look, Theodora, what's the problem? What do you want from me?"

I said, "I want to know everything that's going on and everything you're planning."

He gave a short laugh. "Is that all?"

We looked at each other. "As soon as I get the chance," he said. He turned to Seth. "Thank you, and say thank you to the Hall Manager for me. You'd better get back and get a little sleep."

"Wait a minute, Seth," I said. "I think that they'll let Vale go once they find out we've left—"

"They already have," he said.

"He's all right?"

"I heard that he was."

"Good." I pulled out my notebook and tore off a sheet of paper. I wrote "Good-bye" and handed the page to Ran. "Put the symbol for "Teacher" next to that," I told him.

He took the pen. "Vale will know it's not your handwriting," he said.

"But he'll get the message."

Ran wrote and passed the sheet to Seth, who folded it and stuck it in the pocket of his robe.

"Good-bye, tymon," he said.

"Good-bye, Seth. You're a prince of storytellers."

"You make things up, tymon," he said, and vanished into the trees.

Ran picked up our packs. "We've stayed here long enough," he said. "We're better off out of this whole area." He handed me my pack. "Well, tymon? Want to stand here all night?"

Tymon, eh? "It's almost morning," I pointed out.

"So it is."

And so we started walking north. All four of us.

Karlas and Tyl pulled their weight, I had to give them that. In fact they pulled more than their weight, for they often passed my pack between them, and after the first few hours I stopped offering to take it back. (Would Grandmother offer to take it back? Would Kylla offer to take it back? Certainly not. Anyway, as time passed the aching in my shoulders and lower back made abstract ethical considerations seem more irrelevant.)

That inglorious tumble from the Mullets' window had jarred me more than I thought. I was thrilled when we finally sat down. We stopped that afternoon for a rest and I didn't wake up again until the next morning.

Ran woke me just before sunrise. "There's a town just a quarter hour away. Karlas is going to get us some supplies, is there anything you need?"

"Uh, I'd better go with him."

"Are you joking? You're too recognizable."

"Come on, Ran, I'll wrap a scarf around my head and I'll just be a short, pale person." I got what I needed from my pack; it would be less noticeable if I left it here.

"It's not a good idea," he said.

"I've seen blonds and lightskins every day in the capital."

"This isn't the capital. It's the back-end of nowhere."

Karlas said, "It *is* a fairly large town. I mean, if the gracious lady has her heart set on going, I think she could blend in. As long as she kept on the scarf, you know."

Ran shrugged. So Karlas and I set off for Jerrinos, which was a fair-sized river town over three times as big as Teshin. Karlas was impressed with it—the streets were paved, at least in the center of town, and the lighting around the square was modern. He told me that he'd always dreamed of going to the capital, that it offered more opportunity for a man of scope, and he saw from Jerrinos that it was just the sort of place that would suit him. Then he went off to buy some new cloaks, shoes, and, I assumed, pistols. I thought about getting boots, but it was nearly spring and my present pair were still sturdy. Then I toyed with the idea of getting a pistol of my own . . . but they *were* expensive. If the prices for the ones on display in the market were firm, I'd clean myself out, and for what? I wasn't experienced in using them, and if anyone pulled one on me it would be too late to do anything about it. Possibly I could get one secondhand, but I didn't know whom to approach. In the end I compromised by getting a new energizer for my hotpencil, a covered warming bowl for food, and a larger canteen.

Then I sat down on the town hall steps and waited for the indigent's breakfast to be handed out. No point in wasting money on a meal. It was rice and meat, with celery and ground tasselnuts sprinkled over the top, not bad for a place like Jerrinos. I put half of it in my new warming bowl to share with Ran. Then I met Karlas back at the square and we returned to the woods.

"No problems," I said to Ran when we got back. Karlas handed a pistol to him, and one to Tyl. There was a new green cloak for Ran, lighter than his old winter coat. He rolled it up and put it in his pack to wait until the weather got a little warmer.

"Are we going?" asked Tyl, standing up.

Ran said, "In a few minutes." Then he took my arm and pulled me off to one side.

"What's the matter?" I asked.

"Nothing," he said. "You wanted to hear my plans."

I grinned. "And you're actually going to tell them?"

He said, "I never know what you think is funny. Listen, this is what I want to do: First, I want to get to the capital as soon as possible. I know the territory there, I have contacts there, and I think there's a better chance of protecting us both in the city than in some little village where nobody feels any obligation toward us. It only took two Imperials to get all of Teshin on good behavior. All right so far?"

"So far, yes, the capital is a good idea. I was heading there anyway before Teshin."

"All right. Once in the capital I can look up old friends, do some research, see what I can do about fixing things with the family council. I can't make any specific plans until I see just how it looks. Satisfied, tymon?"

I said slowly, "But look, Ran, assuming Eln is responsible for our troubles—and I guess he has to be involved—I don't think he's going to let you get anywhere near the council. Or anybody else who might help."

He didn't say anything.

I said, "This must have occurred to you."

He said, "Don't worry about it," and picked up a twig and scraped mud off the bottom of his boot.

"Look," I said.

"Here's the problem." He took the twig, squatted down on his heels, and scratched a vague map on the earth. "We can go all the way around Mountain's End, and up through the pass along the coast. That's the way everybody goes, and it'll take us a good three months by foot. Or we can take a straight line through the Simil Valley, and be in the capital in six weeks. The problem," he said, "is the timing. Every spring the ice along the range melts and turns Simil Valley into a lake. It drains into the Silver River, that's why they've got dikes all the way from Verger's Ford northward to the valley.''

I said, ''It's almost spring now.''

''Yes, that's the risk. We'll have to walk very quickly. I've spoken to Karlas and Tyl about it, they're willing to take the chance.''

''I see.''

He waited. I said, ''Well, if everyone else wants to go, I may as well go, too.'' He looked pleased. ''I mean, why get picked off by Imperials all by myself when I can die in company? I'd rather be done in by the forces of nature anyway.''

''I appreciate it, Theodora, I really do. How are the cards coming?''

''Oh, wait.'' I took out the warming bowl. ''I got this in town. May as well start on a full stomach.''

He opened it and swept up a mouthful with his fingers. ''Mmm. Good tasselnuts.'' He ate some more and said, ''But this is supper-food. Are they serving dinner for breakfast these days?''

''Well, in a way. It's leftovers from the hall—it's the indigent's breakfast.''

He stopped chewing and for a second I thought he was going to spit it out. For another second I thought he was going to dump the bowl. ''What?''

I said uncertainly, ''The indigent's breakfast?''

''Are you trying to insult me? What can you have been thinking? Are you begging on provincial steps now—a Cormallon house member?''

I found coldness creeping into my voice. ''Look, friend, you may have been the First in Cormallon, but that doesn't buy you a dinner roll out in the sticks. If you'll think back to your recent *incapacity,* you'll remember sitting on a lot of hall steps between here and Issin—and you wouldn't be alive today if we hadn't. Just what do you mean by criticizing me? I'm an outlander. How am I supposed to know you've got a fetish about free breakfasts?''

Ran was staring at me. It was the first time I'd ever told him off. What's more, I couldn't seem to stop.

"And as for today, I got us a free meal. Do you want me to apologize for that? Do you know how many bakras I've got left in my wallet right now? Not very precious many, I'll tell you that. And where do you think our finances are coming from? Do you think your two new allies are going to throw their life savings into the pot— not that it would amount to much, I'm sure? Not if they've got any brains they won't. They'll be holding most of it in reserve in case we fail. Which leaves you and me, and I don't know how much you've got on you, but . . ."

I found myself trailing off and starting to sniffle. Ran looked horrified.

"I'm sorry, Theodora. I beg your pardon." He put another handful in his mouth and chewed. The look on his face suggested he was chewing sawdust, and not very good sawdust either. He swallowed manfully.

"Oh, gods who watch over scholars." I no longer could tell if I were sniffling or chuckling. Ran finished the bowl and wiped it clean with a cloth.

He handed it back to me. "Thank you very much," he said. Then he said, "I'm sorry for my behavior. But, Theodora—we're not going to do this again."

"All right," I said.

We rejoined our two allies, who tried to look as though they hadn't heard anything of the last five minutes. We took up our gear and started moving. Try to look at it as a camping trip, I told myself as we walked.

Chapter 13

As it turned out, our new ally Tyl was almost neurotically shy, so it was some time before he brought himself to tell us that he'd turned his ankle. Even then he mumbled the information to his uncle Karlas, who passed it on to Ran and myself. I didn't appreciate it at the time, but this was the best thing that could happen to me—already I was having difficulty keeping up with the others. Not surprising; the three men I traveled with were all taller than I was, their legs coming up well past my waist, so that I had to jog to keep pace. Nor was this good jogging country. But we all had to slow down for Tyl, who made shift with a stick to try and keep the weight off his left foot.

That first night after Jerrinos I took out the cards. Ran saw what I was doing from across the campfire, but he went on arranging the undertunic he'd just washed so that it was closer to the heat. I started the configuration with a center-card for Ran, not something I usually did, but I suppose his condition was still bothering me. The card that turned up was the Aftermath, a scene of people running down a city street, one woman holding a baby while others crawled out from the rubble of destroyed buildings. It symbolized rebirth. As I touched it the buildings recoalesced into the house at Cormallon, the street became a hill, and the woman with the baby was Kylla holding a torch. She joined Eln on the hilltop under a night sky and they began reciting something. Like all my pictures it was silent, but I knew they were enacting Ran's official disownment.

No new information here. But as I kept my fingers on the card it occurred to me that perhaps I wasn't going far enough. I treated the cards like Net transmissions, I took what came over the lines and assumed that was all there was. What if there were more? Studying with Vale had meant finding level after level . . . now there was a thought. I still felt that "de-energizing my na'telleth" was so much double-talk, but calming down and opening up had seemed to help my performance at tinaje. Perhaps it would help with this as well. I took a few deep breaths and made myself as still as possible. I tried not to think about anything at all, and after a bit I let my mind creep up slowly on the card, gently, not grabbing for information but more as if I were just wondering. . . .

At once I was pulled away. It was like falling down a well. I was on the hilltop again, but this time it lacked the air of solid reality it had held earlier; strange, since now it felt as though I were actually present, not simply watching a picture. But present at what? Kylla was holding a torch again—or was it Kylla? Her face was older, and not as kind. She took Eln's torch away from him and handed it to someone standing behind her. Then she lit the kindling in the huge marble bowl on the crest of the hill. Eln said—and I could hear him!—"I'll light the rest of the funeral fires." She said, "It's too late. You don't have a torch." She sounded angry with him. I remember thinking that it hardly seemed fair of her under the circumstances.

The card was jerked out of my hand. Ran was bending over me, looking unhappy. "Theodora? What are you doing, are you all right?"

"Yes, of course. I was running the cards, what's the idea of interrupting me?"

He said, "I *couldn't* interrupt you. You didn't hear me. What were you doing?"

I told him. I thought he would say at once, "Try it again"—he was fond of information, and he'd been after me to run the cards for days. But he just looked thought-ful and said, "I don't know if this is a good idea."

"It was working all right until you pulled the card away."

"Working how? I never heard of card-reading like this. You say it didn't feel like a real event—"

"No, more like something symbolic, or something from the future—"

"I don't like it. How sure can we be about that kind of information? I've never thought much of oracles—and it might not be safe for you."

"It felt all right. I wasn't scared."

He said, "No. We don't know what would have hap-pened if I hadn't been here to take the card away from you."

"Presumably the scene would have finished." I sounded a little irritated even to myself, like someone whose terminal shorted out at the end of a mystery story.

Ran said again, "No." So I put the cards away for the time being. Karlas had been squatting on the other side of the fire, waiting politely for us to stop talking; now he came over to me.

He said, "My nephew would like to ask you to give him tinaje. He hopes to ease the pain in his ankle."

I looked over at Tyl. He sat with his face averted, one hand clasping the ankle in question. I said to Karlas, "There's no guarantee the pain would be reduced. It's possible, but not certain." According to Vale's teach-ings, I wouldn't touch the ankle itself tonight, even if I did full tinaje, but direct the energies around it instead, which might or might not be of help.

Anyway, that's what Vale would have said to do. Karlas said, "I know. This is why Tyl wants to know something of your moral character."

"I beg your pardon?"

"Your character. Obviously the success of a tinaje ses-sion depends heavily on the moral character of the prac-titioner. This is well known."

The mind reeled. "It is, is it? Look, Karlas, you've got it backward. If it has anything to do with personality, it depends more on the attitude of the person receiving the tinaje. If he can relax and participate, it's reflected in his body and his body receives the benefit. But that's as far as it goes.''

Karlas went on, ''But I've already reassured him that your character is exemplary, or you would not be on this journey with us. I'm sure that the sir Cormallon would not have brought anyone into this who is not of the highest sort.''

''Well, thank you,'' I said, as I gave up on achieving communication. ''That's kind of you to say.''

''So will you have a look at my nephew? He is a fine boy, I know he doesn't complain, but he is troubled by this.''

''All right.'' I got up and went over to Tyl. ''Hello,'' I said.

Tyl shifted his hulking shoulders and mumbled back. I assume it was hello.

Ordinarily I would talk to a client, to learn about him and put him at ease. It would probably have the opposite effect here, knot up all those hard-gained muscles. ''Turn over,'' I said, making it an order.

He turned over gratefully.

Ran came by as I worked. ''Can I watch?'' he asked. ''If you like.''

Working on Tyl, I could see what Vale meant when he said that people who built up their muscles had a different energy flow than dancers like Pyre. Both had trained their bodies sternly, but Tyl's energy was in separate pools, while Pyre's had leaped along like a river. ''It doesn't hurt, does it?'' I asked Tyl. I was going in more deeply than I ever had.

''I barely feel it, you're like a butterfly,'' he said. My goodness, he really could talk. I gave his back an affectionate slap when I was through, and he smiled. There was a pleasant feel to Tyl, like a large family dog.

Ran said, ''You've studied hard, haven't you?''

''Yes, I have.''

He nodded, as though figuring something out. Later he brought over a blanket from his pack. ''I know you're too cheap to buy an extra one for yourself. Still, it's not spring yet.''

"Thanks.'' I took it from him. It was dark red wool, Karlas must have picked it up in Jerrinos. "Well, good night.''

"Yes, good night.'' He paused a moment. "Do you still have that onyx cat?''

"Yes, it's in my pack. Do you want it?''

"No. I just wondered. Never mind, tymon, sleep well.''

Tyl's stride picked up over the next couple of days. They tried to slow down for me, but after keeping pace for half an hour or so he and Karlas would pull ahead, and Ran and I would meet them much later, sitting on a log or a boulder, waiting for me. "Sorry, my lady,'' said Karlas. "It's difficult to hold back.''

I resented them for it, and it felt bitter to think of Ran going slower for my benefit. Not that he said anything about it—and I resented that, too. My feet ached and my back ached, in one continuous pain. One night I sat dully by the fire, thinking unhappy thoughts, when Ran sat down beside me. "You look more miserable than anyone I have ever seen,'' he began.

"Thank you.''

"It's not you, it's the expression on your face. You should see it.''

I grunted.

He said, "I know it's difficult for you, but . . . do you want to talk about it?''

I scuffed up some dirt. "I have,'' I said, "no physical endurance at all.''

He seemed to be waiting for something more. "What of it? It's never bothered you before.''

"I never *knew* it before!'' And there I was, yelling at Ran. I said, "I'm sorry. Please excuse me for a little while.'' I went off a short distance into the trees where I could be alone in misery.

I hadn't known it before. I'd always done pretty well at whatever I tried to do, always comfortably in the top twenty percent of my class—and anything I hadn't done well at I'd figured wasn't all that important anyway. I hadn't known that my body was designed along such unheroic lines. Nor had I had any inkling of the shameful way one's mind would follow the physical state—making me resentful and short-tempered with people who hadn't done me any wrong.

When I'd told myself off sufficiently, I got up to rejoin the others. Then I had a major scare. There was blood on the boulder I'd been sitting on. I quickly checked my robes and found blood on my undertunic and between my legs. I was shocked and frightened, sure that I was hemorrhaging internally. Could I get to a doctor quickly enough? And *was* there a Tellys-trained doctor anywhere between here and the capital? I was shaking.

I'd taken a couple of steps back to the camp when I suddenly remembered there was another and less harmful cause of bleeding in a female. It would be hard for an Ivoran to understand that I'd forgotten about it, but after all I hadn't menstruated since the first time, when I was thirteen. I'd had the usual implants to inhibit ovulation, right on the dot, every three years. The implants were supposed to last from three to five years, but I liked to be prudent. My last one must have just worn off. Great Plato, what was I supposed to do now?

It occurred to me that besides the inconvenience, I was now capable of becoming pregnant—*involuntarily* pregnant. What a concept! I was capable of screaming my way through childbirth on a planet where the nearest medical facility I would trust was geographically and financially way out of my league. And what about Ran? Not that I was thinking, specifically, about Ran—but what if Ivory and the rest of the universe had indeed gone their separate ways, and we were different species? The definition of species was that they were able to mate and produce fertile offspring. But there were plenty of separate species that could mate and produce, well, *something*. There was no guarantee what. It might require sophisticated medical technology even to bring such a child to term.

Well, there was no point in thinking any further on that topic, or I would lose heart entirely. But, gods who were supposed to watch over scholars, this was really the final straw. I climbed back up on my rock, avoiding the bloodstain, and thought about crying. I just felt numb, though.

I didn't have the faintest idea what to do about menstruation, either. I wasn't sure about bringing up the problem to the others; maybe it was a taboo topic on Ivory, I'd never paid any attention to it before. Why doesn't anybody ever warn you about these things? I thought about all those marvelous stories I'd read back on Athena, the legends I'd fallen in love with—the heroes setting off to seek fortune and adventure. Knights and damosels rode forth to do battle at castles perilous, and the damosels never had this problem. And hobbits and tall elves strode swiftly over the earth, and the hobbits never had any trouble keeping up. Of course, hobbits were supposed to have great endurance.

If only I were a hobbit. A *male* hobbit.

Oh, well, I was just going to have to go ask. If they thought it was an unrefined topic to bring up, they would just have to live with it. I couldn't stay here on this rock forever.

I went back to camp and told Ran about my problem. He looked blank. "Don't you have an idritak?" he asked.

A what? "No," I said.

"I assumed you picked up some in Jerrinos," he said. "Well, it's late, but we can't avoid it. I'll have Karlas go into Spur, it's just a couple of miles away, and he can get you some. Really, Theodora, I would have thought you'd anticipated this."

"How can Karlas pick me up anything? Are we talking about an implant?"

"A what?"

Some confused exchanges of information followed. Eventually Ran shook his head and went over to talk to Karlas, who shrugged and left the camp. He came back in an hour with a small pouch containing a lot of little white things. They seemed to be made of absorbent cloth.

"What do I do with these?" I asked.

Karlas looked blank. "Whatever it is you women do with them," he said.

"You put them inside," said Ran.

"Actually inside me? How many at once? Are they sterile?" I looked at them distrustfully.

Ran and Karlas were at a loss. Apparently this was something they had never given much thought to, either.

Tyl spoke up. "If I may," he said quietly. Then he gave me explicit instructions. Ran and Karlas looked at him. "I have five sisters," he said, shrugging.

So I took the idritak pouch and went off to "do whatever it is we women do with them." It was more difficult than it sounded. I told myself as I worked at it that it was all part of being a primate. But since that day I have often thought I would rather be a marsupial.

I believed that I had reached the low point of my life so far. I was wrong. The following morning we arrived at the lip of the Simil Valley.

It was a long, narrow, bare-looking place; filled with undergrowth in the summer, they said, but just muddy now. We were lucky, they said, that it wasn't summer and we didn't have to pick our way through it. I didn't join in these congratulations, saving my breath for the descent. We went down the long hillside trail, boots on in spite of the warm weather.

"Almost spring," said Ran quietly to Karlas.

"Um," said Karlas. His expression was serious.

The valley looked long to me—too long to get through in three days, which was the schedule we were working on. But we tramped down into the heart, and I swore to myself that I would keep up, regardless of how I might have to run through the muck. Being too slow here would put all our lives in danger.

I had said I would ask for no more rest periods, and I didn't. I knew I wasn't going as quickly as the others could, but I went on. And on. Soon the pain in my feet and back spread to my neck, my calves, and my chest. I pushed a fist into the small of my back to try to minimize it, and walked that way. I didn't complain—but that was small credit to me. I didn't have the wit or the energy to complain after a few hours. Speech was beyond me. At first I thought longingly of the trip up from Issin, when I set my own pace and rested whenever I liked; it was another world. Soon enough I stopped thinking at all. It was one long dreamlike horror, step after step after step. I no longer moved to wipe away sweat. One foot after the other, that was enough to deal with.

Ran's hands were on my shoulders. "Theodora," he said. "You can stop now. We're stopping here. Do you hear me?"

I dropped down into the mud and lay there.

At once he knelt beside me. "Are you all right?"

"Yes. Go away."

He seemed to sense that I meant it, and went away. After a while, I don't know how long it was, he returned with Karlas. "Help me get her up," he said. They each took an arm, and we went on. That was how it was in the daytime. At night I took no part in setting up the fire or cooking. They left me alone, for which I was grateful. As for my body, it ached through the night; there were blisters on the soles of my feet and there were rashes on parts of me I had never known about before. It itched terribly, but when I saw the effects of scratching I tried to stop.

One day, two days, three days. We were still in the valley. Ran and Karlas were worried, always listening now for the sound of rushing water; but I was beyond that. In fact, I was the only person in the party who wasn't frightened. But something gave out on that third day. I had no notion it was coming; if I'd been asked before I entered this valley, I would not have thought that one's limits could be reached so quickly. Between one step and another it happened: I stopped. I sat down.

I said nothing to anybody, and it was several minutes before they realized I wasn't with them. Then they came back and stood around me.

Ran said gently, "Theodora, we have to get on. We can't even go back, it's too late. We're in danger here.

We could be flooded out at any time, and it's a vicious flood, I've heard about it. Theodora? It'll cut through here like a knife through paper. We couldn't possibly survive."

"Go," I said.

"What?"

"Go. Save yourself."

They looked at each other.

Ran said, "Theodora—"

"Go. It's all right. I don't care." And I didn't. It's hard to enter now into my feelings on that day, at that moment, but I really didn't care. Things had simplified for me enormously: I couldn't continue. Therefore everything else had to follow from that point. Death just didn't seem like the thing to be avoided it was when I was in my right mind.

They went away and spoke to each other for a few minutes. I could hear them, but I wasn't interested. After a bit Ran came back.

"I've sent them on ahead," he told me.

"You go, too." Conversation was an effort but it had to be said. I didn't want the responsibility for his death. On top of everything else it was just too much. If he stayed, I might try to get up in a while, and I didn't want to.

"No."

"Please."

"*No*. Listen, Theodora, sweetheart, you don't have to talk. Lie down if you want to. Pretend I'm not here."

I sat there dully, resenting him for making me deal with his presence. After a few minutes—or maybe it was longer—I realized he'd pulled off my boots.

"What are you doing?"

"If you won't lie down, this will at least help." He poured water from his canteen over a tunic he'd pulled from his pack; then he started washing my feet with the tunic. He was crazy, but it would take too much effort to stop him. "Your feet look horrible," he said conversationally. "I didn't know a person could have this many blisters and rashes in such a small area. Athlete's foot, too. My, my—sensitive skin for a barbarian.'' When he'd finished washing off the sweat and grime he lifted one foot and began pressing against the sole with his thumb, using a tinaje grip.

"I didn't know you knew that," I found my voice saying.

"I watch and learn," he said, "much like yourself."

We sat there like statues for several hours. I said, finally, "I'm very sorry."

"Sorry about what?" He seemed genuinely blank.

"I've slowed everybody down. I'm not the stuff heroes are made of, Ran. I'm not even the stuff Karlas and Tyl are made of. I'm not worth wasting your time over."

He was quiet for a minute, then he said, "I have often had difficulty understanding you, Theodora, but never more than right now. I don't see what the question of how quickly you can travel through the Simil Valley has to do with how good you are. You're not a hiker, at least not with these people and in this terrain. Too bad, but I always took you for a city kid anyway, tymon. I'm strictly urban, myself, and when I go to the country—as you've seen—I bring plenty of comfort along with me. You'll probably never be called on to do something like this again, you know. And in the capital, who's going to care if you take shorter steps when you walk?"

I hadn't thought of it that way. Still, it was easy for him to be polite about it—he hadn't failed.

Then he was going on. "I know you have no reason to listen to me. I fell apart just when you needed me. When I found out that I wasn't going to have every move I made backed up by the family, I just gave up living. I know, Vale claims that it was an attack by sorcery; but I know, myself, that I wouldn't have been vulnerable to it if I hadn't given up first. You had to take care of everything. That wasn't what you signed on for, was it? Don't think I haven't thought about it every day since Teshin—"

"Are you crazy?" I don't know how long he would have gone on with that nonsense if I hadn't stopped him. "Look, I understand that this family business means more to you than to a tymon from Pyrene. Your world was hammcrcd down in front of you, Ran, how were you supposed to react?'' He looked so miserable. I raised his head. ''I was irritated, of course, when you checked out like that. But I get irritated by a lot of things. That's all I thought about it. Really.''

We sat there holding onto each other for a while. Eventually I noticed the particular aches and pains that had receded for the past few hours into generalized misery were making themselves known. I sighed. ''We'd better go,'' I said.

He got up and held out a hand. We went limping off into the mud. I felt pretty miserable, but I really didn't feel too bad.

I must have thought I heard the sound of water a dozen times before we reached the halfway point on the trail up the pass out of the valley. ''We're safe at this height,'' Ran said. When we got to the top of the ridge, I turned around.

''I wish I could see the water come through,'' I said. ''After all that trouble, I'd like to see what could have killed me.''

''Well, there's no hurry now,'' said Ran. ''Do you want to wait?''

We sat for a time looking out on that lousy valley. I felt as though I'd spent a lifetime in it. The sun swung behind the mountaintops to our left. ''I guess we should go on,'' I said.

He shrugged. ''Sorry, tymon, it doesn't come on cue.''

''Yeah, all things being equal I suppose I should be glad we missed it.''

He laughed and helped me up. We crossed over the ridge. On the other side I stopped.

''What is it?'' he asked.

''I thought I heard water. Never mind,'' I said, as I started walking again. ''It's probably all in my mind.''

Behind me the roaring got louder. Ran looked at me questioningly.

''No, thank you,'' I said. ''We're out of it now. Believe me, Ran, you haven't got enough in the family treasury to get me in that valley ever again. That sound," I added firmly, "is in our minds."

"As you say," said Ran; "Grandmother taught me never to contradict a lady of Cormallon."

Chapter 14

We met up with Karlas and Tyl in the town of Tenrellis, a few days away from the capital. There were a lot more towns now, and a lot more traffic on the roads. They'd booked themselves into an inn—the sort of place that was as inexpensive as we could go without offending Ran's sensibilities. It was all right by my standards, anyway; which is to say, vermin were kept to a minimum. I ask for little else.

Ran agreed that we could stay for a couple of days and rest up. While he was eager to move, he didn't want us staggering into the capital in rags, too tired to deal with whatever we might find there. The morning after our arrival I went out to the market, leaving Ran behind with Karlas and an old, battered chessboard they had dug up somewhere. Chess has never interested me, probably because I'm such a bad player, and I wanted to buy something good to eat and sit under the striped awning by the market and think about how I didn't have to do any walking today. It was a beautiful springlike morning.

I was sitting under that striped awning, licking a lemon ice, when I heard a voice I knew very well. "Have you shrunk," it said thoughtfully, "or have I gotten taller?" It was Kylla, standing over me in her best go-to-the-city robes, hair demurely braided but with wide gold hoops in her ears and a hint of gold swirl on her cheeks. I looked down at the sandals that peeped out from under her robes and saw her toenails were painted gold, too.

"I'm sure I've shrunk," I said, blinking up at her face

in the sunlight. "I really don't think there's much left of me."

"My, my," she said, and sat down tailor-fashion by my side. "We'll have to do something about that. How's my brother?"

"Well."

"And yourself?"

"Shrunken, but otherwise unharmed."

"Good." She played with the hem of her robe. "Theodora, I think we should talk. How would you like to check into the local Asuka baths with me? We could order in food and masseurs and anything else we like, and make a day of it."

The idea of hot water in bulk was very tempting. "Uh, you would be paying for this, Kylla?"

"Naturally."

I took perhaps a second to make up my mind. "Done. Let me leave a note for Ran at the inn."

She shook her head. "If you don't mind, I'd rather you didn't tell him about it. I'm not supposed to have any contact with either of you . . . and very likely he wouldn't take it well if he learned you were talking to me."

"I gather Eln doesn't know you're here."

"You gather accurately. But let's not destroy a beautiful day by digging into all the decaying details, all right?"

"Whatever you say—you're the one paying."

So we went down a few streets until we came to a cavelike entrance built into the hill on the north side of town. This branch of the Asuka business was very different from their glass-and-steel tower in the capital; it actually was built into a cave, and much of it had been cleaned, but other than that left in a natural state.

"We'll take a suite," Kylla told the woman in the front. "The best one on the women's side. What's your security like?"

The woman, a burly, middle-aged top-sergeant sort, raised an eyebrow at the coins Kylla was counting out on her table; but she appeared otherwise unimpressed. "Solid rock, as you can see for yourself, gracious lady. At least two feet thick in every room, usually thicker.

We've put steel reinforced entryways to each room, too. No windows." She took out a pipe, lit it, and added, "We're bonded against listening devices. There's a sorcerous sweep once in the morning and once in the evening to see that it's clean of tampering. And, I will say that we're the best in this town or any other—face paint if you're going out tonight, masseurs, you name it."

"Tinaje?" I asked.

She hesitated a moment, then said, "Of course. My girl Celia is a tinaje specialist. Have you tried her before?"

"No," I said, "I've never had a full professional tinaje session. She's specifically trained?"

"Of course, or she wouldn't be here. Will you be wanting her before or after your bath?"

Kylla looked at me. "After, I think," she said. "We'll be letting you know."

We were taken to a large room carved out of rock—by nature or man I couldn't tell, nor did it seem important. The important thing was the pool in the center, a thing of beauty with stone steps leading down to a steaming, rock-heated bath that came past my chin when I stood up at its midpoint. It was wide enough for eight or nine people, and you could sit against the walls and have the water lap up to your chest. Which of course I lost no time doing.

"Mmmm," I said to Kylla, when I felt the urge for conversation.

"Yes," she said. We were leaning against a wall of the pool, arms up on the sides, floating out straight from time to time and dropping back down. It was nice to have that as the sum total of my responsibility for the day.

"You want to talk about Ran and Eln?" I asked eventually.

"No," she said.

"Neither do I," I said, and floated some more.

After a while I said, "So what did you look me up for?"

"Well, actually . . ." she wrung out her braid and

pinned it atop her head. "Grandmother told me to come."

"She did what? How did she know? I thought she was sick."

"She is sick. But she holds on, Grandmother does. She called me in last night and said, 'Cherie, our Theodora is going to be in Tenrellis market tomorrow morning, and she's going to be very tired, and she's going to need cheering up.' So I sort of borrowed an aircar, and here I am."

"My. Grandmother stays on top of things, doesn't she?"

"She tries."

I felt around the stone below my arm. "There are some switches here. Do you think we can make this a whirlpool?"

"You want everything, don't you, Theo?"

"I wasn't complain—"

"Of course we can make it a whirlpool." She lifted the casing and pushed a button. A current started to run clockwise through the water. "So, do you need cheering up?"

"Maybe. It wouldn't hurt, I guess."

She clucked and picked up the housephone by the steps and called for lunch. When it arrived, we climbed out and dried off on the enormous gray Asuka towels. We ate on the couches beside the pool, tiny meatpies and bread and cakes, and a potful of green tah. Then she clucked over the state of my body, which was still fairly blistered and rash-ridden, and sat down at a low, mirrored desk in the corner of the room and began pulling boxes and vials out of the drawers. "Here we are," she said, and started handing them to me.

So I put powder on all the parts of me that tend to get too damp, and oil on all the parts of me that tend to get too dry, and it was glorious beyond literary expression. Some of the itches I had picked up in the Simil Valley even faded away, and I vowed never to leave urban civilization again.

"Now let's play," said Kylla, and she got out yet more

vials from this miraculous desk, this time tiny containers of face paint and nail colors and body designs. "Just hold still," she said. "Believe me, I can do this better than the house designers."

I could well believe it, and I held still. When she was finished, a full hour later, the mirror showed me a total stranger. This person was taller than me, and more fine-boned, with larger, darker eyes; and she obviously knew no fear, because she was wearing face and body swirls that I myself would never have the nerve to put on. I stood up and walked over to the floor-to-ceiling mirror on a nearby wall. "Wait a minute," said Kylla. She went to the pile of jewelry she'd discarded before entering the bath, picking up here a hoop of gold and gems, tossing aside there a handful of tiny I-don't-know-what's. "Hmm, your ears aren't pierced, are they? Well, try these." And she hung the hoop around my neck, and pushed two wide, delicately banded bracelets up my arms, and clipped a twisted strand of gold to my earlobe. Then she stood back and said, "No, you need symmetry." And she pulled the strand of gold off again. "Now look," she said. I turned to the image in the mirror.

It gave me an odd feeling. I could see that I was still at the bottom of this theme Kylla had created; but maybe because she had done so many changes, I could see things I usually missed in my own reflection. It was a shivery experience, half objective and half not knowing what to think. I was lightly tanned, darker than I'd ever been, and I'd lost my baby fat somewhere on the northward trail; probably in the Simil Valley. No more Teddy Bear nicknames—it was quite possible they wouldn't recognize me on Athena. They certainly wouldn't recognize me with this pirate booty draped all over—I'd had no idea I could handle jewelry this gaudy and not appear a fool. I looked as though I could pass for one of the so-phisticated ladies I'd seen coming out of private dining rooms in the Lantern Gardens, with wealthy, family par-ties.

"Oh, *Kylla*," I said finally.

"Not bad," she said, as she appraised the finished

canvas. "We ought to outline your eyes in blue or green next time—better for unusual skin like yours, make you look more exotic."

Exotic was not a word I had heretofore thought of in relation to myself. I looked back at the image in the mirror. It was lovely, I had to admit, although the idea made me nervous somehow; but it wasn't, well, *Athenan*.

I said, "It bothers me a little."

"Think of it as a play," she said. "You can scrub it off and leave the role any time you like; this just expands your options."

They would read me out of the Ethics in Scholarship Group if they ever found out about this back on Athena, where it was a well-known fact of good society that a single black or gold ring, with perhaps a simple necklace for special occasions, was all a person of taste should require. Still, how likely were they to find out? I said, "How about the tinaje? It'll mess up the body paint, won't it?"

"Not unless the girl uses oil. I don't think they use oil for tinaje, but I'm not sure."

"They don't," I said. She looked at me. "It's just one of the things I happen to know in this life, " I explained.

"Ah," she said, and she rang for the manager and asked if the tinaje specialist was available.

A few minutes later Celia came in. She looked like the daughter of the manager, and perhaps she was. She asked me no questions—which Vale would not have approved of, but not all systems are the same—and simply told me to lie on my stomach on the couch. Then she started on my upper back, without preliminary.

"Ow," I said. "That hurts."

"Some people like it hard," she said, pouting.

"I know some people like it hard. I'm not one of them."

She went back to work and I tried not to groan. But courtesy has its limits and after a few minutes I stopped her. "You're not a tinaje specialist, are you? You're perthes-trained, maybe even bratelle."

She knelt back on her ankles and looked at me suspiciously. "You said this was your first session."

Kylla got up from her couch. "Never mind, dear." She gave the girl a coin and dismissed her. "I didn't know I was dealing with a connoisseur," she said, and she sounded amused. She was probably thinking I'd come a long way from the stranger Ran brought home grimy from an inn fire and stuffed into his sister's robes. Well, it doesn't hurt to remember our beginnings.

So we just lay back on the couches and talked, about the latest scandal of the Emperor's wives, the rumors of the Emperor's impotence, and the accusations about the Emperor's progeny. A corrupt government at least provides food for conversation, particularly if personal topics are too painful to bring up on a pleasant day at the baths.

I told Kylla I would be glad to get back to the capital, and would be just as happy never to look up through the trees at the winter constellations again. She laughed—by then she had brought out a bottle of wine, which we were making use of without glass or wine bowl—and declaimed, "Too long, too well I know the starry conclave of the midnight sky; too well, the splendors of the firmament, the lords of light whose kingly aspect shows, what time they set or climb the sky in turn, the year's divisions, bringing frost or fire."

I applauded. I wanted to stamp my feet, but it would have meant getting up off the couch. She said, "Thank you. That was the play I was in at Lady Degrammont's School for the Sage and Cultured Upbringing of Most Valuable Young Ladies. I was just the watchman," she added. "I wanted to be Agamemnon, but they gave it to Edra Simmeroneth because her family paid for the new wing."

Some things in academe are the same all over, I thought vaguely; then it caught up with me and I said, *"Agamemnon?"*

"Yes, it's a play about a king who comes home from a war—"

"I know it, I know it. It's in partial form at the Antiquities Library on Athena. How do you know it? I thought Ivoran history had gone its own way, I thought all that material from the past was lost—''

"I don't know how old it is," she said, and the thought didn't seem to interest her. "But it's a good story, Theo. You don't think anyone would forget a good story, do you?"

I said, "If you had that translated into Standard, the classics branch on Athena would pay you hard money for it. I don't think they have the least idea it exists anywhere."

She shrugged. "A lot of trouble to go to," she said. Then she said, "Before I forget," and pulled a piece of paper from the pocket of the robe she'd thrown over the couch. She wrote on it and handed it to me.

It was an address. "What is it?" I asked.

"In case you need to get in touch with me. This is a friend of mine in the capital. He'll see that any messages get through to me quickly."

A friend? The name above the address was Lysander Shikron. Not a Cormallon name, or any ally of the Cormallons that I had heard of before. I remembered Eln taunting her that night at dinner, when he said that she'd brought a lover within Cormallon boundaries. I decided not to ask.

Kylla looked, for the very first time, just a little guilty. She said, "Theo, take good care of that address. It's something that neither Ran *nor* Eln should know about."

When I got back to the inn later, I found Ran and Karlas still on their third game of chess.

"I'm glad I didn't stay," I said.

They looked up at me. "What happened to you?" Ran asked.

"I went to the Asuka baths, and the house designer painted pictures on me."

"You look beautiful, my lady," said Karlas.

"Thank you. What's the matter, Ran, don't you like it? It didn't cost all that much."

"I don't know," he said slowly. "You don't look like a barbarian any more."

"Is that bad?"

"I don't know," he said again. He looked down at the board and frowned.

Three days later we were in the capital. It was the first month of spring, a full Ivoran year since the day Ran sat down across from me in Trade Square and asked me if I wanted a job.

Chapter 15

We rented a house in one of the cheaper quarters of the city. The first thing Ran did after signing a false name on the rental agreement was to circle the building, squeezing his way down the narrow alley between our place and the tavern next door, and then crossing round back and inching through the crawlspace by the clothing store on the other side, all the while with a look of fixed concentration. The rest of us stood just inside the entryway while he worked. It gave me the feeling you get late at night, when lightning has flicked brilliance into your room and gone again, and you wait for the rumble to follow.

Then he put a neat printed card on the front door that read: "TRADESMEN AND VISITORS UNWELCOME. This constitutes fair warning that the first person to violate this property will accrue seven years of ill luck."

I said to him, "Sorcery is still illegal, isn't it? Should we be calling attention to the fact you've put a spell on the house?"

"Everybody does it," he said. "Anyway, the cop on the beat isn't going to cross the property line to arrest us—not unless he's an idiot. And he won't be an idiot if we pay him regularly."

So we moved in. It was good to have a roof over my head again, even if it was the rotting one we'd gotten here. During the first rainfall I put a pan down on the floor under the most major leak and said to Ran, "What are we going to do when the real spring rains hit?"

"We'll need a lot more pans," he said calmly.

And that was the spirit of the season. Ran went first to the Street of Gold Coins to see if he could set up shop as a sorcerer. He used the name he'd put on the rental agreement, and was arrested the first day. Arrested, he described later, by two very bored policemen who had no interest in pulling in one minor lawbreaker on a streetful of minor lawbreakers but who claimed they had no choice. An anonymous informant had lodged an official complaint against him with the Bureau of Urban Affairs. A bored judge, who sat court in an extra room at the police station to save time, pronounced him guilty, levied a fine, and apologized to him in one sentence.

Ran tried it all again two days later, under another name. He was arrested again and fined. We were running out of money.

The next day Ran went to Trade Square, rolled out a blanket on the ground, set down Karlas' battered chessboard, and offered to take all comers. He came home with three tabals.

"You should charge more per game," I said. "Considering how long a game takes."

"My dear tymon," he said, in one of his less acceptable flights into aristocracy, "it's not a question of *charging*. This is a wager. When you make a wager, you have to have the cash on hand to back it up. We are in no position today to risk more than three tabals. Now, logically, as the days go by, we will accumulate enough capital—"

"All right, all right." It was true, and I ought to have thought before I said anything, but his tone was irritating. I had been playing rather guiltily with the thought that I should open up the coffers I'd squirreled away with my nonNet banker before the trip to Issin, and make the coin generally available to the household. I felt some obligation, but at the same time it would mean consigning the homeward trip even farther into a murky future. Already Athena was becoming too abstract for comfort.

However, I knew I ought to be bringing some money into the house. So I went to Trade Square myself next morning, with a length of rope and some green cloth, and looked for my old vendor-mate, Irsa.

"Hello, youngster," she said when she saw me. "Wondered when I didn't see you—wasn't sure if you were too high-rung now, or if you were dead." She put down the fruit she was holding and hugged me properly.

"How are the kids, Irsa?"

"Trouble. Big trouble. Never get married, believe me." Which is what she always said. "How about you? Lost a little weight, haven't you? You've not been sick?"

"Well, Irsa, as you say, the wheel always comes around. Which is why I wanted to ask you about renting a few feet off your market space, and what the Merchants' Association would do if I asked for my old membership back."

She shook her head. "It's the way it always is, isn't it? Well, sweetheart, I wish I could say no charge on the space, but times are hard, so . . . ten percent of the take?"

That was steep—steeper than I expected from Irsa. She'd only charged three percent in the old days, and sometimes not even that when things were bad.

I was in no position to bargain, so I said, "If that's how it has to be."

She grinned that broken-toothed grin. "But don't let the Association bother you, sweetheart, you're still a member in good standing."

"What?"

"I kept up your dues, is what I'm saying to you. I thought, well, if things go wrong, and they always do, why try to talk them into letting you rejoin? And they're a mess since the chairman resigned, the committee members all want separate bribes. Too much trouble, my dear."

"You mean you've been paying them for me right along, all this past year?"

She nodded. I was overwhelmed. What she must have paid out covered far more than the ten percent she was asking. "Irsa, I don't know what to say. You're a life-saver. Thank you."

"Well, let's not dwell on it. Go on and set up your cards, you're losing customers."

"Actually, I didn't plan on doing the cards. I lost that old deck anyway, a long time ago."

"So what then—"

"Tinaje."

She blinked at me. "How—"

I said, "I figure I can set up a sort of tent if I run a rope from the top of your cart to the pole over there. I've got enough cloth and I'll just put down a mat inside."

"I didn't know you were healer-trained," she said.

"I've spent part of the last year studying tinaje with one of the best healers I know."

She frowned. "I thought you went off with that good-looking boy with the fancy clothes."

"It's a long story, Irsa."

She sighed and said, "Well, the wheel comes around sometimes and doesn't leave you in the same place. I don't know." She turned back to her cart. "Tinaje . . . at least we'll be getting some tone in this part of the market."

That's how we started the spring, with Ran and me in different corners of the Square. He never bothered with the Association, preferring to defend himself from thieves and cops. Nor did they bother him about joining, or anyway not after the first two representatives they sent. I knew that he was busy in other ways, too, but I didn't nag him about his secretiveness, mostly because when I remembered my own private bank account I didn't feel in a secure enough moral position.

It wasn't too bad in Trade Square. I'd been pretty hesitant about charging money for tinaje; Vale never had given me permission, but then, I'd left Teshin in rather a hurry. I told myself I was better than the girl at the Ten-rillis baths, and the Asuka people had been willing enough to charge. And it seemed to work out; if a client looked too scruffy I simply turned him away, and I kept my knife in easy reach. Anyway, one yell from me and Irsa would have had the curtain down and the Association running our way. And in fact I had far less trouble than I anticipated. Dancers are big customers for tinaje, and dance students had a hard time affording the more reputable practitioners; they were always on the lookout for a new one. I found in a short time that I was developing a reputation with the Imperial Dance Academy.

Soon after I set up in the Square, a client came to see me. He was about thirty Standard, tall and well-dressed, and I mentally raised my fee a bit when I saw him. He sat down on the mat, and I said, "Is there some particular problem you want to tell me about?"

"Not unless you count deceit as a problem," he said, and handed me a piece of paper. "I didn't come for tinaje. This is a message for you."

I read it. It was the address Kylla had given me at the Asuka baths, with a date and time underneath. I looked at the visitor and said, "You wouldn't be Lysander Shikron, would you?"

"Your servant, gracious lady."

He was good-looking, with sharp, dark eyes and a wry smile. Kylla didn't seem to have chosen too badly; maybe he didn't have the family's approval, but so far he had mine. "This is today's date," I said.

"Today is when you're wanted."

"All right," I agreed. "I'll be there, unless something goes wrong."

He rose to leave. I said, "I assume you came in here to divert suspicion. You didn't want to hand me a note in full view of the market."

"Yes?"

"Well, don't you think it will look strange if you leave after a couple of minutes? Tinaje usually takes at least half an hour."

"Maybe I changed my mind," he said.

"And that won't look good for my reputation."

"All right, what do you suggest?"

I pulled out my notebook. "Do you know any good stories?"

* * *

The address was in a better residential section of the capital. As I expected, Kylla was waiting for me there. She didn't have much time, she said, but gave me thirty tabals (all she could get away with at the moment) and told me Grandmother was about the same and that Eln was spending a lot of time on the Net lately. She also had a basketful of groundhermit, red eggs, and a bottle of Ducort wine. We moved these hurriedly to a sack for me and exchanged a good-bye kiss, followed by a different sort of kiss on her part for Lysander Shikron. I spent at least a full minute looking through my sack while this was going on. Then we left the house in separate directions, me back to Ran and Kylla off to the relatives she was supposed to be staying with.

When I got home, I found Tyl cooking a supper of vegetables and fried bread. "Fine as a side dish, but we can do better than that," I told him, and handed him my sack of goodies. His face lit up.

"How did you do it, my lady?"

"Foreign barbarians with no manners," I said modestly. "We have our methods."

"I haven't seen wine like this since the Emperor's Anniversary. Ah, lady, I was wondering—my shoulders have been hurting since I did the extra set on my stretch bars this morning—"

"No problem, Tyl, do you want me to work on you now or after supper?"

"Food first," he said, surveying the riches.

Later when Ran and Karlas came to table they stared at the array disbelievingly. "Tyl?" said Karlas. Tyl looked to me.

"Theodora?" said Ran.

"A lucky day in the market," I said.

Ran picked up his wine glass, took a sip, glanced at what he was holding, put it down and raised an eyebrow at me.

I did not choose to respond. It was difficult enough trying to figure some way of explaining our new possession of thirty tabals. And I did have to bring it out some-

how; Ran could make much better use of it than I could
to achieve our mutual goals, and besides there are some
ethical lines I will not cross. I really didn't believe Kylla
had meant the thirty tabals to go into my Athena fund.

When dinner was over, I still hadn't mentioned it. I
did some tinaje work on Tyl's shoulders and helped him
clean up the supper dishes. Ran would look at me from
time to time, but not in any way that let me know what
he was thinking. Finally he said, "You do tinaje for everybody else, but not for me."

"I'm sorry," I said. "I didn't think you had any interest in it." Which was better than coming out with the
truth, that doing tinaje for Ran would just confuse me. I
had come to accept, back at my start with Vale, that
tinaje was a nonsexual form of art. In that definition, I
understood it. I require consistency in my life, I don't
like to blur definitions, I keep mental categories separate
. . . in short, I didn't want to do tinaje with Ran.

"Well?" he said.

"Sit on the mat," I said. "I'm too tired for a full
session."

He sat down obediently. I knelt behind him, took a
minute to gather concentration, then went into the ritual
for partial tinaje. I focused my attention on the necessary
movements only. It was going well, I'd done the shoulder
muscles, the arms, the upper back, when I moved to the
head. There is a movement to help loosen tightness in
the neck, where the person doing the tinaje places one
hand on either side of the head, just above the ears, and
rotates it. I placed my hands in the proper position and
suddenly I forgot the whole session and thought: What
nice, soft hair you've got.

As the thought crossed my mind I felt his neck muscles
tighten.

Vale had warned me about the occasional telepathic
experiences one has in tinaje, but I'd discounted it. I
finished the session in professional manner, ruthlessly
trampling on any personal thoughts and concentrating on
the ritual.

"All done," I said, thinking, damn it, just what is it

about my thoughts that annoys you so much? He'd closed
all up after he took the onyx cat away from me, too.
Evidently telepathy was overrated as a means of bringing
people together.

Well, enough of stepping softly. I said, "I have something to show you," and I went upstairs to my room and
got out Kylla's bag of coins. I brought them down and
emptied the bag on the floor in front of Ran. He stared
at them.

"Thirty," I said, when he started to count. He looked
up at me.

"Pieces of silver?" he asked. Ivory is not a Christian
planet, but I should have known they wouldn't forget a
good story. I got up to leave. He reached out an arm and
held me back. "I'm sorry," he said.

I waited.

"I would like to know how you got them," he said.

"Are you sure?" The only time since Teshin that I'd
said Kylla's name, he'd told me never to mention it again.

He considered the matter. Maybe we were still in sync
from the tinaje; I could almost see her name rising in his
eyes. "Not necessarily," he said. He picked up a few
coins and let them dribble through his fingers. "All right,
tymon, we'll leave it alone."

I got up to go to my room. He called, "Theodora."

I turned. "Yes?"

"Whose side are you on, anyway? I never asked."

I wanted to say, why do I always have to be on somebody's side? But to Ran that would be as good as saying
"not yours." I said, "I'm going to bed now. If you think
of any other interesting questions, hold them till morning."

Traditionally, rudeness is an acceptable answer to having one's loyalty questioned. Ran said, "Good night."

I woke up next morning knowing that I'd had bad
dreams, but not knowing what they were. I stood at the
wash basin, not moving, trying to remember; something
about a dripping sound, and an echo, and being in a bad

place. Nothing else. I dismissed it and went on to the market.

It was an uneventful morning, not many customers, so when Irsa asked me to watch her wares for her I did so. It started to rain soon after she left, and I put up the sides and top of her cart and went and sat under my tent, keeping an eye on things as best I could through the narrow opening. One of the flash rains of early spring, it probably wouldn't last more than ten or fifteen minutes. Meanwhile the market emptied like an overturned cart.

I felt the tent shake and stuck my head out front to find the cause. Eln Cormallon was there. He was seated on his floater, dry and perfectly turned out in the midst of the downpour, and standing beside him was cousin Stepan, holding an umbrella over his own head and looking silly. The floater was dry, too; it must have been a spell-shield.

"Hello, Theo." Eln smiled, the same look of gentle complicity he'd always shared with me, as though we'd just done a practice set in the garden only yesterday. "Put your head back in, you'll get wet."

"If I put my head back in, I won't be able to see you."

"True. Stepan, can we raise this rope, so I can get the floater inside the tent?"

Stepan appraised the situation with an expression of dutiful misery. "I don't think so."

"Well, then," said Eln, "I'm dry enough, so if I lower to the ground I can talk to our Theo comfortably, and you can hold the umbrella over her head."

"I don't have an extra umbrella," said Stepan.

"Yes, I know," said Eln.

So he lowered the floater, and Stepan squatted grimly beside me with his umbrella.

"Long time," I said.

"Yes, I'm sorry about that. You've often been in my thoughts, though."

"Same with me."

He said, "I never thought to see you doing tinaje. Kylla would approve, she likes the old ways. I don't mind tradition myself, when it's not at the expense of profit. . . ."

He hesitated, thinking his own thoughts. "Theo, here's the problem. You shouldn't be here."

"I've been in Trade Square before. If you don't mind my saying so, Eln, your family is more than a little snobbish about the ways people can make a living."

"I meant," he said, "that you shouldn't be on Ivory." I froze. "Oh."

"You ought to be on Athena, getting your degree."

I relaxed, a very little. "You have a point there."

"And it's my family that's mucked around with your life, so I feel some responsibility. I've done some checking. There's a liner due from Tellys in a couple of weeks, one of the *Queens*. It'll be in port for ten days, and then go on to the next leg of its run."

"To Athena."

"Yes, to Athena."

"Well, I appreciate your notifying me of the schedule, Eln, but if I could have afforded passage on a starship I would have left here quite a long time ago."

He laughed gently. "I had that impression. What I've come here to tell you is that your passage is already paid."

"What?" It came out as a choke.

"Your ticket and your ID are registered with the Port Authority. All you have to do is show up." He paused, and when I didn't say anything he went on. "What I would suggest is that you wait till the last day it's in port, less trouble all around that way. Now, the thing is, darling Theo, fond though I am of you, I can't afford to buy passage on every Athenan-bound liner that puts into this city. So this is a one-time deal, this ship only." He turned suddenly to Stepan. "I forget the name."

"The *Queen Emily*," said Stepan. By now he was thoroughly soaked.

"The *Queen Emily*," Eln repeated. "So there you are. By the way, if you're feeling especially grateful to me when you get back home, you might talk to a couple of people I've been dealing with on the faculty there. Let them know what a fine and trustworthy person I am, see if you can get them to stop dragging their feet."

He paused again, but I still couldn't seem to come up with anything to say. "Well, there's no need to go into all that now. I'll leave you some notes on the subject in the Net link in your cabin, and if you feel like giving me a hand, that's fine; if you don't, that's fine, too. Theo?"

"Yes."

"You're getting all this information, aren't you?"

"I'm getting it."

"Good." He seemed uncertain. "You know, I would have paid your fare a lot sooner, if you'd just gone with the Issin people back to the capital. Still, no harm done, I suppose."

I said, "No, no harm done. Eln—"

He looked attentive. I don't really know what I would have said at that point, because that was when Stepan shot to his feet, rainwater started to pound me in the face, and I heard Ran's voice say, "Theodora, are you all right?"

I called, "Yes, I'm fine."

Through the sluice of heavy rain I saw Ran standing with Karlas and Tyl. They were standing warily, rigidly, by Irsa's cart, and if they were in anything close to the same mood Stepan was in, their nerves were stretched taut. Stepan's knuckles were by my face, and they were white. I hoped no one was armed. What was I thinking? They were all armed, I only hoped nobody was too nervous.

I said, "I think they were leaving."

Ran started to walk slowly toward us, followed by Karlas and Tyl. Eln raised his floater. He said, "As a matter of fact, we were just about to go." Ran kept walking. When he reached the floater, he stopped.

"Well, then," he said, "go."

Eln regarded him. Finally he said, "Don't blame Kylla for any of this. I didn't give her a choice."

"Everybody has a choice."

A funny sort of half-smile raised itself on Eln's lips, as though he couldn't keep it off. He looked down at me.

"It must be nice," he said lightly, "to believe that."

The rain was starting to slacken. Followed by Stepan, he rode slowly out of the market, the only dry person among us.

Chapter 16

"What did he want?" Ran waited until we were home and the door was shut before he turned to me. His green cloak dripped on the floor. Tyl tried to take it from him, but Ran waved him away.

"I don't know exactly," I said. "We didn't have long to talk before you showed up. He was suggesting that I leave Ivory."

"I'll bet he was," said Ran. "Talk about nerve." He paced a few steps over the parlor floor, then pulled off his cloak, rolled it into a ball, and tossed it to Tyl. Tyl shrugged at me and took it away to dry.

I didn't know why I wasn't telling Ran about the ticket arrangement. I needed time to think . . . my impulse was to ignore it, try to pretend the ticket wasn't there. Was that because I was looking for an excuse to stay on this planet? Had I been kidding myself the past year? That didn't feel right either . . . it was the circumstances . . . the feeling I got from my talk with Eln was that I was perfectly free to go, provided I left my honor behind when I boarded.

I didn't plan to leave that way, and yet I felt guilty about the whole scheme. Why? And why was it dishonorable to leave now, and not later? Even if Ran got through this crisis, he would still be in a semi-lethal position without a card-reader. Didn't the argument that I'd been tricked into all this still hold?

Ran went to his room, presumably to brood, and I did the same. I have never liked ethical complexity.

That night I had more bad dreams. I woke up with the feeling that I'd been through a recurrent nightmare, one I'd had before but couldn't remember. Probably just as well, I thought; there was enough to deal with in my conscious life.

I met Kylla a few days later at Lysander Shikron's. We sat in the servants' pantry, off the main kitchen, surrounded by shelves of sealed jars. She was jeweled and painted, no doubt for his benefit, but underneath it all she looked tired and drawn. She brought more money, twenty-five tabals.

"Eln spends his life on the Net terminal," she said, "and when he's not there, he's with Stepan. I never gave much thought to Stepan one way or another before, but now he gives me the creeps. He follows Eln around like he's waiting for raw meat."

Lysander was out of the room just then, and Kylla pulled aside her robes and put her perfect, bare legs up on a bench. She leaned back against the wall. "Oh, how I wish I could get out my pipe right now. But I'm trying to introduce Lysander to my vices gradually." She glanced at me and added, "I think we'll save some of this knowledge till after the wedding."

I was surprised. "You're planning to get married?" Implied in my tone was, you can pull this off with the family?

She smiled. "Give me some time, Theo. So far, the lead role in *Agamemnon* is the only thing I've ever wanted that I didn't get."

I shook my head and she suddenly gave a guilty start and dropped her legs. "Is that Lysander?" she said, as there was a thump on the door to the kitchen. But no one came in and she returned the legs to their former royal seat. "One of the house servants," she said. "I see that giggle, Theo, you may be holding it in out of courtesy, but you ought to keep your eyes down. You don't think I should be keeping these habits from my future husband, do you?"

"It's really not for me to say, Kylla."

She laughed and lit an imaginary pipe. "Isn't this the

best way to break it to a beloved? Wouldn't you give him time before you exposed your, well, more unfortunate character traits?''

"No."

"What would you do?"

"I'd print out a list, and tell him to speak now or not bother me about it later. Then I'd have him initial it.''

She really laughed at that point, not the ladylike silvery laughter she usually produced, but sheer guffaws. She put a hand over mine as she let go. "Theo, sweetheart," she said finally. "I can see why you get along with Ran.''

I waited till she'd calmed down. "How's Grandmother?" I asked.

Her expression faded like a doused candle. "She never leaves her bed. And the only people she'll let into her room now are me and Tagra." She stared at the wall. "I wonder sometimes. It's frightening to think of Grandmother as powerless. Does getting old scare you, Theo? It does me.''

"I don't know," I said honestly. "Death scares me. Getting old, the loss of beauty—I never had that much beauty to begin with. And getting older in an Ivoran family means gathering more power . . . anyway, up until near the end. Your people treat it with respect. Ivory is a good planet to get old on, Kylla, at least if you have a family like yours.''

She went on staring at the wall. "Thank you," she said softly. "I'm glad to know that.''

Lysander came back, and she put down her legs hastily.

Kylla had told me some things about that period of Eln's life no one at Cormallon wanted to talk about, the time when he declared ishin na' telleth on his family and went to live in the capital. Apparently he'd been here for two full years, longer than I'd somehow expected; how had he made a living? There were ways, I knew, and at least he could read and write—but without family connections it was damned hard. And he'd had no Tellys-imported floater then, something difficult to imagine, and

which I didn't want to imagine. Kylla said he'd made do
with a jerry-rigged board on wheels when he was in the
city. It was an insult to Eln to think of him looking eye-
level at people's knees.

I wanted to see the place where he'd lived. Kylla told
me that he'd been retrieved from a room above a store on
Marsh Street, on the other side of the business quarter.
It was a store that sold secondhand jewelry, halfway a
pawnbroker's, she said; there were two on Marsh Street.
I chose the less prosperous looking one.

Inside there were bins of cheap trinkets, foreign-made
necklaces of the sort tourists don't mind parting with,
false gold and tarnished silver. The counters edging the
walls held the better stuff. They were locked. There was
one man behind the back counter, reading through some
papers. No Net terminal was in evidence; it was a place
that dealt in cash.

I walked up to the man. He was young, perhaps twenty-
four or five; which made him a couple of years beyond
me, but somehow I felt the elder. He was light-skinned,
more gold than brown, with blond hair and gray eyes.
He put down his papers when I approached.

"Can I help you?"

No "gracious lady" here, although the tone was quiet
and polite. Perhaps I should try to dress better. "I don't
know," I said, wondering what in the world I would say
next. "I'm looking for something for a friend."

"Male or female?" he said.

"Male."

"We have a good selection," he said, gesturing to a
nearby case. We moved over to it. "Rings, necklaces,
earrings, belt-ends . . . did you have something particular in mind?"

"Not really." How unfortunately true that was. He
wasn't a bad salesman, directing me at once to the more
expensive material. But maybe he assumed I wouldn't
have bothered him if I just wanted junk from the bins; I
could have rooted through them by myself.

"Well, this belt-end is unique. A diving gryphon, you

won't see many like it.'' He pulled it out and laid it on the counter for me to examine.

"Yes, it does appear unique." The gryphon looked as though it had eaten something that disagreed with it. "What about those gold things over there?"

"These?" He laid them beside the gryphon. "Spurs, shaped like salamanders. Ornamental, of course. You wouldn't have much use for them in the city."

"Oh, I don't know. They might strike my friend's fancy."

"He rides?"

"In a manner of speaking. Perhaps you know him— Eln Cormallon."

The hands over the spurs froze, then a tremble went through it, convulsively, like a ground tremor. I stared. I had never seen anything like it. He seemed tightly controlled, distant, unaware of his own reaction. His face remained impersonal.

"Eln Cormallon?"

"Yes," I said carefully. "He might like the spurs. He has an unusual sense of humor."

"Did he send you?" His face raised from the jewelry, his eyes looked into mine. "Do you know where he is?"

"I don't know. I suppose he's at Cormallon." Now I was the one who looked down. I was wrong about the control; I didn't want to see eyes like that.

"He's not in the city, then."

"I don't really know."

"And he didn't send you."

"No. I'm sorry." I wasn't sure what I was apologizing for, but I was sure that I owed it to him somewhere down the line.

He put the pieces back in the case, moving stiffly. "No. Of course he didn't send you." He looked up suddenly from what he was doing. "I'm sorry. Were you really interested in the spurs?"

"No. No. Put them away." I waved them back. "Pay no attention to me. I'm leaving anyway." I started edging down the main aisle. Interfering in people's lives—you'd think I would have learned my lesson from Pina. I felt as

though I'd just broken into this store with two large men
and had him beaten up.

"Uh, gracious lady?"

I paused, unwillingly, by the door. He stepped out from
the dim light behind the counter, and I saw that his left
arm, the one he hadn't used, was made of metal. I noted,
for no reason, that there were rings of gold and gems on
the metal fingers, and none on the biological arm. "Gracious lady, if you see Eln, would you tell him that . . .
tell him that he's always welcome here?"

I nodded and went out the door. I wasn't two steps
down the street when the door opened behind me and his
voice said, "Gracious lady!" I turned.

"Never mind, gracious lady, please don't say anything.
All right?"

"All right."

I turned back and started walking very quickly, before
he could follow me and tell me he'd changed his mind
again. I had the feeling he would have given me twenty
different messages if I let him.

I went home that evening to find that we had a visitor.
It was Karlas' brother Halet, a middle-aged, middle-
class, slightly more respectable businessman in a striped
cotton robe. He ran two stores back in Summring, the
town nearest to Teshin, and had stayed behind to arrange
their new management. Now he was here to throw in with
our cause.

"Honored," he said, as Ran introduced us. "I have
the best hopes for our success."

We traded a few flowery compliments, and I said to
Ran, "How did you get him over the property line?"
Saddling an ally with seven years of bad luck seemed not
in our best interests.

Ran sighed. "I had to break down the whole spell, get
him inside, and then redraw it."

I frowned. "Then how did I get in? I wasn't inside
when you redrew it."

"Trust me, Theodora, I'm a professional."

I hoped so. Halet pulled on my robe at that point. "My lady, I have something of yours."

"What?"

He opened his wallet and took something out. He placed it in my palm; it was small and hard, wrapped in tissue paper. I opened it and stared.

He said, "The Old Man of Kado Island is dead."

It was the pendant, the piece of delicately lined river-bed stone on its thin silver chain. The lines were like blue veins on skin of alabaster.

Halet said, "It's a bluestone pendant, isn't it? I've never seen one."

"How did you get it?" I asked.

"It was brought to me by Vale the healer. The Old Man sends it to you."

I didn't know why he used the present tense, he seemed to have good grammar—it made me nervous. "Why didn't he give it to Vale?"

Halet shrugged. "I can't say. Perhaps he didn't want it to stay in Teshin."

I snorted at that. The Old Man waits until he's dead, to leave Teshin the only way he can. I kept the paper between my hand and the stone.

"He must have known someone else, somewhere, that he could have sent it to."

Halet said, "You're a tinaje artist, I understand. No doubt he wanted it in good hands, with someone of high moral character."

That was even sadder and funnier. And it was the first time someone ever entrusted me with a responsibility based simply on my profession. That was even more of an ethical burden to bear than the pendant.

I said, holding the stone carefully, "Can I send it back to Vale?" Knowing the answer already.

Halet, and even Karlas, looked shocked at such a suggestion. Ran said, "Yes, you can. You can do anything you like, Theodora. Do you want me to send it back?"

"No," I said. "If he wanted Vale to have it, he would have given it to him."

Halet relaxed, and gave me an approving look. No

doubt he was glad to share a house with an unregistered alien of high moral character.

It was a responsibility, but it was also a comfort. I took the pendant out that night (still wrapped in tissue paper) and placed it under my pillow when I went to sleep. I don't know why I did it. But for the first time in a long while I didn't have bad dreams.

I was afraid of losing it, so I made up a little bag of red silk (Tyl did the sewing) and tied it around the stone; and I wore the pendant that way, under my tunic and robes. After a few days I almost forgot it was there.

Ran came to me one night and said, "I want you to run the cards."

I said, "You didn't like it the last time I ran them."

"It has to be done," he said. "Look, I'll be with you the whole time."

"Oh, it doesn't bother me. I was just wondering why you changed your mind."

He looked uncomfortable. "Everything's dangerous," he said. "You can walk down the street and get kicked by a cart-horse."

"Yeah, no doubt."

"All right, something's very wrong here. I put on a mirror-spell not long ago—"

"A mirror-spell?"

He gestured impatiently. "Back-reflex. So physical harm done to me would be reflected back, duplicated on the person doing the harm. Well, on Eln actually, he's the one I designated."

"And?"

"It didn't work." He started to pace. "It doesn't make sense. It was as if he were already in a mirror himself."

"So, maybe he is. He had someone cast a spell, got in ahead of you. Everybody keeps telling me how bright he is."

Ran looked at me, and I shrugged. He said, "He can't be in a mirror. That can only be self-cast, by its nature. Only a sorcerer can do it, and he's not a sorcerer."

"All right, explain it, then."

"There *is* no explanation. Are you carrying the cards on you?"

"Ah." I took out the deck. Ran settled himself on the floor and I did likewise.

The center card was the Charioteer with paired horses, one black and one white. Well, that was an identity card for Eln, if one existed. Then I thought again, and wondered who I was kidding—it could really stand for anyone in this schizophrenic family. I took another card without dwelling on it. This one was the Water-Drawer, a young man, bare-chested, with a bucket of water from a brick well. He was pouring the water into a jar, and there were more jars by his feet. I placed it beside the center card, keeping one finger on it, and let myself go.

I was in a room walled in ancient, jagged stone, with a flat stone floor. There were no windows. I felt somehow that it was underground, there was something dark and earthy-smelling about the place. It was damp and rooty, like wet flowers. In the center of the room were two couches, low and without sides or arms. A person lay on each couch. They lay like corpses, faces turned up, arms limp. I moved closer to the couches and looked down on them: One was Stepan, the other was Eln. Somehow I'd known that. There was a plastic tube running between them, one forearm to another, and as I watched the tube turned from transparent to red. Then there was a dripping sound that echoed off the stones. Suddenly I remembered my dreams, my recurrent nightmares of the last few weeks, and I knew that in the nightmare I was in this room.

I didn't want to be there any longer, and somewhere far away I took my finger off the card and gazed up at Ran. He said, "You looked upset for a minute."

"It wasn't important." I described the room, the people on the couches.

He said, "It sounds like the cellar at Cormallon. But what was it? A blood transfusion? Why?"

I shook my head. "It's not like the regular pictures, remember. It may not be literal."

"When you drew the cards," he said slowly, "you

were thinking about the problem I just gave you? The mirror-spell?''

I said, "Trust me, Ran, I'm a professional."

He gave a half-grin. "All right. Thank you, Theodora. I'll go away and think about it until it drives me crazy." Then he picked up my right hand, kissed it, and went upstairs.

Well, well. I got up off the floor, made my way to my own room, hit the bed like a felled oak and slept heavily till dawn. It had been a confusing night all around.

The next morning Ran walked into the kitchen happily. Tyl was serving me more fried bread; it was cheap and one of the few things he knew how to cook well. I hoped Kylla would send me another message soon, we could use more eggs. "I've got it," said Ran.

"Oh?" In the morning my verbal ability is limited at best. Things would improve mentally after breakfast . . . if only Tyl would use butter instead of oil. . . .

"Theodora, you're not paying attention. This is it, I've figured it out."

"I'm glad, Ran. Tyl, can't you get butter at the Square? There must be a market for the tourists—''

Ran walked over to my place and lifted my plate. "Hey!" I said.

"Are you listening?"

I put down my fork. "All right, you have my full attention. But I'm telling you now that I'll make better sense if you let me take in some food."

He handed me the plate. "Eat, and listen." He sat down next to me. "Logically, why would a mirror-spell not work? The answer is because the target is already protected. All right, logically, how could the target already be protected? Because he cast his own mirror-spell." He was spilling out the words quickly and cheerfully. "It's the only answer."

"You already explained to me last night why that can't be," I said. "Eln would have to do the spell himself, and he's no sorcerer."

"He's a theorist. He knows everything there is to know

about sorcery on a theoretical basis. He's not a sorcerer because he has no talent.''

I finished my last bread slice. "That's a major obstacle, isn't it?''

"All right, but listen. He's got a mirror-spell, and that can only be set by oneself. It's the very nature of the spell, it's part of the basic fabric of the way things work in magic, it's just . . . indisputable. It's easier to believe that Eln could get what we call 'talent' from someplace than that all the laws of magic no longer apply. That would be believing that stones fall into the sky and water runs uphill—'' He stopped. "I'm starving," he said, as though he'd only just noticed. "Is there any more of that? Tyl—''

"In just a minute," said Tyl.

I said, "You can't just walk into the market and buy talent in a jar.''

"Exactly, that's where your card-reading comes in. You know what Grandmother did when she cursed me? She shifted my ability in that one area from me to you—not you specifically, I mean, but someone who fit your parameters. Well, that's not so strange, in a way all she really did was link us up using a physical common point, the deck of cards. No different really from shifting good or bad luck from one person to another by seeing that an object that was in the first person's possession passes to the second person. You remember all this from the textbook, don't you?''

"Vaguely." Extremely vaguely. It was really Eln who used to explain all that sort of thing to me—Eln the theorist.

"It's been said for years that there must be a way to shift sorcery itself from one person to another. But until now no one's been able to do it.''

"Eln? I don't see why you should think that he could—''

He shook his head impatiently. "If anybody could figure it out, it would be Eln. He's the best mind working in sorcery. Think what it could mean for the family! People interested in joining Cormallon could buy into the family and be trained, and we could guarantee them to be sorcerers when we finished. People born into the family and talent, but who want to be, I don't know, traders, could sell their talent to someone more interested in developing it. It would change the whole face of the business, and we would control it—it would still be the Cormallon specialty."

"Eln doesn't seem eager to make his knowledge public. If that's what he's really done."

All the animation seemed to drain out of Ran. "No." Tyl brought over a full plate to him, and he stared at it with uninterest. "No, he hasn't made it public. Why would I expect him to? I wonder when he worked it all out." He looked at me. "He hasn't bought his talent, he's stealing it."

"How do you figure that?"

"Well, stealing it in some sense anyway. I can't believe Stepan would agree willingly. No real sorcerer would."

"Ah. The transfusion tube. I begin to see where you're going."

He got up and started pacing, the way he always did when he was on the trail of something. When he was after an answer he was a walker, a hunter; all that energy had to come out somewhere. In similar circumstances I became a go-sit-in-the-corner-and-think-things-over person. And I don't talk about it till I've got it straight.

He said, "We have to know. We have to know how he's doing it. There's no way around the problem; we need to cut him off from his source, and to do that we have to know how he accesses it."

The word "access" brought it to mind. I said, "I understand he's been spending a lot of time on the Net lately."

Ran looked at me. "How would you have heard this?" he asked.

"How do you think?" I said.

He drummed his fingers on the table. "If only I had five minutes with his terminal! If I were at Cormallon—"

I said, "I think we can safely assume he put a confinement on his work so that only his own terminal could access it, and a lock on the terminal so only he can get in.''

''If I were there . . .'' His voice trailed off. ''Money,'' he said, in a new voice. ''We need money.''

Well, that was something I always agreed with. The connection with Eln's Net work escaped me, though. Ran picked up his cloak and started off immediately for the Square, apparently eager to accumulate tabals as swiftly as possible. I followed, more calmly, but in much the same spirit.

Given Ran's new state of mind, it was only a matter of time until I broke down and told him about my nonNet account. In fact it was that very evening.

''How much?'' he said, at once.

I told him. His face fell. ''Well,'' he said politely, ''I'm sure it's a fine amount for the purposes of one person.''

''You always told me I was saving too much and spending too little!''

''Naturally I said that, I didn't want you to buy a ticket offplanet.''

Here we were both silent, for different reasons. I was thinking of the ticket registered in my name, waiting with the Port Authority. The *Queen Emily* was due to touch down the next day, not that that should hold any relevance for me.

Ran said, ''But you've got a banker. Presumably you've both checked on each other.''

''I can't speak for him. But I asked around, and he was okayed by the Merchants' Association. And Irsa said he had a good reputation. That's all these unregistered bankers have to go on, their reputation; they don't play around with it if they want to last in the business.''

He nodded, and held out a hand. ''Come on,'' he said. ''I want you to introduce us.''

''You want me to introduce you to my *banker*?''

He pulled me up, and we left the house and went off toward the Street of Gold Coins. I said, as we walked through a spring evening in the capital, breathing in the scent of cinnablossom from every gutter, "Why the sudden obsession with coin? I thought we were doing all right."

"We need backing," he said. "More backing than you've got in your personal account, and more than Karlas or Halet have to give—or anyway, are willing to give, if they're sane."

"Just what is it you've got in mind? And why should my banker be willing to contribute?"

"They do loans."

"Yes, but the loans they do aren't anything we want to be involved with. I don't consider my body as collateral, Ran."

He smiled. "Relax, tymon. Under the right circumstances, they do loans on a noninterest basis—business loans, for a percent of the profit. Let's say, Theodora, that we wanted to rob that little office at the foot of Marsh Street that does Athenan-Ivory money exchange. And let's say that the office wasn't insured by the Merchants' Protective Group. We'd go to your banker, then, and show him all our plans, and if he thought they were feasible he'd put up the money to carry it out. Simple as that."

"And if he didn't think it was feasible? Why shouldn't he turn us in?"

"As you say, tymon—their reputation is all these people have." He laughed. "That, and a whole lot of money."

We reached my banker's office in the Street of Gold Coins. There was no emblem on the door, nothing to say this building was any different from the houses on either side. Ran knocked. He said to me, "After you introduce us, wait out here while I talk to him."

I said, "You're willing to tell your plans to a perfect stranger, and not to me?"

He looked surprised. "He has the money," he said reasonably.

Chapter 17

"What we want you to do," said Ran to me," is break into the house at Cormallon."

We were sitting in the parlor: Karlas, Tyl, Halet, and Samanta, the wife and partner of my banker. I gathered she was here to safeguard their investment and see if we showed signs of doing anything stupid. I was tempted to behave stupidly then and there, but I managed to hold it back.

"Uh," I said, "are you craz—I mean—what do you mean?"

Ran said, "This is how I see it. We need to access Eln's information. Now, *I* can't go through the barrier, I've been ritually disowned. Nobody else here can go through the barrier, they're all strangers to it. That only leaves you, Theodora."

"It's always possible the barrier was set against me, too," I pointed out.

"Not likely," he said. "It's not set anew each time someone passes—it recognizes what's been defined as a friend, that's all. My definition changed when they read the disownment ritual. Your definition *could* have been changed. I'll admit it, but it's a lot of trouble to go to; and for what? To stop one little tymon from coming on the grounds? The goldbands could put you out just as well."

I saw the reason in that. And Eln didn't think me much of a threat anyway. He probably expected me to be on the *Queen Emily* any day now.

I said, "The goldbands certainly will put me out. Assuming they don't kill me on the spot."

"It's not probable." He gave me a level look. "Eln likes you."

"How long will he like me when he finds me breaking into his house?"

"Yes. Well, it's not without danger."

I said, "And the barrier isn't the only thing in the defense arsenal."

"True," he said, surprised. "How did you know?"

"I know the Cormallons."

Ran leaned over. "I guarantee that I can coach you through the rest of the ground defenses. If you're caught, it won't be through them."

I glanced around at them all, waiting; at Karlas and his relatives, looking tense, at Samanta, looking uninvolved.

"All right," I said.

Karlas smiled. Halet bowed his head to me. Tyl frowned.

Ran said, "There's still the lock on the terminal data."

"There's a lot more than that," I said. "But it's all right, we'll work it out."

Right, here we go—warrior queen Theodora of Pyrene sets out with lance and steed to storm the castle of the green knight. I felt stupid quite often the next few days, wondering how I could have agreed. I found I was checking off the days the *Emily* was in port, too, adding fantasy treachery to fantasy heroism. And while I was wandering around the house in mental turmoil, Ran was always out *buying* things.

"You're running through that loan like water," I said, when he came home with the aircar. We were standing on the roof.

"Just get a tarpaulin," he said. As I helped him to cover it, he added, "Wait till you see the other one."

"Other what?"

"Other car."

He didn't sound as if he were joking. "I beg your par-

don?'' Aircars are enormously expensive on Ivory because of the tax. They're still trying to get back what they
had to pay to Tellys for the first model.

"We'll need two, Theodora, this and a one-seater for
you to take through the barrier. It'll be easier to maneuver, and Karlas and I will be just outside Cormallon territory in the larger one.''

I stopped fooling with the tarpaulin. "Ran, I don't
drive.''

He stopped, too. "What do you mean, you don't drive?
You come from a highly industrialized planet.''

"Yes, it is highly industrialized—with big, crowded cities. If everybody had their own aircar it would be chaos.
That's why we use mass transportation.'' He kept staring
at me. "I've never had to fly one of these in my life.''

"I don't believe it.'' He said down on the rim of the
aircar.

"I hope you're starting to see why it's better to let me
in on your plans at the beginning.''

He said, "Never? In your life?''

"Never.''

He stood up. "Get in,'' he said.

"Look, Ran, it's a little late to start teaching me
now—''

He said, grimly, "Our bankers will understand failure—
intellectually—but they won't understand it if we back
out now. Unless you want our bodies used as collateral
after all—get in.''

I got in. He sat in the other front seat. He'd named half
a dozen controls and their functions when he stopped and
said, "If I weren't letting you in on my plans at the beginning, this would be the night of the break-in, and it
really would be too late.''

"You're right. For you this is an improvement. I beg
your pardon.''

He nodded, and went back to the controls.

The ground defenses were next on my worry list, but
Ran refused to talk about them. "There's no need,'' he'd
say, whenever I brought it up. "They're very simple.''

Fine, if that was the way he wanted to play it. Meanwhile I was becoming a real whiz at the aircar; Ran had to dive on the controls twice to keep us from crash landing in the meadow outside town. He didn't yell at me, though, he just got very pale.

The *Queen Emily* touched down in port, and we set the date for my exercise in thievery. Ran gave me lists of potential passwords to try on Eln's data lock, and at my insistence Tyl took apart a couple of my robes and made me a pair of new trousers. "You look like a provincial," said Ran when he saw them. "You're not going fishing, you know."

"I'm the one doing this," I said. "I'll set the dress code."

I thought, I'll bet he never gave Kylla a hard time about her hunting trousers. But then, Kylla is the sort of person who gets away with a lot.

The day came. Ran made a big point about not allowing there to be any witnesses for the operation; we didn't want the Cormallon council officially on our backs. I didn't ask him what I was supposed to do if there was a witness—I had a feeling he expected me to know.

We'd fixed on two hours after midnight as the proper time. Cormallon wasn't really an armed camp, despite indications to the contrary; basically it was a country home, and practically everybody went to sleep at night. There were no patrols, no guards as such—they left the defenses to sorcery and their reputation. And why not? No one had been silly enough to try to break in for at least two centuries.

"Eln might very well be awake," I said. Ran and Karlas were sitting with me in the kitchen after sunset, checking their gear and finishing up the bowl of rice and vegetables that Tyl had just made. I couldn't eat more than a couple of mouthfuls, and they lay like lumps of mud in my stomach. "Either I'm very nervous, or Tyl should stick to fried bread."

"Both," said Ran, as he slid a pistol into the holster on his belt.

"Eln has a reputation for roaming the halls at night," I said.

"He used to," said Ran. "But that was before he became the—before he had to handle all these new administrative duties. No doubt he keeps more normal hours now."

"You used to leave the administrative duties for days on end."

"Grandmother and Kylla could pick up the slack then." He handed a pack to Karlas.

"But if he *is* awake, he's very likely to be . . ."

"Right in the room with his Net terminal. Yes, I was going to mention before you left that you ought to enter that room very carefully. Thank you for reminding me." He glanced at Karlas. "Have you got the material?"

Karlas said, "Right here." He took a small vial from his robe. "Took the last of the money," he added.

"Reliable?" asked Ran.

"Believe me," said Karlas, "I checked very carefully."

"All right," said Ran.

He put his elbows on the table and leaned over toward me. "The ground defenses," he began.

"Oh, the oracle speaks," I said.

"Do you want to hear this before you go in? The ground defenses. There aren't any."

"Now, wait a minute—that isn't what—"

"Not any that are really there. The defenses are strictly illusory. There are set traps at various places on the property, and they're tripped by trespassers. They present sensory illusions of danger—things that inspire fear in the person receiving the illusion. The victim's fear is then fed back into the trap on a positive circuit, projected back at the victim at a higher intensity, and so on until they lose their mind. With me so far?"

"More than I want to be. But look, if they aren't really there, why can't I just ignore them and walk straight into the house?"

"The feedback circuit," he said. "You're walking through some trees at night, you hear a roar just behind you—your first reaction is panic. A second later, true, you'd say to yourself that it's just a trick. But it's a second too late, you're already hooked into the circuit.''

I thought it through. ''Then why are we contemplating this merry expedition? It sounds impossible.''

''Not impossible. For instance, if you could turn off the fear first at your end, not let the circuit start, there would be no danger. Unfortunately, you're not na' telleth enough.''

''Who says? I'm as na' telleth as anybody here.''

They exchanged looks. ''So that's why,'' said Ran, ''we got this for you.''

He handed me the vial. It contained a great many little white pills. I inspected it, then Ran and Karlas, with narrowed eyes. ''I don't know what this stuff is.''

''Anarine,'' said Karlas. ''Very good quality. I used to deal in some of it in Teshin—not as good as this, though.''

Tyl came in then, carrying a bottle. ''Is this what you wanted?'' he asked Ran.

''Ducort ninety-nine,'' said Ran, pleasantly. ''If this doesn't work, we'll have gone out in style.'' He took down glasses from a shelf and set one in front of me. ''It has more of a kick with alcohol.''

''I'm sure. Will I wake up tomorrow?''

He poured one for himself, then filled glasses for the others. ''Concentrate on getting through tonight,'' he said. ''We'll worry about tomorrow then.''

A half hour and a half dozen little pills later, things were pretty fuzzy around the edges. There were only two glasses of wine, though; I think. Anyway, when Karlas tried to fill my glass again, I glared at him and said, ''Do you want me to stop in the middle of this highly complex robbery and ask to use the toilet?''

''No,'' Ran answered, ''we wouldn't want that.'' He took the bottle away from Karlas. ''I think she has the basic concept,'' he said. ''We'd better get into the car. Anarine is supposed to wear off quickly, isn't it?''

"The alcohol will keep it going a little longer," said Karlas.

We all went up to the roof. "Are you coming, too?" I asked Tyl.

"Sure I am," he said, and went over to the one-seater parked in the corner. There wasn't much room left on the roof.

"Hey!" I yelled. "You don't know how to pilot these things either."

Tyl grinned and went on. Ran said, "Get in the car, Theodora."

I did so, and said, "He doesn't know how to work that thing, Ran."

We took off, Tyl following perfectly. I don't recall most of the trip, except that periodically someone would hand me another little white pill. We must have been cruising at extremely high speed, though, because I remember going "Wooooh!" at one point, when we were crossing over a village.

We set down near a stand of trees just outside the barrier. Karlas took out another pill, but Ran said, "We want this to wear off, don't we?" and he put it back. We got out and stood between the two cars. Ran said, "Are you all right?"

"I'm fine," I said.

"We're going to be right here," he said. "That's directly south of the house. Just aim in this direction when you take off. See those hills over there?"

"Sure."

"Use them to steer by if you have to. I mean, I've preset the auto to return here, but it's better to be ready in case anything goes wrong."

"Fine."

"You can fly for about five minutes after you cross the barrier. You don't want to have to walk too far. But you want to put down *out* of line of sight of the house."

"Right."

"You remember all the passwords I gave you?"

"Uh-huh."

He seemed worried, but I wasn't. "Well," he said.
Then he kissed me and said, "Good luck, Theodora."

"Queen Theodora, to you," I said.

He frowned, confused. "Hand me my trusty lance,"
I said, gesturing to the back of the aircar. He took out
my data-case and handed it to me. I strapped it over one
shoulder. Then he paused and took off his holster and put
it around my waist himself, pulling the belt taut. He
stepped back.

"Do you know where you're going?" he asked uncertainly.

"North through the barrier. Straight arrow to the main
house. Land out of direct line of sight. Be careful going
in the Net link room. Use the auto when I take off or else
line up with the two hills."

Karlas said, "I told you it doesn't affect intelligence.
Much."

I started toward the barrier. Ran said, "Don't you think
you should use the car?"

"Right," I said.

He was looking pale again.

The one-seater wasn't that hard to maneuver. I set down
behind the south hill outside the main house, on the other
side of the front garden. The front garden was a massive
project of streams, tall hedges, tiny bridges, marble
benches, and pavilions. I'd always preferred the back garden, where things grew up wild and tangled, and the
sa'ret equipment was set up. I started on the pathway
through the maze that led up to the lawn. The night air
was bracing, head-clearing, direct and sharp; all I didn't
want to be at this particular moment. I noticed a little
white pill caught in the cuff of my tunic. "What the hell,"
I decided, and swallowed it.

It was more enjoyable after that. I decided I was glad
to be there. I was thinking how lovely the garden was by
night, when I noticed that the entrance to the Crimson
Bridge was blocked by a giant with a scimitar. It was
eight meters tall, and stood waiting for me menacingly,
tapping the blade on the wood of the bridge. It growled,

low in the throat, as I came nearer. I started to giggle; it was clean out of period with the rest of the garden. "Atrocious taste," I commented as I walked through it and went on to the Center Maze of Flowers. Rooting among the flower beds, snuffling up the path toward me was a gray rat about the size of Ran's aircar. It followed me through the Center Maze, occasionally nipping at my heels, and when I reached the entrance to the Path of Many Stones I turned and pretended to thrust with an imaginary sword. "Take that," I said, but it vaporized. "Damn," I said.

I went down the Path of Many Stones, looking for the door Ran had told me about. Somewhere around the quartz boulders, wasn't it? I counted them off, lost track, and had to start again. Seven, eight, nine. That must be the one. Hell, there was another huge rat, sitting on the boulder and baring its teeth. How annoying. I began to declaim, in a louder voice than was wise, "Why are your traps so barren of new pride, so far from variation or quick change? —Hey, I didn't know I remembered that. It must be the pills." We regarded each other. I went on, "All your best is dressing old rats new, spending again what is already spent." It licked its neat white teeth. "Move," I added. It sat there. I took out my pistol and rapped it on the snout with the butt. It vanished. I pushed the boulder over, grunting, and examined the damp earth beneath. Using my forefinger I drew a pentacle in the ground, and covered it with the sorcery symbol. A second later there was a large hole in its place, with steps leading downward.

I descended into a dusty, foul-looking tunnel. The floor was lit with greenish luminescence, showing the cracked stone and remains of vermin. Ran said the emergency exit to Cormallon hadn't been used in generations, and it smelled like it. I followed the tunnel to a wooden door at the end, opened it, and found myself in the back of a garden-supply closet, among rakes and hoes. I opened the closet door very slowly.

I was in the cellar. I looked around at the jagged stone walls, the floor with its carefully fitted blocks, the ceiling.

I almost expected to see two couches there, but there were none. Nevertheless I was nervous simply being in the room and I wanted to get out. I reopened the closet, just to check my potential exit, and saw that there was no door visible at this end. I put my hand against the far wall—it felt like wall.

Still, I wasn't worried. I'd taken too much anarine for that. I headed for the cellar steps, walking as quietly as I could. The stairs came out in the kitchen; huge, deserted, and dark. It was another country entirely with the lights out, a different place from the friendly pocket of food and conversation I'd found when Herel the Cook was holding court. I tried not to knock anything over.

Nobody in the passageway, nobody on the main stairs. My heart was beating faster, I noticed. Given my present rate of pulse, who knew what state of nerves I'd be in if I hadn't gotten blessedly tranked up ahead of time. Eln's Net link was on the second floor; I'd never been in the room, but Ran had drawn a map . . . here we were. There was just a curtain in the doorway, and no sounds coming from inside. Of course, some people can be awfully quiet when they use a terminal. There's no law that says you have to use the audio switch; if you're doing math, it's easier not to. Would Eln be doing math? I dithered in the doorway for a couple of minutes, getting up the nerve to look inside. It was the idea that someone could come along the second-floor passage at any time that finally pushed me to stick my head in and take the risk.

Empty. I hadn't realized I'd been holding my breath. I walked in and steadied the curtains behind me.

Now, let's see. His keyboard was covered with dust. Evidently he did use the audio switch, or else the screen pad and pencil. Not surprising—this was another heirloom terminal, first-generation import, and the keys were Standard letters. Tellys had gone to a lot of trouble to get the Net to accept phonetic renderings of Ivoran words in Standard letters. Ivoran just had too many damn characters, it drove the Tellys technicians crazy. As a result hardly anybody on Ivory used the actual keyboard, they preferred to talk or write on the screen pad. Ran was one of the few people I knew who punched the keys. Probably something to do with his aggressive instinct.

I needed the keyboard. I would leave dust tracks if I hit the keys, and Eln would know someone had been there. I actually stood there for a moment wondering if there was any way I could put the dust *back* on the keyboard after I was finished, before I realized I was being an idiot. It was the anarine, I would like to think. I activated the terminal, sound off.

-CAN I HELP YOU? the screen said. At least, I assume that's what it said. I typed, in Standard, PLEASE USE STANDARD.

-CAN I HELP YOU? it said, obligingly, in readable letters.

-YES, I said.

-PLEASE IDENTIFY YOURSELF.

I typed, ELN CORMALLON, 53462.

-ELN CORMALLON, YOUR NET MATERIAL IS ALL PASSWORD-PROTECTED. TO ACCESS ANY SPECIFIC INFORMATION, YOU WILL HAVE TO PROVIDE SPECIFIC CODES. WHAT AREA DO YOU WISH TO GO TO?

-ACCESS BY SUBJECT.

-VERY WELL.

-SUBJECT IS SORCERY-TRANSFER.

-VERY WELL. PLEASE GIVE ME A SPECIFIC CODE.

-HOW MANY INCORRECT CODES CAN I TRY BEFORE THE SIRENS GO OFF?

-I BEG YOUR PARDON?

-HOW MANY TRIES FOR SPECIFIC CODE DO I HAVE BEFORE SECURITY PROGRAM KICKS IN?

-THREE. BUT YOU CAN TERMINATE YOUR SESSION AND TRY AGAIN AS OFTEN AS YOU LIKE, SO WHY BE COY ABOUT IT.

-I LIKE YOUR SECURITY INFORMATION PROGRAM.

-THANK YOU. FOR AN ADDITIONAL 86,000 TABALS IVORAN A TIGHTER SECURITY PROGRAM MAY BE PURCHASED FROM SOFTSTAR OF TEL-

LYS, AND INSTALLED FOR YOU AT NO EXTRA
COST.

-SUBJECT IS SORCERY-TRANSFER.

-VERY WELL. PLEASE GIVE ME A SPECIFIC
CODE.

I typed, STEPAN.

-INCORRECT. PLEASE GIVE ME A SPECIFIC
CODE.

-I typed, BLUESTONE.

-INCORRECT. PLEASE GIVE ME A SPECIFIC
CODE.

-I typed, RAN.

-INCORRECT. CODE "RAN" IS NOT A
SORCERY-TRANSFER SUBJECT. THIS INFORMA-
TION RESIDES IN ANOTHER BRANCH.

END, I typed. Then I logged on again. We went
through the routine, I asked it to speak Standard, gave
Eln's name and ID number, and tried three of the passwords Ran suggested. None of them worked. I tried
the whole thing again, with three more passwords. Nothing. I did it all again, still no result. Within half an
hour I had gone through Ran's entire list of forty-eight
passwords. Many of them were genuine Cormallon
codes—Eln had apparently wiped them all when Ran was
disowned.

I logged on again, and thought about it. I typed,
KYLLA.

-INCORRECT. PLEASE GIVE ME A SPECIFIC
CODE.

I typed, THEO.

-INCORRECT. CODE "THEO" IS NOT A
SORCERY-TRANSFER SUBJECT. THIS INFORMA-
TION RESIDES IN ANOTHER BRANCH.

-WHICH BRANCH?

-PERSONAL RECORDS.

It was very tempting, but I was pressed for time. SUB-
JECT IS SORCERY-TRANSFER, I typed.

-VERY WELL. YOU HAVE ONE REMAINING TRY
FOR CORRECT CODE.

This session, anyway. But I was running out of guesses.

I thought of the shopkeeper in the jewelry store on Marsh Street. Kylla had told me his name, what was it? While I was trying to remember I decided to do one more code and log off and on again.

I typed, MARSH.

-VERY WELL.

I was about to type END, when I froze.

-VERY WELL? AM I IN SUBJECT SORCERY-TRANSFER?

-YOU ARE IN SUBJECT SORCERY-TRANSFER.

-THANK YOU.

-YOU'RE WELCOME. DO YOU WISH TO CONTINUE WORKING ON THE TIME/INTENSITY GRAPH?

-NO THANK YOU. I WANT TO COPY ALL INFORMATION ON THIS SUBJECT TO PORTABLE MEDIUM.

-WHICH MEDIUM? PLEASE NOTE THAT YOUR PRINTER DOES NOT POSSESS STANDARD CHARACTERS.

-PELLET.

-PLEASE NOTE THAT PELLET GENERATOR HAS NOT BEEN USED SINCE ITS INSTALLATION 53 YEARS AGO. WITHOUT MORE CURRENT TESTING, IT IS POSSIBLE THERE WILL BE DIFFICULTY IN GENERATION OR DISRUPTION OF DATA.

-GO AHEAD ANYWAY.

-VERY WELL.

I looked at the pellet generator beside the terminal, a small glass case with a spindle inside. Real glass, not plastic; that's Cormallon style—it could just as easily have been cut crystal. Sometimes this family got on my nerves.

While I watched the spindle started to turn. It revolved faster and faster, accumulating soft gray material at its base. The gray material grew. When it was about a centimeter wide and three centimeters high, the spindle stopped. I waited another moment for the pellet to harden, then I opened the glass and took it out. I placed it in one of the pellet-holes inside my data-case.

I typed, THANK YOU, I'VE GOT IT.

-DO YOU WISH MATERIAL ON RELATED SUBJECTS ALSO?

-WHAT RELATED SUBJECTS? I asked.

-SORCERY, THEORETICAL

SORCERY, HISTORY

SORCERY, PRACTICAL

SORCERY, CORMALLON

SORC—

I hit the "cut" button. -NO THANK YOU. Then I got a bright idea. I typed, ACCESS BY SUBJECT.

-VERY WELL.

-HOUSEHOLD SECURITY.

-THREE SPECIFIC CODES ARE NECESSARY TO ACCESS INFORMATION. YOU HAVE TWO MINUTES TO ENTER THE FIRST. IF THIS CODE IS INCORRECTLY ENTERED, OR THE TWO MINUTE MARK IS REACHED, THE HOUSEHOLD ALARMS WILL GO OFF. TIME BEGINS NOW.

Great gods of scholars! I leaped out of the chair. Then I stopped, leaned over, and typed END.

-THIS DEFENSE PROGRAM CANNOT BE INTERRUPTED.

I started to sweat.

I ran down the main stairs, skidded to a stop in the passageway and wondered if I should make for the front door; it might not open easily and would start the alarms that much sooner. I wasted half a second thinking about it and then, for no really good reason, kept running through the kitchen and down the cellar stairs. But the emergency exit just wasn't there. I pounded on the closet wall in desperation, and as I did the alarms began to sound. I took the cellar steps upward, two at a time, and headed for the front door. Then I skidded to a stop again—there were people starting down the main stairs. I reversed direction and headed back toward the kitchen. I would have to use the back entrance, although it would mean yet more alarms going off, and then a long sprint around the east wing of the house to get to the front and try to reach the aircar before everybody else did; a hope-less task, but this was no time to think about it. I hit the kitchen running flat out. As I rounded the table, the door to the other passage opened.

It was Kylla. She was wearing a nightrobe and holding a pistol. She stared at me.

Under the circumstances, I didn't know what to say. I opened my mouth, paused, and she said, "Come on."

"What?" I said.

"Follow me," she ordered, with intensity in her voice, and turned away. Having no other alternatives, I did.

She took me down the hall to a door I'd never paid much attention to; it led up some stairs to a garage. There were two aircars there, both four-seaters. She said, "Get in that one. The other one needs repairs." Then she hit a switch and opened the roof doors. "C27 activates it," she yelled to me through the car window. I punched it in and watched the board light up. Then I took off.

There was no time to ask questions, no time to say thanks, no time to look back and wave. I had my hands full just maneuvering.

This model was different from the ones I'd been taught on. The altitude control was foot-operated; what could the manufacturers have been thinking of? I kept dipping groundward as I flew. And while I tried to make sense of the controls I kept thinking, what if they've done something to the barrier? I increased speed with one hand and adjusted the altitude yet again. And where were those damned hills I was supposed to steer by? And why did I have to get stuck in a clumsy four-seater obviously de-signed by the Marquis de Sade Research and Develop-ment Corporation? And where *were* those hills?

I crashed through the barrier. It felt like that, but all that really happened was the familiar tingle as I passed harmlessly through. Just in time—let them do what they wanted to it, now. I scanned right and left, looking for any landmarks, and as I did I must have lost control of the altitude. Suddenly I was a lot lower than I thought I was, and a hillside was rushing up to meet me.

In rapid, useless succession, I jerked up the altitude, I veered sharply left, I saw that neither of these were going to be enough to help; I froze for perhaps one very lengthy millisecond; and I felt a burning sensation in my chest. Then I hit the brakes.

Maybe it would be obvious to people who know what they're doing that the brakes were the first thing I should have gone for. But ever since I'd tripped the Cormallon alarms I'd been operating on a single looped program that said, GET OUT, GET OUT, GET OUT. *Stopping* had, momentarily, seemed like a foreign concept.

It worked. I still came down rough, there was no avoiding it. My teeth jarred in my head. I pulled off the safety web (the de Sade people had gotten one emergency measure right) and rolled my neck tentatively. Everything still seemed to be there, albeit in somewhat bruised condition. At this moment, though, it was perhaps more important that the car be all right. I switched on the control-check and thought, as I waited for the green light, well, it's lucky that in a crisis like this you held together long enough to hit the brakes. Pat on the back for you, Theodora, and we'll overlook the fact you lost control of the thing to begin with. But the pain in my chest continued, and I opened my tunic to see what was wrong.

I was still wearing the Old Man's bluestone pendant. It felt warm. But the back of the silk cover had burnt through, where it touched my chest, and the patch of skin underneath it was blistered, as though from a bad sunburn. I wondered if Annurian knew anything about driving an aircar; maybe I didn't deserve as much credit for hitting the brakes as I thought. I didn't want to speculate about it now, there were too many things to deal with in my immediate future; but I also didn't want the pendant in physical contact, so I pulled it off and stored it in the data-case.

The control-check came up green. I thought I could make out the hills in question farther over to my left, which would make the rendezvous just a few kilometers east. As I was looking out the window, I saw something move in the bushes, like a person's head ducking. At once I snapped my attention to the spot, although it really wasn't fair, I thought; I'd been through enough just now. Nothing else happened, but I was sure that I'd seen it, it hadn't been nerves. I got out of the car, pistol in hand.

"Come out," I yelled.

Nothing. Another bush rattled.

"You'd better come out, or I'll start shooting at random."

Slowly a man's form straightened up from the bushes. He walked out. He was the thinnest person I'd seen in a long time, and his clothes were obviously makeshift. His hair was gray, but he didn't look more than forty-five.

"Who are you?" I said.

"Arno Serren, noble lady," he said. "Please don't hurt me."

His accent was very thick, and I didn't recognize it.

"What are you doing here?" I asked. "And you'd better talk quickly."

"I'm from Tamas District," he answered.

"So?"

"Tamas? Have you heard of it, noble lady? Things are bad there."

So they were, I'd forgotten. There'd been some kind of trouble in Tamas District and Imperial troops had been called in. It had nothing to do with me, I'd never given it much thought; nor had anybody else I'd known.

"You've come a long way, sir Serren." Out of the frying pan, into the fire.

He shifted feet nervously. "I have a long way to go, noble lady, I didn't mean to interrupt anything you might be doing—or to trespass—or to do anything to annoy you. I'd better be on my way."

"Where?"

"Uh, I was going to the Northwest Sector, noble lady."

Oh, gods, what an innocent. To leave Tamas District and go to the Northwest Sector. I couldn't shoot him, I just couldn't. "Sir Serren, I'm going to do you a favor."

"Oh?" The idea didn't seem to make him happy.

"You wouldn't last a week in the Northwest Sector.

And I can't leave you hanging around here to answer questions. So, I tell you what—I'll take you with me."

"You don't have to do that, noble lady. It's too great an honor, believe me. I'll just be going—"

"Get in the car."

"Really, noble lady—"

"Get in, now. I'm in a hurry." I gestured with the pistol. He began moving, very slowly, toward the car door. As he touched it, I heard a squeal from the bushes, and a short, brown human figure raced out and joined him. It was a woman. She was similarly dressed, and clearly very upset. They started talking very quickly, too quickly for me to follow their accents.

"This is my wife, Heida," said Arno Serren.

"Honored by this meeting," I said. "Get in the car, fast."

And so we all took off. It had been a very eventful six minutes.

Three minutes later I touched down at the correct spot. I got out of the car and Ran grabbed me by the shoulders. "We saw the car go down," he said. He looked sick. "Are you all right?"

"Just shaken."

He let out his breath, the same way I'd done when I found the Net link room empty.

I said, "We have to hurry, I tripped the alarms."

He cursed. I said, "It's not that bad, Kylla said the other aircar needed repairs—they'll have to use ground vehicles or horses, it will take longer."

"Kylla?" he asked. "Never mind, you can tell me later."

Meanwhile Arno Serren and Heida were getting out of the car, very uncertainly. They had the look of people who try to stay in the background, wherever they find themselves. Ran's eyes widened.

"Who are these people?" he said.

I told him. He said, "You brought strangers with you at a time like this?"

"You said no witnesses."

"I didn't mean for you to bring them along!"

I said, "I'm not going without them, Ran."

He stood there, breathing hard for a second. Then he said, "Karlas. Tyl. Get over here."

Karlas got on one side of me and Tyl on the other. Karlas' hand touched my elbow, preparatory, I suppose, to picking me up and throwing me in the other aircar.

Ran said, "Get those two back in the car. Tyl, you can drive them to the city. Karlas, you ride with us."

Karlas looked confused. He went over to help Tyl get my two new responsibilities into the stolen vehicle.

Ran called, "Tyl, be sure and ditch the car somewhere far from our house. And don't lose track of our guests."

"Yes, sir," said Tyl. He held out a hand to help Heida Serren enter the car.

"Well," said Ran, "shall we go?"

I climbed in, followed by Karlas. Ran handled the controls. When we were a good twenty kilometers away, he said, quietly, "Kylla helped you get out?"

"Yes."

"Well," he said.

We were all silent for a few minutes. Then Ran said, "What went wrong?"

I told him about the closet door that wasn't there, and about setting off the household security alarm program.

He frowned. "I just don't believe it. How could you have done anything so stu—so risky, Theodora? You're usually so careful. Weren't you thinking? Didn't you realize that if there were anything in the household security program you should know, I would have told you? Of course it's tighter than the general security program, it was set up separately, as part of the package, when Grandfather got the Net links put in. I've been in it a hundred times. Theodora—"

"Look, I know I screwed up, but really, Ran. You fill me up with Ducort and anarine, and then ask me why I do something stupid?"

He bit his lip. Karlas said, "It doesn't affect intelligence."

"Much," I reminded him.

Ran looked over at him. Karlas said, defensively, "She's just a little tiny barbarian. Maybe her system didn't have the capacity to handle it."

A while later Ran said, "Still, bringing those two refugees along was not perhaps our wisest move. I respect your sentiment, Theodora, but we really ought to get rid of them."

I said, "Oh, give it a chance. Isn't it a Cormallon tradition to take in the cream of the ones heading up the Northwest Sector route?"

He considered that. After a bit he stared to smile. He probably missed all the servants he left behind at Cormallon, I thought. Karlas and Tyl were all right, but they didn't wait on him hand and foot. And I suppose he also missed the idea of *household*. He wanted one, even if it had a leaky roof and the noise from the bar next door never stopped.

He said, finally, "I wonder if either one of them can cook."

I grinned. "We can always ask."

Chapter 18

When we got back, I went straight upstairs and fell on my bed. Ran had to sit up waiting for Tyl and our two refugees to reach home, so he could redraw the circle of protection. I slept through their arrival and through the subsequent reshuffling of bedrooms. Most houses in the capital have plenty of rooms, but five sleeping chambers was our present limit; Ran had no intention of sharing his room or letting me share mine, and as a married couple the Serrens seemed entitled to their own. So Halet was routed out of bed and asked to move in with Tyl. When I got up, late in the morning, I found Halet rolling fitfully on some cushions in the parlor, red-eyed and irritable; apparently Tyl snored.

Ran at least was happy. He was up ahead of me, as were the Serrens, and Heida was setting a huge plate of hermit's eggs, smoked saffish, and half a pellfruit in front of him. Arno was still working at the stove. They must have been up hours ago and at the dawn market.

I sat down beside Ran. "Impressive," I said.

He said, "It tastes good, too."

And just last night he'd been implying a quick shooting would be in the best interests of all. Yet once they were in the household they were members like anyone else, and here he was sitting smugly over this breakfast as though he were personally responsible for it.

"Hermit's eggs for me, too?" I asked.

"Ask your sycophants," said Ran, through a mouthful of saffish.

"They're not my sycophants," I said.

Heida hurried over with a cup of tah. "Noble lady," she said, setting it in front of me. "We'll have yours ready in just a moment. We have spices, too, if you want salt or pepper."

"Heida, I'm not a noble lady, hasn't anyone told you?"

She looked flustered. Ran smiled around a forkful of egg.

"I'm sorry, noble lady. I didn't mean to be impolite."

I had the feeling that "Theodora" would be a long time coming from this woman, and that even if I succeeded, I'd be the only one in the house she called by name. I gave up the attempt to foist my outworld principles on her. "How about 'my lady'? We're house members now, you know."

She smiled in relief. "Yes, my lady. We have sliced red peppers, if you would like them?"

She went off to help Arno and I said to Ran, "It reminds me of the first time you told me to call you 'sir.' "

"Undisciplined little tymon, weren't you?" he replied.

I ignored that and took a sip of tah. "I take it you'll be analyzing the pellet data today."

"Of course."

"Do you want me to stick around? I did some analysis on Athena."

He shook his head. "Go to the Square, as usual. We'll look guilty if we break our patterns too obviously."

"Does it matter? Eln's going to have a pretty good idea it was one of us."

"The council won't, and there's no need to get their attention."

I didn't want to bring it up but felt it had to be said. "They've acted without proof before."

"Not without manufactured proof, and that sort of thing takes time."

"And you don't have a Net link code."

"I'll be using Halet's."

Well, there was nothing more to be said. I sipped my tah.

* * *

Apparently he was dead serious about keeping to pattern because he showed up in the Square in late afternoon. He dropped by my tinaje tent before going to set up among the games players. "How's it going?" I asked, when I'd sent off my latest customer.

"Huh," he said, sitting down for a minute. "A lot of numericals, a lot of charts. It's going to take a while."

"We do have the right data, though, don't we?"

He looked tired. "I dearly hope so."

"I can help, if you need it."

"It's not just the analysis, it's what it means. We've got a fine graph, for instance, and I can tell you the formula that describes the curve on it, but what it's doing here I have no idea. I thought from the points on the vertical axis that it was some kind of lunar cycle; but it isn't, quite." He ran a hand through his hair. "Eln's had years to study this, I'm just beginning."

Someone rustled the tent wall; a customer, asking admittance. "Damn," I said.

He rose. "I have to go anyway. I'll see you tonight."

That night was spent going through printouts. We sat on the floor of the parlor staring at one sheet after another. None of it meant anything to me; I could see why Ran hadn't leaped at my offer of assistance. This was heavy going.

Some time after midnight, Ran put down a roll of charts, leaned back against his pillow, and closed his eyes. "No," he said.

"Get some sleep," I said. "You'll do better when you're not so tired."

"Look who's talking. It was just last night you were crash-landing a car outside the Cormallon barrier. A very expensive car, I might add."

"Would you want me to crash a cheap one? Get some sleep."

He smiled, very distantly, eyes still closed. I left him there and went upstairs.

* * *

Someone was shaking my arm. "Wake up. Come on, Theodora, wake up."

"What? What?" I opened my eyes. Ran was standing over me, and a dim light was coming through the window slit. "What time is it?"

"Almost sunrise. Listen, I've got it."

"What?" I said again. He went over to my basin, poured water onto the sponge and brought it back to my bed-mat. He started wiping my face with it. "Hey!" I said. "Hey, that's cold."

He threw the sponge back onto the washtable. It hit the towel with a spongy splat, like a wet snowball. "Listen," he said. "The graphs. They're time-intensity graphs."

"So?"

"Intensity of sorcery," he said impatiently. "On a time axis, because it changes over time—waxes and wanes, just like the moon."

"I don't see why."

"It's not his, you see. He doesn't get it in one lump sum—he has to draw on it continuously, and some times he can draw more than others. So he has to time his plans to fit with how much he can draw on, do you see?"

"I guess. Sort of."

He smiled. "Which gives us the obvious corollary. We time our plans to fit how much he can draw on, too."

I sat up in bed, beginning to get the idea.

Ran and Karlas started disappearing for long periods of time. This did not surprise me. I continued my time in Trade Square, keeping up the pretense of normality over the next several days. Ran told me, over dinner, that the graphs showed the worst low point of the next two months coming—for Eln—in two days' time.

"What does that mean for us?" I asked. "You said he might have a mirror-spell, didn't you? What can you do?"

"For that matter," he said, "what can he do to me? He's taking sorcery from Stepan—what if I aimed my own mirror-spell at Stepan? I've had years of experience in laying boobytraps; I've been in the field and Eln hasn't. He'd be an idiot to do anything directly.''

I said, ''Why don't I feel like applauding? You're both invulnerable, is that what you're saying? And yet somehow I think you have something in mind.''

''All right,'' he said. ''It's nothing you have to worry about. You're not involved in this one.''

I put down my fork. ''What *is* this one?''

He said, uncomfortably, ''I've been meaning to say—you know, Theodora, that I didn't tell you about the Cormallon ground defenses for a reason. If you'd spent days worrying about them ahead of time, you would have been working against yourself in terms of the feedback circuit.''

''Yes, I understood that. What's the point?''

''I just wanted to be sure you knew.''

Was this in the nature of a last will and testament? I hoped I was just being nervous. ''Tell me what's going on,'' I said.

''Look,'' he said, ''we've been struck close to home before. It took months for Vale to dig me out from under. And when it happened, you lost control of the cards first. In terms of magic, we're linked. I don't want to open up any doors right now that we may not want open.''

I leaned back. ''I'm a security risk, is that it?''

''I knew you'd say that. You're not listening. Eln's the best theorist on Ivory in this generation—he's doing things people aren't supposed to be able to do. His point of attack might be the cards. It's nothing personal.''

I looked down at my empty dinner plate. ''He hasn't tried anything before,'' I said.

''He's never been under this much pressure before.''

I was silent. He said, ''It's dangerous. Particularly with this new facility you have with the cards. I don't know what you're tapping into, but it worries me. You can't control it, and we don't have time to study it.''

''All right,'' I said.

''You understand, I'm not being arbitrary—''

''Yes, all right.''

He studied me. He said, "We've got more Ducort in the kitchen. Would you like some?"

"No, thank you."

"Well—Halet's got us a second loan from the bankers, and we might not have much longer to spend it if things don't work out. Would you like to go to the Lantern Gardens?"

"No, thank you. It's late." I rose from my place.

"The show will only just be starting."

Tyl had come in halfway through the meal, and gulped down his food in his usual silence. Now he looked up and said, "Won't you, my lady? I've never been to the Lantern Gardens. I'd like to come along."

So two nights before whatever was going to happen was going to happen, I went out to the Lantern Gardens, escorted by Ran and Tyl. I painted on all the cosmetics Kylla had given me, and not just to make it a grand occasion. I was also hoping the manager wouldn't remember me from the last time I was there.

I was in the Square as usual the next day when Eln came to see me. Stepan was absent this time. He came alone on his floater, maneuvering carefully through the market crowds. It was a fine sunny day, not like the last visit when he had the place to himself.

I was between customers. "Hello, Eln," I said.

"Beautiful day, Theo, and I'm happy to see you're no worse for wear."

"Worse for what?" I said. Was he going to accuse me of the Cormallon break-in?

"For the two and a half Pink Ringers you downed at the Lantern Gardens last night."

"Oh. Barely felt them, I assure you."

"I believe it. And you struck me as such an abstemious girl when you first appeared at Cormallon. For a little outlander, you're developing quite a capacity. Have you been gene-tested for alcoholism? Something to bear in mind if you're going to go on this way."

I squinted up at him from where I sat. "Yes, it is a beautiful, sunny day," I said.

"Sorry about the excess sunlight," he said. "Can't stand it, myself. If you'd let me into your tent here, we could both be in the shade."

The rope I'd tied to the pole might just be high enough today to accommodate him. "Come on in," I said, crawling backward.

He managed to maneuver inside by holding the floater about a centimeter off the ground. "Snug, but service-able," he said. "I suppose you'll be glad when you don't have to squat under a makeshift canvas anymore."

"Oh?"

"The *Queen Emily*. She takes off at the end of the week."

"Oh, yes."

He cocked a head in my direction. "I don't detect that scholarly enthusiasm, Theo. Is there something I should know?"

"Eln . . ." I said. "How's Grandmother?"

He looked serious. "I don't think she has long. She hasn't let me into her room in months." He paused, then said, "I grew up with the idea of Grandmother. She's like a mountain or a rock, you don't imagine anything will happen to it in your lifetime. Now it's like she's gone already. You know, I used to go to her room every night after dinner—even when I didn't show up for dinner—and talk her down so she wouldn't be mad at me."

"Mad at you for what?"

He smiled. "For whatever I'd done."

"I'm sorry," I said. "I don't know much about fami-lies. Or death. I don't know what to say."

He said suddenly, "You're not leaving, are you? On the *Emily*, I mean."

"Maybe I haven't made up my mind. Give me a couple of days, and you'll see for yourself."

He nodded. "You're not leaving. I thought you might not."

There was a tug on the front of the tent just then, and I called, "Busy! Come back later!"

He glanced briefly at the tent opening and said, "You do tinaje for everybody else, but not for me." It was the very echo of what Ran had once said to me, and I tensed. Was he trying to let me know that he had our house bugged? But he seemed to mean it just as he said, could it be a coincidence? "Why not, Theo? I've got some extra time, and riding in the same position every day is hell on my back."

I thought, you ask why not? Because I'm withdrawing from you, and I don't want to do anything to bring us any closer. I'm not going down with you. I may be like you, but I know when to let go.

I sat back on my heels, and he sighed. He looked around the tent, and his gaze rested on my notebook. "May I?" he said.

He leafed through it. "A varied collection," he said. And we spent the next hour talking about my notebook stories. He was probably the only person on Ivory who could have talked to me about my work the way an Athenan would. We agreed that there had been very little drift in the oral storytelling lines over the centuries, and after we compared the northern and southern thematic differences, I said suddenly, "Were you responsible for the aircar fire? Did you know I was inside?"

"Yes," he said, and his voice was unhappy but unashamed. His eyes met mine easily.

"Yes to both questions?" I asked. Never willing to let well enough alone.

He said, "Are you going to send this collection to the University Press on Athena?"

"Yes."

"Then let me tell you a story, too. It would be nice to think of something I've said being read by other people, even if they are barbarians."

I said, "If you make up the story yourself, I couldn't honestly include it. The book is supposed to be folktales."

He smiled. "This is an old one." So he told me a story, short but neat, and I wrote it down as he talked. And I wondered, which is Eln, the one sitting beside me now or the one who tried to kill us? I tried to imagine Ran on a murder attempt one week and teaching his victim sa'ret the next. Imagination failed utterly. He was too straightforward emotionally; the idea of being a friend and an enemy at the same time was beyond him. (And that, I realized suddenly, was how Eln had gotten so far so quickly. Ran had iron rules. He couldn't let himself distrust his brother, not till his face was rubbed in the evidence.)

When he was finished I said, "I've heard this story before; there's a version from Earth. Several versions, actually. But it's got Ivory written all over it."

"I'll take your word for that. You'll keep it, then?"

"I'll keep it." And I got the point of the story, too, which was not to ask questions you don't want answers to. So I shelved matters of guilt and responsibility for the time being.

He said, "I must be going. I'm sorry about this, Theo, but as they say, it's one of those things that happen because we are in this world. I won't be so rude as to say it's for your own good, although, as a matter of fact, it is." He was maneuvering the floater out as he spoke. I followed him outside.

"What are you talking—" I stopped short. Four uniformed Imperial officers were standing outside the tent. *"Damn* it."

"Thank you for waiting," said Eln courteously to the officer in charge. "Please take this for your trouble—" he handed a small bag to the man "—and convey my thanks to your captain. I'll send him my regards as soon as I can."

"Our pleasure," said the officer. He turned to me. "Please come with us, gracious lady."

I looked at Eln. "It's all right," he said, "it's nothing lethal. Best just to accompany these good men, Theo."

For some reason I believed him. And the officer had thrown in that "gracious"—he'd been told to be polite, and why waste that on a soon-to-be corpse?

"Be seeing you, then," I said to Eln.

"I'm afraid not," he replied, "but don't forget those notes I left in your ship's cabin link." And to top it off, he waved as they led me away.

* * *

I thought we'd be going to jail, but instead I found myself being taken up the steps of the Athenan Embassy. "Hey!" I said. The officers ignored me. I was led through those well-lit corridors decorated with tasteful Athenan minimalism I'd learned to know so well, back when I first became stranded. The ambassador's secretary, a young man with an unattractive blond mustache, told the officers that the ambassador would be happy to see us; which was more than anybody had ever told me.

We entered the ambassador's office. He stood up to greet us, smiling for the benefit of the Imperials. It was the same man I'd dealt with in my first year on Ivory, whom I'd last seen in the Lantern Gardens under unusual circumstances; silver-haired and distinguished, everything an ambassador should be. He said, "Won't you gentlemen have a seat?"

My captors eyed the straight-backed Athenan chairs warily; "No thank you," said the officer in charge. "We won't take up your time, gracious sir. Can you identify this woman with us?"

"I can," said the ambassador.

"Theodora of Pyrene?" asked the officer.

"Yes," said the ambassador.

"A distressed Athenan citizen, without a work permit?"

"That's correct," said the ambassador.

"You pig," I said.

"Thank you," said the officer. "Any objections to deportation?"

"Wait a minute—"

"None," said the ambassador.

I said, "You officious pig. You were too regulation to send out my loan request to Athena, and now you've got your hand out under the table like anybody else."

"Will that be all, officers?" he said.

"You sure you want me back on Athena?" I asked him. "The Board of Ethics might not like what I've got to say."

He looked slightly pale, but said, "Well, then, offi-

cers, thank you for consulting me. My secretary will
show you out.''

One of the officers took my arm. "You kanz!" I was
losing my temper, I really hated this man. Eln might kill
me, but he'd do it for a good reason. This one was just
careless and nasty. "Kanz," I said again. Another officer
took my other arm, and they started to pull me away.
"Pig! Ethical moron!" I found my vocabulary running
backward chronologically as my fury mounted. By the
time we reached the door I was throwing in Pyrene epi-
thets. "Anti-social! Enemy of unity!"

They pulled me out.

So this was the *Queen Emily*. Of course I hadn't
planned on staying in the brig, but at least it was clean
and well-appointed. There was even a Net link here, although its security protection was rather stringent. I could
read a few novels and get into the ship's itinerary, but
that was about all. Eln had said something about notes,
but maybe they were time-contingent; or maybe they were
confined to the terminal in the cabin I should have had.

I sat down in the cushioned chair by the link—a soft,
adjustable, Tellys chair, that conformed to my back; it
was lovely, and made you wonder what the first-class
cabins were like—and I considered my situation. My personal effects, including "jewelry" (the Old Man's stone)
and "one deck playing cards" (guess what) were in the
purser's safe, somewhere on the administration deck. I
had a receipt for them. Meanwhile, what was happening
to Ran while I was in here? Eln wouldn't have had me
picked up now for no reason—improvisation was not his
style at all. I ought to have run the cards for Ran, whatever he'd said; maybe I could have seen this coming.

So here I was, on a first-class liner, bound for Athena,
and I wasn't even paying for it. This was where I'd been
aiming for over three long years. This was the culmina-
tion of all that planning and working and constant attention to money.

This was what they called irony.

Chapter 19

I spent the night on a bed that was higher up from the floor than I was used to, so that I banged my knee painfully when I rolled out in the morning. Then I took a shower in the wash stall that appeared when the wall button was pushed. Then more sitting around.

It worried me. Take-off wasn't until tomorrow; Eln had gotten me out of the way ahead of time—why? I wished for the thousandth time that I had my cards.

In late afternoon the door opened. Two men came in, in Ivoran robes, holding pistols in a way that suggested they were very ready to use them. At once I thought two things: one, that Eln wasn't taking any chances, and two, that I shouldn't have threatened the ambassador yesterday. Scared amateurs can do anything.

"Theodora of Pyrene?" asked one man. He was tall and bearded, older than the other.

"Why do you want to know?" I said.

"I'm Hedron, this is Pory—"

Pory interrupted. "She looks like just another fuzzy-brained foreigner to me," he said. "How do we know this is the one?"

"Kylla sent us," said Hedron to me.

"Prove it," I said, as I backed up toward the Net link.

He smiled. "This is the one," he said to his companion. He turned back to me. "Too long, too well I know the starry conclave of the midnight sky; too well the splendors of the firmament—"

"All right, all right." For a second there I'd thought he'd lost his mind. "Why are you here?"

"We're to take you off the ship," he said.

"Then what?"

Pory said, "Then we give you some money and a message, and let you go. Can we get moving?"

"Well?" said Hedron.

"Right," I said, and picked up my empty wallet-pack and followed him out of the room.

The detention section was automated, and I was the only guest there; so we didn't even see any ship's personnel until we were two decks up and heading for the exit locks. The people we passed ignored us, assuming I suppose that we were new passengers for the Ivory-Athena leg, and had a right to be wherever we were. But before we got to the exit, I pulled on Hedron's robe. "Wait a minute," I said.

"What's the matter?"

"I left some things in the purser's safe. One thing in particular, that I need."

Pory said, "We're not supposed to look after your personal possessions. We're just supposed to get you off the ship."

"And we ought to hurry," added Hedron.

"If Kylla had known about this, she would have had you stop for it. It's important."

They looked at each other.

"It's important," I repeated. "In fact, she probably wouldn't want me at all, without this."

Hedron said, "The administration deck isn't too far. All right."

Pory looked unhappy. I said, "One other thing. Can I ask a favor?"

"What now?" said Pory.

"I've got a reputation to think of on Athena. If there are people around the purser's office, and there probably will be—could one of you hold a pistol on me, as if I were your prisoner? I'd appreciate it."

They muttered, but agreed. Lucky thing, too; I didn't

like the way the purser looked at me when Hedron asked him to open the safe. He didn't look any happier when Hedron took off his shirt, tied him up with it, and locked him in.

We lost no time in getting off the ship after that. We marched quickly through the port, off into the city, and didn't slow down till we reached the maze of alleyways behind the Lavender Palace. "All right," said Hedron. Pory stopped, opened his wallet, and brought out a small bag of tabals. I accepted it.

"What about this message?" I said.

Hedron said, "Pory, go over to the jeweler's shop there, and see what's good in the window." Pory left, not without giving me a sulky glance. When he was out of earshot, Hedron said, "You're not to go back to your house. You're to use the money here, buy whatever weapons you think necessary, rent a solo-driving cart, and leave the city by way of the Ostin road. About two hours' ride there's a stand of tasselnut trees on a hill to your left. You'll be met there."

"Met by whom?"

"I don't know; but Kylla said to say, by just who you think. I hope that's clear to you."

"I hope so, too. Thanks for all your help."

He bowed. "Honored by this meeting. Next time you're going to be rescued, try to keep all your possessions in one place."

The sensible thing to do was to go to the wagoner's first; no point buying weapons without a place to stash them. The wagoner was small, pot-bellied, and earnest— he was very earnest about renting me a four-team cart with driver, at only (he said) half the going rate.

I said, "Just a solo, please."

"A solo, gracious lady—believe me, no one in the capital will respect you if you drive a solo. A driver, now, and a fashionable looking team—"

"Friend, I'm no tymon just off the ship. I know what

I want. How about that blue cart with the canvas cover?
Is it available?''

"A wheel was being fixed," he said.

"So is it fixed?" I asked, jingling my coins.

"Of course, gracious lady, it's in perfect condition.
But you'll need at least a paired team—"

"I want one animal, modified for strength, with a drive
implant. Of course, if it's not available . . ."

"Not available! We have every drive animal on the
market in this establishment. See for yourself." He led
me over to the pens, and we quickly settled on a modified
six-legger. I liked this one; it didn't have horns, and regarded me with a look of uninterest which was reassur-
ing. The wagoner handed me the control box. "Ten tabals
a day, and it comes to you fresh fed."

"Thanks. I've never driven one of these before. Which
button does what?"

"I beg your pardon, gracious lady? You're not saying
you want to take my best cart and you don't know how
to drive it?" He looked horrified.

"Oh, come on, sir. It's all straightforward, isn't it?
The animal's trained and implanted? Really—I've piloted
aircars, sir, I can certainly handle a wagon." And
crashed aircars, too, but there was no need to bring that
up at this time.

So at last I was driving the wagon, rather tentatively,
through the city streets. My six-legger was rather large,
but the wagoner had sworn up and down it was herbivo-
rous, and besides, implanted animals have never bothered me deeply; they're practically machines anyway.
There was an arms shop on the northwest wall, by the
exit to the Ostin road. I picked up a couple of short
swords, four rifles, four knives, four pistols, and four
hotpencils and energizers. Then I thought about it and
picked up a pistol and holster for myself. Call me paranoid, but my short stay in the *Queen Emily*'s brig had
gotten me thinking about where I was going in life and
how the plans of mortals come to naught, and a lot of
other things that the philosophical tomes of the university
had proffered; hypothetically, I'd thought at the time.

I drove out past the remains of the old city wall, into the meadows just outside the capital. The sun was still high, in spite of the hour, and the ground I rode over smelled sweet. It was nearly summer. I was on the Ostin road, heading west—this was the easy part, just follow the road until I came to the stand of trees on the hill. Unless I passed it when it became dark; unless I wasn't ready at the right time, because I was driving too fast or too slow to know when I was "two hours" out; unless there was no one waiting for me there—or worst of all, the wrong people were.

It was past twilight when I reached the hill. I stopped the cart and waited. There were no villages nearby, and the last town had been an hour ago; no farmhouses, no inns. It was deserted. The evening air blew against the back of my neck.

After a few minutes a figure detached itself from the grove of tasselnuts. I jumped off the cart and drew my pistol as it walked down the slope toward me. "Hello, tymon," said Ran's voice. "A bit late, but good to see—" He saw the pistol and hesitated. "Were you planning on shooting me?"

"I didn't know it was you, idiot." I dropped the pistol back in its holster, ran up the slope and threw my arms around him. Maybe the stay in the brig had had more of an effect on me than I'd realized, but a good long kiss seemed the logical thing to do.

"Well," he said, looking rather silly as an expression of embarrassed pleasure suffused his face. "Well," he repeated. After a minute he said, "I suppose we'd better get going; we are on a time limit."

"Oh, are we?"

He helped me up into the seat and climbed in behind. He turned to survey the back of the cart, now full end-to-end with newly purchased weaponry. He started to smile.

"I got your message," I said.

"So I see."

"Well, I didn't know what you might need," I said defensively.

"Did I say something ungracious?" Still, he looked suspiciously near amusement.

"Are we meeting Karlas and Tyl?"

"No, they're taking care of other concerns." He picked up the wagon control box. "You know, when I told Kylla to have you rent a solo, I really wasn't sure you could drive one of these."

"This is my first time, actually."

He'd been holding out the box for me to take, and now his hand froze. "Your first time?"

"Yes, but I must say I think I'm every bit as good with it as I am with an aircar."

"I see." He returned the box to his lap. I hid a grin; this made us even for his superiority over the excess weapons.

We continued northwest along the Ostin Road. "How far are we going?" I asked.

"A few hours' ride. There should be enough moonlight tonight to get by. We don't want to miss the turnoff, though; I'll tell you when to start looking for it. Then it's a quarter hour through the trees, and up the Na'telleth Road. Tevachin Monastery is on top of a hill, it shouldn't be difficult to find."

I turned to look at him. "Why are we going to a monastery? Are you withdrawing from the world?"

He laughed. "You say that with such irony. I must be a lot farther from na-telleth-rin than I thought. All right, as you've noted, I'm not joining up; I'm going to avail myself of the monastery's services. They're famous as a meeting place; they provide supervision, security, even arbitration if it's requested. Their reputation is spotless—they see that the rules for a meeting aren't broken by anybody. They're completely disinterested, totally incorruptible, and open to anyone who'll pay their fee."

"Very professional," I said, after a moment. "You're meeting Eln there, aren't you?"

"Does it bother you?"

I shook my head. "It's about time. This situation can't go on forever." I was glad he was willing to attempt negotiation, though surprised Eln had offered it. Or had he? "Whose idea was this?"

"That's the odd thing. I'd been thinking about it for weeks, but only settled on firm plans a few days ago. Before I could make any arrangements, one of the Tevechin monks came to me in the market with Eln's preliminary offer." He frowned. "Our dates coincided. I don't like that. He should be at his weakest point now; why risk coming out? But he *is* at his weakest point," he added with quiet intensity, as if he were talking to himself. "I know he is. I'm sure of the analysis."

"Numbers don't lie."

"No. Unless the data was faked—no, that's too far-fetched."

"Anyway," I said, "I'm glad you and Kylla are on speaking terms again."

"So am I." He stretched his legs out on the foot-rim, and smiled happily. "I suppose she decided that the time for this pretense of neutrality was over."

I raised an eyebrow. *"Pretense* of neutrality?"

"There's no such thing as neutrality, Theodora," he said calmly. "There's indifference, and there's choice."

We came upon Tevachin Monastery at midnight. Pools of rust-colored granite blocks showed under the torches set in the walls. Despite the hour, people were crossing the yard by the main door, leading horses to stable, carrying waterjugs, and seemingly intent on every kind of errand. Trade Square was deserted at this time of night— if these people were leaving the world behind, they certainly seemed to have brought a lot of it with them.

A boy in a brown tunic with no outer robe ran down the front steps toward us. He paused breathlessly by the wagon, putting one hand on the driver's steps. "Ran, declared-to-be-Cormallon?"

Ran said, "Yes."

"And this is your witness?"

"Yes," he said again.

"Honored-by-this-meeting," he said quickly. "Please

come with me, gracious sir and lady. You're expected inside.''

We dismounted and started to follow him up the steps. ''Your wagon will be taken care of,'' he said.

Ran said, ''Do you know if the one I'm meeting has arrived yet?''

''He's not expected till morning,'' said the boy. ''They say he's been delayed by some problem. Or rather, that's the gossip, gracious sir. No one tells me anything official; you'd be better off asking the abbot.''

Ran smiled. ''I'm sure your gossip's right. He's probably dealing with a major problem right at this moment.''

The boy looked at him. As we were in the hallway then, I said, ''These portraits along the walls, are they members of your order?''

''Past abbots and teachers, gracious lady.'' He led us down another corridor. Interesting order; half of them looked like schoolmasters, and half of them looked like horsethieves. I stopped to peer at one unshaven countenance who had particularly shifty eyes. ''If you could move along, gracious lady,'' said the boy.

''Sorry,'' I said, and followed. I wouldn't have bought a used wagon-beast from that man. Or a used virgin either.

''Here we are.'' he said.

The sign over the old wooden door read: ''If the fool would persist in his folly, he would become wise.'' The boy pushed it open and stood aside.

''That sounds familiar,'' I said to Ran, frowning. We entered the room.

The abbot was a tall, heavyset man, more physically suited to be a wrestler than a spiritual leader. Maybe he *had* been a wrestler before he declared na 'telleth. He bowed to Ran and held out a hand to me.

''The outworlder! Athenans shake hands, do they not?'' And he enveloped mine in a hurricane-force, but somehow friendly, crush. ''I trust I performed it correctly,'' he said as he peered at me hopefully from beneath bristly red-brown eyebrows.

''Oh, perfectly,'' I assured him, glancing at my flushed

knuckles. Perhaps one day he'd be introduced to the Athenan ambassador; let that gentleman get his share of what I got.

Ran said, "I understand the person I'm meeting isn't due till morning."

The abbot sighed. "So much for secrets in this House. Still, sir, you may be assured that whoever mentioned this to you would not have brought it up if you were not one of the principals. It's only among ourselves that we can't seem to keep effective security."

"Quite all right," said Ran.

"Believe me, private matters never leave Tevachin."

"Your reputation assures it," said Ran politely.

The abbot motioned us to some red silk cushions. "Well, it is true your man is delayed. We expect him before sunrise, though—I hope this doesn't disturb your schedule unduly."

"It's within my parameters," said Ran, "I can adapt."

"Good, good. And we have beds ready for you if you wish them; food, baths, meditation rooms—whatever is your preference. Or, Brother Camery could take you on a tour of the monastery. He's quite used to dealing with those who are still tied to the wheel—he's the Master of Novices. Does a lot of negotiating with the families; he doesn't mind the company of the unenlightened, I assure you."

"That's very kind of you to say," said Ran. "But first, do I take it that the sunrise meeting seems to be firm?"

"Circumstances would support such a view. Two of our monks are accompanying your man at this very moment; and he's given his bond to appear during this day." An Ivoran day is from sunrise to sunrise; so the latest Eln could show up was in about six hours. "What can I say?" added the abbot. "It's as firm as anything is in this life."

"In that case," said Ran, "I would like a meditation room. My witness might want to see the tour, though."

I looked at him in surprise. He said, "Unless you'd rather have a bed, Theodora. But you seem pretty awake."

I turned back to the abbot. "The tour," I said, "Thank you very much."

Brother Camery was an apple-cheeked old gentlemen with wings of thick white hair that went back on each side of his head, leaving a rosy baldness on top that matched his chubby pink face. He was talkative, charming, and sharp-eyed, with that "retiree look" I was coming to associate with many of the monks. "Happy to oblige," he said, when I apologized for the lateness of the hour. "I often don't sleep until dawn in any case. Many of my duties are night duties."

"Oh?" I said. What do novices do at night, polish the breakfast silverware?

"Here we are," he said. He shook out a large ring of keys. "We can see the kitchens first, or the dining hall, or the gardens, or the library—"

"Is that a library with books?"

"What other kind would there be? Or we could see the Arena of Magic, or the Hall of Delights, or the Initiation Wing. Most outsiders," he lowered his voice confidentially, "wish to see the Hall of Delights."

I said warily, "Maybe we could work up to it."

"Then perhaps the Arena?"

"As you say," I said, and we started down the red-tiled corridor. "I understand the meeting I'm to witness won't take place till morning."

"So I hear," he agreed. "Dawn and sunset are the traditional times for a meeting. I'm to be one of the outside observers myself; quite looking forward to it."

We were passing more portraits. There was a wide doorway with another sign above. I didn't know all the words on this one. "What does that say?" I asked Brother Camery.

"The Road of Excess leads to the Palace of Wisdom," replied the master of novices. "It's the entrance to the Hall of Delights." He chuckled. "Given the hour, probably half my novices are in there right now, gathering wisdom." He leaned over and put his ear to the door. I joined him, unable to resist.

There was either an orgy or a torture session going on inside. From the occasional punctuating giggles, I decided it was an orgy; unless the torturers were both sadistic, and from the tone of their voices, about fourteen years old. "I thought you left the world behind when you came here."

He laughed. "There is more than one way to purge desire. It's a disease we're all born with, and here we inoculate against it. 'You never know what is enough until you know what is more than enough.' "

"Do all your novices spend time here?"

"Most do. For some, this is not the way. But the majority of people have a great deal of foolishness to root out. 'He who desires but acts not, breeds pestilence.' "

I looked at Brother Camery with some impatience. These sayings were beginning to get on my nerves; and they were very familiar, somehow. The brother smiled back at me benignly; it was hard to imagine him as a pimp, but I suppose he saw his duty and he did it.

On the way to the Arena, I said, "The furnishings here are very impressive. I didn't expect a monastery to be so well-appointed."

He shook his head. "The taxes," he said mournfully. "You have no idea. But we do the best we can. As the inductor of novices, young lady, I can say with some pride that my services bring in a fair sum each year."

"How so?" We were going down stairs, and more stairs. It was making me jumpy, being this isolated with a stranger. I tried to determine if there was reason for my discomfort or if I'd just picked up the natural paranoia any Ivoran feels in unusual circumstances.

"The novice fee," explained Brother Camery. "We generally charge fifty percent of the individual's net worth at the time of application. He can dispose of the other fifty percent in whatever way he wishes."

By now we must be a good twenty meters underground; way too far to yell for help. I said, "I didn't know the families allowed individual property, in that sense of the word. I thought everything was held communally." The whole point behind Eln's mudslinging against his brother was that Ran had separated his money out from theirs, a clear sign that he no longer identified his interests with the family's.

"Most families practice communal financing," agreed the Novice Master. "But one can always ask for his share and resign."

"Share?" It was the first I'd heard of it. "I didn't think a family membership could be converted to money."

"Everything can be converted to money," said the Novice Master.

It was probably the closest this planet came to a universal religious statement.

He continued, "Often the applicant will put the other fifty percent back into the family treasury, as a goodwill gesture, although there's no rule that they have to. So the families usually come out with a profit of sorts, and they think well of the monasteries and don't make a fuss when people come to us."

The corridor was blocked here by two immense wooden doors. They were bright crimson, with the sorcery symbol painted half on each, and an iron bar drawn across. Brother Camery reached for the bar. As he touched it, sparks flew and the sound of electrical sizzling came and went. He drew back his hand sharply, grasping it hard with the other.

"Oh, dear," he said.

"Are you all right?" I asked. The hand that had touched the bar was turning an unpleasant shade of pink.

"Yes, thank you. Nothing to be concerned about. I should have thought—but the meeting isn't scheduled until sunrise. I hoped we might enter the outer rings. I suppose they put the protections up when they thought it might be used at midnight, and when your party was late they just left them up." He raised his voice toward the door. "May we enter?"

The answer was an ominous rumbling, like a stormy sea. It swelled until it filled the corridor, then faded away.

"Not promising," he said. "Well, I must apologize for having brought you this way for nothing. Still," he brightened. "You'll see it all at dawn, won't you? And at its best, which few visitors do. I've only seen it used twice, and I've been here for fifteen years. Of course, I'm often away gathering up my novices when duels are taking place.''

"When what?" I froze.

"When duels are scheduled to take place. My duties involve a great deal of travel—"

"What duels? What do you mean by duels? And what do they have to do with me?"

He seemed at a loss. "You're to be a witness, aren't you, at the sunrise meeting?" I must have given him a look as blank as his own, for he went on, "I understood—unless I was mistaken—that there was to be proper duel magical, to settle an internal Cormallon matter. We were to provide the arena, the outside observers, and the arbiter.''

I continued to stare.

He said, "I'm sure—yes, I *am* sure—that I'm not mistaken. Certainly there's a duel scheduled. We have everything set up and ready. And I must say, they could not have chosen a better House. No rule-breaking here; not in five hundred years. And we handle everything, so there's nothing for the principals to worry about but their performance. We open the rings to magic, we seal off the arena, we have clean-up crews, even provide burial with our own services, should the victor not want the responsibility." He paused. "Always providing there's something left to bury. Are you all right, child? You look terribly pale.''

I said, "I have to go."

He said, "Of course. This way, my dear."

Chapter 20

By the time I'd climbed the third flight of stairs I was dead-angry. I left the Novice Master far behind, clanking his keys, as I stalked down the main hall. I saw the boy who'd first shown us in, and stopped him. "My companion is supposed to be in one of the meditation rooms. Do you know where he is?"

He was startled by my tone. "Uh, yes, I can show you—"

"Then show me." I was grinding my teeth.

He led me down the hall to a room in another wing. One of the younger monks was sitting on a stool just outside, and rose to stand between me and the door.

"Excuse me," he said politely. "This is a meditation room."

"I know," I said, and aimed for the door again. He moved to block. I stamped my sandal down on his bare foot and reached for the knob.

His arms clamped around my shoulders, pinning me against his chest. "Excuse me," he said in the same courteous tone. "Would you be Theodora of Pyrene?"

"Yes," I said, tentatively. I stopped struggling, partly because I felt guilty about his foot, which would be black and blue by dawn, but mostly because it wasn't working.

"I have a message for you." He turned around, taking me with him, and we both faced out into the hall. Then he released me.

"Oh?" I said.

"Your companion asked if you would mind leaving him undisturbed until dawn."

"I mind," I said.

"He said, if you have any interest in keeping him alive, you would please respect his wishes."

Damn damn damn. "Were those his exact words?"

"Virtually. He did not say 'please.' "

"All right." I turned away, then looked back briefly. "Sorry about your foot," I said, not really with graciousness.

The monk returned my gaze. "What foot?" he asked.

I walked away followed by the boy, who had stayed to watch the entire encounter with frank interest. I was glad somebody around this place beside myself wasn't na'telleth.

"Where are you going?" he asked. It was a good question.

I said, "Are there any other meditation rooms free?"

"Dozens," he said. "It's a big place."

"So I've heard. Could you take me to one?"

"Of course." He took the lead. "How did you like the arena?"

"I haven't seen it yet, but I gather it's just a matter of time."

"Oh. I thought Camery took you there."

"It was locked."

He seemed disappointed. "I was hoping you could tell me about it, I've never been in there. I don't think old Camery's been there twice since he lost his name."

"His name is Camery, isn't it?" I asked.

The boy looked up at me with that "we-have-to-excuse-the-tymon" look I'd seen so often. "Camery is an old word that means 'counselor.' It's the traditional reference-name for the Master of Novices. Other brothers have other nicknames; they shift around a lot. But nobody keeps his birth name, gracious lady. It would confine his behavior."

"Confine it to what?" I said.

"To what he expected of himself." He looked confused, more by my needing to question it than by the topic. "Here we are, gracious lady. Meditation rooms can be locked from the inside, if you want to."

"Thank you. Listen, could you, or could somebody else, come by before dawn and get me? I don't want to lose track of the time."

He grinned. "No fear of that, the bells will toll half an hour before the duel. It's a big event here, you know."

"Oh," I said. He bowed and sauntered off down the corridor. I went inside.

The room was small and bare, with a gray woven rug and a pile of pillows. There was no window. An iron lamp hung from the center of the ceiling, flickering.

Maybe I was making a major mistake. Maybe this was not the time to ignore Ran's advice and leave the road of caution. But I was at a loss, I needed answers, and there was one place I'd been taught to expect them.

I pulled out the pack of cards.

Sitting there on a faded blue pillow, under the lamp, I held the cards in my left hand until the warmth of my body heat penetrated the deck. I was not going to snatch. I was going to creep up on them gently, bearing my destination in mind every step of the way. Above all, I was not going to think about how many hours remained until dawn.

It had never taken me so long to begin a reading before. Finally I drew the center card and turned it face up on the rough gray rug. The illustration was the Evening Star. Four-pointed, hanging low on a dusky horizon of shadowed hills, and watched by two figures facing away, toward the star, too indistinct to identify even as male or female.

The star drew me up to it like dew from the grass. I was hurtling through the twilight, the sky around me growing blacker and blacker. The star was many-pointed now, with arms stretching in all directions, touching the earth and the heavens in a blaze of incandesence. Energy surged up the arms to the center, where I was pinned like a butterfly in helpless joy. It was beautiful and frightening.

Back in Tevachin Monastery, the small and worried part of me that watched came to a decision and broke physical contact with the card. Abruptly there came a sensation like a blow to the back of the head, and all of me was sitting on the pillow in the meditation room, unsettled and a bit sick, wits scattered in all directions. Along with the blow to the head came an afterimage: Eln imprisoned in the center of the star. His arms and legs were the star's arms, pinned down somehow and yet reaching in all directions. It was as if he were a starfish— or a spider—even as I'd thought it the image shifted to a luminescent web, and I was kicked out of heaven and back to Tevachin.

Gods. That was one to give you the shakes; I'd never felt anything like *that* before. And did I have any idea what it meant? Not a clue.

This is doing no good, said one part of my brain to the rest; best put these cards away and let Ran handle things whatever way he wants. Doubtless that was the part of my brain responsible for my sanity—I noticed that my left hand, still holding the rest of the pack, was trembling. I made an effort to stop it, to no visible effect.

How many hours left till dawn? I drew out another card before I could change my mind.

But I was no longer relaxed. Too much information, I thought vaguely, on too many levels. I realized suddenly that accessing what I would call the "symbolic" level of the cards was like reading a line of poetry. There was a lot being communicated—and it was subject to interpretation.

Enough of this, I thought, snapping shut like a clamshell. I'm not one of these na'telleths; give me plain language. And finally I brought myself to look at the card.

It was the Prisoner card, I'd drawn it before. The man in chains melted into a man in ropes even as I watched; it was Stepan. Another man, about the same age and wearing a cheap brown overtunic, walked behind Stepan's chair. He pulled on the ropes as though testing their strength, then nodded and said something to someone outside the frame. I bent over closer, trying to get a better look.

The man in the brown overtunic was Tyl, and it didn't take sorcery to know the person he was speaking to was Karlas. I sat up straight and considered the matter. So Ran had Stepan tucked away somewhere; that wasn't surprising when one thought about it. He would have done that, if he didn't kill him.

Then this was his method of preparing for the duel; to separate Eln from his magic source. In the meditation room Ran could take care of the spiritual side of preparation, but he was not one to overlook the practical.

I drew a third card and laid it right of center. The Traveler, with her rucksack and her staff, striding through a forest in red fisherman's trousers. That brought back memories. Was this supposed to be me? I didn't want it to be; the thought of involvement made me nervous. Then the clothing changed to an embroidered robe, and the staff disappeared, and the figure was mounted—and it was Eln. Mounted, but he and his floater were both inside an aircar, and a pretty luxurious one it was. Traveling fast. The night sky flashed by behind his image. The seats on either side of him were occupied by two brawny men in monk's robes. I watched for several minutes and could see the sky lighten to pearl and Eln's features coming into relief. He was talking to the monks, no doubt trying as host (since I assumed the car was his) to amuse his escorts. The last thing I saw was the jumbled stone mountain of Tevachin Monastery growing in the window beyond.

Almost here, then, or would be by sunrise. What kind of preparations had *he* made? You would think the cards would be more forthcoming.

I packed the deck away in its case and left the room. The corridor was deserted. There was a long, narrow window at one end, and a few stars were visible through the bars. It was still full night, then; maybe what I'd seen in the final card was the future. Unless it was the past . . . but it had been on the right side of the center . . . no, you could drive yourself crazy second-guessing the deck. Keep your first impression, it's usually the right one.

I found my way back to Ran's room. The monk I'd argued with earlier still sat on guard outside, in the same position I'd left him; I decided not to stop.

Eventually I found the main hallway and the entrance. It was not a comfortable place to wait: no benches, no cushions, just a stone floor. Thinking it over, it occurred to me that this was not a place where people stood heavily on custom, nor indeed where they cared much one way or another what a tymon might do. So I sat down in the middle of the hall, facing the entranceway, and waited.

At least the floor was clean.

There was no way of judging the time from where I sat. Hours seemed to pass. A few of the lamps had begun to sputter, and I'd had a lot of time to think, when the main doors opened and Eln came in with his two escorts.

Typically, he was still talking as he entered, his head half-turned to face one of the monks; then his gaze moved over me and he fell silent.

"Theo," he said a second later. "What are you doing here? If you'll forgive my triteness in asking," he asked.

"They tell me I'm a witness," I said.

"Ah," he said, and nodded. "I might have known, sacred custom and all. Wish I had time to talk with you, sweetheart, but I'm running late. You wouldn't believe the problems I've been having . . . maybe you would. Still, we'll laugh about this someday, if we're drunk enough. Maybe we can get together in the Lantern Gardens some night and give it a try." He seemed ready to go on his way.

I said, "This is *stupid*, Eln."

"I agree completely. Was there anything else? I really am late—"

"Then *why* are you going through with it?"

He sighed. "When something has to be done, it has to be done, Theo; that's the only universal law there is. I'm as weary of all this as anybody, believe me." And he did look very tired at that moment, not just in body but in mind. "I want it to be over. It's worth going through all this, to be able to say that in a few hours it will be done. Settled. Behind me." He started to move down the hall, then stopped and smiled wryly. "Say, Theo, shouldn't you be lifting off around now?" I blushed. He said, "Nobody ever stays where I put them." He moved on a little farther.

I yelled, "Damn it, Eln, go home!"

He turned back for the last time. From the look on his face you'd think I'd said something funny. "When I remember all the times I said the same thing to you. Listen, Theo, I lied when I saw you in Trade Square. The deal's still open. When this is over, I'll get you another ticket, if you want one." He left.

It was so unfair. I wanted so much to hate him wholeheartedly. The gods knew I ought to hate him, after what he'd done. Why was it so easy to forget what he'd done, and what he'd tried to do? Not to mention what he would *still* do if he could . . . Eln and his sister were very much alike in some ways, I saw suddenly; they were both the sort of people who got away with a lot. I couldn't see Ran doing the things Eln had done and still being loved, still being the favorite. What must it have been like growing up in that family? Why, I couldn't even total up the treacheries Eln had committed, against his brother, against me, against Ran's first card-reader, against (for all I knew) Stepan. There was a jeweler on Marsh Street who still wanted to know where he was.

So why was it so easy to forget all this? Because he was charming? Did that give him the right to hurt people? Or was it because he hurt so much himself? Sometimes I couldn't look at him without cringing.

I hadn't stood when Eln came in. I still sat in the shadow of the open door, feeling helpless. Tears were starting down my face. I needed an hour or two of mental collapse, but the patch of light on the floor beside me was gray with the threat of sunrise.

I got up and walked very quickly toward Ran's room, wiping my face. As I did so, the bells began to toll.

* * *

The monk on watch was gone, and I felt a stab of panic. What if Ran was gone, too? I pushed open the door.

Ran stood there, dressing with the help of two monks. They looked up briefly as I entered. One monk handed him a crimson-and-gold belt, with gold tassels, and he clasped it over his tunic. "Do you think the white outer robe?" he asked them. He looked at me. "What do you think, Theodora?"

My face must have been a puckered and reddened mess—it always was from the least bit of crying—but Ran was studiously careful to avoid comment. I said, "What the hell do you think you're doing?"

One of the monks got up from where he knelt around the back of Ran's robe and started toward me. Ran said, "No." It was only one syllable, but I could feel the enforced calmness in it. "I'll take care of it. Theodora, I can see you're upset about this, but we did discuss it on the way here—"

"I didn't know this was what you meant! I'm a tymon, I don't know everything about your stupid culture!"

"I'm sorry if I was unclear—"

"And now that I know, I'm telling you it's *stupid.*"

Ran said to the monks, "Would you do me the courtesy of waiting outside? I'm almost done anyway."

One of them said, "The procession is supposed to start in ten minutes."

"I know," said Ran. "I'll be ready."

They left, ignoring me. I said, "Ran—"

He cut me off. "Listen, because I don't have a lot of time. It's too late to do anything now. Understand? The contract's been signed. We're both under monastery enforcement. It's past time to back out. With that in mind, do you think it's a good idea to push me into an argument when I've spend the last six hours calming myself down for the duel? I have to be totally in control of myself to get out of here alive, and *I am not at my best under pressure.* If you want to kill me, getting me upset right now would be a good way to do it."

I lowered my voice, and forced myself to speak as if I were commenting on the weather. "I really would prefer that you didn't do this. I don't know anything about contracts, but there must be some way of getting out of it. What's the penalty for noncompliance? Confiscation of goods? We've gone without before—"

"The penalty is death," he said, in an equally disinterested tone of voice.

It was the strangest argument I have ever had. It was the one I most wanted to win, and the one I tried hardest not to care about when I had it.

"You can't think of any way out? Tell me the truth," I said, not as if I really wanted to know.

"Face it, Theodora. It's settled. It will happen." He was pulling on the white outer robe as he spoke. "See if the back is even?" he said.

I checked. "It looks fine."

"Was there anything else you needed to say?" he asked.

For the life of me, I couldn't think of anything beyond grabbing him by the sides of the robe and shouting "Stop this, you idiot." But that didn't seem to be wise, under the circumstances. "Nothing," I said.

He opened the door, and held it for me to go first.

The procession started from the main hall. Eln wore dark blue silk, and a white outer robe much like Ran's. Maybe it was his, and maybe the monks spared no expense when other people picked up the fees. Probably cheaper in the long run to have each duelist already decked out in a decent burial robe. Someone handed me a candle.

I followed directly behind Ran. Someone from Cormallon must have met Eln here; a young man in gray, vaguely familiar, walked behind the floater. He couldn't have shown up this late; he must have been here the whole time Ran and I were. Apparently the monks could keep news about outsiders to themselves after all.

We filed down the halls to the back of the monastery. There seemed to be more than the usual number of monks hanging about in doorways, watching us pass. We did not turn to the stairways, as I expected, but continued out of the building and into a covered tunnel of gray stone that led downward into the hill. By this time there were about twenty of us in the procession; I recognized the abbot and Brother Camery. A half dozen of us on line were women, but I was the only one who looked to be under the age of ninety. The ramp spiraled downward interminably.

At last we came up against double doors with the sorcery symbol half on each, twins to the ones Camery had shown me last night. The man at the front of the line stopped, reached into a velvet bag, removed a red cap of three cylindrical sections, and placed it gravely on his head. "The Protocol Master," he announced. The doors creaked open.

As each person entered the Protocol Master would say, "Eln Cormallon, principal. "His witness, Jermyn Cormallon." "The Master of Novices." "Duelmaster and Arbiter." "Ran, declared-to-be Cormallon." He put out his hand to stop me.

"Disarm, please," he said, in a more conversational tone.

Ran looked back. "She's not wearing anything," he said. "She never wears anything."

I pulled open my outer robe to show the holster underneath.

Ran sighed. "Once they start," he muttered.

"I was nervous," I said. I pulled off the holster and pistol and handed them to the Protocol Master. "What about my knife?" I asked, before anyone else could bring it up.

"You call that fruit-cutter a knife?" asked one of the witnessing monks after me on line. Monks left the rules of courtesy behind when they dropped their names, and were rude or polite according to whim. They could get away with it because nobody took na' telleths seriously.

"We're only interested in energy weapons," said the Protocol Master more kindly, seeing my discomfort.

"They might disrupt the force-patterns inside. That would be most dangerous."

"Oh," I said, not understanding. He let me pass through the doors.

I was totally bewildered. We'd gone *down*, hadn't we? So what were we doing outside, on what appeared to be a hillside? We were standing in what seemed to be some sort of amphitheater, on the edge of the center arena, and around the sides steps rose up to three or four times the height of an Ivoran. Beyond that, I could only see sky.

The monks filed out into the amphitheater and lit torches around the inner wall. It was still dark down in the arena. I looked around and saw the other monks had gone up into the seats, and as I peered up at them they seemed to become fuzzy and indistinct. I turned slowly around, frowning at the seats.

"As observers, they are not allowed to intrude on the event." The voice startled me. It was the Duelmaster-Arbiter, standing beside me. He was a tall man in silver, with an old, old, face. He reminded me of the Old Man of Kado Island, and I liked him, perhaps unreasonably.

He said, "Do the principals have anything to say to each other? This will be their last chance to do so. No record will be made, either by writing or on tape, of any words spoken now."

Eln was about to make his way to the other side of the arena. He halted and turned, an expression of polite interest on his face. Ran stopped also. He said, "I have nothing to add."

"Nor I," said Eln.

"I trust you're in good health," said Ran.

"Adequate. I trust you're the same."

"Yes." He turned. "Duelmaster-Arbiter, I think we've said all there is to say."

"Apparently," he agreed. The Duelmaster motioned them to move to their places.

I followed Ran. For all their surface coolness, there was a great deal of emotion in that moment, emotion of the sort I have never liked, mixed emotion. Hatred beneath good manners is an Ivoran specialty, but here there was something both familiar and repellent to me; it was as though they were too close to each other to breathe and extreme feelings were the only kind left to them. I wondered if such strong and confused emotion was rare, or if I had simply never been close enough to another person to be aware that they were capable of it. I wondered if I were capable of it. I wondered if it would be a good or bad thing if I were. And I wondered fleetingly and for no logical reason what my guardian-mother on Pyrene had thought when I left without looking back. It was the first time that any thought of leaving Pyrene which was not tinged with relief had ever crossed my mind.

I turned with some haste to the Duelmaster-Arbiter. "Where do I go?" I asked him. "What should I be doing?"

"Stay here on the side, under the pillars. Be ready to help your man if he needs it. Watch everything."

"That's all?"

"That's a great deal." He looked down at me. "You're an outlander. Has anyone explained the event to you?"

"No, Duelmaster, they haven't."

"Well, it begins when I declare it begun. There are rounds of combat followed by periods of rest; a round lasts about five minutes."

"Five minutes doesn't seem very long." I said.

"When two sorcerers are trying to kill each other, five minutes can contain eternity. I've never seen a duel that lasted beyond fifteen."

I didn't like the bald way he put it. But what I really didn't like was the bald fact of what was happening.

"I must go out now and read the contract," he said. "There's a bench, if you want to sit."

"Thank you, I'll stand."

He moved out into the center of the arena. Ran came over to stand beside me; across the ring I saw Eln and his witness waiting, too. The Duelmaster-Arbiter called, "Attention, principals and witnesses. The contract has been signed and agreed to this day, under the enforcement of Tevachin. All mirror-spells have been stripped.

No vengeance is contemplated against anyone for anything which may take place today. Let all witness.''

Ran sat down on the bench. I didn't know how he could. The Duelmaster said, "Tevachin attests to the fact that papers have been left with responsible Cormallon parties, absolving Ran Cormallon of any infractions and passing inheritance back to him; these papers to be opened at noon unless word saying otherwise reaches the main estate. Tevachin attests to the fact that arrangements have been made to release one Stepan Cormallon, and to terminate the employment of all other persons, unless word saying otherwise reaches the capital. Let all witness.''

He lifted an hourglass, turned it gently up and down again. The sand, if it was sand, glittered like gold dust. "This is the measure of one round," he said. "When the sand is falling, all rules of the duel apply, and will be enforced by Tevachin. Between, before, and after the rounds you may do as you like—once the first round is over, you are free to leave, if you like, and not come back. But once a round begins, you are bound to stay in the arena until the end. Am I clear?''

I saw Eln nod, across the way. Ran stood up. "Clear," he said.

"Ran—" I said, and bit it off. He walked down into the dueling pit. Eln came in from the other side. The Duelmaster came up and stood beside me, briefly touching my hand.

The arena was a granite hollow, a grainy gray-white surface that sloped to center. The floor was dingy with ancient dirt. "The sun," whispered the Duelmaster to me, and I looked over my shoulder to see the brightness in the east. The top rows of the other side of the amphitheater were exposed in the light, showing three old nuns swathed in robes against the morning chill. "Now," said the Duelmaster, and because his voice was so low I thought he was still talking to me. There was a muted rumbling of distant thunder that seemed to come from all directions. It fused and intensified until it came to sit underneath the arena. I thought, "earthquake." I wanted to run, but no one else seemed disturbed. I glanced up toward the three nuns, but the top row was dark again; I turned hurriedly to look behind, and the sun was gone. There were no clouds, it was just gone!

It hit me then at last, far too late. All the figures, all the calculations, all the driving engine of rational thought that made the outrunners of the theme; I'd forgotten that what we were dealing with was *magic*. As electric power lived in the massive force of water breaking through a dam, as it lived in lightning, the force retains its essence. Ivorans had come to terms with magic, they let it serve them and give them comforts, a wolf-creature tamed to a dog. They took the idea of passion and made legal marriage out of it, and so were able to make daily use of it. And I could see now that they were right to do so; I would rather room with a dog than a wolf. But the dog still had its teeth, and beneath the marriage sheets the bodies and hearts were unchanged.

They were still in the arena, like standing stones, in their white silk robes. Then Eln moved somehow—I couldn't see it, but there was a flash of midnight blue from his tunic in the midst of all that white and gray— and he rose into the air; and all at once there was an eagle there, a huge thing only a few wing-beats from the bottom of the pit. And not quite an eagle, for the claws were enormous. I was too startled for a second to look at Ran, and when I turned back to him I saw a blood-red dragon, at least ten meters from top to tail, its narrow head stretched into the air. The jaws opened and a stream of fire jetted out, scorching the eagle. It backed up hurriedly, the feathers on one side turning a grayish black.

"Oh, gods," I said weakly. I heard the Duelmaster's voice, as though from very far away, saying, "Yes, mythical creatures are always best for a beginning. Use them while you have the strength, that's the strategy."

I must have groaned. He said, "Are you all right, little outworlder?"

"How can this be happening?" I asked.

He said proudly, "Tevachin has the greatest dueling arena in all the world. It has been used for nothing but magic for the last fifteen hundred years, and all the thoughts of generations of monks and nuns have gone to building its power. I'd like to see a transmutation of such size and speed as that eagle was be tried in any other arena! And I don't care how good the sorcerer is.''

The eagle was circling the dragon, looking for an opening. Another approach, another stream of flame. ''Eagles aren't mythical,'' I said dully.

''I beg your pardon?'' asked the Duelmaster.

I grasped his robes and tugged. ''Is any of this actually happening?'' I begged.

''You should really enroll in the morning novitiate's class on the nature of reality,'' he said. ''However, I know what you mean, and the simple answer is no, it is not. Like all simple answers that is a lie; but it's the best I can do for you, child.''

''What happens,'' I said, ''if the eagle kills the dragon?''

He seemed faintly surprised. ''Why, I don't know, outworlder. Are you asking me to speculate on the change in linear events that occurs when one person dies? As someone who appears to be acquainted with both the dueling parties, you should know better than I.''

The last stream of fire hadn't gone as far as the others, and the eagle hadn't seemed to have minded it as much. Now it stooped for a run at the dragon's side. The dragon swivled its neck around, but too slow and too late; a rip ran through its hide, tail to throat. Blood started to drip, starting at the tail. The blood was black.

The eagle made another run, still avoiding the head. This time it didn't pull back at the final moment, and the force of the collision knocked the dragon half over. Another slash of the talons. A futile stream of fire, way off target; the dragon was immobilized. The eagle began to slash at the underbelly, pulling out the guts onto the floor of the pit.

And suddenly the dragon was gone. On the other side of the pit stood, of all things to find on this planet, a grizzly bear. It stood three meters tall, brown, a perfect copy of what I'd seen in the Zoo of Past Species on Athena.

It growled. The eagle beat its wings, just once, and seemed to compress itself into a ball; when it opened out again, it was a lion in mid-spring, heading for the bear. It was hard to follow this phase of the combat; for a moment I wasn't even entirely sure who was what. But the golden blur was Eln, and the snarling mass of fur was Ran. They rolled down the side of the pit, brown and gold, and streaks of red.

"I thought the dragon was dying," I said to the Duelmaster.

"Each one can change as often as he likes—that's generally whenever he's losing. The opponent must transmute to follow. Until, of course, the loser has no strength left to change. Then he must stay to face the consequences."

The bear's fur was matted, but I couldn't tell whose blood it was. It tried to swipe at the lion, but they were too close; still, there were strips of red on the lion's back. As I peered closer, trying to see what was happening, the lion fastened its teeth on the bear's throat and shook it. The bear's head moved back and forth, its paws waved feebly—and it escaped in a flash of silver. An arc of shining metal, like a spit seed, and a fish was flying through the air. The floor of the pit was covered now in a foggy sort of water.

I let out my breath. I hadn't realized I was holding it.

The fish was less than a meter long. It hit the water beautifully and came up in a leap a moment later. I looked around the pit. Where was the damned lion? The fish leapt and swam its way through the foggy carpet, searching. Then something broke the surface. A moist, reptilian worm, rising higher—and higher—and higher. A sea serpent, gods, and it was enormous; as big as the eagle had been. Wouldn't he ever run out of energy? The tongue flicked out, the worm head turned from side to side. It slid beneath the mists again. The fish made another leap, and the serpent broke through the water as it did. It grasped the fish in the curve of its own body and started to squeeze.

Change again, dammit, change to anything! It looked useless even as I thought it; who would change to a defenseless thing like a fish unless his power was so low his choices were few? The serpent squeezed harder. I couldn't even see the fish, suffocating in the wet wormy flesh.

"Time," said the Duelmaster. I'd forgotten he was there. The word "time" echoed off the walls, and the misty water rolled back. The fish was dropped, gasping, in the center of the pit. The serpent melted and shrank and became Eln once again, on his floater, in the immaculate silk robes.

"Why isn't Ran transforming?" I said to the Duelmaster.

"I don't know," he said, and as he said it I was running down into the pit. What I would have done, I don't know; the fish began to waver and stretch into a robed figure before I reached the arena floor. He was still gasping, though, and his robes were marred from lying in the dirt. He grabbed my arms and tried to rise. We stumbled out of the pit, up to the first ring, where he quietly collapsed on the floor. I looked over at the Duelmaster to see if he could help; the man had seated himself on the bench and taken out a book!

"Ran? Are you all right?"

He nodded, choking.

"Do you want me to do anything?"

"Wait," he got out at last. A minute later he said, "I'll be all right."

"Do you want water?"

He got out a strangled laugh. "I've had enough *water—*"

I sat down next to him on the granite. "How long have you got?" I asked.

He shrugged. "Maybe five minutes. I don't know. It's at the Duelmaster's discretion."

"Let's hope he's got a good book."

He seemed to be pulling himself together. I said, "Ran,

this doesn't make sense. You've got Stepan away from him—don't give me that look, it's obvious—so where is he getting his magic from? He's made three transmutations, and he hasn't lost any power at all!''

"It doesn't matter.''

"Kanz it doesn't matter. Shit it doesn't matter. You can't go back there, he'll kill you.''

"I need to get Cormallon back.''

"I'm talking about your *death,* you idiot.''

"It has to be done.''

"You monomaniac, you won't get anything if you go back. Did you see the size of that sea serpent? Maybe it was hard to tell when you were being suffocated—''

He looked up at me. "Theodora, listen. If anything happens to me, go to the Abbot. He's got a letter for you, I wrote it in the meditation room. There are some things in it that might help you get to Athena, if you still want to.''

"The hell with that! Everybody wants to help me. Help yourselves!''

I wasn't getting through. That was all there was to say; I wasn't getting through. I'd never had an all-consuming passion in my life, I was always the reasonable one, and I could give out all the logic and rationalism in the world and I had to face that *nobody was going to stop what they were doing.* Somebody was going to die here, within the next few minutes, and it was beginning to look more and more clear who that was.

The Duelmaster looked idly at us, playing with his bookmark. I got up and walked over to him. "Finish your chapter,'' I said.

He turned to me a face with the merest hint of amusement. "Very well,'' he said. He opened his book again and dismissed me from his attention.

I stepped away from the Duelmaster, to go back to Ran, and I caught sight of Eln across the way, beside his witness, untouched, unconcerned, as though he were the center of the universe.

He *was.* Eln in the heart of the star, energy traveling up the arms—all at once I understood.

I went to Ran, squatting down beside him on the cold granite. "Listen." I said urgently. "I know what it is now. He has more than one source."

"What are you talking about?"

"As soon as he drains one, he moves onto the next one. You've cut him off from Stepan, but he's got others—he can just keep going while you get weaker and weaker. Today may be the low point in his draw from Stepan, but he could be anywhere in the cycle with the rest."

He frowned. "How do you know there's more than one source?"

"I *know*. Anyway, what else can it be? His third transmutation was just as powerful as his first—that's because you were fighting three different sorcerers in there, Ran. And who knows how many more he's drawing off?" He looked thoughtful, and I pressed it. "You can't go back in—he might have a dozen more to fall back on."

He considered the matter. "It can't be a dozen. He'd never find a dozen people to agree to give up their magic, even temporarily. With luck he might find four besides Stepan . . . which would mean there's only one left. I can handle four."

"And if there are five?"

His face was stubborn.

I got up. "Fine," I said, and started toward the arena floor. Eln was at the opposite edge, looking interested.

"Will you come back here?" came Ran's voice, annoyed. "That won't do any good." I kept going. "Whose side are you on, anyway?"

I knew he was saying it to irritate me into returning, but it *was* irritating just the same.

Across the arena Eln was waiting with a quizzical smile. "Theo, sweetheart, you're supposed to be on the opposite side; ceremonially speaking, of course."

"You're winning," I said.

He laughed. "Does that mean you're changing sides?"

I shook my head. "You and Ran come from another universe; ethically speaking, of course."

"Well, then? Sorry, do you want a seat?" He motioned to the bench nearby.

"No. Tell me, how many have you got?"

He didn't ask how many what. "Been at the cards again, haven't you? Have you mentioned this to Ran?"

"Naturally."

"Naturally," he agreed.

"So how many?"

"If I tell you, will you tell Ran?"

"Yes."

He grinned that morning sunrise grin. "Really, Theo, I think under the circumstances you can hardly blame me for declining to answer."

His witness had been hanging around the fringes of our conversation. Now he moved in uneasily. "Eln, you shouldn't be breaking your concentration. Send her back."

Eln didn't look at him. "Thank you, Jermyn. I thought you were going to behave yourself if I let you come along?"

The young man dipped his head, embarrassed, and walked away.

"Overenthusiastic," said Eln, "but a good heart."

"Not like the rest of us, then. Why are you here? You've got what you wanted, why don't you go home and enjoy it?"

"I don't have everything I wanted," he said simply.

No, not with Ran still around as a thorn in his side. What should I say? Go home and try to ignore your brother? Maybe if you don't kill him he won't kill you? Was there one chance in a thousand that I could talk either of them into stopping?

No. All my life, when I found myself in a situation I hated, I withdrew. Light years, if necessary. Was that wrong? If the Cormallons had spent some time learning the art of withdrawal, none of us would be in this position.

So withdraw, then. Leave Eln, leave the whole arena— you know what's going to happen, you don't have to witness it as well. "Good-bye," I said, and turned to go.

"See you," he said, unrepentantly.

I was a few steps away. I looked back at him, I don't know why—to try to imprint his image in my memory, maybe; I had no intention of seeing him again, and it would no longer be possible to see Ran.

His clothes hadn't even gotten mussed in the first round; blue silk suited him, his hair was light for an Ivoran. Rare in every way, I had to admit—physically, mentally, emotionally. I still wanted to protect him if I could. A crazy feeling—he wasn't the one who needed protection.

But there was still that disarming sense of tenderness. Damn it and damn this stupid planet, too, because I didn't see any way out of this that would leave any of us whole. I glanced back at Ran, who was sitting on the wide ledge at the other side of the arena, watching, breathing deep with visible intakes of breath, preparing everything he had for the next round. Which wouldn't be enough. Why couldn't Eln have left things as they were? Why couldn't he follow custom and confine murder to strangers? In that instant I wanted to stop him—to kill him if necessary— to see that he couldn't hurt anybody ever again. I felt the stone around my neck pulsing warmly with my heartbeat. Ran was going to be dead as soon as the Duelmaster put down his book, and I didn't have any idea what I could do about it.

But Annurian of Kado Island knew very well. "Eln," I said, and I took my hand from the pack strapped to my side and tossed him a round, black object. He caught it neatly. It was the onyx cat. Fresh from my bare hands, the scent of it all on its stony skin: the tenderness and the understanding and the gratitude, the hatred and the wish to end all this. An emotional confusion more than equal to his own. He looked up from the cat, his dark eyes widened in surprise. "Theo, sweetheart—" he said. "I can't—" And he looked down at his chest, at the knife handle suspended there, and I looked down, too, at my empty fingers and the empty sheath under my robe. "Theo," he said again. The bluestone pendant was a fire against my skin. I ignored it.

What had I been thinking? For a wild second I tried to convince myself that I hadn't done this, that I wasn't responsible, although I could hear my thoughts still echoing: the mechanical choice of target, Vale's remembered voice telling me the location of the heart, tracking the nipple line, at the fifth intercostal space. The abdominal aorta would be easier, but the head of the floater masked it. The carotid artery, then, I seemed to hear the Old Man's voice: but I rejected it. Cut throats were the way cattle were killed.

I knew Eln's upper body intimately, from all the days of sa'ret practice in the garden. Now a red spot was spreading over the blue silk, just above his left nipple. Beads of sweat appeared on his forehead. His face was drained of color. His eyes met mine in disbelief. He lost consciousness as I watched, his body sagging down awkwardly off the floater, the straps on his legs holding him to the seat.

Ran pulled me out of the arena. The Duelmaster was talking, making some kind of announcement. "The Cormallon matter has been settled privately," I remember him saying; "Thank you for your time and attention."

Ran grabbed hold of my upper arms, his hands like ice through the robe. "Are you all right?"

I pulled away. "Of course I'm all right." It occurred to me that he might yell at me, that he might think I'd usurped his male prerogative to slaughter, or something like that; but I'd underestimated him. He was of a practical mind. Eln was dead and Cormallon was legally his; the details were not relevant.

"Come on," he said, "I'll get you out of here. Can you walk?"

"Of course I can walk." It wasn't clear even to me quite why I was so angry at him. I strode past him, up the ramp and out of the arena. I walked all the way up the tunnel, into the monastery, through the halls, and out the front doors. Once there I didn't know where to go next.

I paced in the yard, from the trees to the front steps

and from the steps to the trees. After some amount of time had passed, Ran came out. He said to me, "I've arranged to borrow an aircar from the abbot. You can rest at Cormallon. By the time we get there, they'll have read Eln's documents. They may not be sure, but they'll let us in."

"I don't need to rest." And I didn't; my system was throbbing with energy.

"Come along anyway." He took me by the hand. "I know *I* do."

It was a long ride to Cormallon. Ran said once, "That was an amazing throw. I didn't know you had it in you."

I grunted. With help, apparently I did. I fingered the stone around my neck. I suddenly wondered what would happen to Eln's stone. It was a pretty good guess that it wouldn't be laid in honor in the library at Cormallon. Swept up with his clothes, by the monks, to be burned or sold? What about his witness? Would he take care of it? I hadn't looked back at either of them when I left the arena. How convenient things were on Ivory, when you paid the proper people; we would never have to think about these details again.

We rode for an hour or so. After a while I said, "You'd better land this thing, I'm going to be sick."

We landed on the dirt hills near Amshiline. I was ill, on and off, for the next couple of hours. Somewhere in between the waves of nausea I got this crazy idea: That I had to go and talk to Grandmother. She saw herself as the moving spirit of Cormallon, and I guess the rest of the house did, too; there was nobody else who could give me absolution. Maybe she wasn't supposed to see visitors, but Kylla would find a way, I knew, if I let her see how important it was. Not that there was much chance of forgiveness in that quarter, really. Eln was always her favorite.

Ran rolled up his outer robe and placed it on the dirt under my head. I wanted to tell him he didn't have to help me. I wanted to say that I was as na'telleth as anybody, that I wasn't upset, that what made me sick was the decision; that I was contaminated by the act of choice. Luckily I was too weak to say any of those things. He got a canteen from the car, poured water over a cloth and wiped my forehead. He held me when I was heaving sick and said things like, "There, now, get it all out, you'll be all right." And all the while he had a pinched, abstracted look on his face, as though he wasn't even there.

It was afternoon. Ran called ahead and found that Eln's documents had been read, and that several hours ago Grandmother had sent a letter with them to the Cormallon council giving Ran her full support. I thought resentfully that if she had given Ran her support a lot sooner, maybe we could have avoided this past day. We rode in silence through the gray, rain-filled clouds of early summer. Below, on the hills ranging toward Cormallon, was a line of fires. I looked down and my mind flashed to the bowl of fire I'd seen in the cards, the torch Kylla took from Eln. I looked at Ran's face, drawn now and white as my own.

"What are they?" I asked.

"They're funeral fires," he answered.

"For Eln? How could they know?"

"They don't," he said shortly.

We landed in the front compound, and the goldbands who came out to bow Ran inside all wore black.

They were Grandmother's funeral fires.

Chapter 21

No absolution, no higher judge.

I am a person who makes lists. This was something to add to the list of things I'd noticed changing as I got older. I'd noticed that making a fool of myself no longer seemed to be the soul-rending experience it once had been; that when I was badly treated by others, I understood when to make a fuss and when not; and now, I saw the third item: the knowledge that there was no court but the one in my head, and its judgments were all life sentences. I suppose I'll find other things to add as I go along . . . but the first two bits on the list had been a comfort to me; I saw now it would not all be that way.

I didn't go to the ceremonies, not the family ceremonies that went on for a week (and to which I would not have been invited in any case) or the House ceremony that took place two days after we arrived. I stayed in my room, mostly. Nobody expected any duties from me, and Ran and Kylla were busy. It was several days before people started to notice me beyond polite inquiries as to my health and my room.

I wasn't eating at that time. I want to be clear about this; I wasn't trying to commit suicide, or anything so dramatic—it was simply that the sight of food made me feel ill. I drank, water, milk, and tah in great quantities, but although from time to time I could feel hunger stirring in my belly, as soon as I looked at a bowl of soup or a cake, I had to turn away. I was perfectly aware that human beings can last for many days without food and that the time would come when my hunger would be great enough to overcome the revulsion. However, I was beginning to alarm the household, which made me feel badly.

I accompanied Kylla down to the kitchen one evening in an effort to set her mind at rest. She said that Herel had made me a light casserole of egg, cheese, and bacon, and although the very thought of it made my stomach turn over, I agreed to go with her and give it a try.

"Here she is," said Herel, pulling out the bench for me to sit. "It's warming in the oven. Just you wait a minute." I hated being treated like a patient, but they'd gone to a lot of trouble. I sat down beside Kylla and Herel brought the dish from the oven with great ceremony and set it before us. Then she called, "Tagra! I asked you to bring the plates." And Tagra stepped out of the pantry doorway and carried two plates to the table. She planked them down with just enough force that one couldn't, quite, call it rude. I looked into the scarred face for a moment and met eyes just as wounded.

I hope my own eyes didn't have that trapped look. Gods, when was the last time I'd used a mirror?

She raised one eyebrow, beautifully ironic, just the way Eln used to. "Was there something else?"

"No, thank you," I said, and she left the kitchen. I picked up a fork. "I didn't expect she would still be here," I told Kylla.

She was cutting a wedge off the casserole, with difficulty. Without looking up, she said, "Where else would she go? This is her home." She got the slice onto my plate. "There we go," she said with satisfaction, handing it to me. She licked a finger and said, "Beautiful work, Herel. Go ahead and start, Theo, don't wait for me."

I put down the fork again. I said, "I'm sorry, Ky."

It had been two weeks, and I was walking through the back garden, smelling the aroma from the kitchen, thinking that maybe the human race hadn't gone so wrong after all when it decided to get energy from food. Maybe

I should try it. Ran joined me there just as I was sitting
down under the sa'ret equipment.

"I was thinking about having all this pulled down,"
he said, motioning to the bars and the platforms. "But
then I thought you might want to use it for arm-work
when you go back to doing The River. What do you want
me to do?"

"Leave it up," I said. The sun was high, and the shadows of the bars made cross-patterns on his face and robe.

"All right," he said.

After a while I said, "It's a nice day for summer. Not
too hot."

"No," he agreed.

Herel's voice filtered through the trees, calling someone. A moment later a goldband came by, carrying a
tray. He was familiar, but I couldn't remember his name.
He inclined his head to Ran and said, "Call for you on
the Net."

Ran signed. "Probably more expressions of sympathy.
I'll be back in a little while, Theodora." He pulled himself up and brushed off his robe.

The goldband put down the tray on the ground beside
me. "Excuse me," he said, "but Herel sends these to
you."

There were three small pastry-cakes. Ran lingered for
a moment looking down on them. "I'd steal one, but they
were obviously cooked for you." And so they were; there
was a thick coating of dark icing on each one. Everyone
"knows" that barbarians like lots of sugar. Herel was
going to destroy me with her polite attentions—not a day
went by but she fired up her oven to make me something,
and how could I get rid of it nicely? I couldn't even crum-
ble up her offerings and hide them in my room or stuff
them in the trash; one of the goldbands on cleaning duty
would be bound to notice and tell her. There are no secrets in a house with servants.

The goldband who'd brought out the tray said, "She
said to leave it here for you."

"And not to take no for an answer, I'll bet," said Ran.
He grinned. "Don't worry, Theodora, there are lots of

boulders to hide it under. Just wait till we're out of sight.''

I hoped he wasn't adding telepathy to his other talents. They left, and I lay down under the bars and let the sun warm my face.

The cakes were fresh and smelled delightful. After a few minutes I sat up and said, ''well,'' to myself. I picked one up. Try as one will to be sick, I thought, health gets the better of us all. I took a bite.

And I was shocked when Ran jumped down beside me and knocked the cake out of my hand.

''Spit it out,'' he said.

''What?'' I said through a mouthful of icing.

''Spit it *out*, '' he said, and even as he started to repeat it I spat out the mess onto the dirt.

''Did you swallow any?''

''No,'' I said. ''Who—''

''Tagra.'' He sat back on the ground and ran a hand over his forehead. ''I thanked Herel for the cakes and she said she hadn't made any. Jad said that he'd gotten his orders relayed by Tagra. I checked her room; all her things are gone.'' He was breathing hard.

The goldband—Jad—came running up. ''Medical?'' he asked. Ran shook his head. Jad said, ''I sent someone to ask at the stables. Tagra took a horse about an hour ago— that would be just after she spoke to me and asked me to take the cakes out of the oven for Herel. She must be a good fifth of the way across Cormallon territory now . . . if she's heading northwest.''

''And of course she is,'' said Ran.

''The aircar's in good shape. There's a lot of cover in that direction, but we're used to spotting people heading for the Sector. We can hunt her down, sir.''

Ran closed his eyes. He took my left hand in his. After a moment he said, ''No. Let her go.'' He opened his eyes and looked at me. I nodded.

Jad said, ''As you say.''

It was three weeks after Tevachin that I happened to wander into the Cormallon library. I'd been taking reg-

ular meals, to Herel's great relief, and to my own, in a
way; breakfast, lunch, and supper at least provided some
structure to my rather rootless days. I'd been avoiding
the library, perhaps because it was where I first met Eln.
But it began to look like a potential refuge now, where I
could get a measure of personal relief in the sometimes
bloody-minded, joyfully conscience-free memories of
past Cormallons. Nobody in the household mentioned
Eln's name—not *once*—and it was getting on my nerves.

It was easy to see the new addition to the room. There
were bouquets of flowers all around it, vases standing on
the floor and tucked with difficulty into the shelf. There
were flowers that I'd never seen before, sent in from other
parts of the continent, expensive fire-lilies from hot-
houses in the capital, and in one vase there was even
hearthwhistle from the meadows around Cormallon. And
only one lonely bluestone pendant on the shelf. I picked
it up.

And had one of the major shocks of my life. I heard
my name.

I had the presence of mind to keep hold of the pendant
as I found a cushion and sat down.

"Theodora, cherie," I heard, in what was not quite a
voice, but had the tones of Grandmother running all
through it. "Theodora, I am repeating this over and over
again in the hope that you can hear me. You are the only
one who will receive this; if my grandson picks up the
stone, he will hear something quite different. I would like
to ask your forgiveness."

What?

"When my first grandson was born, his father had his
cards read. The cards said that Eln would cause great
trouble in our House one day. The configuration was certain; I know, I was the card-reader. I couldn't lie about
a reading, but I put my foot down when his father talked
about sending Eln away to be raised. Send the child out
of our control, where we couldn't see what he was doing?
My son was always an idiot. One would think he had
never heard of old stories.

"But I couldn't let Eln be killed, either. It put us all

in danger, but I could not allow it. He was my first grandson, and he was a beautiful child. After all, we did not know how this trouble would come; perhaps not by Eln's choice, perhaps not his fault. This was an excuse, I know. What difference did it make to the safety of our House whether it was his fault or not?

"He was always a delightful boy, I loved to talk with him. Doubly precious, when I thought of the trouble I'd gone to to keep him alive.

"But I had to watch him, just the same. I knew when he made up his mind to regain his place in the family; I knew when he decided to kill his brother. He was going to wait until I was out of the way and then he was going to bring murder to our House. And by the time I was dead, he might be strong enough to succeed—I couldn't wait for that to happen. I began to exaggerate the effects of my illness; not much of an exaggeration, I knew I was dying. With Kylla's help I began to shut myself out of the day-to-day affairs of Cormallon. I retired to my rooms. And I *held onto life*.

"As I hoped, Eln felt safe enough to begin taking over in earnest. It was dangerous for you and for Ran, but the danger would have come anyway, and this way I could keep an eye on things. Kylla kept me informed of everything that went on in the household. I did what I could; it was through my intervention that you were not killed in the aircar fire—Ran was not quick enough in his shielding—and it was I who had Kylla arrange for you to be taken off the *Queen Emily*.

"I know today that it is over, my duty is performed, finally I can let go. Finally.

"I beg that you will not judge me too harshly. You will think, perhaps, that I have interfered in your life. But something had to be done, there was a choice to be made. I loved Eln best, but I could not allow him to retake Cormallon, nor kill his brother for that end. This is Ivory, Theodora, we cannot trust our courts and police as Athenans can; those institutions exist here mainly to collect taxes. Families must make their own justice, and the tragedy of it is that the prisoners we judge are the people we love.

"Well, there is something I can do for you. If you truly want to return to Athena, I do not think Ran will stop you. Keep the onyx cat, if you like, it has performed its service for me in keeping me informed of my grandsons' minds. More importantly, from your point of view: I have removed the curse from Ran's cards, so you are free. Although, you know . . . there is no need to tell him that, little one."

The message faded with a brief visual image of Grandmother's bedroom, the table with the star-maps, and the awareness that Kylla was coming in with a tray.

I sat and thought about things for a long time.

After a while I picked up the pendant again. The message was fainter this time, tinged with other thoughts, other memories. A tah plantation to the south, plants with huge leaves, as big as I was. Faces with labels attached like a faint perfume: father, mother, husband. Eln as a child. Ran, too . . . the label was "young brat," but it was affectionate, and I was glad of that. If there was a message for Ran, I couldn't read it. Finally I returned the pendant to the library shelf.

Things were coming together that had never made sense before. I was beginning to see that Grandmother's plans had gone way beyond controlling possible harm from Eln. That damned onyx cat . . . no wonder Ran had drawn away in Braece. He grew up in this house, he knew Grandmother for the unrepentant manipulator she was. He knew she wouldn't have given the onyx cat to anyone if she didn't expect it to stay in the family.

This needed thinking about.

I left the library and headed for the back garden. In the downstairs corridor I met Ran, coming the other way. I put up a hand, and he stopped.

I said, "Have you been in the library since Grandmother died?"

He knew very well what I was asking. "No," he said, with the slightest touch of embarrassment. As a dutiful grandson he should have been, but I could sympathize with a wish to avoid this particular mark of respect.

"I think you should go up there."

He said, "You've never given me a hard time about family custom before."

"I think she left a message for you," I said.

He paused. I said, "I don't know the retentive quality of bluestone. If you wait too long, could it get lost in the stream of life memories?"

He said slowly, "That's possible."

"Well," I said, "It's up to you. I'm going out to the garden."

I left him standing by the stairway.

An hour later he joined me by the mirelis vine, one of my favorite spots in the back garden. I couldn't tell if he'd been to the library or not.

It was a tall mirelis, in summer bloom. I sat with my back against a rock, and Ran lay down on the grass. It was a companionable sort of silence, but I made no assumptions from that.

Mirelis flowers have a sweet center, so I'd heard. Ran pulled down a blossom, opened the petals, and pulled out the tiny silver bulb inside. He offered it to me. "Have one?"

"Thank you, no. I'm already addicted to tah."

"This isn't addictive."

"Not technically. It's a euphoric, though, isn't it?"

"Coward," said Ran, as he popped it into his mouth. He put his head down on the grass again. After a while he said, "I've been wondering, Theodora. The funeral's just over, I know, and there's still a half-year mourning period . . . but these things take time, and I was wondering if we should start making arrangements now."

"Arrangements for what?" I toyed with the idea of trying a mirelis anyway.

"For the wedding. Kylla's been asking me, too, and we ought to set a date."

I sat up with a bounce. "I beg your pardon?"

He turned his head. He looked perfectly serious. "I understand wanting to put if off, I've felt the same way.

All the fuss and the relatives and the arguments over details—it's like holding two jobs at once, and we shouldn't
postpone reopening the sorcery practice, either. But we
have to get it over with eventually."

I continued to start. "Did I miss something here?" I
asked. "When did we get engaged?"

He blinked. "I thought you expected it. Everybody
else expects it. You're my card-reader, you have to come
into the family sooner or later . . . and I assumed that
we . . . uh, that is to say, we . . . get along . . . you're
a little old to adopt, Theodora. I'm not bringing you in
as my daughter, that's definite."

"Well, I should hope not!"

"Well," he said, "there you are." And he smiled. "A
barbarian in the family is just what we need. Speaking
personally." He pulled himself up on one elbow. We were
dangerously within kissing distance, I thought, but then
I considered all the time we'd spent harmlessly together
on the road from the south, and decided he wouldn't take
advantage of that.

He did. About ten minutes later—or maybe it was fifteen—I became aware a goldband was standing over us.

It was Jad. He appeared totally unconcerned and unem-
barrassed. "Sir," he said, "Supper's ready."

Ran rolled over, sighed, and said, "Whatever happened to discretion?"

"Herel told me not to come back without you. She
made two dishes just for you tonight."

"You're more afraid of offending Herel than you are
me?"

"Yes, sir," said Jad calmly.

Ran nodded. "We're coming." He stood up and offered me a hand. I took it.

That must have been quite a message Grandmother left
him. On the way back to the house I decided to spend
the next morning on the Net, looking up ships' itinerar-
ies.

Chapter 22

Certainly Ran was taking a great deal for granted. I wondered if he'd come upon any of the "young brat" imagery yet.

I hadn't eaten much at supper (to the minor alarm of Herel, who feared I might be backsliding) and woke in the middle of the night ravenous. I made my way down to the kitchen, where I found the lights on and Kylla, sweaty and blood-spattered, standing at the sideboard in her trousers plucking a groundhermit. Two naked hermits were piled on the trestle next to her, their heads beside them. Her bow was propped against the wall.

She looked up. "Theo!" she said happily. "Just in time. I didn't dare wake Herel. Grab a bird, start plucking, and maybe we'll be out of here by dawn."

"Uh, I just came down for a glass of water."

She laughed. "I only wanted to scare you. This is the last one. But if you want to be helpful, you could wash those two and wrap them up and put them in the icer."

So I did. When she finished the last groundhermit, she handed it to me and said, "Be right back." She vanished while I cleaned it and put it away, then reappeared in her nightgown. She'd found time to splash water on her face and arms. "Oh, sweetheart," she said, "what a night. I love it like this, two moons out and stars all over the place." She threw herself down on the bench. "It must be the wild romance of the night that kept you awake."

"Hunger," I said. "I skipped most of supper."

"You know, I see why you and Ran get along."

"You said that to me once before," I said. "Listen, Kylla, about this getting-along stuff—"

"What about it? You mean you've already heard? I wanted to be the one to tell you."

"Tell me what?"

She gave me a satisfied smile. "Lysander Shikron's been officially accepted by the family as my fiancé. Ran gave his blessing and argued the council around. The Cormallons and the Shikrons are as of this moment on speaking terms."

"Kylla!" We hugged. Then we talked about the wedding plans, about Lysander Shikron's physical characteristics, and about the general quality of life. Kylla still had not told her promised husband that she smoked a pipe and liked to sit with her feet up. ("We'll work up to that," she said.)

"We'll have to be careful not to get married the same day," she said. "Bad luck for two weddings in one family."

I frowned. "Ky—" I said.

"Hasn't he brought it up yet? Heavens, try to get a man to set a date for a social function. I'll have to have a talk with him—"

"That's not the point, Ky."

"What *is* the point?" She seemed genuinely puzzled. "Is there something wrong? Theo, darling, whatever it is, we'll carry it out with the trash and never mention it again. You're not already married, are you?"

"No!"

"Well, that's all right, then." She smiled. "Although if your husband were on Athena, we could just pretend he didn't exist. Change your name, pay off the necessary officials, or hire someone to make him behave. Not to really worry . . . I'm thirsty. Would you like some tah? It's my own blend, half green tah and half Ducort tah, mixed."

"Yes, thanks."

She came back in a minute with two wine bowls and two tah cups. The wine bowls were very old, with painted scenes on the inner rim. "The tah's boiling," she said, "but I had a better idea." She poured wine for us both. "Ducort tah and Ducort wine," she said, "two things that make life worth living. Anyway, that's what Eln always used to s—"

She stopped.

"Go ahead," I said.

"I'm sorry, Theo."

"Kylla, what nobody here seems to understand is that I *want* to talk about it. You people—this planet—when you don't want to deal with something you ignore it, pretend it doesn't exist. That's not the way I am. I need to understand things as they really are. Or were."

"You'll never make na'telleth that way."

"Maybe not."

She leaned over. "All right. Nobody's here. Let's talk."

Four hours later the sun was rising. Across the room, on Herel's huge range, sat a pot with the remains of old noodles stuck to the bottom. There were dirty plates all over the table. Kylla leaned back against the wall and patted her belly. "I think I might be sick," she said.

"Me, too."

"You know, I don't think you're supposed to put oil with noodles when you boil them."

"They did taste a little funny. But the sauce helped."

She nodded. "I don't know if I can make it upstairs."

"I don't know if I can move," I said. But I helped her up and we headed for the door. "Anyway," I said, "If I do end up trying to run the estate, you'll be around to tell me what to do."

"Don't count on it," she said sadly. "I'll have my hands full with Shikron."

"A cheery thought," I said.

She grinned. "Try not to let it influence you."

According to the Net, no ships were due to lift for Athena for at least three months. Two freighters would be going in late summer, and a few weeks later two passenger liners were scheduled to go. I wiped my question from the Net just in case Ran decided to check up on me; Grandmother might think he would go along with this, but I wasn't going to take any chances. I would relax and enjoy a vacation until the departure date.

Well, not quite a vacation, for two reasons. The first was a bound volume I finally held in my hands, with a Standard title: *A Branch of the Common Tree: Riddles, Proverbs, and Folk Tales of Ivory.* Collected and Translated by Theodora of Pyrene. It wasn't my original notebook, of course; that had been in Ivoran, in a combination of real characters and my phonetic renderings. I had the Net print out the final version and a shop in the capital bound it for me.

I wanted to dedicate it to Eln, but Ran might find out and he would never, never understand. I thought about dedicating it to Vale, or Irsa, or even Seth, who'd told me most of the stories. But that didn't feel right either, and anyway none of them would care.

Nor did I know what would happen to it when it reached Athena—maybe the Board wouldn't like it. Maybe it violated some pet theory of somebody's; it was possible. But the hell with all that; it wasn't important enough to worry over.

Important enough . . . I opened to the dedication page and wrote, in characters, "Ishin na'telleth."

Now the only problem was whether to send it in storage or deliver it personally.

Meanwhile, there were other calls on my time. Ran had won his fight, and there were people to be paid off. I know these details because he began to instruct me in the household accounts (the very heart of the mystery) and seemed to feel that tracking the rewards for our allies would be a pleasant introduction.

"You want me to do accounts?" I said, with wariness.

"It's money," he said, laughing. "How dull can it be?" ("It's numbers," said Kylla to me later, "and it's boring.") Two people in every branch could access the Cormallon treasury directly; here it was Ran and Kylla. " 'For a peaceful life,' " quoted Ran, " 'let the women worry about the money.' After the wedding, I'll transfer my access to your name.''

I grunted noncommittally.

He said, ''Kylla can show you how to set up my expense account. I like to draw an allowance every week or so. Not a good idea to carry around too much coin, you know.''

''Very true,'' I said. And he went away and let me play with the cash flow.

Karlas, Tyl and other involved members of their ex-family were in receipt of Cormallon House and family shares. They were setting up an import company to deliver things up from the south to the capital; what they were delivering, I did not ask.

The Serrens made a quick speech about their eternal gratitude to the House of Cormallon; then they asked for their shares, resigned, and opened up a cookshop (on-premises dining, with tables and benches) in one end of a building on the north side of Trade Square. It was a good location; not only would they pick up the spillover from the market crowds, but a lot of tourists made their way along the north side of the Square to get from the port to the Lavender Palace. Heida and Arno asked if I would drop in from time to time during the first few weeks, and let them know what dishes foreign barbarians preferred; although they did not phrase the invitation in exactly those terms. I decided they had what it took to make it in the Square.

We never heard about Tagra. I assumed that she was in the Northwest Sector by then. Ran thought that she was probably dead, but Tagra never struck me as the sort of person who let go of things easily, and I wished her the best, within reason. It hadn't been much of a murder attempt, anyway, more of a game of chance. She left it in my hands—if I still felt too miserable to eat, I would live. If not, there would be one barbarian and one gold-band less in Cormallon.

* * *

So the weeks passed. We entertained Lysander Shikron regularly, and when he wasn't in Cormallon I was often invited to the capital to dine with his family. Ran asked me along to all the places he was asked to, and it seemed easier to accept. I would have dearly liked, however, some advice from someone I could trust.

I returned to the library often those days; there was something comforting in touching the rhythm of Grandmother's mind. Unfortunately it was becoming more clear with each visit that to her dying moment she regarded Ran as the same boy who refused to behave on initiation day. She thought he needed spurring to perform his duty. And to her dying moment he resented it.

"You spend a lot of time in there," he said one day, as I came out of the library.

"Trying to understand things," I said.

"Try asking me," he said.

How could I let that go by? We went out to the courtyard. A light drizzle was falling in the pool.

Ran said, "There's a banquet in the capital six days from now. A couple of officials and a delegation of Cormallons from the Serenth Peninsula. I hope you'll attend."

He'd been like that the past few months, thoughtful and considerate. Either that was the way one was with a future wife, or he still wasn't entirely sure that I wouldn't skip out.

But if there was any uncertainty in his mind, he wasn't showing it. I said, "Ran, tell me, when I first gave you my onyx cat, you thought it was some kind of trick of Grandmother's, didn't you."

He paused and looked uncomfortable. "I'm sorry about that. It's just that . . . you seemed fond of me, apparently. So I assumed that—look, Theodora, you're not going to ever mention this again, are you?"

"Not if you answer now."

"I assumed," he said, "that Grandmother had put an attraction spell on the cat. And that was why you—I mean to say, you were only going along with the spell. Look, is this funny?"

"Sorry," I said, trying to stifle the laughter. "You

mean all those symptoms I memorized, like increased heart rate and all that—you thought I'd fallen for a spell?"

He didn't answer. I said, "Ran, I'm afraid I have to set you straight. I was experiencing those symptoms within about three minutes after you sat down by my pitch in Trade Square."

For once he looked surprised. Maybe Kylla's right about men.

This is the story Eln told to me that day in the market before my arrest.

There was once a rich merchant who married a wife who was, many said, too young for him. One day he returned unexpectedly from a business trip and found his housekeeper waiting for him at the door. She said, "For some time now my lady's behavior with men has given me cause for alarm. Today I took two trusted servants and entered her bedchamber without warning, in an attempt to discover the truth of the matter. It took several minutes to break the door. When we entered we found the mistress sitting on the great wooden chest in which she keeps her linens. She will not allow any of us to open this chest, even though we told her it would be best to establish her innocence before your return." The merchant thanked the housekeeper for her efforts, and went, most unhappily, to see his wife. He said, "My dear, I think perhaps I should unlock this chest of linens." She replied, "Do so, if you have no intention of trusting your wife and the mother of your children." And she threw him her keys and stalked away. The merchant thought for a while, then called his servants. He had the chest carried outside and buried, unopened, in the garden; and no one ever brought up the matter again.

It was a story I'd heard in three similar versions before, when I'd studied on Athena; one was from a place called France. Maybe Eln had even heard it from his Grandmother. But it struck me that it was the tale most redolent of Ivoran thinking that I had ever heard.

I didn't know if I wanted to be *that* trusted.

The banquet with the Serenth Peninsula delegates was in late summer. I went as Ran's guest. Our seating arrangements changed every three courses, and between the third and seventh course I enjoyed a delightful conversation with a dog-breeder from the Marble Cliffs on the north side of the peninsula. We didn't find out we were both Cormallons until our last course together. I finally woke up to my obligations and turned briefly to the woman on my left, whom I'd been ignoring, and introduced myself.

She looked at me strangely, which made me look at her strangely, and I realized that I knew her. I said, "You were with the Athenan party I met in Teshin Village. . . ?"

"Yes. We're due to leave on the *Queen Gretchen* in a week."

"I'm sorry, I've forgotten your name."

"Annamarie."

"Yes. I'm sorry I didn't recognize you—you look older in Ivoran clothes."

She said finally, "Your name is really Theodora?"

"Yes, I'm afraid things were rather complicated in Teshin—"

"Theodora of Pyrene."

I laughed nervously. "I don't owe you money, do I?"

She said, "But Theodora, haven't you been to the embassy?"

"Many times. What about it?"

"The *fund*, hasn't anyone told you?"

I said, "No."

So she told me. Since I left Athena, the Board of Student Affairs (prompted by my companions of the trip out, now suffering unexpiated guilt) had instituted a fund in my name. It revolved with the other theater and dance funds, and over the last few years they'd collected three hundred thousand dollars. At the going rate of exchange—

"That's over half the price of a ticket," I said.

"Yes, that's the point." said Annamarie, smiling broadly. "We brought the bank draft with us and deposited it at the Athenan Bank here in the capital. We told the ambassador all about it, didn't he tell you?"

That filthy kanz. With the tabals in gold I had with my own banker, this put me over the top. And with no charity from any Cormallon.

"Let me get this straight," I said. "All I do is establish my identity at the bank, and they give me three hundred thousand dollars?"

She said, "Yes." And she added, "They've got your finger and retina prints."

I grinned back at her. Just then the sixth course ended, and we all had to get up and change seats. "Well, thank you very much," I said.

She looked puzzled. "Don't you want to stay and talk?"

"It wouldn't be polite." Besides, I had some thinking to do. The nice dog-breeder on my right tugged at my robe.

He said, "Will I be seeing you again?"

"I don't know," I said honestly.

And then I had to sit beside one of the Imperial officials, who smiled and said, "You're engaged to young Cormallon, aren't you?"

"Yes," I said, to cut it short.

"A tinaje artist, too, I hear."

Oh, damn, was he trying to prove how thorough his background checks were? Just what did he want? Was I about to be offered a bribe on some Cormallon business?

He leaned closer. "Maybe you could do me a favor."

"Oh?" I leaned farther away.

He looked embarrassed. "I have this problem with my lower back. . . ."

* * *

Well, what are we to do with all these facts? They float
in and out of consciousness, seemingly unconnected, just
when I most need a pattern.

Do you know that I think about Ran all the time, even
when I'm doing other things? I can say that because I'm
going to erase this section from the record when I'm done.
I've heard about this sort of obsession though (the archaic
term is *infatuation*), and they say it passes. I hope to the
gods that it's true, because it can become very wearing.

As for Ran, who takes me for granted in a way that is
a great compliment, who is willing to ally himself to me
for life although he knows *nothing* of my genetic background, who assumes I'm far more competent than I think
I am . . . he's not infatuated, in the sense of the word I
implied above. The Ivoran word for that kind of mind/
body obsession would translate as "crazy." I've run the
cards, and I know him. His erotic adventures have been
varied, to say the least, but his emotional life always
comes up surprisingly barren. He's never loved anyone
in his previously too-easy life . . . too easy before he met
me, that is to say.

But I think it was in the plans Grandmother had for
him. I think maybe she held herself responsible for his
problems. I think she had some kind of lifetime design
involved, and we've only gotten to the tip of the iceberg.

Or am I falling into paranoia? What do we do with
these facts?

They all seem to think this marriage makes sense. But
what Ran doesn't seem to realize—or Kylla, or Grandmother—is that the water has become too tainted to drink.

I've been badly shaken, not only by the idea that I'd
killed someone but by the dawning realization that I was
not the same country scholar who'd left Athena. All this
time I'd thought I was compromising, when what I was
doing was *changing*.

Be honest. We're not talking about tolerant views on
bribery. We're talking about killing a human being. A
consciousness that's not there any more, and that was the
point of the exercise. There's no use confiding in Ran
about this; he's Ivoran born and bred, he knows that

there's always something gnawing away at your vitals, no matter how happy things look; unless you're a true na'telleth. It was an act performed, to him, a thing done. To Grandmother it was a necessary thing. To Ran it was a reasonable thing. But at bedrock, at my core, I find I still have the soul of an Athenan, and the question I must ask myself is this: Was it a good thing, or a bad thing?

And the answer is *yes*.

All right. I understand now, I admit I will be forever detached from whatever culture I live in—very like Eln. I've lived on Ivory now for over half the time I lived on Athena, and how can I change that fact? And I'm not going back to Pyrene, no matter how confused I become. There is no "home," there will never be a home in the way other people take one for granted.

Two roads, then. Ran can be difficult when his desires conflict with mine, but of course it's taboo to kill a member of the family without good reason, so I won't have to walk on eggshells around him. And my position is quite a strong one, thanks to Grandmother. I wonder if she saw something like this coming when she placed her curse—doing something in a fit of temper has come to seem less and less like the old woman.

But is that a happy ending? What sort of children, if any, could we have? And how dangerous would it be for me? Or given the statistics on male life expectancies in the Great Houses, what happens when Ran dies young, leaving me this little kingdom I am not qualified to run?

On the other hand . . . I have the money. I have the expertise, given my tutoring in Ran's tricky ways, to get aboard the *Queen Gretchen*, now due in port, without leaving a trail. But if I do return to Athena, it won't be as a scholar. Too much has happened for that ever to be more than a hobby. It hurts to acknowledge it, but university life has come to seem, well, boring.

Athena must have spies on Tellys and Ivory, though I don't know how I know that. Surely there are job opportunities for someone who can talk like an Athenan scholar and bribe like an Ivoran aristocrat, and who speaks several languages (albeit some of them dead) with colloquial accents.

It doesn't sound unpleasant. My classics teacher used to say that the ancients believed you could tell if prophetic dreams were true or false only if you knew how they came to you; false dreams came through the Gate of Ivory and true dreams came through the Gate of Horn. Trust me to get it backward. Still, maybe it was a fitting reversal, for an ex-scholar. The trouble with telling true dreams is you never really know, not for twenty years or so, if you were right.

But whatever happens, there's too much history here.

I boarded the *Gretchen* five days ago, an hour before take-off, under an assumed name. I'm in my cabin now, on a first-class deck, dictating this to my terminal. You don't know how dry your throat can get in five days; there were hours at a stretch when I had to give up and use the keyboard.

I left a note for Ran, telling him where to pick up the cards and the onyx cat. I told him that Grandmother had lifted the curse. I said I would miss him. And I apologized for not attending Kylla's wedding.

Many weeks ago I sent to Tevachin to see if the monks retained any of Eln's effects, particularly the bluestone ring he used to wear on his left hand. They still had it—it had looked valuable—and they were willing to send it to me for a nominal handling fee. It arrived in a small wooden box, lined with velvet. I made sure it was there, then closed and locked the box. I had no intention of touching this one. Perhaps I'm oversensitive, but dealing with Annurian's mental reflexes seems more than enough for one lifetime. I wrote out a letter to the jeweler on Marsh Street who'd been Eln's companion, and sent the letter and the box to him by messenger. I'm sorry to say that I didn't remember the jeweler's name. I didn't want to send a letter telling the death of someone close to a person whose name I'd forgotten. But he needed to know, and I had no right to censor the information.

The messenger came back saying that the store was

closed and the jeweler had moved, no one knew where. So now I have a carved wooden box, four centimeters by six centimeters, which I have no plans to ever open. What else could I do? I could hardly send it to Cormallon and ask them to place it in the library.

I think Eln would have liked to go off-planet. I hope someday I find a place for him.

The cabin I've drawn is pretty sumptuous, but I haven't brought much to it in the way of personal objects. The wardrobes and drawers are empty. I didn't take any Ivoran clothes when I left, just a couple of tunics and trousers to wear aboard ship. Beyond that, I have in my possession one cut-rate dagger, a stone pendant belonging to a rebel, killer, and ex-prime minister, and a ring from a person whose mental problems I will not begin to try to define. Just some mementos from friends. Souvenirs from a trip that lasted a little longer than I planned. That is the attitude to take, I think.

I finally went to the dining room tonight. It was the first time I'd been out of my cabin since I watched the world of Ivory fall away from us in the lounge monitor. Table 53A, my assigned dinner seat. It was a very small table, since I'd not signed up as part of a party when I boarded.

Ran was sitting there, inspecting the menu. I don't know if anyone reading this is surprised; I found that I was not surprised. I was not expecting him, but I was not surprised.

He looked up as I took my seat. "Do barbarians really eat snake?" he asked.

"Some do. I understand it's a delicacy on Tellys."

"Amazing." He reached into a pocket, brought out a pack of cards and placed them on the tablecloth. "You left some things behind recently. One should be more careful."

How had he gotten my message out of the Net before-time? And even harder, how had he gotten the cards away from Irsa? I'd told her to hold onto them until after the ship left.

"Ran, you could read them yourself."

"Not as well as you." He said, "Do you realize I've been sitting here alone for five days? I was beginning to think you'd keeled over and died in that cabin of yours."

"I'll bet you didn't expect to see me in first class." I said, assuming he knew perfectly well how much I'd had stashed away here and there.

He said seriously, "Theodora, I always expect to see you in first class."

"Well, the feeling is mutual, but can you afford to be away from home for this length of time? Do you know how long this voyage is, one-way?"

"Forty-one point six standard days," said Ran, who may or may not have had an hour to prepare for it, but who would not dream of setting one foot on board without knowing these things.

"You think you've got thirty-six days left to change my mind." I stated.

"Me?" He smiled. "I'm going to Athena to register as a student. They take all ages, I understand. I've always said to Kylla that our House should open its doors, scan new horizons . . ."

"So you're going to let yourself be taught by barbarians? You're going to live in student housing and share space with superstitious people who won't know what a sorcerer is? They'll confiscate your pistol when you land, and anything else you've got on you, by the way." I didn't believe it for a second.

He had picked up the fourth formal vegetable fork by his plate, and was regarding it with amused contempt. The ways of the barbarian, I could see him thinking. No, I didn't believe that story and I wasn't meant to.

Still, it was an interesting image. Would he really go through with it if I didn't agree to come back? Just how stubborn was he?

Student housing . . .

"What's so amusing?"

"Nothing important. I was just wondering, Ran, have you tried any magic yet? Does it work in space?"

He gave a slight smile. "That's the sort of information,

tymon, that I really wouldn't feel comfortable sharing with someone who wasn't of my House.''

Point one for his side. He said it very courteously, too. And when he was finished speaking, he lifted up my right hand from the table and kissed the inside of my palm.

Thirty-six days. I wouldn't want to make any bets on who would be holding the deck of cards when I finally made it back to Athena.

DAW

Savor the magic, the special wonder of the worlds of
Jennifer Roberson

THE NOVELS OF TIGER AND DEL

☐ SWORD-DANCER   (UE2152—$3.50)
Tiger and Del, he a Sword-Dancer of the South, she of the
North, each a master of secret sword-magic. Together, they
would challenge wizards' spells and other deadly perils on a
desert quest to rescue Del's kidnapped brother.

☐ SWORD-SINGER   (UE2295—$3.95)
Outlawed for slaying her own sword master, Del must return to
the Place of Swords to stand in sword-dancer combat and
either clear her name or meet her doom. But behind Tiger and
Del stalks an unseen enemy, intent on stealing the very heart
and soul of their sword-magic!

CHRONICLES OF THE CHEYSULI

This superb fantasy series about a race of warriors gifted with
the ability to assume animal shapes at will presents the Cheysuli,
fated to answer the call of magic in their blood, fulfilling an
ancient prophecy which could spell salvation or ruin.

☐ SHAPECHANGERS: BOOK 1   (UE2140—$2.95)
☐ THE SONG OF HOMANA: BOOK 2   (UE2317—$3.95)
☐ LEGACY OF THE SWORD: BOOK 3   (UE2316—$3.95)
☐ TRACK OF THE WHITE WOLF: BOOK 4 (UE2193—$3.50)
☐ A PRIDE OF PRINCES: BOOK 5   (UE2261—$3.95)
☐ DAUGHTER OF THE LION: BOOK 6   (UE2324—$3.95)
